FROM PAIN TO FAME

FROM PAIN TO FAME

A Congo Boy Story

Ndala Mamadou

Copyright © 2019 by Roland Butsitsi.

Library of Congress Control Number: 2019904175
ISBN: Hardcover   978-1-7960-2655-9
           Softcover   978-1-7960-2654-2
           eBook   978-1-7960-2653-5

All rights reserved. No part of this book may be reproduced or transmitted in any form or by any means, electronic or mechanical, including photocopying, recording, or by any information storage and retrieval system, without permission in writing from the copyright owner.

This is a work of fiction. All of the characters, names, incidents, organizations, and dialogue in this novel are either the products of the author's imagination or are used fictitiously.

Scripture quotations marked NIV are taken from the Holy Bible, New International Version®. NIV®. Copyright © 1973, 1978, 1984 by International Bible Society. Used by permission of Zondervan. All rights reserved. [Biblica]

Any people depicted in stock imagery provided by Getty Images are models, and such images are being used for illustrative purposes only.
Certain stock imagery © Getty Images.

Print information available on the last page.

Rev. date: 04/10/2019

To order additional copies of this book, contact:
Xlibris
1-888-795-4274
www.Xlibris.com
Orders@Xlibris.com
777743

PREFACE

HOME, THE SOCIAL unit formed by a family living together or a place one lives permanently especially as a member of a family or household, according to both the *Merriam-Webster* and the *Oxford Dictionary*, is something I have gotten a little taste of but never did experience to the fullest throughout my childhood as I never truly had a place for me to call home.

If you ask me what is home? My answer to you will be no other than home is more than just a place; home is indeed a fortress, the zenith of all places to be, the only place in the world you can only have one of.

A person who has more than one place to call home has none as a result. One can only have one home.

Whereas family, which is the basic unit of society, a group of individuals living under one roof usually under one head, united by certain convictions or certain affiliation, according to the English dictionary, just like home, is a very sacred entity, which I had been lucky enough to experience many times throughout my journey on earth. I have been a part of so many families without actually risking losing being a part of another, which led me to conclude that unlike home, one can belong to more than one family without actually running the risk of losing any other as a result.

This book is the journey of a child, a boy, a young man who not only lived in many homes in which none were his to call home but also had the privilege to have been a part of so many great families that embraced him as one of their own.

Buckle up. Let us take a ride on this roller-coaster story.

THANK YOU TO everyone that made any impact in my life directly or indirectly. To my brother and friend, you will never be forgotten. A very special thanks to my other half, as I wouldn't have accomplished this without you. Finally, I would like to take the time to thank my Creator for giving me the strength, wisdom, and inspiration to achieve this project. I thank him for being the potter that made this very intriguing piece of pottery I call my life, which I'm now making into a story for the whole world to see how mighty, graceful, and merciful our Creator is.

IT WAS A very beautiful Saturday afternoon. The sun was up. All the flowers were blossoming. No school. No homework, at least none to be done on that day. It was a perfect day if you ask me. As I was sitting outside contemplating and brainstorming on how to start my weekend, I heard a very loud shout coming from inside the house calling my name. Timu! Timu! Someone who wasn't familiar with that voice would have probably mistaken it to that of God's perhaps! But not me. I knew exactly who it was!

It was Maggie, my stepmother, calling for me. We lived in a one-bedroom little house, which was a part of a duplex. From what I could see, our neighbor had almost the very same layout as ours. The only difference was that our place looked much nicer than theirs, at least from the outside, thanks to my father's creativity. My father had one of the most creative brains that would have made both Steve Jobs and Mark Zuckerberg look simply average. Our house was located at the very end of the street behind a very big house that was unfinished. The house owner planned to build a six-bedroom house in front and a smaller three-bedroom house in the back. Midway to her project, she ran out of money, leading her to abandon her plan of building a six-bedroom house. She settled with barely finishing the three-bedroom house, which she turned into a duplex in a hurry and then made it available for rent.

My family rented one side, while another family occupied the other. We both lived behind this big unfinished house that looked almost haunted at night. The neighborhood kids used the living room part of the unfinished house as an indoor soccer field while using the doors as goals. My father took great care of our side through landscaping. He painted the wall with very beautiful colors. He planted flowers all around our house, making it look like a pretty version of the little house in the prairie. Every visitor was always amazed and full of praise on how beautiful our house looks.

After checking in to find out what Maggie wanted, I have known from experience her calling my name only meant two things: one was that I was in trouble, and the other was that she wanted me to do some kind of chore. This time, again, I was on the money. She wanted me to hold my baby sister, who was seven months at the time, so she could finish whatever it was that she was doing inside.

As I was holding my sister outside, I had a visitor, my friend Christian. Christian and I were the same age. He lived two houses down from mine. He was the only friend I was allowed to have in the entire neighborhood. My father was very picky when it comes to socializing. He had very few people in his social circle. He only had one person he would chat with from time to time from our street. It was a certain Mr. Vuvu.

Mr. Vuvu was a banker, and his wife, a stay-at-home mom. Mrs. Vuvu was a member of the neighborhood Catholic Church choir in which my father happened to be the conductor. Mr. Vuvu had four children: two teenage boys, probably age nineteen to twenty-two, and two younger girls, Francine and Nancy. Francine and I were the same age, and Nancy, about two years younger. The Vuvus lived about five houses from ours. Mr. Vuvu had the habit of sitting in a chair just in front of his gated house every week day between the hours of six and seven. On his way from work, my father will usually stop and chat with Mr. Vuvu for at least forty-five minutes to a full hour, discussing the daily newspaper headlines and the country's politics. Much like my dad, Mr. Vuvu was a very private person; I never knew him of having any friends.

Christian was a part of a very big family, the O'Mangelo. His father, Mr. O'Mangelo, was a very successful businessman who owned about three stores. He had about twenty kids by at least three different women. Most of his kids lived there with him. He had kids with ages ranging from eight to thirty years old; Christian being the youngest of all. He had four boys, and the rest were girls. No set of twins at all. My father used to refer to them as "the Jungle."

Most of the O'Mangelo boys were affiliated to the neighborhood gangs and were responsible for about 90 percent of the neighborhood terrors. The girls weren't an exception either. The O'Mangelo girls were known for their divas-like lifestyle, and some were known for fighting boys.

Unlike the rest of his siblings, my friend Christian and two of his sisters from the same mother, Mamie and Bijoux, were the very opposite of the bunch. Mamie, who was about seventeen years old, was extremely beautiful, very quiet, and above all, a very private person. She fell in love with my baby sister from day one, which led her to coming around and babysit very often. She was very charming. Bijoux was about a year older than I was. Just like her sister, Bijoux was very beautiful, an identically younger version of Mamie in everything but shyness. She was everything but shy. She was very outspoken. For whatever reason, everything always seems to fall her way. Christian was his father's favorite child, the brain of the family. He was intelligent and very polite, and he loved and fancied his education.

As for me, I had a very good reputation in the neighborhood. People thought of me as being very smart to most of the neighborhood girls. I was the perfect bachelor, every girl's crush. My father has forbidden me to have any ties or association with anyone in that neighborhood. My routine only consisted of going to school and sitting at home. My father was to me what Hitler was to Germany or Stalin to the Russian. Only him knew what was best, and his decisions were final and irreversible. My father was very totalitarian. Not following his instruction was as fatal as questioning his authority.

From time to time, I will accompany him to the Vuvus' house. While Mr. Vuvu and my father would carry their long conversation about politics, I would be playing with Francine in her room. After being playmate for quite some time, Francine and I came to the agreement that we were now boyfriend and girlfriend. If only relationships were formed as easily as ours was, this world would have been a far better place romantically. Our relationship was more artificial than anything since Francine and I barely saw one another.

Mr. Vuvu never once stepped his foot in our house, and my father only took me with him to the Vuvus on very few occasions. Although Mrs. Vuvu did come to our house on a few occasions along with the girls, that still wasn't enough for the sake of our relationship. While Mrs. Vuvu and Maggie were inside chatting, Francine and I would be outside playing. Aside from having very little to not time to spend together, there was an even bigger obstacle getting in the way of our relationship. It was Bijoux!

Bijoux had a thing for me. She had already picked me as her boyfriend, and as far as I am concerned, what Bijoux wants, Bijoux always gets, and the earth wasn't going to stop orbiting in my case. Bijoux only lived one house down. Her family was very lenient. I wonder if they even had any rules to follow. The kids in that house had total freedom to leave and return as they wish whatever time suited them best. They were more than welcome to come back home after roaming the neighborhood for as long as time allowed them. So Bijoux had pretty much the luxury of seeing me as often as she wished to. Compared to the O'Mangelos, my house was like one of the Nazi concentration camps. Sometimes, I was left to wonder how great my life would have been had I been born an O'Mangelo. Having to benefit from all that total freedom would have been liberating.

I did master the art of sneaking out. I would sneak out the house from time to time to go watch the neighborhood kids play soccer in the unfinished house. I never dared to sneak out to go see Francine. That was almost mission impossible given the distance. If caught, it could turn out to be a very fatal experience for me. The Vuvus were very protective of their daughters. Mr. and Mrs. Vuvu would never allow Francine to go five houses down by herself, at least not in this lifetime.

Unlike Francine, Bijoux had the luxury to leave her house as she pleased. She would come to my house to babysit just to talk to me. From time to time, she would come to the unfinished house, and we would spend time together a few times. I even managed to sneak out the house to go to her house, which was one house down. It was less risky for me to take a trip there. Bijoux's bedroom window was very close to the wall separating the two houses, allowing me to keep my ears wide open in case Maggie were to shout my name. While at Bijoux's, I would run back as fast as I could after having heard Maggie shouting my name. I would just tell her I was exercising in one of the rooms in the unfinished house. It worked most of the time.

As I began to spend more and more time with Bijoux, Francine started to see less and less of me, which eventually brought our relation to an end. Not only that but also Bijoux was more physically attractive to me. Her availability and freedom were what sealed the deal, and besides, Christian, her brother, was my only friend.

Christian and I became really good friends, although I was forbidden by my father to ever set foot at his house. Christian, on the other hand, was welcome to come see me at my house. My father never knew much about Christian except that he was coming from the house he always referred to as "the Jungle." It was mostly Maggie who, having to rely on the service that Christian's sisters sometimes provided her with, allowed Christian to come often to see me whenever my father wasn't around. Christian and I not only were the same age but also shared most common interest in education and sports.

Christian and I would always tease each other on who was attending the better school. We will have discussions on how far ahead which school was in their curriculum compared to the other. It seems to me that his school was ahead of mine when it came to science, but when it comes to social studies and language arts, my school was ahead. We were pretty even when it comes to mathematics. We both attended honorary private schools.

There was a public school on our street. Christian sometimes claimed that by the time he finishes fourth grade, he could be hired as a ninth-grade teacher at our neighborhood public school. Sometimes while walking together in the neighborhood, I would point at a kid that seemed to me like he might be attending that school. I would turn to Christian and say, "Don't you think you should go introduce yourself to him as his future teacher?" We both would laugh as hard as we could.

That Saturday afternoon as Christian came by to see me, I was sitting outside the house holding my baby sister. As he approached me, he asked if he could hold the baby. While I was giving him the baby to hold, he accidentally dropped the baby. As the baby started to cry, my stepmother rushed out from the house as I was picking up the baby from the floor. She punched me in my eyes and grabbed the baby. She told Christian to leave and told me to go kneel down as a punishment. After the baby fell asleep, she had me get up and took an extension cord and went on to whoop me with it for about thirty minutes straight. After crying for the next hours, I finally fell asleep.

I was woken up by my father, who had an extension cord in his hands, asking me what was I doing having one of the jungle boys at his house. "Didn't I forbid you from having any contact with any of those boys from this neighborhood!" he asked. Before I could even gather words together for my own defense, I was brought down to the floor by a lash of the extension cord. My father whooped me like I was a runaway slave. I cried so much that very day, more than I ever cried my entire life. That's the day I realized that wasn't my home anymore. At eight years old, finding me a place to call my home became my number-one priority.

That's when all the trouble began.

My father was a very private person, but what mostly intrigued me about him was the fact that he was both private and also very sociable. It amazes me until this very day to know that one can be very private while being very easygoing and sociable at the same time. Altogether, I always thought that it was almost impossible to be both, and until now, I have never met a person with both attributes. To me, being a very private person is the opposite of being a socializer. It's kind of synonymous to being a Saddam Hussein or a Hitler that do hold free and open elections every two years. Quite impossible, isn't it!

I can count with one hand how many times we had visits from one of his relatives, or vice versa. The same goes for his so-called friends. There was very little to no contact between him and my aunts and uncles. It seems to me like there was a cold war going on between him and his family. I also had the impression of some sort of a very shaky truce that could have easily be broken by any small piece of conflict at any given moment.

I had four aunts that I knew of: Marthe, the eldest, Monique, Euphrasie, and Mado. I only remember seeing two of them only twice. I saw my aunt Euphrasie once at my graduation from kindergarten and once more when she came to visit us when Maggie gave birth to my sister Jenny. To be honest, she came a few months after my sister was already born. Once, we visited my other aunt Martha at her home. My uncle Danny, my father's younger brother, was the only sibling to attend my father's wedding, and I only saw him once after the wedding. That's when he came to visit my father at home. He brought me a soccer ball and brought my sister a Barbie doll.

As far as I know, my father was the fifth out of ten kids. He had three elder brothers, one elder sister, two younger brothers, and four younger sisters. From what I heard, his eldest brother, Joseph, disappeared a while back, and no one seemed to know of his whereabouts. My grandparents, along with three of my father's siblings, still live in the country, in a village about eight hundred miles away from us. That's where my father and all his other sibling were born and raised. Five of his other siblings lived in the same city with us.

As a child, I was known to be very curious. Growing up, I had always been concerned why our family tree was so short that not even an eight-year-old could even climb it. I made it one of my conquests to get in the bottom of this. What also bothered me the most was the fact that I had a biological father and a stepmother. Nothing was ever mentioned of my biological mother's whereabouts. Is she still alive? Does she live around here? What is her name? All those questions were roaming around my eight-year-old brain. I also made a promise to myself to get some answers. To find answers to such questions as an eight-year-old was almost as big as a task as climbing Mount Everest barefoot.

I started my investigation by one day asking my stepmother if she knew of my mother's whereabouts. She simply told me that she was dead. She died in a car accident and to never ask her such a question ever again. Although I did get an answer to my question, it seemed to me that there was still more to find out. Once again, I was up to the task. At eight, I was already aware that not too much information was ever to be available to a person my age even if I was to be the heir of the throne, which meant that for me to gather any classified information, I had to rely mostly on being very attentive to any adult conversation around the house or wherever that may be. I figured that there were some people, if not at least someone, out there that had answers to my questions. I couldn't wait to get in contact with the person who could have all the answers to my questions.

Through eavesdropping, I did manage to find out the reasons behind my father breaking away from his relatives. There were two reasons. One of them was an act committed by my father, and I was the other one. Until this very day, I am still not so sure how I found out about it or the person that told me about it.

From what I have heard, or to put it quite honestly overheard, was that my father as a kid was very intelligent and gifted. My father was his father's favorite child. Being such an honor to his family, he benefited from special care and affection from his father, who openly put him above all his other relatives, causing a little resentment toward him by all his other relatives except for one, the youngest of all his sibling, my aunt Mado. At a young age, my father really valued his education. He always managed to be the first of his class from primary school to secondary school. It was a very sad day in the house the day he managed to come out second during one school year.

After finishing his secondary schooling, my father attended the seminary, a vocational school for Catholic priesthood. While trying to become a priest, one was required to attend and graduate from the seminary, which was divided to two branches, the little and big seminary. All seminaries were set up as a boarding school. My father attended the little seminary in Kabwe, a town about eighty miles away from his native town. As a seminary student, my father was a member of the debate team, which earned him such a very huge amount of popularity among both the faculty members and his fellow students. He graduated once again top of his class from the little seminary. With everything going his way, the future never ceased to look brighter. He attended the big seminary in a different town the following school year, beginning where he left off, halfway through graduating from the big seminary and actually being ordained a priest.

My father came in contact with a very beautiful young lady named Rose. Their acquaintance quickly turned romantic, and before he knew it, the young lady got pregnant with his child. As the pregnancy became impossible to hide from her family and friends, the young lady was forced to notify her parents of her dilemma. As her mother and father never seemed to recall a day they had ever seen their lovely, shy daughter in the company of any boys, there was only one question to be asked—who indeed was the father of this unborn baby?

The young lady collected herself to tell the name of the man she had been seeing for quite a while now. When she told her parents the name of the person responsible for this saga, she never realized what she got herself into was going to get even bigger than her belly will ever get while carrying that pregnancy. Her family couldn't believe the name that had just come out of their daughter's mouth. She, on the other hand, was to be as shocked to find out that the same name that had brought her so much joy now is causing her so much pain. The person who impregnated her is none other than her first cousin.

As this young couple hooked up, there was nothing in their best knowledge indicating to them that they were relatives. What my father didn't know was that his lovebird was actually his cousin. Rose's mother was my father's aunt, the daughter of my father's mother's younger sister. The last time my father saw Rose's mother, he probably was a toddler.

You know what they say—the only thing traveling faster than lightning is bad news. After making its way throughout the village, it was just a matter of time before the tragic news had reached the seminary faculty. As a priest to be, it was forbidden for one to engage in any sexual relationship with anyone. That was written in fine prints. Breaking that rule alone was a guaranteed automatic expulsion. Even worse, impregnating your own relative, that alone could have you on a guillotine. At no one's surprise, given the circumstances, my father was expelled from the seminary. Just as misfortune never comes one at a time, following his expulsion from the seminary, my father was quickly disowned by his own family.

Even Nostradamus in his glory days would have never predicted such an ending. The man who once carried the family pride in his shoulder, the one whose future was as bright as one o'clock in the afternoon, was now reduced to nothing but a renegade. Outcast by all his family and friends. When everything and everyone leaves you, that's when you truly find yourself and what you are really made of. This wasn't the time for grieving or sobbing, my father thought. In moments like this is when men are born. After picking himself up, my father hitchhiked his way out of town and found refuge about one thousand miles away from his native town.

Shortly after that, the young pregnant lady found her way out of her town very far away from her family and ended up finding refuge about one thousand miles away from her family. A few months later, she gave birth to a baby boy whom she named Benni. She came up with the name Benni by combining two very important names in the history of the Congo, which at the time was under Rwandese and Ugandan's occupation, also known as the darkest era in Congolese history.

The first name was Beni, a city located in North Kivu region, in the northeastern part of the Democratic Republic of the Congo. Beni is also known as the rape capital of the world. Thousands of women and girls are subjected to rape and sexual violence, which was used as a weapon of war. Beni is the worst city in the world to be of a female gender. Mind you, I said female gender, and I did not use the word "female," "girl," or "woman." In Beni, Rwandese and Ugandan's militias are creating so much terror to the Congolese population there. Those militia are responsible for war crimes committed in that part of the country such as the massive rapes of women and children on a daily basis. Infants are being sexually abused, and women are being raped and having their genitals completely dismembered by Rwandese militia loyal to the Kagame's regime of Rwanda.

The second name was Denis, which was in tribute of Dr. Denis Mukwege, the only Congolese to have won the Nobel Peace Prize. Dr. Denis Mukwege, also known as "the man who mend women," was a Congolese gynecologist surgeon, human rights activist, and world's leading specialist in the treatment of wartime sexual violence who, during the Rwandese and Ugandan's occupation of the Democratic Republic of the Congo, devoted his life fixing damaged bodies of degraded Congolese girls and women victims of sexual violence committed by Rwandese militia loyal to the Kagame regime of Rwanda. Dr. Denis Mukwege founded the Panzi Hospital, where he treats thousands of girls and women who have been subjected to all sorts of sexual violence during the Rwandese occupation of the Congo.

As a rape victim herself, she thought to give awareness to the rest of the world of the terror that was going on in the city of Beni, and being one of Dr. Denis Mukwege's patients, she owed that godsend man her life for having performed a miracle in treating her that she was even able to conceive her first child—me! So from Beni and Denis, Benni was formed.

After setting foot in the capital city, Kinshasa, from his exile, my father hooked up with a guy named Jean, who happened to be an old childhood friend who had found his way to the city few years before my father's arrival. Both Jean and my father would later embark on an adventure of a lifetime. My father knew that he had family members in the city, which included a few uncles, cousins, aunts, and among all, his elder sister Martha, who was married to a city official. Given all the circumstances involving his arrival, he chose not to bother checking in with any of his relatives. Instead, he chose to link up with Jean.

One day, my father and Jean drew up a plan to live the country and head to a European country clandestinely, preferably France or Belgium. Jean had earned himself a gig at the train station as a train cleaner. His job involved cleaning trains and sometimes loading and unloading commercial trains. Few months into his new job, he helped hire my father. Both men were in their midtwenties at this time. One night, they both decided that it was time to carry out their plan of immigrating to Europe. The night before, they had learned that the commercial train they helped load that night was on its way to a neighboring country on its way to Belgium, most likely through sea after redocking at some country's main port. The following night, both men decided that it was now or never. They both snuck inside the wagons carrying coal with their little backpack, which contained few extra clothing, canned food, and bread for the road.

The trip from Kinshasa, Zaire, to Port Gentil, Gabon, took about forty-eight hours with one or two stops in between. They made it safely to the port without being caught as they roamed around waiting for the cargo to load into the ship to sneak into the ship that was boarding for Marseille, France. Jean was apprehended by three of the port's guards and was taken to a nearby police station where he spent two nights before being taken to the border and expelled from the country for illegal entry. After Jean was caught, my father turned himself in to make sure he didn't lose sight of Jean. The penalty for illegal entry was about thirty days of jail time plus some fine, which will eventually lead to forcible deportation.

Jean had a very nice watch, a very expensive one. He had purchased that watch with his first paycheck working at the train station. He took that watch and gave it to one of the officers in charge as a bribe, thus cutting their time in custody very short to only two nights instead of serving the minimum thirty days. They were later escorted to the border nearby and expelled from the country. After crossing the border and yet entering another country without the proper documentation, they were quickly escorted by the border police to the country's consulate. Being Zairian citizens on the verge of deportation, they were allocated a per diem sum of about thirty-five dollars with the option of staying at the consulate until the filing of proper documentation to stay in Congo as either tourists or visitors. After spending about two weeks in Congo, they both decided to head back home, leaving behind their dream of clandestine migration to Europe.

Upon their arrival back in Kinshasa, my father and Jean both went their separate ways. My father went on to attend the University of Kinshasa, while Jean went on and enlisted to serve in the army. My father graduated with a degree in philosophy. Shortly after that, he managed to gain full custody of me. I was about two years old at the time. He handed me over to his sister Martha while wrapping up his master's. My aunt Martha was very delighted by the task that was given to her. She even told my father it will be best for her to keep me until

I'm at least a teenager or, better yet, until my father had settled down and maybe, perhaps, married. My father agreed.

The following year, to everyone's surprise, my father came back for me. My aunt refused to give me up, prompting a family emergency meeting. At the meeting, my father was anonymously outvoted, but with an iron fist, he vetoed their decision. "Being the child's father, anything I say or want for my child goes," he said. After storming out of Aunt Martha's house, he took me with him by force. Just like that, I was out of Aunt Martha's care. Together, we both embarked on a new adventure!

The very first thing my father did after becoming my supreme custodian was to change my name. My father changed my name from Benni to Timu-Mamadou. But why Timu-Mamadou? Just like my mother, my father was in one of the most radical anti-Rwandese occupations there ever was. Together, they share a black panther-like spirit. So he combined his two favorite Congolese heroes.

One was Mamadou Ndala, a valiant Congolese army colonel. Mamadou Ndala was a complete ranger who received military trainings from the United States, China, and Belgium. He also completed the highest form of guerrilla warfare training in Angola. At twenty-five, he became a country hero after single-handedly defeating the M23, a military militia composed of Rwandese insurgents loyal to both Paul Kagame of Rwanda and Joseph Kabila of the Congo.

The M23 was responsible for 90 percent of all terror in the eastern part of the country, especially the Kivu region. They were very active in Beni, Fizi, Buhumba, and Kiwanja, all towns in Northern Kivu region. The M23, or the personification of evil on earth, carried out the world's most atrocious war crimes of all time. Even Hitler in all his glory wasn't a match to M23. They burned villages and beheaded boys, and men raped women and children as young as four years old in front of their relatives. They were the most sadistic people on earth. The M23, a proxy of the Tutsi-led Rwandese army, was highly equipped with one of the most updated military equipment, a courtesy of the millions of dollars in military aids from the U.S. government to the Rwandese regime of Paul Kagame, which was implementing its hegemonic vision of setting up a Tutsi-led power movement all along central Africa's Great Lake Region.

One of the major obstacles facing Paul Kagame's plan was the lack of land, as his country Rwanda was very tiny superficially. He was in concert with one of his most loyal acolytes and fellow Rwandese, Hyppolite Kanambe, a.k.a. Joseph Kabila, whom he helped install as the head of state in the Congo following the assassination of Laurent Desire Kabila, the former president of Congo and Paul Kagame's enemy number one. With the blessing of his protégé Hyppolite Kanambe, a.k.a. Joseph Kabila, Paul Kagame was able to deploy his Tutsi-led militia M23 to the eastern part of the Congo under the label of being a Congolese rebel group in violation of the UN resolution 3314, prohibiting the invasion or attack by the armed forces of a country or any military occupation of another country.

The M23, a Tutsi-led militia from Rwanda, was operating mass murder and rapes under the label of being a Congolese rebel group with their only mission being to get rid of all the Congolese population living in the Kivu region of the Congo and replace them with Rwandese population who would later claim those vacated territories as theirs. Why only the Kivu region, one may ask? Simply because it's the only region that shares border with Rwanda and shares somehow some cultural similarity, but most importantly, by occupying the Kivu region, Paul Kagame would have his hands on the region, which is the world's number-one producer of a very strategic mineral called coltan, a mineral much needed for the great operation of all your electronic devices such as smart phones, game consoles such as PlayStation, Nintendo, and Xbox. It is also used in electric cars, and it is in optical and medical equipment. Last but not the least, it is also used in smart bomb guidance control. As the M23 was making their presence felt so deep into the Kivu a region located in eastern Congo, ironically, Rwanda became the world's number-one exporter of coltan, a mineral not found anywhere on Rwandese soil.

At twenty-five, a young ranger in the Congolese army in defiance with the military hierarchy who was ordered not to attempt any military assault on the M23, Mamadou Ndala went against the grain and led an assault against the heavily armed and well-equipped M23; as a result, defeating them with a vast majority of the survivors opting for a retreat back to Rwanda. Mamadou Ndala's heroic victory over the M23 was widely celebrated by the Congolese people. Men, women, and children took it to the streets of Beni and surrounding towns to celebrate the rise of a national hero. Few years later, he was brutally assassinated, burned alive in his jeep in an ambush orchestrated by some Rwandese militia operating in that region. He died at the age of thirty-four and still stands today as the reincarnation of Congolese patriotism, something the Congolese people have lost since yet another assassination of another hero, Patrice Emery Lumumba.

The other name was that of Mukendi Tshimanga, a human rights activist who dedicated his adult life advocating for political freedom and basic human rights, which was being denied to the Congolese people by the occupying regime, which had its roots deep into Rwanda. He was assassinated by a sniper while leading a pacific demonstration demanding human rights nearby a Catholic church. His last words before passing were "Le Peuple Gagne Toujour!" which can be translated to "You can kill, you can torture, you can even imprison and try to silence us, but at the end, the will of the people shall prevail no matter what!"

To my father, I was Timu-Mamadou. To my mother and any other family relative, I was still Benni. As for me, I mostly went by Timu.

My father and I were very close. I went wherever he went. At three, I knew of no other superhero besides my father. He was both my mother and my father at once. I went with him everywhere. He would take me with him job hunting, He would even take me with him at some of his job interviews. He would dress me up and have me wait for him at the lobby until he was done. He only had one instruction for me—do not move even if the place was to catch on fire or even if the pope had instructed me to do so. My father's instructions were as straightforward and final as the Ten Commandments. I was my father's trophy.

My father landed a job as a vice principal in one of the newly established local private schools, Pegase. The school taught grades K–12. "Education gives wings" was the school's motto. In addition to being the vice principal in charge of discipline, he also taught music at the school. As a school faculty member, one of the incentives that came with the job was free tuition for me. Pegase was owned by one of the city's prominent union syndicates, along with his associate, a childhood friend and longtime business partner. One of the owners' wife, Mrs. Petruc Helena, a Romanian national, was the school president. My father was the fourth-highest-ranked school faculty member.

Up until this point, I have no recollection of having our own home. As a matter of fact, I believe we spent the night wherever the night found us, whether at different friend's house, sometimes at various places staring at the blue moon. It wasn't until my father had that job that we had a place to sort of call our home.

As a faculty member, my father was one of three people that had the key to the school. We will come in late at night and enter one of the classrooms. He would put up some cardboards together and line it up on the floor. That was my bed. He would cover me with a blanket and read me a fable every night until I fell asleep. He would pull up a chair and fall asleep next to me. He was my king. I was his prince. That were the best nights of my childhood.

He would wake me up at about 5:00 a.m. at the very first rooster's sound. He would bathe me outside with cold shower. By 5:30 a.m., he would have my backpack ready for school. We would check everything together: crayons, check; colored pencils, check; notebooks, check. He would have me gently close my backpack. We would both recite a prayer and put our cardboard away. By 5:45 a.m., we were on our way to the nearest place to get us breakfast, which mostly included muffins and coffee with milk. At around 6:45 a.m., we would make our way back to the school. School for grades K–6 was from 7:15 a.m. to 12:15 p.m., while grades 7–12 was from 12:30 p.m. to 5:30 p.m. My father worked with grades 7–12, so he would drop me off for kindergarten, and once school was out, I would wait for him at the school office, where he would have me take a nap after serving me lunch, which mostly consisted of canned food and a bottle of Fanta. During his break time, he would come and help me with my homework.

At 5:30 p.m., when the bell sounded to mark the end of the school day, I would gather my stuff together and meet him by the schoolyard.

From there, we would wait until the last parent has come and picked up his child. Then we would lock the school entrance and be on our way to our next adventure, which was usually at one of his friends' house where we would eat dinner. We would stay up to 10:00 p.m., and by 11:00 p.m., we would make our way back to the school to spend the night. Our routine lasted for about two years. I graduated from kindergarten at age five. My second year of kindergarten was very eventful as I became best friends with Joel, who happened to be biracial. Joel was the lone child of the school owner. Joel's mother, Mrs. Helena, a Caucasian from Eastern Europe, was the school president. Joel and I were in the same grade, but I was about a year younger than him. Joel was a little taller than I was. We both went through grade K together.

Shortly before the start of the first grade, I had a surgery in my thumb, which kept me from attending the entire school year. I was born with an extra thumb in my left hand. Since that was seen as an anomaly by most, my father had a surgeon perform a surgical operation that would remove the extra thumb. It took two surgeries to achieve that goal. Everything seemed perfect for a while until we started to notice that my thumb was growing facing the opposite way, but by this time, my father didn't have the financial prowess to do anything about it surgically. Therefore, my father left it alone.

When I was five years old, my father acquainted a family that became very fond of me. Every time they would ask my father to let me spend the weekend at their house, he wouldn't budge. After a while, my father finally caved in and allowed me to start spending some weekends there. My father took great care of me. I was healthy, always neatly dressed, and sharp. He took great pride into shaping up my appearance. But something about our society wasn't very accepting of a single father taking care of a child. For most, it was something not customary, and most people felt like my father being single in his late twenties or early thirties shouldn't have any business raising a child alone. Although everyone was amazed at the job he was doing raising me, they still thought I would have been better off being raised as a normal kid in a kid-like environment. There were even offers from some friends begging him to let them take me in to live with them. One family that was very financially established even offered to take me to Europe and go live and study there, giving him time to find himself and perhaps find a good woman. My father, being the stubborn man he was, wouldn't even consider such a thought. To him, I was his jewel, his only reason for living, and no way would he ever let anyone else raise me but him. It took him a while to even consider leaving me in places.

As there always is an exception to everything, there was this one particular family that my father became accustomed to as he started to push for a second gig on top of the teaching one. He started leaving me over to this one family. Although I do not recall their names individually, it was a family of seven. There were this very nice lady and her husband, along with her four children, three girls and one boy, and the lady's youngest sister who was around eighteen years old. The three girls' ages were ranging between seven and thirteen years old, while the boy was about three years old. The wife's little sister watched over all the kids and performed almost all the household chores. She cooked, cleaned, and babysat. Come to think of it, her name was Sophia. Her name was the most called name of the household. Every five to ten minutes, it was always "Sophia! Sophia this, Sophia that, Sophia come take this, Sophia bring me this, Sophia bring me that."

The lady of the house was very sweet and nice, but most of all, she was the laziest person known to mankind. Her only hobby was sitting on the couch watching show after show and taking naps in between. Sophia was very fond of me. She likes me a lot. I was like her personal teddy bear. As a matter of fact, she likes me a little too much. As I started spending most weekends there, I began to spend more time under Sophia's care. She wouldn't let me be anywhere else but by her side. Around nighttime, after she had finished all her chores, she would take me to her room, have me in her bed, and begin to fondle me, putting her hands and reaching under my pants and then placing my fingers in her genitals.

Sometimes, she would have us play hide-and-seek. During hide-and-seek, she always made sure I was her partner. She would take me in the backyard where it was very dark. She would undress herself and rub my genitals against hers from time to time. She would ask me how it felt. She would ask me if it hurt. I would say no. She would keep on rubbing my genitals against hers for about fifteen minutes. Here I was, a little six-year-old being repeatedly molested by an eighteen-year-old for months. I never told anyone about any of this, not even my father. It carried on for a while. For whatever reason, my father eventually stopped leaving me over there.

After skipping the entire first grade because of my thumb surgeries, I came into the second grade, where I was reunited with Joel. We started back up where we left off. In second grade, Joel and I were the two most popular kids around. We were both intelligent and very outspoken. We pretty much ran the whole school. We were both the class clowns. Sometimes, when the teacher would have enough of the both of us, he would hand us over to Mrs. Helena to deal with us. Even as class clowns, Joel and I were always among the top three with the best grades in our class. Joel and I, along with a boy named Tresor, who was now part of our crew, made up the top of the pyramid. We also were the topic of every girl's mouth, even elder girls from grades that were ahead of us.

The beginning of second grade came along and saw some changes in my father's daily routine. At the sound of the bell marking grades K–6 dismissal at 12:15 p.m., now, instead of staying at school until the end of the school day waiting for my father, I started going home with Joel. Mrs. Helena's chauffeur took us back to Joel's house. Joel's family was part of the higher middle class. They were doing great financially. Mr. Mbele, Joel's father, was the vice president of UNTZA, the country's union of laborers. Mrs. Helena, Joel's mother, was a member of a wealthy family back in her home country of Romania. Her father, a former advisor to Nicolae Ceausescu, the former president of Romania, was one of the pillars of the Communist regime.

Joel's house was very big. It had about five bedrooms. As the only child, Joel was very spoiled. He had everything, Nintendo video games, every toy one could possibly dream of. I have heard stories of Michael Jackson's Neverland Ranch. Maybe aside from the little zoo at the ranch, Joel's house wasn't that far behind in commodity. Above all, Joel had luxury I never had up until this point. His own bedroom was equipped with a large king-size bed made up of the finest oak. It had big dressers. His room alone could easily be taken for somebody's home. As soon as we got home, Joel and I would change into house clothes. I would wear some of Joel's clothes. Afterward, the cook would feed us snacks. Then we were headed for a nap. Our nap lasted for about an hour and a half. As soon as we woke up from our nap, we went on to play. At around 4:30 p.m., we were served dinner by the cook. Roasted chicken and smoked sausage with mashed potato and ketchup and sparkling water were at the menu most of the time at Joel's.

At around 5:00 p.m., the chauffeur would take the both us back to the school, where I would join my father at the end of his school day, and Joel would go back home with his mom, who had also finished her day at the same time as my father. My father and I would once again embark on a new adventure until dawn, when we would make our way back to the school to spend the night.

I started out second grade very slowly academically. Given that I missed the entire first grade, I found it very hard to impose myself academically. Since the first part of the trimester consisted mostly of review lessons from the first grade, I started the first trimester ranked among the bottom half of my class. I was very far behind in reading, writing, and science, but I quickly recovered my pace when it came to math, social studies, and language arts. By the time the second trimester ended, I was already in the top ten of my class, thanks to some very intensive tutoring from my father, which mostly involved hours of homework sessions and constant whooping. Aside from the school's curriculum, my father had me working on some lessons he had set up in all different subjects, math, reading, and calligraphy. My weekends became more and more unpleasant, since it mostly involved long tutoring lessons. I was moving at a very fast pace in all other subjects except for writing and reading.

As a kid, I was born left-handed, although at no fault of my own. I was just unfortunate to live in a society where being left-handed was seen not only as an anomaly but also as a sign of weakness. So being left-handed meant you were somehow inferior. My father was a perfectionist. No way was he going to live with that. My father was such a perfectionist that, to him, if you weren't first, it only meant one thing—you were last. He sure wasn't going to have a child who is a left-handed and was behind academically.

My father's tutoring session not only were long but also were mostly brutal. I would get severely beat up with extension cords during lessons for mispronouncing words during a reading lesson or for not writing my letters correctly as it was shown to me during calligraphy lesson. He would make me stay up till 3:00 or 4:00 a.m. until I got it right. I became very traumatized. At some point, I started looking forward to going to school as a means of escape. As Christians look forward to heaven, I was looking forward to Monday, and to me, it seemed like Mondays were never on time when I needed it to be. Sometimes, I wish school hours were from 6:00 a.m. to 5:00 a.m., Monday to Sunday.

By the time the second-grade school year was over, I finished among the top five in my class. Had I not started so far behind, I definitely could have finished first or, worse, second. I can honestly say that my father whooped me into finishing among the top five of my class. By the end of the school year, there wasn't a better reader, math problem solver, or calligrapher in my class or even the next class.

My school was among the top five prestigious schools in the city. Government officials and most business elites had their kids enrolled there. We were a part of the Ivy League of our city' educational system. We had very highly qualified teachers. They were, as a whole, a big family that was interconnected with each other by the love and passion of teaching. I remember, for instance, in many occasions, the fourth-grade teacher who was best friends with our second-grade teacher would come to our class, pull me and one other classmate to go to his class, and try to see if we could solve a math problem that students in his class weren't able to solve, or sometimes just to answer a trivia question. The level of competition among students, which was set by our teachers' such high standard and their educational style, made it more than enjoyable and raised the standard and zeal for higher learning to the sky. Whenever there is zeal, there is also a will; and where there is will, things always seem to get done as a result.

When it comes to interaction with not only people but also the right group of people, my father was a genius. My father was very intelligent, sociable, eloquent, and very intellectually gifted. To the ladies, he was very charming, polite, and well put together. My father always looked sharp whether he had $100 in his pocket or was $10,000 in debt. Never before in my entire childhood had my father shown any sign of weakness even when facing any dilemma. Even when defeated, he always stood strong against adversities.

One thing that is very certain is that if our lives were a poker game, my father would have been the ultimate bluffer that always managed to get away without a trace. Even though my father was financially poor, he never settled for less; nor did he ever seek charity from anyone. On the contrary, he was so proud he'd rather die before asking anyone for anything. Above all, he hated borrowing. He always says there is no surest way to a wealthier life than not being indebted to anyone. He had set one of the highest standards ever seen in a human being. My father had so much ambition, one of the great qualities that he possessed that I've always been envious of. Ambition was his strength. Being stubborn and totalitarian was his weakness. My father hardly ever compromised if ever; it had always been his way or the highway. At times, bad luck played major parts into his misfortunes.

My father was very highly educated. He held a master's degree in philosophy. Unfortunately, by the time he finished school, our country was under the rule of a ruthless dictator who was running the country under a one-party rule. The mid-'80s in our country saw a wave of political uprisings from factions advocating for democracy and an end to the one-party ruling. Even though those movements were nonviolent, they were brutally crushed by the ruling dictator who would have protesters jailed, tortured, and sometimes even killed, leading most of them to either be forced to abandon their cause or go underground.

As a young man, my father was very passionate about bringing changes to the country. One of his primary concerns was to rid the country of a dictatorship that has crippled our nation for over two decades. He went on to join the opposition movement. There was a high shortage of jobs in the private sectors. Majority of jobs were mostly government-run businesses or were affiliated with the government under the one-party rule. It was a Communist-like regime.

My father's refusal to adhere to the ruling party MPR meant that his chances of landing himself a job anywhere in the country were as slim as saying the alphabet backward without catching a breath. Damn near impossible. Managing to land that teaching job was more a sign of bravery in his part than anything else. Considering the fact that he was highly overqualified for the job, he was still highly underpaid. Although his salary didn't reflect his credential. He still took that job given its incentive. So long as he was a faculty member at that school, I was guaranteed free tuition at one of the most prestigious schools in the country. That alone was a great achievement. His gross salary apart from my tuition exemption was hardly enough to raise a child out of, let alone support him.

Midway through my second grade, my father met a beautiful young lady in her twenties named Maggie. Maggie was a college student. She attended one of the city's technical colleges where she was studying to become a teacher. They met one day at a bus stop. Maggie was coming from doing some grocery shopping, while my father was on his way to a friend's house. After introducing themselves to one another and having acquainted for about half an hour, they both made plans to see one another once more. Maggie invited my father at her sister's house, where she lived. My father cheerfully accepted the invitation. After seeing one another a few more times after that, they started dating each other.

Few months later, I got the privilege to finally meet Maggie, who made a very nice first impression. She was slim, tall, with a lighter skin complexion, and most of all, she was very charming and quickly warmed up to me. She even brought me a box of my favorite cookies the first time we met. Maggie and I hit it off from the start. We were already best friends. She was the very first female I saw my father with on a regular basis. As time went by, Maggie would pick me up from school. We would both go to her sister's house. When we got to her sister's house, she would first give me a snack and then have me take a nap. After waking up from my nap, she would feed me dinner and then help me with my homework. As soon as I finished my homework, I was outside playing with her little nephews and the neighbor's kid until around eight o'clock. That's when she would run the hot tub and give me a bath. After the bath, she would then read me a fable or sing me a song to put me to sleep, marking the end of the day.

The home belonged to Maman Agnes, Maggie's elder sister. Her husband, Papa Nestor, was a very successful businessman. He owned quite a few supermarkets around the city. Papa Nestor's house was very big and very beautifully designed. He had one of the city's most prominent architects design it for him. It was located in a very rich neighborhood. His neighbors were either high-ranked senior officials of the country's military, government officials, or some foreign businessmen. Papa Nestor, as I called him, was very nice, and he really loved showing off his assets. He never missed out on an opportunity to show off. Anytime he bought a new car, he would have an open house. New furniture—that was a perfect call for an open house. He once had a special reception at his home where he invited families and friends just to show off his newly installed bathtub. To borrow one of his famous quotes, "It's very hard to be humble when you are as great as I am." I loved that man.

He had a lot of children, and by a lot, I mean around twelve, if not a little bit more. He had some of them studying abroad in France and Belgium. Living with him, he had about five daughters and three sons. Jean-Claude, his youngest boy, was about four years older than I was, or maybe more, but he was my closest playmate. Papa Nestor also had a few of his relatives' children living with him. He had a few nieces and nephews under his care. As is customary in most African traditions, if one of the family members happened to have earned himself a very comfortable living, it is his duty to care for the rest of the family members that are less fortunate than him. As a sign of gratitude, he would have to show his support to the family by offloading them with the task of having to struggle to take care of their own offspring, thus enabling him to become the leader of the big family. Whenever any family member that was in his care happen to prosper financially, he or she now had to carry on the same tradition of helping other less fortunate family members.

As it has been said, the road to hell was created with great intention, so was this old tradition, which, over decades, have shown to create more harm than good. The bad part of it usually arises when one who has done well for himself by virtue of sacrifices and self-discipline for the sole purpose of becoming somehow successful. Once he or she becomes successful, he or she ends up with the task of caring for a multitude of people with little or no interest in trying to work half as hard as their provider. These moochers have no intention whatsoever to make it on their own. You would have family members who would continuously flood the person with more dependents. Those dependents wouldn't stop there. They will get so comfortable being taken care off and go as far as starting to have kids at someone else's expense, making it very overwhelming and somewhat uncomfortable. This malpractice always ended up tearing the family apart and creating more resentment among family members.

Although this old tradition has shown to be very ineffective to many families, it also had worked wonder to the exception of those who have managed to use it properly as it always been intended. One of the perfect examples was my aunt Martha, whose house hosted so many of my uncles and aunts who took advantage of the opportunity given to them and ended up flying with her own wings. Another example of the system's success was Papa Nestor's home. Everyone at the home adored me. They all took me as one of their own. I even started living there at one point. I would get driven to school in the mornings and picked up after school. For as long as I lived there, I was one of them. They were all impressed about how intelligent I was at six. I was a trivia machine. Politics was my strongest topic. I was the only six-year-old who had interest in the news and who could spark a debate with anyone about our country's politics. I had my father to thank for that. At six, I was able to spot any government official on the street and call him or her by their name.

In one occasion, while walking around with my father, we were passing by in front of the chief commander of our country's air force. He was sitting in front of his gated house. Behind him, there were two of his bodyguards. My father looked at me and asked me as we were approaching the man, "Do you know who that it is?"

I said, "Yes," and loud enough, I said, "That's General Kikunda, the chief commander of the air force."

The general looked at me and asked me to come. "Who am I?" he asked.

I repeated. "You are General Kikunda, chief commander of the air force."

"How do you know that?" he asked.

"I see you on TV!" I said.

Being really amazed by what he had just witnessed, he reached out of his pocket and pulled out two bills of 500 zaire, our country's currency. I was handed what I believe could have been the equivalent of $200.

On another occasion, Papa Nestor was sitting outside on the patio, chatting with a certain Mr. Lukoji, a friend of his who happened to be the country's prime minister. As I was passing by, I yelled out his name. "Mr. Lukoji!" I said.

He looked at me and said, "What can I do for you, son?"

I said, "Do you know you are the worst at your position?"

He took a second and then asked, "Who told you I was?"

I said, "My dad!" Papa Nestor had a smirk in his face as to tell his guest that he wanted absolutely no part of that.

One of my father's greatest successes while raising me single-handedly was the ability to expose me to a wealthy life without actually being wealthy himself. That alone, I believe, should count as success. It's like growing up with the Rothschild or the Rockefeller children while being a nobody. Growing up, looking around me, all I could see left to right were kids from all those elite families. It was amazing to me that even though for many nights, we used one of the classrooms in my school as a bedroom while using a collection of cardboards as a bed, at the end of the day, the genius that was my father put me in a position where I was as equal as those kids from those prestigious families with the opportunity to even achieve greater things than those friends of mine who came from wealthy families. If one day, I fail in my conquest to live a successful and balanced life, I would have no one but myself to blame, since as a child, my father did everything plus more to guarantee I never fail in my quest to achieve greatness. I was well trained and strongly equipped.

My childhood at this point was the best one could've possibly ever dreamed off. I was the heir prince of an everlasting kingdom that carried from all extremity—an empire that knew no borders. As a child, I had everything I ever wanted and wished for. I was this little adorable figure that everyone seemed to always be fond of. I was the perfect child to anyone that loved or wished to have a child. As a child, there were no limits to what I could ever achieve.

My father was a lady's man. He fared quiet well with the ladies. Not only did he have a very good taste when it came to the ladies but he was also very picky. He had a thing for slimmer ladies with body shape almost as identical to runway fashion models. He always knew exactly what to say to gain a lady's hand, and they all were very fond of him. He would occasionally use me as a bait whenever he felt the necessity to do so. I remember at four years old, when one day waiting for a bus at a bus stop, he had me go approach a lady that was standing about twenty yards away from us. He instructed me to tell the lady that there was this gentlemen standing back there that was dying for a chance to compliment her on how beautiful and well-dressed she was. For some reason, I never fail on my missions. I believe it was because he knew exactly when and whom to strike.

I remember a share of his targets that ultimately ended up in short-term relationships up until Maggie. I never knew of any of my father's relationship that lasted as long as three months. At first, I thought that mostly came as a result of him having to care for me twenty-four hours a day, seven days a week, and the fact that he had technically no place to call his own residence, or maybe he was just a little too demanding and too picky. Then later on, I realized it was just a combination of many things that factored out together to his own detriment.

At his early thirties, my father was already at a stage of his life where he wanted to settle down and build his family. Like a very smart shopper, he knew exactly what he wanted and needed no time to waste in getting it. But unfortunately for him, a lot of his first choices were a few steps behind him when it came to commitment.

I remember, for instance, there was a case involving a very beautiful young lady named Marceline. She was in her midtwenties, just fresh out of her first few years of college. She was the daughter of a well-respected surgical doctor. I could see through her eyes how in love Marceline was with my father, and from the very first day I met her, she fell in love with me too. She was very charming. It was almost as if she was the elder sister I always wish to have. From time to time, my father would drop me off at her house. Marceline and I would have so much fun together. She always managed to take me out for a cone of ice cream, which always was my favorite. One time, while in her room, I even told her that I will start calling her mom. She was so happy, and from that day on, she would always tell people that I was her son even if most people found it very hard to believe. I had no doubt I wanted her to be my mother.

My father wanted to marry Marceline right away, but there was only one problem. Marceline wasn't opposed to marrying my father, at least not until after she finished med school. My father wanted her to put her studies on hold until at least a year or two after the wedding. They were both at a deadlock, and since neither Romeo nor Juliet planned on making any concessions for the greater good, the whole relationship ended up being called off, and they both went their separate ways. I don't know how much hit my father took from the breakup. All I knew was that I was badly emotionally affected by the split. I lost a best friend and potentially the greatest mother I could have wished for.

My father had a few more very short-term relationships after Marceline that were very irrelevant to me, as for me, whoever wasn't Marceline wasn't worth the time or the affection. There was this French lady that used to work as a telemarketer. There were also rumors going around that my father was having an affair with Mrs. Helena, Joel's mother, our school president. Whether that was accurate, I wouldn't be surprised if that was the case given how close and cozy they were together.

During the summer that followed, the end of my second-grade year, my father and Maggie finally tied the knot. But few weeks before the wedding, a tragedy did hit close to home. Maggie's mother, who has been living in Brussels, Belgium, passed away at the hospital after suffering from a very complicated illness. The burial was held in Brussels. Maggie had to fly to Belgium to attend her mother's funeral. She was very emotional the night of her flight. My father and I accompanied her to the airport. She had been crying throughout the whole way there, and all attempts of consoling her were all met with even more sobbing. About two weeks later, she made it back in great spirits just in time for her wedding.

It was a double wedding also involving one of Papa Nestor's daughters who was marrying her high school sweetheart. It was a very nice wedding with a lot of guests. The wedding reception was held in one of the city's luxurious hotels. Papa Nestor, out of his gratitude and since it was both his daughter and his sister-in-law getting married on the same day, he offered to pay for both receptions. The proud man that was my father politely declined his offer. Being somehow never accustomed to the word "no" being told to him, Papa Nestor felt somehow deflated. That incident alone put a lot of damage into my father's relationship with Papa Nestor. To my father, it was nothing personal, just a matter of principals. That was too much of a debt to be owed to one man, and he hated owing another man. Papa Nestor, on the other hand, was just trying to make his financial prowess felt and idolized. They both did made some concession, and it was rumored that my father did accept their honeymoon to be paid for by Papa Nestor as a wedding gift, thus ending the friendly feud.

The wedding was extraordinary from start to finish. I was the ring bearer at the wedding. One of the things that caught my attention at the wedding was the fact that among the many invited guests, only my uncle Danny, my father's younger brother, and one of my father's distant uncles, a former diplomat whom my father picked to act as his caregiver, accompanied by his wife and children, were the only family members to attend the wedding. The low turnout from the groom's family, whether it was accidental or coincidental, sure did not go unnoticed to my or everyone else's eyes. On the bright side, the turnout among his friends and colleagues was far more impressive. He even had one of his exes in attendance.

Maggie was glowing on her wedding day. Dressed up in a pink-and-white specially designed low-cut wedding dress, she lit up the place and made the very best out of her most important day. From the church ceremony to the reception, this was by far the greatest day of my life. I got to meet so many unfamiliar faces. From state officials, high-ranking men in the military, to very successful businessmen, the reception was full of VIPs. There was a live performance from a very popular local band, Wenge Musica, which lit up the night with their exuberant performance. The unlimited alcohol and food supplies had the party going until seven o'clock the next morning. To all, it was indeed a night to remember as Papa Nestor went all out in guaranteeing a very successful ceremony.

After the wedding, my father, Maggie, and I moved in to our place. It was a huge four-bedroom house that belongs to one of Maggie' elder sisters, Rosalie, who lived in Belgium. For years, she rented out the house to a few different tenants. The house was located in a swampy area not very far off from the river. This area was very susceptible to severe flooding, causing many tenants not to honor their lease. For years, Rosalie tried to put up the house on the market, but no one ever seems to come up with a good offer. She had purchased the house at a very high value, but now with the economy being down and all, along with the constant flooding in the area, the house had lost about 40 percent of its market value. Rosalie still wouldn't budge on the price. She still demanded the same amount she had previously put up on the house, which by this time was about 40 percent above market value. She would rather no one lived in that house than having it sold far below her asking price.

Maggie and my father had talked her out of letting them rent the house until a suitable offer came along, giving a them a little time to find a nice place to move into. My father and Maggie rented the house from Rosalie. The house was so huge we didn't have enough furniture to even cover half of the house, so we only managed to occupy about a quarter of the house, while the other three-fourths was left unfurnished.

My father was very culturally hip. His discography collection was very expanded and resourceful. He had record albums from various artists such as Elvis Presley, Michael Jackson, Luther Vandros, Lionel Richie, Bob Marley, Whitney Houston, Celine Dion, Boys II Men, TLC, Julio Iglesias, you name it. Michael Jackson, Julio Iglesias, and two local artists, Papa Wemba and his Viva la Musica band, and Koffi Olomide and his Quartier Latin band, were his all-time favorites. They both were the two pillars of Congolese music. Music had a big part in his everyday life. Being a fan of both Papa Wemba and Koffi Olomide was somehow contrasting. Not only were these two artists the biggest archenemies in Congolese music but also they both had two different styles in their music.

On one hand, he had Jules Shungu Wembadio, known as Papa Wemba, the father of the Congolese hip-hop culture. He had a very distinct style of music in which he combined both traditional folkloric rhythm and sounds with what is known today as world music. His style of music, which mostly emphasized the street life, also walked parallel with the excessive love of fashion.

Papa Wemba was crowned the Pope of Fashion, a code religiously followed by all his fanatics. He is responsible for promoting the street life through his music, and above all, he is accredited for propelling la Sapologie, also known as la Sape, a movement that magnifies one's physical appearance through fashion rather than his or her character or intellect all over Europe and Africa. You had people spending more than 80 percent of their income in name brand clothing, such as Gianni Versace, Dolce & Gabbana, Giorgio Armani, Gianfranco Ferre, Jean Paul Gaultier, Yohji Yamamoto . . . just to name a few, while they still live in total poverty. And those who didn't have any source of income turned to shoplifting at those name brand fashion stores just to stay hip. Being hip was so much glorified in those days. To fit into the new culture, one had to abide by the rule, which was none other than spending as much money in name brand clothing to stay relevant.

With that came the war of fashion, which had individuals going against one another just to see who had the best collection of brand name clothing. Those fashion warriors were known as Sapeur or Sapologue. You had on one side Sapeur, such as Papa Wemba himself, Kester Emeneya, Stervos Niarcos, General Defao, Tresor Ngando, Clam

Franchi, Spadjarhy Tembo, Ya Dieu Watshambu, all representing the Democratic Republic of the Congo.

On the other side of the Congo River, the competition was made up of great Sapeur such as Djo Balard, Norbat de Paris, Rapha Bounzeki, Diodel Bilamba, Mesma Mabonza, and Stany de Paris, all representing another heavyweight fashion country Congo-Brazzaville.

On a group level, you had groups such as Les Leopards de la Sape, Alkaida, Jet Set, and Les Anglais. Those were your front runners. Those groups were made up of about seven to ten best Sapeur who would travel from city to city just to challenge other groups or individuals in a fashion showboating. Whenever an individual or a group of Sapeur would gather to challenge one another, that event was called Affrontement. Sapologie is a worldwide movement that found its root deep on the streets of Kinshasa, DR Congo, and made famous worldwide by Papa Wemba, one of Africa's greatest recording artists.

Although the movement started out in the late '70s, it was thanks to great media coverage from one of the leading voices in Congolese Diaspora media reporting from Paris, France, chroniclers such as Kerwin Mayizo and his program *L'Analyse* and a certain Papa Rolls under his program *Zwa Nga Bien* who were the first music chroniclers to be filming live Affrontements, with the famous of all Affrontements, which took place by the Eifel Tower in Paris between Norbat de Paris of Brazzaville and Tresor Ngando of Kinshasa in front of a very large crowd. Norbat de Paris's authentic blue alligator shoes, which was estimated at around $9,000, was the knockout punch that brought down the king of Sapologie, Tresor Ngando. Since that day, Norbat de Paris became the undisputed king of Sapologie. His victory over Tresor Ngando marked the end of total dominance from DR Congo Sapeur all over the globe. With a budget estimated around $100 million annually, Sapologie was able to become one of the leading movements in African music culture especially for the African Diaspora.

With the recession hitting most of Europe, a lot of Sapeur were now unable to afford expensive brand name clothing to keep up with the fashion race because of the economy; some became more reliant on knock offs. Although cheaply made from secondhand materials, most knockoffs, which still had the logo of original brands, still look good but cost a fraction of the original brand. Those knockoffs were usually coming from Turkey, Thailand, and China. As knockoff brands started pouring into the market, it became somehow difficult to tell them apart from the original brands, but thanks to Sapologie connoisseur, that task was made easier, since only they were able to point out a knockoff brand even from miles away.

Those who were reluctant to go the knockoff route found themselves creating a new fashion movement, which they called Chic et Rebel. Unlike Sapologie, which required a large budget and constant Affrontement, Chic et Rebel was less costly and very affordable. Chic et Rebel emphasized in looking clean and sharp at very little to no cost without recurring to name brand. The pioneers of the Chic et Rebel movement were Alain Mbolela, BobCarlos Kalala, Bora Malega, Jean-Paul Luabeya, Platini Manzambi, Michael Ruguge, Giresse Samabi, and the only girl in the group, Didistone Olomide, known as the princess of fashion for her blossoming style and great looks. All together, they were known as the G8.

On the other hand, he had another celebrity who is arguably the most controversial icon in Congolese music history—the legend, Antoine Christophe Agbepa Mumba, also known as Koffi Olomide. Unlike Papa Wemba, a product of thug life growing up on the streets, Koffi Olomide was a college graduate. He held a bachelor's degree in business economics at the University of Bordeaux in France and a master's degree in mathematics from the University of Paris also in France. His passion for music led him to juggle between both school and music. He started out by being a songwriter to various artists including providing hit songs to none other than his former friend and mentor now turned archenemy Papa Wemba. He decided to start his solo career and put together his famous band Quartier Latin, bringing aboard young talents who arguably had the best musical voice in the country.

Unlike Papa Wemba, Koffi Olomide's trademark was lovemaking and the glorification of the Congolese and African women in a vast majority of his songs through his trademark music style, which he named Tchatcho, a style of music he invented and is now emulated by many across the globe. With his poetic lyrics combined with his charming and, most of all, very unique voice, it led so many women to orgasm through their ears while listening to his songs. He is the Congolese artist with the most greatest hit songs. One of his recording albums, *Loi* is Africa's number-one selling album of all time, making him one of the continent's best-selling artists of all time. With his Tchatcho style, there was not a single woman or girl who wasn't a fan of Koffi Olomide. In addition, he also introduced his fans and everyone else to his love of luxury cars. While Papa Wemba was the undisputed king of fashion, Koffi Olomide was the king of luxury automobile. His collection of luxury cars was second to none. From Mercedes-Benz, Ferrari, Ranger Rover, Lamborghini, you name it, he had it all.

So if you wanted to be hip and street smart, Papa Wemba offered the type of music suitable to you; but if you wanted to score with the ladies and grasp a good understanding on how to leave a good mark on a woman's body, Koffi Olomide was your guy. With both Papa Wemba and Koffi Olomide at the peak of their music career, the DR Congo was the undisputed dominant force in music throughout both Africa and the Caribbean. The rivalry between Papa Wemba and Koffi Olomide was Congo's biggest rivalry in music. In a city where one was only either a fan of Papa Wemba and his Viva La Musica band or a fan of Koffi Olomide and his Quartier Latin band, my father went against the norm by being a fan of both artists.

Maggie's family loved my father. Her niece and nephews would occasionally spend the weekend or other school holidays at our house. My father was such a good host when it came to guests.

The beginning of my third-grade year was marked by very unfortunate events that brought chaos in our country. The early '90s started out very badly for our country. We had a dictator as a head of state who has been in power for over twenty-five years. He went by the name of Mobutu. Mobutu came into power in 1965 by means of a coup d'état. With the backing of the CIA, he overthrew a democratically elected government following our country's independence from our colonial ruler Belgium. In June 1960, the Congo, a former Belgian colony, gained its independence, thus installing its very first democratically elected government with Joseph Kasa-Vubu as president and Patrice Emery Lumumba as the country's prime minister. Once in power, the new government found it very difficult to implement its agenda, which came mostly as a result of foreign interference to its internal matters and foreign policy. Patrice Lumumba opted for a more nationalistic approach in trying to help build a stronger nation based upon a stronger economy.

The young leader ideology was parallel to that of other promising Pan-Africanism leaders such as the likes of Kwame Nkrumah of Ghana and Anwar Sadat of Egypt, who all believed in setting off the whole African continent as a major power among the world elite such as the USSR and the United States. Those people had the blueprint to develop and unify the whole continent as to become what the EU is to Western Europe. They envisioned a United African Union that would compete in the world stage with the likes of USA, USSR, and all other developed countries. That was the goal of Pan-Africanism.

Given that the Congo was a vast country very rich in arable land and natural resources, diamond, gold, copper, cobalt, uranium, manganese, oil, and natural gas, all are found in the Democratic Republic of the Congo. The Democratic Republic of the Congo is a geological wonder, a paradise on earth. It is the only country in the world to possess all the minerals found in the periodic table. It is the world's number-one producer of cobalt, a mineral very essential for the production of electrical automobiles. Cobalt is used to treat some form of cancer and is also used as a medical tracer. The Democratic Republic of the Congo is also the world's number-one producer of coltan, a very strategic mineral used in every electronic devices. It is one of two countries in the world to be located in both sides of the equator; Brazil being the other one. It is home to the okapi, an artiodactyl mammal also known as the forest giraffe or zebra giraffe, an animal only found in the Democratic Republic of the Congo. The Democratic Republic of the Congo is home to the Lake Tanganyika, the world's longest lake. It is also the only lake in the world that hosts more than 350 different species of fish. Last but not the least, it is also home to the Congo River, the second-largest river in the world by discharge and the world's deepest river.

Lumumba knew one thing the only way to a very prosperous Congo was by securing foreign investment and guaranteeing a very proportionate equitable sharing of internal revenue from big mining concession to the import of our goods abroad. One of Lumumba's first move was seeking the renegotiation of all mining contracts with foreign companies. At the time, foreign companies were making so much while paying the state very little to nothing, making it near impossible for the Congo to boost its economy. In some cases, a foreign company would be benefiting from 80 to 90 percent of the revenue, while the state would be left to get by with 10 to 20 percent if that. All those multinational companies backed by Western interest had no challenge under colonial rule. Lumumba sought to put an end to that. Now that the country was under nationalists, the table was quickly turning against multinationals.

Lumumba, one of the most passionate nationalists the Congo has ever known, identified the lopsided mining contracts and revenues from those multinational companies as the number-one threat to national interest. According to Lumumba, with the Congo now being independent as sovereign country, the Congo was now master of its own destiny, meaning that any precolonial contracts were doomed obsolete and needed to be renegotiated. From now on, the new partition of all mining revenues would be as follows: 65 percent of all mining revenues was going toward the country's treasury, while 35 percent was going to foreign companies.

All the foreign companies and investors didn't like that idea a bit. According to them, there wasn't going to be any changes at all. One of the country's leading foreign investors even went as far as stating that an independent Congo was just the same as a Congo under colonial rules. There were no changes to be made. All foreign companies' previous contracts were to be maintained and never to be messed with. No way were they going to renegotiate any contracts. With neither parties willing to concede to another's demand, one thing became very clear to Lumumba. Although the colonial powers did concede political independence to Africans by granting them their independence, they still held on to the economy. All they did was take the noose off the neck and replace it with one in the leg.

Lumumba was not going to give up so easily. Gaining a total independence from those colonial powers was a task worth of dying for, he thought. He sought to establish the country's sovereignty over Western powers. He brought the fight to them by threatening to nationalize all the mining companies that were under foreign management if no one was willing to renegotiate any contracts. In his first month in office, Lumumba has already made himself more enemies within the Western world. He became so isolated, leaving him with very little to no support at home. His approval rating was at an all-time low. The United States, along with other colonial powers who were enjoying such unlimited amount of profit under the previous status quo, identified Lumumba as the number-one threat to their national interest, meaning that now, the elimination of Lumumba in the political scene was more imminent than ever.

As American and Europeans investors pulled out of the Congo, Lumumba moved to attract Chinese and Soviet investors, earning him to be tagged a Communist. With the cold war between the United States and the Soviet Union at its peak, the Congo, as a potential game changer because of its large deposit of natural resources, was a very strategic country that neither the United States nor European powers could effort letting it slip under Communist hands, which could pretty much decide the winner between the capitalistic USA and the Communist USSR. Seeing the danger posed by Lumumba to its economic interests, the United States moved quickly with a plan to destabilize the Congo under Lumumba by supporting and supplying proxies groups within the country to undermine stability in the Congo with mutinies, thus weakening Lumumba's ability to govern.

Few months after, Lumumba, along with two of his collaborators, was assassinated in a CIA-sponsored coup. A couple of years following Lumumba's assassination, Joseph Mobutu, a lieutenant in the Congolese army and a former CIA covert agent, overthrew the government in a staged coup d'état.

Lumumba's death marked a setback to a dream, the dream of seeing a strong, unified, and prosperous Congo—a Congo independent from any sort of foreign interference and dependency. His loss was a big blow to Congolese sovereignty and African unity. On that day, the whole Africa lost a continental hero.

Mobutu came into power as a very strategic ally to the United States during the cold war with the Soviet Union and also a vital partner to Western Europe as Europe was struggling to recover economically post–World War II. Mobutu proceeded by forcibly eliminating anyone that was posing as a challenge to his autocratic rule. Political opponents who didn't share his views or visions were brutally assassinated, leaving him to become the sole uncontested ruler in the land. As Africa's most strategic U.S. ally, Mobutu benefited from multimillion dollars in foreign aids from the U.S. government because of his allegiance against Communist expansion in Africa. Above all, he also received millions of dollars in military hardware and equipment and trainings, making his military the best trained and equipped army in Africa. As a dictator, Mobutu took great advantage of American money that was being poured on him to strengthen his grip onto power.

To his credit, his first fifteen years in power were marred by great accomplishment such as the building of Africa's largest suspension bridge, known as the Pont Marechal, located across the Congo River at the port of Matadi. He also built La Voix du Zaire, Africa's largest radio and television broadcasting tower, and both the Palais du Peuple and the Palais de la Nation; the former was the seat of the National Assembly, and the latter being the seat of the Senate in the capital city, Kinshasa, both of them being Africa's largest congressional buildings. His vision for building a stronger and greater country competing for supremacy in the international stage among the western hemisphere's great countries such as France, the UK, Western Germany, and the United States was second to none. He started out in the right path by bringing about one of his greatest accomplishments, if not his greatest ones. In his first decade in power, he was able to unify the country, which was composed of more than five hundred different ethnicities molded into one nation. He established a sense of dignity and patriotism into the Zairean citizen.

During that time, to be identified as a Zairean was something of greater esteem. He introduced the country to his new state of ideology, which he named Zairianization, or a recourse to ancestral roots socially and spiritually.

Zairianization, according to Mobutu, was an idea based on Pan-Africanist philosophy with more emphasis on authentication of African values such as the adoption of ancestral names, customs, and culture against Western ones. Through Zairianization, every citizen was urged to abandon their Christian names for true African ones. As he put it himself, it wasn't logical for African men or women to carry on Europeans names in which they had absolutely no history or connection to. He once asked to name a Caucasian or a Jewish person with an African name. There was none, he said, and why should an African be named Michael or Jeanine while he or she has absolutely no connection to those names? He led by example by changing his own name from Joseph-Desire Mobutu to Mobutu Sese Seko Kuku Ngbendu Wa Za Banga. He also proceeded by changing all former colonial names to African ones. He eventually renamed the country from Belgium-Congo to Zaire. The capital city, which was known as Leopoldville, was renamed to Kinshasa, and so did other cities and streets in accordance to the new doctrine.

By the early '70s, he was able to propel the country to becoming among the world's best economies. Zaire, which was also the name of the national currency, was worth twice as much as the U.S. dollar. In 1974, one zaire was trading for two U.S. dollars. In that same year, Mobutu took it a step further in gaining our country recognition in the world stage by paying $10 million to bring the fight of the century to Zaire, the historic boxing bout held in Kinshasa in October 1974 between the undefeated world heavyweight champion George Foreman against the crowd-favorite Muhammad Ali. The sixty thousand plus spectators, a record then for a live boxing event held outside the United States, were all in favor of the Louisville, Kentucky, native Ali, whom they embraced as being one of their own. The Stade du 20 Mai Stadium was electrified with what is known today as boxing's most famous trademark chants of "Ali Boma Ye, Ali Boma Ye, Ali Boma Ye," which means, "Ali, finish him," in Lingala, the number-one language spoken in Kinshasa.

To name such a historic event Rumble in the Jungle is just another way for Western geopolitics to undermine great achievements by another race, especially a black one. The fight was held in the capital city, Kinshasa, one of the most flourishing cities in the world at the time, home to the world's twenty-second-best economy at the time and holder of the world's fourth-strongest currency. The country Zaire wasn't a jungle, let alone its capital city, Kinshasa. I never quite understood which jungle they were referring to.

In 1974, the city of Kinshasa was ranked the sixteenth best city in the world to live in. Kinshasa was home to the leopard of Zaire, the first African nation to make it to the World Cup featuring the most prolific striker to ever come out of the continent, a guy known as Ndaye Mulamba, a.k.a. Mutumbula, the only player to ever score nine goals in one major tournament, a record that is yet to be broken.

One of Mobutu's many great accomplishments also came in the world stage where he delivered his famous 1973 speech at the UN general assembly, a speech that is by far the greatest speech of all time by a head of state at the UN. In his speech, President Mobutu painted a true picture of imperialism and capitalism and its negative influence in the African continent. In his speech, he defended African values and stressed the need of a more collaborating approach between developed countries in the western hemisphere through the sharing of knowledge and technology with other underdeveloped countries in the African continent. He also tackled the Israeli and Palestinian conflict by breaking diplomatic ties with Israel for its role in escalating the Arab and Israeli conflict. One of the most important parts of his speech was his elaboration of the many problems Africa was facing such as Apartheid in South Africa, Western colonialism, global warming, just to name a few. The whole continent of Africa, he said, has the form of a revolver with the trigger located in Zaire; therefore, it is the duty of this great nation to propel the whole continent to economic development. That was arguably the greatest Pan-Africanist speech of all time.

Those were Mobutu's greatest accomplishments, which are still unmatched by any of his predecessors. But as time went by, Mobutu became more and more interested in keeping a stronghold into power. Accumulating more wealth became his priority, while the welfare of his citizens was nevertheless becoming more of a surplus requirement in his agenda. As Mobutu and his entourage's wealth was skyrocketing at a record rate, the rest of the country was getting poorer and poorer. There was lack of infrastructure, no funding was made available for education, no roads were being build, teachers weren't getting their salary, and corruption was at a record high, leading the country to become one of the worst economies in the world.

The early '90s saw a shift in the world stage with the collapse of the Soviet Union, thus marking the end of the cold war. The end of the cold war also brought in a shift in U.S. foreign policy toward most of its strategic cold war allies. The United States winning the cold war meant it no longer needed Mobutu's service, subsequently putting an end to all financial and military aids to Mobutu and his regime. The early '90s sought an overwhelming state of anger and displeasure toward the Mobutu regime from a large majority of the population, with the gap between the haves and have-nots becoming as wide as it had ever been, and the middle class going toward extinction. There were no jobs available; corruption was at an all-time high, leading to the rise of prostitution even among minors. The whole country was in crisis. Nothing seemed to work. It was a disaster politically, socially, and economically.

The beginning of my third grade saw a rise of political uprising within the country. There was a lot of opposition to the government leading to a lot of political rallies and strikes all in favor of more political freedom and democracy. People were very fed up with the Mobutu regime, which had a total disregard of its own people suffering, while Mobutu and his entourage were getting richer and richer, leaving the population in starvation mode. One day, people all over the country took up to the streets looting businesses, stores, and residences of government elite. Foreigners were robbed of their goods, bringing chaos to the country for about a week. Many foreign investors, along with some foreign officials and their families, fled the country. Most foreign embassies were closed for a long period.

About a week later, calm and order was restored, thanks to the heroic intervention of Marc Mahele, the army chief of staff. General Mahele, as he was known to all, was a national hero. He was a former army ranger who received training from Special Forces in Israel and Russia. General Mahele was the highest decorated man in the military, the only man never to have been defeated. He had won every battle he ever was involved in. General Mahele was very popular and beloved by the people. General Mahele was to Zaire and the Zairean people what George Washington was to the United States and the American people.

Mobutu, being out of idea, had to seek the help of General Mahele to quell the uprising. Using his popularity among the population, General Mahele was able to convince the people to stop looting and go back to their respective activities. But even with his intervention, the looting, which was nationwide, had already made so much damage to the country. With no foreign investors willing to come back and invest into the country, the country's economy went from bad to worse. There was no foreseeable hope for the country.

All prayers now were aimed at one thing and one thing only—the end of the Mobutu regime. No one had a clear idea how an end to the Mobutu regime was going to come about, but one thing was certain—whether by might or by miracles, Mobutu and his regime being gone will be the greatest thing to ever happen to this country postcolonialism. The Mobutu regime disapproval rate was at a record high. Public schoolteachers around the nation all called for a nationwide strike demanding back pays that had been owed to them by the government from months leading to all public schools across the country to be shut down because of teachers' absence. The only school left opened were some private and Catholic schools. Eighty percent of the population, which relied on public school as the only means of education for their children, were forced to keep their children at home. The schools were closed for a whole school year.

My third-grade year saw major cuts in school faculty staff. Some teachers were let go as a means to balance the books. To fill up some vacancy as a result of the budget cuts, now, my father had to pick up more responsibility. Aside from being both music teacher and director of discipline, he was now promoted to school principal.

In third grade, Joel and I still ran the show, but we were challenged academically by the arrival of a new kid in the class with the name of Junior Kakese. Junior was very smart in his first year at the school. He already occupied the top spot in the class, which caught Joel and me by surprise. Junior was somehow quiet and, most of all, very savvy. Joel and I were mostly known for being the class clown, me especially. Whenever the teacher would step out of the class, I always took it upon myself to fill in the void. It was my duty. I thought to keep the class up and running through funny jokes and buffoonery, creating a state of pandemonium in the class. Throughout the school year, Joel and I managed to introduce Junior as a new member to our crew. We were no longer a duo, but instead, we became a trio.

Junior was one of four siblings attending that school. His younger brother François was in the first grade, his sister Jenny in fifth grade, while his eldest sister, Bijoux, was in seventh grade. Amazingly, they were all top of their classes, respectively. Junior's savviness was one of the attributes of his intelligence. While Joel and I always had trouble finishing our assignments on time given how busy we were entertaining the class with our goofiness, Junior always managed to finish his assignments first before joining us with the foolishness.

The third grade, one of my greatest years academically, was overshadowed by a long record of disciplinary reprimands as a result of being the undisputed class clown. It was almost ironic. With my father being the head of discipline in the entire school, I was the student with the worst disciplinary record in the entire school. Being the class clown at school came with a heavier price to pay as I was receiving a lot of whooping at home for all the demerits I was receiving in class as a result.

Despite all the disciplinary trouble at school, the third grade was very memorable and pleasant for me. For the very first time in my childhood, I had a place to call my home. I had my own room and had two lovely parents that seemed to care a great deal for me. At school, I was surrounded by the best duo of friends in Junior and Joel. Together, we were the inseparable trio, a band of brothers. I had it all. Life was great. As they all say, good things don't last forever. Then came the fourth grade.

The fourth grade started out quite badly for me. As the school was going through some more budget cuts, meaning most of the faculty staffs were asked to take a significant pay cut or else they were shown the door. This time around, my father wasn't exempt from it given the fact that my father was already carrying more responsibilities at a very little to no cost from the school budget. He felt very insulted by being asked to take a pay cut. He was very well deserved of a raise being so overloaded as he was. The school ownership didn't want to lose my father. Not only that my father was overqualified but he was also a workhorse, a very dedicated one to say the least. Ms. Helena tried her very best to persuade my father to stay without taking a pay cut, but all that fell on deaf hears.

My father had made up his mind—it was a raise or nothing. He later handed his resignation to the school ownership. Even though I didn't agree with his sudden resignation, I strongly respected and supported his action. I totally understood his motive. Unlike years ago, when he only was a single father, now he was responsible for a family of three, which was soon to become a family of four given that my stepmother was weeks away from giving birth to a baby girl. This wasn't the time to take pay cuts especially that he was already working on a discounted salary. My father's work hours at the school were from 6:45 a.m. to 6:00 p.m., from Mondays to Fridays, and 6:45 a.m. to 12:45 p.m. every other Saturdays. The school kept him very busy. With his salary, he couldn't afford public transportation; therefore, he and I had to walk to and from school every day. The walk to and from school was about one hour and fifteen minutes each way. We left home at five thirty every morning and didn't get back home till around seven at night. Just like great warriors, we managed just fine.

Few weeks into my fourth-grade year, we were out of the house that we were renting from Maggie's sister. My father being unemployed caused him to fall so far behind on rent, leaving Maggie's sister with no choice but to put up the house back in the market and ended up selling it. After the house was sold, we moved in to a smaller house not very far from the previous one. The new house was a pretty little two-bedroom house with a spacious lawn. It was gated. There was one huge problem—the house being built in a swampy area caused it to flood whenever there was heavy rain.

One night, as we were all sleeping, we were awakened by a heavy large amount of water covering the whole house. The heavy rain that had been pouring for hours had caused the whole house to be flooded, with the water about two to three feet high everywhere. Everything was underwater. We lost about everything in that flood, from furniture to personal belonging. About 80 percent of our belongings were gone with that flood, prompting us to relocate once more.

We eventually moved away from that part of town to a smaller place. We rented the other part of a small house, which had been turned into a duplex. The house was owned by a widow who was in her sixties. A few weeks after settling into our new place, Maggie gave birth to a beautiful baby girl, Jenny. It was I who came up with the name Jenny. I became very fond of the newcomer of the family. We were so close that her very first word, instead of being "mommy" or "daddy," was "eh moo." That was her way of saying my name, Timu. My baby sister was the most adorable creature I had ever seen. I couldn't help but love her more and more. She would cry her lungs out whenever I left for school in the morning and was as excited to see me coming back from school, just like a sailor's wife would be when seeing her husband back from long naval duties. I couldn't wait to come home to hold her.

My father's unsuccessful attempt in landing another job was quickly translating into frustration. One of the greatest lessons life has taught us is that financial stability and love always walk parallel to one another. Whenever there is financial stability, love seems to blossom; whereas love always seems to be very shaky when financial instability is making its mark on the horizon. My parents did the best they could to keep everything under control, but as they say, fire always brings about smoke. In this case, the smoke coming out from the fire underneath was starting to cause cancer.

As the financial trouble was persisting, perhaps turning into a nightmare for my father, so did my father's attitude, which basically transformed his character to something I couldn't recognize. It was as if the devil had traded places with my father. He became very neglecting and mostly abusive, both verbally and physically. It seemed like nothing pleased him at all. As for me, it seemed like everything I did earned me a beating. When it came to punishment, I believe not even Saddam Hussein could have rivaled him in inflicting such pain to anyone. My relationship with my father was already deteriorating shortly after the birth of my baby sister. It seemed to me that baby Jenny took all the love and affection. Even my relationship with Maggie was at its lowest with Jenny's arrival. Maggie became a totally different person from the person I liked so much. I had trouble understanding how a person who seemed so sweet and energetic and caring at first can turn out to become so indifferent and dull in such a short period. Everything was hitting me at once. I had trouble digesting what was happening around me.

Up to this point, I always consider my father to be something more than a parent. He was my best friend, my hero all in one. He was like a spiritual figure to me. At this point, my father became more and more interested in disciplining me than actually caring and showing affection as a caring parent would do. We were falling further and further apart from one another. It became obvious to me that it would take a big miracle just like the one in the Bible where the Red Sea opened up from side to side, making a path for the children of Israel to cross while escaping from Egypt, to get our relationship back at least close to what it used to be. All I could think of was asking myself where it all went terribly wrong.

It became more apparent that Maggie was now enjoying her new role as the devil's advocate to my father by making sure that she had at least one or two bad reports on me to tell my father about. Every little thing was exaggerated just so to make a case for a whooping, and she never failed to get what she wanted. It seemed to me that the more whooping I was getting, the clumsier I became, which undoubtedly led to more and more whooping.

Even though I felt like I was being unduly punished for what seemed to be very minor offenses, I still put all the blame on myself, thinking I could have prevented it one way or the other, and I could have done more to eliminate such terror that was being inflicted upon me. Unfortunately, the more I tried, the more my task was becoming unrealistic. Little by little, I began to despise my parents. My baby sister was my only comfort at home. From then, I began to feel like a stranger in my own home. For whatever reason, I began to cherish every minute being away from home, whether I was at school or was sent somewhere. Anywhere but home felt like a paradise. More and more I contemplated of life away from this hell I call my home. I had built in my mind this fantasy world, a beautiful place I called home, a place with no tears, no whopping, a place of total joy and excitement, a place where I had a purpose, a place where all the love flowed like waterfalls. I wouldn't go a day without imagining it. I would say to myself, there is, somewhere maybe very far away from here, such a place. just not here, a place I will call my home.

One weekend, I decided, enough of the beatings. I decided to run away two houses down over to my friend Christian's house. I told neither my parents nor Christian's parents of my plan. Since Christian's parents were very lax when it came to rules, spending the weekend there pretending that it was in accordance with my parents was as easy as multiplying any number by zero. Christian's house was so big that you could even hide two more families of five there for years before anyone else could ever run into each other's way. That weekend while I was MIA at home, leaving everyone at home to think nothing but the worst that could have possibly happened to me, I was having the time of my life at Christian's. I would say it felt like the day after the emancipation of slave to a former slave. What a day. Unfortunately for me, as they all say, the good things sure do not last forever.

Sunday night came, and as everyone was expecting me to go back home to get ready for school the next day, it became apparent to them that, for whatever reason, I was showing very little to no interest in going back home. That's when the bell must have rung in their head that something wasn't quite right given the fact that only twice have I ever been there, and on both occasion, thirty minutes was the longest time I ever spent there, combined. But this time, I spent the whole weekend there. Whatever it was that was going on, they were sure to find it out before any more time goes by.

As the night was approaching, I spoke a little with Christian, briefing him a little on my situation at home, what I was going through without really getting into any specific details. As it started getting late, everyone around Christian's house was getting ready for school tomorrow by starting with their homework, or in other cases, others were starting to look for their homework. Christian's mother was a reminder of Winston Churchill. She was very friendly, spoke very softly, but at the same time carried a big stick when she needed to. That was probably the only way to manage that multitude at her home. Even though she was the kids' best friend and ally, she still left no doubt about showing off her being in charge. I could see it through her eyes that she was getting a little frustrated with me. Not only was it getting late, but also she did let me know that it was time for me to go home twice indirectly and once directly, and at her greatest astonishment, I had yet to leave the premises.

Just when she was about to let me know how she felt about my reluctance, Christian stepped in by telling her why I was showing little to no interest in going back home and begged her to let me stay the night. Even though she felt very moved and touched by her son's testimony on the cruelty I was exposed to at home, letting me stay there beyond the weekend wasn't going to be a responsible thing to do on her part. She would have been harboring a fugitive in her home, something she didn't want to have any part of. But instead, she did come up with an alternative. She decided to accompany me back to my house and have a few words, woman to woman, with Maggie.

Once we reached home, to my delight, I was so relieved to find that only Maggie, the baby, and her sister Rosaline, who had been staying with us for quite a while now, were the only ones at the house. My father, the Terminator, as I had been referring to him as of late, was not around. As Christian's mom and Maggie were engaged into what seemed to me like a very deep conversation, I was hoping and praying that Christian's mother could stay the night to shield me against any punishment that was coming my way when my father would make his way home. To my own demise, the hour-long conversation between Christian's mom and Maggie, which to me felt like five minutes, was already over. After saying her good-bye to everyone in the house, Christian's mom assured me that everything was going to be just fine, and no one would lift their hands on me. Then she went on her way back to her house. Shortly after Christian's mom's departure, Maggie sent me to bed.

At midnight, I was woken up from my sleep by my father. With his finger, he motioned to follow him in the living room. As I was gathering myself very fearfully, the ten-yard walk to the living room felt like the walk Jesus took carrying the cross on his way to his crucifixion. When I made my way to the living room, I could already predict that I was in for something bigger than I could have possibly imagined.

"So where have you been this weekend?" my father asked.

As I started to gather my thoughts to give whatever answer that could possibly overturn a murder conviction with all evidence pointed against me, all I could manage to say was "I was next door over at Christian' house."

"And who said you could go over there?" was the next question quickly followed by "Why did you even bother coming back? Did you forget something that's why you came back?"

Just when I was thinking whether those were rhetorical questions or they were real questions that deserved real answers, I was grabbed by the throat and slammed against the wall. When I tried to get up, I was met with lashes from an extension cord. I had both blood and tears coming all together, joining forces in my face. There I was lying down hopelessly, wishing that either death or the worst natural disaster ever known to mankind could come and rescue me out of my misery. Never in my life have I ever felt so much pain. After enduring so much pain, I finally passed out around close to 5:00 a.m. I didn't wake up till quarter after ten with every part of my body sore as if I just woke up after taking both Mike Tyson and Muhammad to a twelve-round boxing bout consecutively. I missed two days of school as a result. From that moment on, I hated everything about that house and hoped a day will come when I would leave all this behind me.

It took a little while for things to go back as close to normal around the house. In the meantime, there have been some changes around the house. Maggie was now a new member of a sect. She had been converted to this new form of Christianity that was quickly expanding throughout the whole city. Now, every Tuesday, Thursday, and Sunday, I was forced to attend church meetings and sermons with her. I hated the fact that we had to walk about ten miles, back and forth, for those church gatherings that were about four hours long. It felt like torture to me, and I hated everything about it just as much as I hated Maggie's gut. And the fact that I couldn't hide my displeasure didn't help but make matters even worse for me.

This new church was one among the new generation of new faith that was coming around, created by former Catholic faithful who, all of a sudden, miraculously found their callings to lead a new denomination away from the Catholic Church. Their beliefs were mostly based around the Bible and rejecting everything about the Catholic Church, which, ironically, they were once affiliated with. They had one mission—to win every lost soul that was out there until Jesus comes back. Their doctrine was plain and simple—Satan was the root of all evil in humankind. Every misfortune, shortcoming, or sickness was nothing but the work of the devil combatting God's children. Last but not the least was witchcraft, the devil's number-one weapon according to them. According to this new sect, if one was unemployed, sick, or single, it was either Satan or someone's witchcraft holding you back. There was absolutely zero accountability regarding anything. You don't study for a test and you get a failing grade—it was all the devil's fault.

Most of their services were always lasting an eternity. They had a total disregard of time. You always know what time the service started, but there never was an exact time when it will end. I was always sleeping throughout most of their service, either as a sign of defiance or just purely out of tiredness after all those long walks. For being so indifferent and unfazed by their ritual, I was labeled a witch by one of the young pastors. He even took it a notch further by telling Maggie that God had shown him in a vision that my witchcraft was the reason behind all the problems we faced at the house. I was the one responsible for both my father's unemployment woes and the trouble in their marriage. Basically, I was the reason for everything that was going wrong, and she needed to set up an appointment to schedule a séance in which they will free me from my witchcraft through hours and hours of prayers.

The country was going through an era of Great Depression. With that came the rise in fear of witchcraft. Thought of witchcraft was going around the whole city like Communism during the McCarthy era. Churches would have people that supposedly used to practice witchcraft or were once witches appearing as special guest speakers, speaking to the congregation about their involvement in witchcraft and how witchcraft-free they were after being saved. Most of their stories all sounded similar no matter who was telling it. It all involved being exposed to cemetery during late nights, performing satanic ritual, sometimes even drinking blood and eating human flesh spiritually, more like a spiritual buffet with human flesh and blood as the main dinner course. It eluded me how such a multitude of people could be fooled all at once by such amateurism. All the theatrical performances meant big revenue and publicity for the church.

Maggie took me to the church where I spent three days with two of the leaders of the church. Those young pastors where in their late twenties. They were two of the biggest scam artists of their generation if you ask me. The deliverance session to rid me of all my witchcraft or the equivalence of exorcism, as they called it, was held at an annex behind the church, a one-bedroom small house that was used as a prayer room. For the first two days, all they did was pray constantly for hours and hours. From the moment we wake up, we will eat breakfast from about 10:00 a.m. to 10:30 a.m. Then they would start praying right after breakfast till about 1:00 p.m. and then take about two hours' break and then start praying again from 3:00 p.m. to 6:00 pm. We would have dinner at around 7:00 p.m. Right after dinner came the last session of prayer, which lasted about an hour to an hour and a half, max. After that, it was bedtime. I slept on a mat in the living room, which was usually very hot and made it very uncomfortable to sleep, while those two guys slept very comfortably in a room that was well equipped with a bed and ventilation.

Maggie came by once a day to drop dinner off and have a little chat with them to see about how things were progressing, perhaps to check on how many demons I had left in me. At the end of each prayer session at night, they would stop and ask me if I was ready to give up witchcraft and accept the Lord Jesus as my Savior. Most of the time, I would defiantly look at them and give them the meanest look as if they were some kind of virus. As I was fed up with those long endless hours of prayers, something came to mind. I realized that the more cooperative I can be, the quicker I can free myself from this nonsense. Just like Keyser Soze in the movie the *Usual Suspects,* I thought about playing right to their hand by using their own techniques to put an end to this charade. I already knew exactly what they wanted to hear—a confession, a renouncement to witchcraft followed by a willingness to accept Jesus Christ as my Lord and Savior; maybe not exactly in that particular order, but that's for sure what this whole thing was all about, and I knew it. Having heard so many confessions of allegedly former witches and people who were once possessed by evil spirits or demons at the church, I was ready to improvise my own confession.

At their own astonishment and delight, I caught them by surprise when on the second day, at the last prayer session, when asked if I was ready to give up witchcraft and accept Jesus Christ as my Lord and Savior against all odds while perhaps expecting the same belligerent attitude, I said yes. Their facial expression told it all. What seemed to be mission impossible was turning out to be mission accomplished. As unbelievable that yes sounded, they had to ask me once again just to make sure their ears weren't playing any tricks on them. It was like asking the most popular girl at school out on a date for the very first time and hearing her say yes with no hesitation.

"I'm ready to accept Jesus Christ as my Savior and be saved," I said. My statement brought about fifteen more minutes of praying.

One of them took me by the hand and said to me, "Don't be afraid—the devil won't have any more power over you. You are safe with the blood of Jesus." He told me, now, I needed to repent and make a confession, and after that, they will pray for me to guarantee my salvation.

"Praise the Lord!" the other one shouted.

Those two clowns, as I always refer to them, were best friends who supposedly got their calling from God in college, and they were given a mission from God to lead a new apostolic ministry. Since doing God's will was far more important than getting a degree, they both decided to drop out of college and follow God. Those were probably two friends who once had failed to establish themselves well enough academically and instead chose to take a short cut by starting a well-organized scam. In this age of uncertainty and economical drought, what can be a better scam than one involving the Bible as the ultimate bait?

After saying yes to accepting Jesus Christ as my Lord and Savior and renouncing to witchcraft, they had one request for me. They wanted to see if I didn't mind telling my confession in front of Maggie. "That's no problem," I replied, and they told me once again how proud of me they were and not to worry about suffering any repercussion from anyone as a result of my testimony.

On the third day, which was the last day of the session, a Saturday, surprisingly, I saw my father along with Maggie. They came to assist the last deliverance session. It was a very nice day out. The sun was out at its best form, the wind was blowing through the trees, and the birds were chirping in the trees. It was a beautiful day. I was more shocked than surprised to see my father entering the premises as the front gate opened up. My father was once a very devoted Catholic. First of all, he was once a few semesters away from being ordained a priest before getting expelled from the seminary. Even afterward, he still didn't give up on his Catholic faith. On the contrary, he became even more involved in the church. His knowledge of music led him to become a conductor in the choir. He played a few instruments, keyboard, guitar, accordion, with the saxophone being his favorite instrument above all. He also had such a great voice.

During this time, the Catholic Church in my country suffered one of its most devastating losses in believers or faithful. For whatever reasons, a lot of Catholics decided to break away from the church with most creating their own Christian church based on different beliefs. There was a rise in church creation. In some area, you would have three to four different churches in one street, sometimes even two churches next to each other. It became a big cacophony.

My father did leave the Catholic Church, but instead of joining one of those newly formed churches or perhaps creating his own, he decided to stay put and become churchless. He labeled those newly formed churches as nothing but opportunists who were using the Bible as a means to prey on the weak minded. I did agree with him on that one. This new church thing was really getting out of control from left to right. Everybody was getting a calling from God to lead a church as either a pastor or a prophet. One will wake up some morning and claim to have had a dream in which God or some angels came by and spoke to him, and from then on, he or she would give oneself a title, which most of the time was pastor or prophet. They all had one thing in common. As a matter fact, I will even go a little further. They all had two things in common. Their sermons were all based upon giving, giving, and more giving. On the other hand, they preyed upon women tricking them into performing sexual favors while claiming that it was all in accordance to God's words. They did fool so many.

After her conversion, Maggie tried her very best to attract my dad into this new doctrine, but my father never gave her the time to even get anything past him. To be frank, I am pretty sure he was even against her embracing this new sect. That's why I was very shocked to see my father attending my deliverance session. *That couldn't be my father*, I said to myself as I watched him entering the church's gate. As it became obvious that my eyes weren't playing any tricks on me, I had goose bumps all over me. For some time now, I have grown to become very petrified of my father. I always felt very uneasy being anywhere near him. He became the symbol of terror. It didn't matter what mood he or I was in. Whenever he was anywhere around, it was code red for me followed by complete state of fear. That's how traumatized I became.

It was around 3:00 p.m., after all the commotion from greetings to small chitchats followed by about half an hour of more prayers, when one of the guys spoke, telling everyone how successful the session had been and how Jesus helped achieve the ultimate goal of saving a soul of a lost child who had been taken away by the devil. After he was done speaking, he motioned to me as to let me know that now it was my turn to speak and deliver my confession. In other words, it was now "Showtime at the Apollo."

As I gathered myself in front of my audience, preparing for the most important performance of my life, all of a sudden, I became fearless and less nervous. Having to avoid eye contact with anyone in that room was beneficial. I collected myself and took the stage just like little Michael in his very first live performance with the Jackson 5. All eyes were on me, and from the look on their faces, I sure didn't disappoint. My confession was made up of a collection of previously heard confessions from various people and a little improvisation by changing settings and naming a few other names that were supposedly my accomplices. After speaking for about close to an hour, they followed up with thirty minutes of prayers. Then after the prayer, I was hugged by my father, who was almost in tears. We ate the food that was prepared by Maggie. A few hours after the meal, we made our way back home.

Following my little retreat, everything seemed to be as perfect as it has been for me at home. I had both the devil and my fake confession to thank for that I returned to school the following Monday. Missing a few weeks of school didn't really affect me much, since I wasn't that far behind at all with schoolwork. My father got all my assignments from my teacher, and I turned in everything on my first day back. I felt great going back to school being in company of all my gang. I missed them greatly, and from the very warm welcome back and the very loud ovation I received on my first day back, there was no doubt in my mind I greatly I have been missed by the class. Judging from my teacher's reaction, I could see she was glad to see me but not really upbeat having me back, since now she had to deal with containing my turbulence. Now that Dennis the Menace was back to pick up where he left off, she probably would be needing more doses of coffee daily.

With about a little over a month left in the fourth-grade school year, I was forced to finish the school year homeschooled. One day, I was sitting outside holding my baby sister. My friend Christian, who lived two doors down from me, came to visit. Christian was the only friend I had outside from school. Although my father had specifically instructed me not to have any friend from the neighborhood, I went against his instruction by secretly keeping a developing a friendship with Christian. I always thought he should have made an exception with Christian, who seemed like a pretty cool kid to me. Having Christian as a friend was very convenient for me. Not only were Christian and I around the same age, but also he was the only boy my age that lived closer to me. Christian and I were almost the same height; I probably had him beat by an inch or two. He was the quiet and observant type. Christian was his father's favorite son. Being the last child, he was very spoiled by his parents. His father never said no to anything Christian wanted, and everyone in the family knew it. Whenever his siblings wanted something, which would normally be denied by their father, all they did was send Christian to ask on their behalf, and it always worked.

That afternoon, as Christian came to my house, I was sitting outside holding my baby sister. Christian asked if he could hold the baby for a few moments. I leaned forward and handed him the baby to hold. As soon as I went back to sit down, Christian stumbled accidently and tripped himself, causing the baby to fall on the floor. As I hurried to pick up the baby, who was crying her lungs out, there was Maggie rushing in from the house. She grabbed the baby out of my hands and then gave me a good slap in the face. I was so shocked I didn't know how to feel. The baby was OK. She came out that little tumble with no bruise or any injury. Maggie told Christian to leave. I was left alone, dissecting what just happened. Little did I know the worst was yet to come.

Later that night, while sleeping, I was woken up by my father, ordering me to come to the living room. When I got to the living room, my father asked me how my day was. Being awakened in the middle of the night by my father only meant one thing—I was in trouble, but how big of a trouble, that was what I was about to find out. Being called by my father was always similar to being called to the principal's office in the middle of the school day. Usually nothing good ever comes up from such call.

"Good," I replied, "my day was good," looking down at the floor, wishing to acquire some sort of supernatural power, the kind that could help me disappear and reappear in a blink of an eye somewhere very far, perhaps in a different planet. My wish was far from turning into reality.

"What did I tell you about mixing in with the neighborhood kids?" my father asked. And just when I was fixing to put some words together to reply, I was met with a blow from a wooden broom straight to my harm, followed by blow after blow. As I lay down on the floor, crying helplessly, I was being beaten down like a thief in a middle of a Turkish market. What had happened was Maggie had told my father about the baby incident. For all I know, she probably told my father I orchestrated the whole thing—it was all a part of my evil plan to have Christian accidentally drop the baby. My father was very furious. I did break one of his rules, and by doing so, his little girl got hurt in the process—a hole in one. He couldn't wait to make me pay. When it came to inflicting punishment, my father was second to none—even Islamic Sharia law enforcers were no match to my father's cruelty. It didn't matter to my father that Christian wasn't anything like those other neighborhood kids who were nothing but thugs in the making. Christian was an exception; I knew that well enough to befriend him. I just wished my father could have seen it. I did get the whooping of a lifetime that night. I even suffered a concussion.

The very next day, which was a Sunday, I was still pretty banged up. I was sore everywhere I couldn't barely move to even make it to the bathroom. I was still lying down while everyone was getting ready for church. I wasn't feeling too good. I was coming down with a fever, so as everyone went to church, I was left home alone with more instructions to go by. "Don't go anywhere. Don't have anyone in the house, not even the pope," said my father. I watched them exiting the house and then went back to sleep for few more hours.

When I finally got up, I was still very sore but feeling a little better the moment I sat back down on the bed. I started thinking about everything that had happened the day before. I tried reliving every second of each incident that had occurred from the moment Christian walked in to the moment I received the beatdown from my father. I started having very deep thoughts. I realized that I was now being constantly physically abused between Maggie and my father. It felt like no matter what I did, everything surely ended up earning me a beatdown. Mind you, I use the word "beatdown." I wasn't being disciplined anymore. I was being severely punished. It didn't matter whether I spilled something by accident or dirty my clothes. I still received a beatdown as if I purposely burned the house down.

It didn't just stop there. On a daily basis, I was accustomed to verbal abuse from Maggie. It seemed to me that for whatever reason, she hated me so much and never missed on the opportunity to let me know of it. To her, I was a scum who will never amount to anything good in life. Now I was being severely punished for things that were even out of my control. Just the thought of that created even more tears to my eyes.

As I was sitting down sobbing, I cried out loud to God, even though I didn't know much about God, whether he/she was real. At this point, going through all the pain and tribulation, I figured if there is anybody that can come to my rescue, it should be no other than God. With tears still pouring out of my eyes, I knelt down facing the wall, and I said, "If you hear me, God, I pray to you for help, as I have no one else. If you rescue me from my misery, I promise I would never forget you ever in my life." I felt uplifted, calm, and filled with so much confidence in a very short span.

Under no particular circumstance should an eight-year-old be forced to endure so much pain and abuse. They were wrong after all. I said I wasn't deserving of such cruelty. I did develop such hatred toward both my father and Maggie. That hatred was reaching a record high. I couldn't wait to start a new life without them having to play any part in it at all. I was more than ready to take up the next big challenge, which was finding me a place to call home. I knew I was a kid, a great kid at last, no matter what my father or Maggie thought of me. I knew it from the bottom of my heart that there was absolutely nothing wrong with me. At eight, I was more than ready to prove whomever who doubted me wrong, especially Maggie and my father.

I felt a little better the following day and ended up making it to school. Ever since my father had quit his job at the school, I have been walking to and from school by myself. The eighty-minute walk to school now seemed like an eternity now that I had to do it alone. Even though I still was about 60 percent fit for a long walk, I decided against staying at home, as going to school was the only thing that gave me a sense of freedom and kept me sane. After school, instead of going back home, I decided to go home with Joel. I told Mrs. Helena, Joel's mom, that my father was going to pick me up at her house on his way back home.

It has been a while since I have been over Joel's house. Joel's house had always been like a second home to me. Joel and I had been best friends, since we both were four years old. Aside from being in the same classes over the years since grade K till now, fourth grade, we spent most summer vacations together. We did everything pretty much together. To Mrs. Helena, I was pretty much like a second son to her. Mrs. Helena came back home from work at around 6:00 p.m. that day. We were just finishing up our homework when she walked in the house. She seemed a little surprised to see me there, since she probably thought by this time, my father had already come and picked me up.

Joel and I went down to the basement to play some more video games for about a few more hours. At around 8:00 p.m., Mrs. Helena told us to go take a shower and start getting ready for bed. She told me it doesn't seem like my father was coming to pick me up tonight as it started to get really late. After we were done taking a shower, Joel's mom double-checked our homework to make sure we completed all our assignments. She sent us to bed after fixing us a snack. Little did they know I made up the whole thing, and my father didn't even know where I was. I ended up spending the night there.

The following morning, Mrs. Helena got us ready for school. Her chauffeur drove us to school. Everything was smooth and perfect until we reached the school, just to see my father waiting for me outside the school office. For a while, I thought I was having a bad dream. I wish I could close my eyes and everything would get back to normal. Unfortunately, this was reality at its best, and there was no escape route to take, at least not at this moment, without making any scene. My father waited until I got out of the car and picked me up by my arms.

We both left the school together and headed back home. The hour walk back home was a quiet one. Neither of us spoke, sneezed, nor made any sound or gesture to one another along the way.

As for me, all I could think about was after having the perfect day yesterday, today I was in for a real treat. Would I still be alive to at least tell the story to anyone that would dare listen, or is this perhaps marking of the end of my existence? I was for sure I was on my way to the guillotine. One thing I didn't know is that it would be the last time I would be attending that school. Joel was the only and last classmate I would see that day. Just like on an old episode of *Seinfeld,* where the soup Nazi would say, "No soup for you"; in my case, my father was the school Nazi, and there was going to be "no school for me." I was later forcibly homeschooled for the remaining of my fourth-grade school year.

When we finally reached my street, I suddenly became very frightened, with my house only a block away. I knew it was only a matter of time before I get executed. And judging by the silence of the hour-long walk from school, it doesn't take a genius to figure out that this one was going to be a very big—*WWII big,* I thought. As we approached Christian's house, I quickly pulled away from my father's hand holding my harm and ran as fast as I could into Christian's house. Since it was still around eight o'clock in the morning, majority of the household were at school, and those that were at the house were either still asleep or getting ready to leave the house to go to work. I ran straight to the back of the house and hid inside the garage. To be honest, I don't know what went through my mind at that very moment; I felt possessed by some strange entity. I hid inside that garage just like a person of interest in a high-profile murder case would find his way seeking asylum inside some embassy after escaping from custody.

Just when I thought that my father didn't have any jurisdiction inside Christian's house and that I was perhaps safe, at least for the moment, my father came rushing in like a mad dog that suddenly had lost sight of its bone. I was very unlucky that day as Christian's sisters were the only people in that entire house, which meant that my father would have to face little to no resistance to any request he might have.

My father asked the sisters, or should I say pretty much told them that he was on his way to get me out of that garage. As easy as it was seeing my father make his way to my holding spot, I just wished that either Christian's father or mother would've been home. Had either one of them been home, my extradition wouldn't come as such an easy price with little to no negotiation. I watched desperately as my father forced his way to the garage and snatched me out of there. In as little as fifteen minutes, I was back into custody.

Back at the house, my father had both my legs and arms tied up as hard as he could. He had two bamboo sticks with him. That was the very first time I ever saw those monsters. As I lay on the floor helplessly, he began to give me blow after blow from the bamboo sticks. The nightmare that lasted about an hour felt like two weeks to me. After crying my lungs out, there were no more tears coming out. I think I might have used a month's worth of tears on that day. Where is God when you need him! I cried out loud. To top it all off, the last part of my punishment was not being fed that day. So aside from breakfast that I had at Joel's house that morning, I didn't eat a thing until the next afternoon. Yes, you heard it right.

Starvation and forced nudity were the two most unusual and cruel punishments I have been exposed to as a child. Aside from being constantly beaten by either extension cords, wood stick, or whatever stick there was, from time to time, two other methods were employed as a form of punishment. One was starvation, and the other was forced nudity. Sometimes as a punishment, meals were withheld from me, sometimes for as long as two full days. The other method, which was Maggie's favorite one, was forced nudity. She would strip me of all my clothes and put hot pepper around my genitals, and then she would throw me outside, leaving me on the porch, crying my lungs out as I lay there alone, feeling the heat from the hot pepper. These cruel and unusual methods of punishment, although rarely employed, were more common among parents from rural areas. They often used it as a last resort to kids who were far beyond disciplining.

The beating I got from not coming home after school and spending the night at Joel's house was by far the worst beating I ever took. It really changed my perspective on everything, especially on my father. From then on, there was absolutely nothing bounding us together. I completely hated that man forever, I thought. I was still tied up until 11:00 p.m. That's when my father finally decided to untied me. A few hours later, I managed to fall asleep, marking the end of the worst day I ever had. From that day on, I became homeschooled by my father. He made sure I got all my weekly assignments, including all the quizzes and final exams. After returning all completed assignments to be graded, he came back with my grades. I finished the fourth grade fourth in my class. Junior was first as always followed by Tresor, with Joel coming in third.

A few weeks later, while sitting at home by myself while Maggie was gone to the grocery, I sat there reminiscing about everything from my whole childhood to school and my entire life in general, and then came through my mind the most intriguing though I ever had. What would it be like to be free? Free from all these beatings, free from feeling so helpless, and most importantly, free to be a regular kid once again. I don't know if my parents ever realized this, but the constant verbal and physical abuse I became so accustomed to did way more harm than good. For fear of getting beaten, I became clumsier than ever, a compulsive liar. Instead of being a home, to me, that house became more of a reformatory, a symbol of terror. I was stripped of living with two loving parents who were replaced by two interrogators or prison guards. I cherish every second spent outside that house, away from those people that were supposed to be my parents.

The worst thing all those cruel and unhuman punishments did to me was stripping me of my childness. I wasn't a child anymore. I felt like an old war veteran with a body of an eight-year-old. My soul was all bruised up as if I have fought in both World Wars. I looked left to right for a savior; there was no one coming to my rescue. I realized that I was the only one who could help me escape from all this misery and lead me toward the Promised Land. With that being said, I put two pairs of shorts on, two T-shirts, and a shirt. I put my tennis shoes on and grabbed my little pocket-size booklet that my father had bought me, which I had since I was three years old. It had famous people's autograph in it. It had autographs from our country's high political figures, famous sports figures, and two Belgian and French commandoes working as UN peacekeepers. I took my stuff, and I was gone out of that house and didn't look back with only one wish in mind—never to ever step a foot in that house ever again. I pretty much booked a one-way ticket out of my misery.

As I made my way out of the door, I didn't know where I was headed; nor did I plan anything. But I knew one thing for certain—whatever road I was going to take, that will be the road that would lead me to my ultimate goal of finding me a place where I can eat, sleep, awake; a place where I would have the freedom to think, dream, and express my feelings; a place where I could be a part of something, and not something apart; a place where none of my mistakes wouldn't be so monumental where everyone were so judgmental. Above all, a place I could just call home. Once I have reached that place, I said to myself I would do everything in my power to make sure I am not taken away from it. I was so empowered by my own determination I felt so much invincible. There was nothing out there that could break, win, or overcome me. Even without having any concrete plans or knowing where I was going, the road to nowhere never looked so liberating and promising as I was filled with so much joy and pride for breaking away once and for all from oppression.

As I started walking, I decided to take the same paths I would usually take to school every day. Perhaps you can say I was on my way to school, only this time, it was a different kind of school, a school of survival. I was about halfway from my school when suddenly a thought came through my mind. I thought about heading over Junior's house, and since it was summer break, I could just tell his parents that my father didn't object to me spending a few days at their house only if I wouldn't be such an inconvenience to them. After patting myself a few times on the back for having come up with such a brilliant idea I thought to myself, I quickly changed direction en route to Junior's house.

Junior's house was about an hour and half away from my school in walking distance and about two and half hours away from my house. Given that home phones in my country were more of a luxury gadget only available to the wealthy few, most communication was done through word of mouth, so there was no way to check on the authenticity of my story once I got to Junior's house. At that moment, my words were as good as the gospel.

I got to Junior's house a little bit after 3:00 p.m. The sun was shining at its best, a very typical summer day. His house was a very beautiful white house, which stood out amazingly from others with its Romanesque design and fenced gate and entrance. Junior family was wealthy. They belonged to the higher echelon of our middle class. His dad was one of the well-known government officials, so they were pretty well off. When I came into the gate, I was greeted by their butler, who immediately recognized me from having been there a few times before. He escorted me to the house where all the kids were sitting. Junior was so glad to see me. He showed it by giving me a big hug. After saying hello to everyone from Junior's mother to all his other siblings that were present, his younger brother François, his two elder sisters, Jenny and Bijoux, all of them whom I knew well enough from school, I was given a warm welcome by everyone. It felt really great.

Junior had some very beautiful sisters. The fact that they both were older than I was didn't stop me from having a crush on them. Jenny was in sixth grade, while Bijoux was in eighth grade. Many times I caught myself fantasizing about dating one of them, if not both of them at the same time—can't blame a kid for dreaming big. I think I might have mentioned it jokingly to Junior. In fact, I know I wasn't the only one with those fantasies. I can point to about five people at school, including Joel, who had a thing or two for the two sisters. Enough about fantasy world, back to reality.

Junior and I retreated from the rest of his family. We both went to his room to play video games. Junior had a variety of electronic games from GameCube to Nintendo, with Super Mario being our favorite game to play. As we were playing the games, Junior exclaimed, "Man, I wish you could stay here for the weekend!" His words hit me as strong as a nuclear reactor would. I felt as if someone had just read the lottery number with my ticket coming out as the winning ticket to the jackpot. *Bingo!* I thought to myself.

I told him, "Actually, my father had told me he was OK with me staying here for the weekend, since he and Maggie were going on a church retreat and won't be back until Sunday, but only if it's OK with your parents."

"Are you kidding me! My mom would love having you for the weekend, and my dad wouldn't care, as he is barely home during the days anyway. Let's go tell my mom," he said. As we pretty much broke the news to his mom rather than ask for her permission, it ended up being a slam dunk anyway. Junior's mom had no objection. She even offered me a ride back home if necessary.

"Thank you," I said, "but it won't be necessary. My father will be picking me up from Papa Nestor's house, which happens to be only a few blocks away."

The five days' vacation at Junior's house was great. We had so much fun at the house. I could hardly remember the last time I had so much fun consecutively. It was almost unreal to me. We horse played, played video games, and watched a lot of movies. We took walks in the neighborhood. My favorite of all was gazing at Jenny and Bijoux, Junior's two eldest sisters, whose beauty were out of this world.

Sunday afternoon, right after mass, Junior's mother insisted on dropping me off instead of letting me walk to Papa Nestor's house. I couldn't say no to Junior's mom after all; she had been a very good host. When we got over Papa Nestor's house, lucky for me, most of everybody were either still at church or out and about. Junior's mother and I walked out of the car and dropped me off to one of the grown-ups who was at the residence. I thanked her for a lovely stay, said good-bye to Junior, and watched them pull off. As I walked around the house, snooping around, I was so glad to find out that the news about my being missing from my house had yet to reach here. Therefore, I was safe at least for the moment, I thought. After two nights at Papa Nestor's house, I decided to bounce out of there after it became known that I unexpectedly left my house and had never been back since.

I sort of overheard one of the grown-ups in the house telling another family member that Maggie's sister Rosalie, who had been living with us for a while now since her arrival from Brussels, Belgium, came by the day before and broke the news of my disappearance. But she seemed to be more sympathetic toward me throughout her whole testimony on the reasons that might have led to my running away from home. Now that it was no longer a secret that I have run away from home, I figured it was just a matter of time before either I'm sent back home or my father would come brutally looking for me. Either way, I wasn't going to take any chances, not this time.

While everyone were still asleep very early in the morning, about close to eight o'clock, I snuck out of the house and left for good. I started walking once again with no specific plans in mind, not knowing where to go. I just decided against taking any chances of being handed over back home. At this point, I knew of no other places to go except to some of my classmates' house. Given what happened the last time I spent the night at Joel's house, going back there was out of the question, as there was nothing I could come up with as a reason to stay there this time, and having lied to Joel's parent was a mistake that couldn't be redeemed anytime soon. Having already spent five days at Junior's house and with Joel's house now being out of the question, I was left with one last option—my good friend Tresor, another classmate of mine.

Tresor lived very farther away from school, which meant a very long walk for me. Having no money meant I couldn't get in on a bus or anything, and at eight, hitchhiking was as good as committing—a suicide, so I did all my expedition on foot. I walked and walked until I couldn't walk anymore. It took me about four hours' walk to get to Tresor's house. On my way there, the plan was just to feed Tresor's parents with the same story I fed Junior's mom. But for the story to sound more believable, I thought I should wait at least until late afternoon. An eight-year-old showing up at someone's house early in the morning unexpectedly would be a big red flag. Waiting until the late afternoon to get to Tresor's house meant I had to burn a few more hours in between.

I decided to keep walking toward Tresor's house while taking breaks in between. As I was walking, I decided to take a break. I have been walking for about three hours straight. I found myself walking toward a baobab, which stood right across from a soccer stadium. It was still early, perhaps around 10:00 a.m., and there were about twenty people gathered around the tree. The baobab, a huge tree that covered a great portion of the area, was a source of shade for many pedestrians and also a place where heated arguments and debates were being discussed. As I approached the small crowd, I made myself right at home. I came to found out that I have stopped at a very special place, a place like no other.

The area around the monster of all trees was called FEZADI, an acronym for the Zarian Federation of Discussion. FEZADI was located at a very strategic intersection. It was right at the heart of the city. Next to it was the country's second-largest soccer stadium, the 20 May Stadium (Stade du 20 Mai). On one side, there was the road that led to downtown; on the other side, the road to the main highway, which led to the airport; behind it, the road to uptown; and in front of it, the road that led to the Place of Victory, also known as Sin City, where all the city's most infamous bars and nightclubs were located. FEZADI was very infamous for its heated debates and discussions, which covered a long variety of topics ranging from sports and politics to anything you can possibly think of, from why the sky is blue to what came first, the chicken or the egg.

The monster of all trees with its long branches provided a big attraction to many who were trying to get away from the heating sun. People from all around the city would gather around it from as early as 6:00 a.m. till about 6:30 p.m. All types of people—from people who were on their way to work or those on their way looking for work, to students on their way to school or those running away from school, to mobile merchants, vagabonds, and thugs, you name it. There were old ladies who set up small booths all around the monster tree, most of them selling loaves of bread, beverages, bananas, muffins, and grilled peanut. FEZADI was home to great debates, discussions, and arguments, majority of it being soccer, with politics coming second, religion third, and then everything else.

The city had two major successful football teams, The Immaculate, with their green-and-white jersey, and The Dolphins, whose jersey was green and black. Around 90 percent of the city football fans were either V Club Dolphins or DCMP Immaculate. The Dolphins fan base had about 50 percent of the city's football lovers, while about 40 percent were Immaculate, as I was. The other 10 percent was split between undecided fans and supporters of AS Bilima Dragon, which translated to "The Ghost." AS Dragon wore red-and-gold jersey. All three fan bases had a reputation. V Club Dolphin fan base was mostly known for being made up of thugs, gangsters, vagabond, and illiterates. On the other side, the DCMP Immaculate supporters were mostly from the middle or upper class, while about 98 percent of AS Dragon fanatics were people in their fifties or higher. You would have better odds of finding diamond on the street than finding a supporter of AS Dragon who was in his teens better yet in his twenties.

The intercity rivalry between my team, DCMP, and V CLUB is one of the world's most heated rivalry. The two enemies who happened to share the same stadium usually play against each other at least twice during the football season, most of the time resulting to deadly melee between fans whenever the result didn't favor the other. Things were so heated between the two rival teams even when not facing one another. On many occasions, thousands of supporters of V Club would attend DCMP home games against other opposition just to cheer against their city rival, and the same thing went for DCMP supporters when V Club was playing against teams from different countries. Even opposition teams found this practice to be very peculiar if not shocking. It was the equivalent of Duke fans purchasing tickets to a North Carolina home game just to cheer on the opposing team, or Auburn Tigers fans purchasing tickets to an Alabama Crimson Tide home game to jeer its rival, or University of Louisville fans rooting for the University of Kentucky opponents. Although I can keep going on and on, I figured you have gotten the point by now on how ridiculous and out of control this rivalry was.

Fanatics of the two rival football clubs made up about more than 90 percent of the daily FEZADI attendants. Most discussions always started in similar fashion on a daily basis with a fanatic of one team claiming his team as being the best, if not at the very least the best, during the ongoing season, perhaps the best of all time, period. From time to time, there would be fights between overzealous rival fans who strongly believe it was a divine duty to defend their team's reputation at all cost against any facts or fictions. To those die-hard fans, even facts were completely irrelevant when trying to argue with them. Both rival teams were strongly represented in FEZADI.

V Club Dolphin had the greatest of all debaters in a guy named Khumalo. Not only was he a die-hard Dolphin fan but also the guy pretty much had a perfect attendance in FEZADI. Whether it was raining or storming, you bet Khumalo was going to show up in FEZADI to defend his beloved green and black. One of his favorite lines was "You can talk all you want about my family. You can even go as far as calling my mother all kinds of names. I wouldn't lift a finger on you, but if you ever talk trash about my beloved V Club Dolphin, I guarantee you will be picking up your front teeth on the floor." That was Khumalo for you, FEZADI godsend. Khumalo was around six feet two inches, in his late twenties or perhaps early thirties. He was well loved and respected throughout the whole FEZADI community. He was easygoing and very likeable even among rival fans.

Later on, I came to find out a little bit more about his life. He dropped out of school in second grade after the sudden death of his grandmother, who was taking care of him and his two little sisters. He never knew his father, while his mother was never around, too busy selling her body. He learned how to do welding from an old man who lived in his neighborhood. After the passing of his grandmother, they were all kicked out from the family home. He got separated from his two little sisters, who went on to live with some relatives far away in the countryside. He never heard from them since. He lived on the streets for years. He did side welding jobs to get by. As time got tougher, he started scrapping metals to survive. As he stated himself, he lived his whole life on a survival mode.

Khumalo was very fond of me. I liked him a lot too. He was like a big brother to me. We teased each other a lot. Even though we rooted for rival teams, it was still very fun listening to him win argument after argument. He was invincible when it came to defending his beloved green and black. His closest challenger was Manu, who went by the nickname Gorbatchev, one of the biggest DCMP fans you will ever meet, if not the biggest. Gorbatchev was around five feet ten inches, a heavyset guy. He and Khumalo were about the same age, but unlike Khumalo, Gorbatchev was well educated. A college student in his third year of law school, Gorbatchev was very eloquent. FEZADI was between his house and the school he attended, so he would make occasional stops on his way back from class. Although his and Khumalo's schedule didn't really allow them to be there at the same time more often, but when it did happen, the whole FEZADI was in for a treat. It was a thing of beauty listening to those two defending their team colors, respectively. You could even feel the monster tree moving in rhythm.

There was no better place in the entire land to kill time than FEZADI. Whether you were a student who had cut school and was hoping to find hours of entertainment at a priceless rate or you were a poor vagrant as I was in search for a next move, FEZADI was the ideal place for you. Aside from the occasional fights, FEZADI was also a shelter for brotherhood, one of the few places in the land where you could find the true meaning of sharing is caring. Even after long hours of heated discussions and arguments, people who minutes ago were engaged in heated arguments would still find the will to share whatever it was that they had purchased to eat, whether it be a loaf of bread, a muffin, or a bowl of peanuts. At FEZADI, a loaf of bread usually turns out to only a bite or two, since one had to usually share it with the whole crowd. Everything was shared among all regardless of which team you supported or political party you were affiliated with or your religious preference.

I asked around for the time, and it was a little bit past 2:00 p.m., so I decided to continue toward my destination, which was Tresor's house. This time, I only had about an hour and a half left of walking to do. It was around 4:00 p.m. when I made it to the front gate. There was a car on its way out, and it was Mr. Konde, Tresor's father. I politely said hello and hurried my way to the house. As I made it to the house, I was greeted by Tresor, who came to open the door. Seeing that his mother was napping soundly on the couch, I waited until she woke up from her nap to break the news to her. After greeting her, I told her the same thing I had previously told Junior's mom the week before.

"Both my father and Maggie went on a church retreat and won't be back home until Sunday. He had told me to ask you guys if it was OK to spend time here until Sunday. He would rather have me here with Tresor until then than being at home all alone—that's, of course, if you guys didn't mind." I always found the need to add that last line to sound more believable. "He will be here to pick me up Sunday afternoon," I said to her. Just like previously with Junior's mom, it also worked with Tresor's mom, taking my record to two out of two, not bad for an apprentice. I couldn't believe it myself how easy it has been to sound so believable to those parents.

Mr. Konde, Tresor's father, was one of the pillars of the Mobutu regime, which means that he was pretty well off financially. His residence was almost as big as the White House if you asked me. It was a pretty good walk from the front gate to the house itself. Everything in that house was fancy. Being in that house felt like I was in some sort of museum. I almost broke my neck gazing at the whole house. Just like Joel, Tresor was also the only child. Looking at how spoiled he was, one would never have second-guessed it. Once again, I was treated like royalty during my few days' stay at the house. Given that Tresor and I were the best of pals at school, we had no trouble taking advantage of our summer break reunion. We had so much fun that any more fun would have been considered illegal.

As they all say, all fun times sure don't last forever. When Sunday came, Mrs. Konde waited and waited for my father, who once again was a no-show. Little did she know the whole thing was a hoax; she had been lied to. She decided to drop me off herself. It was time for me to get dropped off at my house. Instead of leading them to my house, I led them over to Mr. Vuvu's house, pretending it to be my house. I got out the car and thanked them for having me over. They wanted to come in, but I insisted on them staying, telling them that there was no one at the house at the moment, no need for them to get out of the car, and I was home and safe. I was relieved to see them pull off and drive away.

Once again, I did dodge yet another bullet, a bigger one this time. Had they made their way inside that house, I would have been totally exposed as a liar. As soon as they were out of sight, I quickly left the premises. Mr. Vuvu's house was the very last place I needed to be seen at now that I was officially a runaway.

It has been two weeks since my self-imposed exile. Having previously spent a week over Junior's house the week before and now that I was coming back from spending another week over Tresor's house meant that I was running out of options. Going to Joel's house wasn't going to be an option given what happened last time I was there. I couldn't go to Christian's house, which was too close to my house. At this point, I realized that the sky was closing in on me. My adventure was now in jeopardy. Even though there seems to be very little hope for me in finding another place to stay to keep the streak alive, I still was so determined to keep going no matter what. Going back home was never an option. I would rather live in hell before ever stepping my foot back to that house, I said to myself.

I started walking away toward the soccer field. As I got to the field, I saw kids playing a pickup game. I recognized some of them from the neighborhood. Playing soccer at the field was one of the only hobbies available for kids in the neighborhood. It was the best gateway drug. The soccer field was also the hangout spot to many teenage lovers and friends. On many occasions, kids would leave their home as early as 10:00 a.m. to only return for dinner and then back to the field only to go back home for bed. The soccer field was located about three blocks away from my house, just in front of the only Catholic Church around. As it started getting dark outside, kids who were playing started bailing out from the game one by one, bringing the game to an end. Up until now, I had yet to come up with a plan on where I was going to spend the night tonight. Time was now running out. I decided to follow the last group of kids leaving the field heading back to their home.

Lucky for me, among the group, there were two kids who knew who I was. They were regulars who played pickup games at the haunted house. Rex, one of the two who knew me, asked what everyone else was planning on doing the rest of the night. No one seemed to have any plans. He suggested that everyone meet back at the field in about an hour or so, giving everyone time to shower and perhaps eat dinner. It was unanimously agreed upon. After everyone else had split up on their way home, only Rex and I were left heading in the same direction.

As we walked together, suddenly, Rex asked, as if he was reading a script from my mind, "If you don't have anything to do at home, you could just come to my house and wait for me to take a shower. Perhaps we can eat dinner together and then head back to the field afterward to meet up with the rest of the crew."

"That sound good," I said, trying not to show too much excitement. We ended up going to his house.

Rex was about a year or two older than me but just about an inch shorter than I was. He was a really good soccer player, one of the best in the neighborhood. Rex's house was right behind the church. His father was the church custodian. He had all the keys to the church and was in charge of all the maintenance. Rex was the second eldest out of five siblings. He had an elder sister who was about thirteen years old, two little sisters, and a little brother. Rex's mother was a stay-at-home mom. She ran a small convenience store just outside her house. The house was a three-bedroom house with the girls sharing one room, the boys sharing another. The other room being the master bedroom. When we got in the house, I couldn't help but notice how different his house was compared to anywhere I have ever been. The house was a total wreck. Kids were running around, creating pandemonium. Clothes were everywhere. The kitchen was full of dirty dishes. It was as if hurricane Katrina had just visited the place.

Rex and I went straight to his room. I stayed in his room until he was done taking a shower and ate his dinner. He did ask me to join him for some dinner. I didn't really felt comfortable eating there. I just told him I wasn't hungry at all. Shortly afterward, we were on our way back to the field to meet up with the rest of the crew. I was very amazed at how easy it was for Rex to just get out of that house without even asking his mother for permission, let alone let her know where he was going. I couldn't imagine seeing myself pulling such a stunt especially after dark. I would have been crucified if I ever tried such a thing at my house.

We were the first people to be at the field. About fifteen minutes later, the three others finally came along, bringing our number to five. There were now Patrick, Zak, and Phil in addition to Rex and I. There was no doubt on who the crew leader was ; it was no other than Rex, who happened to be the orchestrator of all things within the crew. He suggested that we go break into one of their rival schools and perhaps steal something, whatever we could find. It took me less than half an hour to realize that there never was any opposition to any of Rex's ideas or suggestions, and I sure wasn't going to be the one challenging his wits or plans. We made it to the school, which was about an hour away in walking distance. We all climbed the fence and began exploring every classroom, finding absolutely nothing worth stealing. We sure were not going to take out any desk, so we just settled for all the chalks we could gather from all those classrooms. Before leaving, we had to make our presence known, if not felt, so we all made big graffiti using every inappropriate words known to mankind.

We made it back to the football field a little bit past 10:00 p.m. As we cruised the neighborhood, I broke the news to the crew about my mistreatment at home and how I haven't been home in two weeks and was never planning on going back ever even if my life depended on it. After I was done briefing the crew about my situation, I could see everyone getting a little emotional for once. Everyone was being supportive, Rex especially, who sort of took it upon himself to make sure I was going to be OK. The vow of me not going back home ever no matter what, as crazy and careless that sounded, was accepted by the whole crew.

Once again, Rex came up with an idea. Since we were all in summer break, I would be staying the night at least once or twice a day over each crew member's house, starting with Rex, at least till we came up with a long-term solution or at least till the end of the summer break. But the only obstacle we could face was clothing. No way was I going to wear the same clothes over and over, week after week, Rex pointed out. It shouldn't be as big as a problem. "We can always come up with something," he said. He even suggested breaking into my house just to get some more clothing, which I respectfully disagreed. I was not about to take any chances of being caught at all—*at least not in this lifetime,* I thought.

I spent the first two nights at Rex's house. Rex's parents didn't care at all. Rex's parents, especially Rex's dad, knew me and my father, since my father used to be the choir conductor at church. The plan worked perfectly the very first week until it became Zach's turn to host me. As the only child, Zach's house only included him and his mom and dad. They lived in a smaller house. His parents weren't as welcoming; therefore, Zach had to wait until both his parents went to bed to sneak me into the house late at night and then sneak me out of the house earlier in the morning.

My lunch consisted mostly of loaves of bread and sugar water from Rex's house. Having to eat two meals a day was somehow a luxury only reserved to the middle and upper class. Most families usually went by with one meal on a daily basis; that was the norm. Rex and I ate dinner together for the most part. On a few occasions, we all ate dinner together at one of the other crew member's houses.

The routine went on perfectly throughout the whole summer, but as the school break was now drawing to an end, we still haven't come up with a long-term solution to my situation. Even though none of us had breached the crew code of conduct, which was to keep whatever was going on only within the crew, no one was to divulge anything at any given circumstances, although no penalty was ever discussed for breaching such a pledge. Everyone kept up with their words when school finally started back up, and I still spent a lot of time at Rex' house, but only this time around, I wasn't freely spending the night there anymore.

Rex was now sneaking me in and out the house, which was becoming more and more difficult now that mostly everyone around the house were early birds as well since school was now back in session. On a few occasions, I could have thought Rex' elder sister had seen me sneaking into the house at nighttime. I even mentioned it to Rex, who seemed not

FROM PAIN TO FAME

to be concerned at all as he assured me his sister wouldn't say a thing to their parents. But after spending more time at Rex's house even now that the summer break was long over with probably caused a few eyebrows to be raised at the house.

Even though Rex and I had been successful in hiding the fact that I was a runaway from my house, I never was so vehement to attribute our success to our skills or cleverness. It was mostly because of a lack of concern from his parents. Rex's parents were so nonchalant. They cared very little. I always had the feeling that Rex's mother knew all along that I had been spending nights at her house quite often. Why she never said a thing, I never quite understood the reasoning behind her silence. I believe each adult had their own way of parenting, although this one was the most unorthodox from anything I have been accustomed to. As long as I was the benefactor, I had no opposition to such method.

One night, after being snuck into the house straight to the room, Rex's mother came by and opened the bedroom without giving us any warning, which caught us by surprise. With no place to hide or run, I was caught red-handed. Just like a bank robber caught in a booby trap, it was all over for me. Rex and I sat there looking at each other, wondering what the future held for us. He sure was going to be in trouble for sneaking me in on a school night, and besides, what was I doing at her house this late at night anyway? Didn't I have school in the morning myself? As we both were trying to each prepare ourselves individually for the worst, none of us knew what to expect, but we both were ready to face whatever was going to be thrown at us with bravery.

It was around 11:30 p.m. when Rex' mom hollered for Rex from the living room. After Rex and I both made our way to the living room, she asked Rex what I was still doing at her house at this time of the night. Rex told her that I came to pick up a school assignment that was due in the morning. I lived a few houses down, so it really wasn't a big deal, he said to his mother. She told Rex to hand me the assignment and I should hurry back home since it was already really late. Once again, Rex had come to my rescue at a very desperate moment after handing me a notebook. As he walked me outside, he told me to go by the soccer field and wait for about an hour and come back by this time; his mother should already be sleeping, and he would let me in the house.

I did just as Rex had said. By the time I got back to Rex's house, his front gate was locked. As I stood there helplessly on the other side of the gate, looking around, hoping for a miracle, Rex was nowhere to be found. I began whispering, "Rex! Rex!" as if to make sure that only Rex or someone named Rex could hear me and come to my rescue. As it became apparent that nothing was happening, tears began to roll down my eyes, and when I realized that crying would only bring more cries and less hope, I just decided to start walking. As dark as it was outside, my sorrow overtook all the fear I had from the dark street with me being the lone passerby.

As I was walking for about half an hour away from the neighborhood, I couldn't help but overhear noises coming from afar ahead of me. It sounded like people singing gospel songs. I even overheard some shouting in between. The closer I was getting to the noise, the more obvious it became that it was a group of church worshippers at some kind of church event. As I walked into the church where the noises were coming from, there were about twenty people gathered around praying. It was very common practice from those newly established churches to hold worship sessions from late night to dawn. Those practices, which usually occurred during weekdays between midnight and 5:00 a.m., were called veiller de priere. I went in and joined the rest of the worshippers, although my goal was different than the rest. They were there to worship, while I was there looking for a place to stay until daylight. I was welcomed into the group just as one of their own, and after singing along on some of the songs and saying a few prayers, roosters were already sounding, alerting the rest of the world to rise and shine. The sunrise was almost here. Shortly afterward, the worshipping session was over with. As everyone was greeting one another, I went out of the door.

By this time around, it had been about three months since I left my house. I went out and spent half of the day in FEZADI catching up on the very latest football gossips. After that, I made my way back to Phil's house. When I got there, Phil had informed me that Rex was looking all over for me. Phil and I went over Rex's. When we got there, we were greeted by Rex' mom, who strangely asked me if I was OK and where in the world I spent the night last night. Before I even opened my mouth to reply, Rex came, and we all quickly made our way out of the house. We were all headed to the football field.

When we got to the football field, Rex told me he tried to go outside and open the gate last night just to be stopped by his mother, who almost confused him to a burglar trying to break into the house and asked him what was going on this time. And after she had mentioned to him that in a few occasions, she saw me sleeping in the room while she was checking on everyone before she went to bed, that's when Rex decided to come clean with the truth and begged her to allow me to stay at their home as I had nowhere else to go, and I swore on my mother's grave that I wasn't going back home ever again. That is when she asked Rex where he thought I went. Rex told her I was at the football field. They both went looking for me at the soccer field, but I was nowhere to be found. They even left their door open for me, hoping I would make it back.

"Well, you guys were about an hour late," I told Rex, "as I came back about half an hour just like you told me, and the front gate was closed."

"I told you to wait about an hour, not half an hour. Besides, I overslept a little," said Rex. "Where the hell did you go anyway?" he asked.

"To some church over there," I said, pointing to the direction of the church.

"Anyway, my mother wanted to talk to you. She said you could stay here until she finds a solution. She probably would have to speak to people at the church concerning your situation at home, as few people, including Christian's mother, who was a friend of hers, kind of mentioned it to her a while ago. The church would have to come up with a solution on that matter, but until then, you're welcome to stay here for the moment." I was so happy to hear all those words.

We went on and found Pat and Zach already waiting for us by the field. We challenged a group of kids that were already playing among themselves into playing against us. We named our team Cinq Sur Cinq, which is French for "five over five." With Rex on our team, we were sure to beat about anyone. Being together the whole summer led us into developing a very solid bond among us, thus making us the inseparable special band of brothers. Soul brothers indeed. Rex and I developed a very special bond throughout. He became the brother I never had.

Since I wasn't in school, I tried to stay on course by doing most of Rex's schoolwork, which I found to be very easy considering that Rex was attending public school. As a result of doing most of Rex's homework, his school grades gradually improved. With that, I made myself more popular around the house. When we got back from the soccer field, Rex's mom gave me a little motherly pep talk and told me to feel as welcome as I can be at her house and to let her know if I ever needed anything. She told me to give her a little time so she can talk to other mothers within the church family in helping to find a solution to my family matters. Everything was nothing but sweet music to my ears. I went to bed that night sleeping like a newborn baby. This time, I didn't have to sneak in or sneak out really early.

About a few weeks later, Rex's mother held a meeting at one of the church's hall. The all-women meetings consisted of several members of the church faithful in the community. Rex's mom was the vice president of the community's church mother, a group of several mothers within the community who belonged to the Catholic Church. The group was mostly involved in setting up events such as fund-raisers, church giveaways, yard sales, cookouts, Easter and Christmas parties, etc. This time, the meeting was called to find a solution to my situation. It was all agreed that the group would send a delegation of about three ladies to my house to come out with a solution to end the standoff.

The following Sunday, Rex's mother led a small group from the mothers' club to my house to have a talk with my father. The meeting with my father was a total disaster as my father told the ladies that since I chose to run away and be free, he cared less about me, and I was never welcome back in his house, telling them since they chose to harbor a fugitive, I was from now on their responsibility, so they can do as they pleased. The ladies, who felt both embarrassed and disrespected by such arrogance from my father, who never had the courtesy to even hear the women out, left as my father was now threatening them to leave his house. As it became apparent that a solution to the situation wasn't forcible, at least for the moment, the ladies now turned to their husbands for help in finding a solution.

About two weeks later, a group of men led by the clergyman himself went to pay my father a visit at home, hoping to come up with a better result. This time, even the presence of the clergyman himself had no effect on my father. My father didn't budge at all from his stance. My father, being one of the most stubborn men known to mankind, wasn't moved by the plea from the abbot.

After both the men and women of the church community failed to gain any concession from my father, one thing was now clear. I was now, without a question, the church's responsibility. With that being said, another emergency meeting was called among few members of both the men and mothers in the church community to come up with a solution that would put this situation to rest once and for all.

At the meeting, a very devoted Catholic faithful, Mrs. Diomi, volunteered to have me in her custody. She asked to be granted my guardianship, welcoming the idea of having me as part of her family. That was an act of a great Samaritan. Mrs. Diomi was a kindergarten teacher at the neighborhood school, which was sponsored by the Catholic Church. She was married with five children. Above all, she was highly respected within the community. Her offer was unanimously approved by everyone, and they all made a pledge to be of great assistance to her if she ever needed any help, whether financially or logistically. From that moment on, you could say I became a ward of the church.

About few days before Christmas of 1995, I moved in with the Diomi family, becoming the sixth newest member of the family, joining Lilly, the eldest daughter who was about twenty; Mwenge, the second and eldest son who was about eighteen years old; Irene, who was about twelve years old; Christian, who was about six years old; and Omega, the youngest, who was about three. Mr. Diomi was a skillful carpenter who worked at home. Also living with us was Uncle Octave, Mr. Diomi's younger brother who was in his early thirties. Mr. Diomi's first name was Gaston, while his wife's first name was Omo. I called

Mr. Diomi Papa Gaston, and Mrs. Diomi Maman Omo. The entire family welcomed me just as one of their own. It felt so great to once again become a part of a healthy family, and having the privilege to have a place to call my home was one of the greatest miracles I could ever wish for.

The Diomis' house was about four blocks away from the football field and about seven blocks away from my house. I loved every part of being a part of that family. I finally started school the following January. I was enrolled in the fifth grade during the start of the second semester at St. Kiwanuka, a community school sponsored by the Catholic Church school, which happened to be where Maman Omo taught kindergarten.

Aside from teaching, Maman Omo also ran two small businesses as a means to support the family, since Papa Gaston, who was a devoted alcoholic, was not reliable financially. Although he made good money as a carpenter, most of his income, if not all of it, were never accounted for. He spent all his money on alcohol, leaving his wife the burden to be almost the lone provider of the family. Maman Omo sold bakery at school during lunch break, and ironically, she also sold beer at home, most of which Papa Gaston would drink alone or with his company. To be fair, he would sometimes pay cash for his purchase, but mostly, he would run a tab that was as large as the U.S. government debt to China, which would occasionally lead to sporadic arguments between the two of them. Even with all that drama, Maman Omo still managed to keep all her kids, with me included, in school and still fully provided for the whole family single-handedly with very little to no support from her husband. If there ever was an award for being the world's supermother, she either deserved to win it or was at least in the running to win it. She did it all.

Irene and I happened to be in the same grade, since I was a grade ahead at my year and she happened to be repeating the fifth grade after being held back a year. The school, which was located on the next street, shared part of its fenced wall with the Diomis' house, which meant, instead of going all the way around to the next street to go to school, I was just able to climb the fenced wall into school premises. We could hear the ring of the school bell from the house. Ironically, that still didn't keep me from being late to school almost every morning. I found my fifth grade being very easy and less challenging, as for some reason, I remember doing the very same assignments in third and fourth grade, giving me the upper hand on the rest of the class.

The atmosphere in the house was great. The only major rules were to be in the house no later than 6:30 p.m. during school nights and 10:30 p.m. on weekends, and Sunday morning mass attendance was mandatory, no exception. No one really stayed at the house that much except Papa Gaston, who did his carpenter work at home, while Maman Omo was always home except when going occasionally to church meetings.

Lilly, the eldest, was in her second year of college. A very devoted church girl, she was also one of the coordinators of a female youth movement within the church called Annuarite, a youth movement within the Catholic Church that advocate good morals and family values among its members. Lilly was good looking, soft spoken, and also well respected among her peers and the community. As a girl, she made her family proud in the way she carried herself. One of the challenges she faced was her health. She had sickle cell anemia, and her health was slowly deteriorating. It was mostly believed that it was just a matter of time, perhaps a few years, before things could turn for the worst, but even with all that going on, she was still fighting her way through life. She was very fond of me, making her my favorite.

Mwenge, the eldest boy, was in his senior year in one of the local private schools. He was very smart. He finished high school on top of his class. Mwenge was very shy. He played the guitar in one of the local bands. Mwenge and I never really crossed paths.

Irene was the star of the family. She was very popular in the neighborhood. She was popular for all the wrong reasons. She hated school, therefore didn't care much about it. At twelve, she had a higher interest in boys, mostly older. One her boyfriends was a pretty much grown man in high school. Sometimes, she even dated men in their twenties. It was debatable if she was dating them or they were dating her. Irene had a really bad reputation in the neighborhood. It was said about two years before I start living there, when she was about ten years old, she was raped by her uncle, her mother's little brother who happened to be staying at the house for a while. The news was known all over the neighborhood as some people saw her running out of the house without clothes on while blood was coming down her genitals. It was also told that she once was sleeping with someone's husband in the neighborhood, prompting some woman to come looking for her to engage in a fight. She was also known for stealing money from her mom. One day, I even caught her myself stealing money and took it away from her and returned it to her mom.

Christian and Omega were the two youngest boys. They weren't that much eventful. Uncle Octave, Papa Gaston's younger brother, was the discipliner. He kept everyone in check, mostly me and Irene, but keeping Irene in check was like fighting the war on drugs, an everlasting conflict with no resolution in sight.

One day, while walking around the neighborhood, I met a boy who introduced himself to me as Roger. He was also ten years old. Roger lived three houses down from me. We quickly developed a very close friendship. Roger lived with his aunt, who also had a big family. Even with Roger as my new best friend, I still kept in touch with the rest of the crew. I would occasionally go over Rex's house or meet up at the football field. We still kept our close relationship pretty much intact. Few times while at the football field, I would see my father passing by, and each time, I would take off, running back to the house. Once or twice, we even made eye contact. I was still very frightened by him. Even though I was no longer living at his house, I still feared him to death. I never knew what he could possibly have done had he come in contact with me. Just that idea of not knowing what could happen terrified me even more. Knowing from experience, I always knew how unpredictable my father was and how he was capable of inflicting serious pain even in the most unconventional places. That fear kept me in constant alert whenever I was out of the Diomis' home.

One weekend, while playing football at the football field, at around 11:00 a.m., my alert system must have failed me that day, as out of nowhere, I felt someone get a hold of my arm from behind. When I looked back to see who and why I was being held so tightly, it was my father. I was a few steps too late. There was no getting away this time. My father took me as everyone on the open field stood motionless. Everything happened so silently and quickly as if it was scripted.

We walked to the nearest bus stop, which was about five blocks away. The whole time on our way to the bus stop, my father was taunting me. "What happened? Why don't you run? You can't run now, can you? Let me see you run like you have been running!" He was holding my arm so tightly that it felt as if I was handcuffed. We got on the next bus.

Throughout the whole ride, I couldn't stop wondering how this could have happened, better yet what was going to happen next. We got off the bus in front of a police station. My father went on and spoke to a guy and handed him some cash out of his pocket. The guy called upon another policeman and spoke a few words to him. The policeman took me with him with my father following closely behind us. We got into this back room, while my father waited outside, looking through the window.

Then the policeman got out a military belt and told me to lie down on the floor. As I lay facedown on the floor, he shouted, "Now you are about to see what we do to runaways." Whoop! That was the sound of the first lash going straight to my back. Then the second. Then another and another. I counted about forty lashes all together. I screamed after each lash as loud as I could, screaming painfully and desperately hoping to attract a rescue from anywhere or anyone. By the time I received the last slash, I couldn't feel my body anymore. I was so disoriented. I even peed on myself.

My father took me afterward. We left the police station. We got to the nearest bus stop and hopped on a bus leading uptown. On the way, there were no words spoken between the two of us. From the time we left the police station until we made it uptown, the hour-ride uptown was in complete silence. As we made our way uptown, I watched him buy some groceries. We made it back to the bus. This time, we were heading back home. Once again, the ride back home was in complete silence. By the time we got closer to the football field, he let go of my hand and told me I was free to go.

I started running as fast as I could back to the Diomis' house. I made it back to the house at around 8:00 p.m. Once at the house, there was a small crowd, mostly adults from church. They were probably briefed by those kids I was playing football with who saw everything that had happened that afternoon. Everyone seemed very relieved to see me. I stood in the middle of the small crowd, and after I told everyone at house about my experience of the day, people were more astonished and filled with sorrow. I went straight to bed after holding what seemed like two-hour-long press conference. I was just glad the day was over with and was looking forward to a regular day tomorrow.

Days went by without any more significant events. I didn't run into my father anywhere afterward. School was going well. I was at the top of my class. I was a step above everyone academically. During the school year, my teacher had me and a few of my classmates working on a play he had written. The play itself was a modified version of William Shakespeare's *Romeo and Juliet*. My character was that of Romeo, while Alice, the prettiest girl in the class, arguably the prettiest in the school, played Juliet. We were set to perform the play at the city hall, where about twenty other schools were all competing in the annual interscholastic show sponsored by the Department of Education. This was the biggest school show of the year. We rehearsed about every day after school for about two hours each day.

My performance and that of my costar Alice were met with a big standing ovation. We had the whole city hall in awe. At one point, I did forget my line; but instead of panicking, I did improvise something off the script in between. I was supposed to say something after a kiss. When I realized that I didn't remember what my line was going to be, I fainted right after the kiss, leaving everyone in the city hall, even my teacher, mesmerized. The performance was a total success. Although we came in second place, that second-place trophy felt like a first-place one. As first-timers, we pulled out a David-versus-Goliath-like performance.

Shortly after that event, Alice and I started dating. I always had a crush on her for the longest time. Spending more time with her at rehearsals helped solidify our bond. For once, I could say I was in love. I finished the fifth grade on top of my class, marking one of the best years academically. Midway through my sixth-grade school year, I fell very ill. I ran a really bad fever for about three consecutive days. None of the medicines I was given were helping at all. The fever wouldn't go down at all. My body was getting weaker and weaker. Five days later, I lost consciousness. I was immediately rushed to one of the city's main hospitals. Everyone was left fearing the worst. I spent three days in intensive care while in a coma.

The first time I opened my eyes at the hospital, I could see a few people by my bed, but I could hardly recognize who they were. As I got better, I started recognizing people's faces. My father was by my side along with my aunt Mado and Euphrasy. I had a few members of the church community who came to visit me. Rex's parents came also. I spend about a total of two and half weeks in the hospital, with Maman Omo being there every day; she never missed a day. I really don't know what caused me to fall so ill in the first place. All I know is that I had lost a lot of blood in the process, requiring a blood transfusion.

I don't know what was said between my family and the Diomis, but when I left the hospital, instead of going back to the Diomis, I found myself going back home with my aunt Mado, the youngest of my father's siblings. My father was devastated by the circumstances that saw me hospitalized. My being in coma four days had brought for the very first time fear in him that at any given moment now, if anything was to go wrong, he was going to lose his only son. This time, it wasn't just leaving his house to go to another; but instead, I would have been gone and buried underground without him having the chance to even say good-bye. He would never have known why I chose to leave his house and why I was so determined never to come back. The guilt of having failed in his duty as a parent was to haunt him for the rest of his life.

But fortunately for him, a miracle happened from very high above, and I was kept alive not by personal strength but, instead, by the grace of the Living God, and with that came a second chance for the both of us—for him, a chance to redeem himself from all the terror he inflicted on me; for me, a chance for a fresh start with the man whom I sought to be my hero, the man who once was my best friend. In other words, having fallen so ill with a good possibility of leaving this world as a result was the silver lining in the cloud. It helped bridge the gap between my father and me. It brought reconciliation.

Although I have blurry recollection of ever seeing Maman Omo at the hospital, even while conscious, I still felt her care and love while I was lying down half dead. She was the real hero. Had she not rushed me to the hospital and stood by me during all that time, I probably would have been dead. On my way out of the hospital, I looked around, and she was nowhere to be found. I just wished I was given the chance to say thank you for saving my life by rushing me to the hospital and many thanks for being the mother I so desperately needed. While leaving the hospital with my aunt Mado, I was still looking around for her, hoping to see her at least one more time. It hurt me to see that she was nowhere near.

My aunt Mado was about twenty-four years old. She moved in with my uncle Danny after her marriage ended up in a divorce. She once married this guy who was about at least fifteen years older than she was. She was eighteen years old when she first married the guy—Julius, that is his name, a businessman who made his money buying and selling diamonds. He was purchasing smuggled diamond at a very cheap price from miners working in government-run mining field in the countryside and selling it back to private jewelers in the city, making himself a pretty comfortable living out of it. The more cash were entering his pockets, the more he could no longer keep his pants up. I am guessing it's from all that money weight in his pocket.

The man had a lot of women, all types, skinny, tall, dark skinned, light skinned, old, and young. If there was a shortage of women in certain areas of the city, it's probably because he had them all. He became very neglecting of my aunt. He even went on to get married to two different women behind my aunt Mado's back. He became more and more abusive to my aunt Mado. He made her become so accustomed to sunglasses to help cover her black eyes from the beatdown he was giving her on a regular basis. Even that didn't really keep my aunt Mado from loving this man—that was, until she found out about a few of his other secret underground marriages, which led to something around twelve children from multiple women. I am guessing that was the straw that broke the camel's back. She finally decided to divorce him.

The divorce was nothing but amicable as the two of them fought bitterly over the custody of their three-year-old daughter. My aunt came on the losing end after her ex-husband forcibly took the child away from her care and moved her to a secret location, probably to one of his twenty other wives' house. After the divorce, my aunt lost everything, from the house she shared with her ex-husband to whatever else she had.

She decided to move in with my uncle Danny following her misfortune. My uncle Danny was the youngest of all my father's brother; it was him and then aunt Mado. Uncle Danny was in his late twenties, perhaps the bravest of all my father's siblings. He was a go-getter who put his hands on trying every profession you can ever think of. He tried to be a professional boxer; it didn't work. He was a photographer for a while and then moved on to become a carpenter afterward. He started a small business, which only lasted a few weeks. One thing about my uncle Danny was he never gave up, I believe, just like Einstein. My uncle Danny never thought of his many shortcomings as failure. He just thought of it as being different professions that were never meant for him to be successful at.

He finally nailed a winner in his latest fight trying to make it when he decided to take up mining. He went to work in a mining field in Angola, one of the neighboring countries that was very rich in diamond. Angola, a country that had been in civil war for over twenty years, was one of the world's top exporters of diamond. The country's large deposit of the mineral was mostly found in regions held by rebels. The country was mostly divided in half with the central government led by a certain Jose Eduardo dos Santos, the leader of the MPLA Party, who had the control of about 60 percent of the land ranging mostly from the western and northern parts of the country, while the eastern and southern parts of the country were occupied by one of the world's ruthless warlords, Jonas Malheiro Savimbi, the leader of the UNITA Party.

Angola's civil war, which dated back from the '70s, was mostly enhanced by the cold war between the United States and the USSR. The two superpower were going at it indirectly by arming opposite factions. The United States provided heavy weaponry and military training to the rebels led by Jonas Malheiro Savimbi in exchange for mining contract in rebel-held area; while on the other hand, the former USSR backed Jose Eduardo dos Santos militarily in exchange for big oil contract in government-held area. The twenty-year-old civil war saw no significant gain from neither side. Both sides still had the full support from their backers, respectively, who, on the other hand, were making the best out of the stalemate financially. Both the United States and the former USSR were making a killing out of the conflict. They both were enjoying such a high profit, while the country was turning into a dumpster. The whole country was a huge shit hole.

Even though Angola was a wreck physically, it was still economically better off than my country, which at that time was among the world's worst economies with one of the poorest standards of living. For many in Zaire who were accustomed to one of the world's highest unemployment rates, I believe at that time it was around 70 percent, I am pretty sure I am even being a little generous with those numbers, Angola, a country in the middle of a civil war, still represent more hope economically than Zaire a country, which wasn't at war at all. In a country where opportunity was as luxurious as a river in a desert for a person in my city who was between the age of eighteen and thirty-five whether or not he/she has earned a college degree or high school diploma, there were only a few ways available to earn somewhat a living.

1. Government sector job. It had the country's highest percentage of employees with nearly close to 70 percent of the workforce. But the only problem facing qualified candidates was that not only it was now harder than ever to find an opening in any jobs within the government sectors, but also the very few times there ever was an opening anywhere, that spot was quickly filled by either someone's family member, girlfriend, boyfriend, or very close friend without taking in consideration whether the person was qualified for the job or at least met all the standards required to hold such position. So if you weren't sleeping with any high-ranking officials or wasn't related to any of those officials in charge of hiring, whether your credentials were as honorary as any Ivy League genius, you sure were doomed to be unemployed for life.

2. The army. Joining the army to most was the only way to somewhat come close to earning a living. Even though about 80 percent of the armed forces were usually underpaid, and most of the time, they would go months and months without getting a paycheck, army personnel still enjoyed a few benefits such as free housing in military bases, free pass in any of the city's transportation system, even the private ones, occasionally free food, and free health care. For the crooks, joining the army had its own hidden benefit. Weapons were used to rob or terrorize the unarmed civilians.

3. Private sectors. Working for privately owned businesses, which really weren't too many as the government owns about everything, except for shops and a few schools.

4. Self-employment: Being a small business owner or contractor.

Last, but not least,

5. Angola. Mostly used as a last resort to many was going to Angola to work in the diamond field digging up diamond in rebel-held area, which paid up pretty well.

Since the rebels needed to keep getting their weapon supplies from the U.S. government, they needed to make sure more diamonds were being produced, which meant they needed more people working on those fields digging for more diamond. To my countrymen, that was an opportunity to stack up money and perhaps go back home to help out families left behind. Working in those diamond fields was not only very rewarding but also very risky. Contractors were paid weekly, and they worked very long hours, sometimes from dawn to sunset with very little to no break. They were constantly watched by armed rebels throughout the work hours, making sure none of the diamonds were making its way out of the field without being accounted for. Death was the penalty for being caught trying to smuggle diamonds out of the field. Every diamond found was to be immediately reported and given to the guard. Failure to do so resulted to being gunned down.

Battle threats were very constant as government forces would launch several assaults to recapture territories under rebels' control. Gun battles would erupt with sometimes heavy machinery and bombing involved, which would leave several unarmed contractors dead while trying to run for cover. Contractors were also subject to all types of abuse from Angolans who were prejudiced against them for reasons ranging from jealousy to anything you can think of. Since some contractors were starting to make a good living from their labor, now they were the attraction of most of the Angolan women, causing a lot of hatred toward those foreigners, eventually leading to some cases of hate crimes.

Majority of contractors' main objectives were to amass quite as much money as they could seasonally and then return back home to take care of their families, perhaps start a business, purchase a home, or even buy a car. Others chose to stay and mix in with the Angolans. Life as a contractor was like playing Russian roulette, as anything could happen from being gunned down while trying to sneak out with a diamond to being killed during one of the battles between the two factions at war to just disappearing and never coming back or to finally coming back home with a large sum of money ranging from $10,000 to $100,000. So depending on your destiny, anything was possible.

The big money came to contractors who, despite the heavy presence of armed rebels surveying them, were still heroically able to smuggle a diamond or a few out without being detected. The most common way to smuggle out a diamond was by swallowing it. Some contractors would swallow the mineral and make sure to retrieve it while using the bathroom. Contractors who had done so wouldn't use the bathroom as usual. They would take a crap on a hard surface and then inspect their residue for pieces of diamond, which they would clean and then take to private jewelers, earning themselves big money ranging from $1,000 to $50,000, depending on the value.

My uncle Danny was one among the few who were getting away with smuggling diamonds out of the field without being caught by the armed rebels. He did so by employing the swallowing method, which he came to master. While Uncle Danny was away in Angola for six to nine months usually, Aunt Mado took care of his home, a small one-bedroom house that was a part of a duplex.

Sometime before I got hospitalized, my father and Maggie got separated, although the reasons for their separation, which was quite mutual, was never known to me. I always suspected that finances was one of the reasons, if not the main reason. One other reason could have been Maggie's unpopularity among my father's side of the family, which might have played a part. For whatever reasons, none of my aunts never warmed up to Maggie at all. Throughout their whole marriage, they only made one or two appearances to the house; one was after Maggie had given birth to my stepsister Jenny. Even then, the visits were more as a diplomatic gesture than a family one, as you could easily feel the tension on the horizon whenever both sides interacted with each other.

After the separation, my father became a regular at my uncle Danny's house. Aunt Mado would usually make him dinner almost about every day. He would hang out with her for a little bit and then take off to who knows where. No one had any idea where he lived since. My father and Aunt Mado were very close. When my father was outcast from his family for impregnating his own cousin, Aunt Mado was the only one who still stood up for him. One other thing that kept them pretty close was the fact that Aunt Mado was just like a female version of my father. They both shared so many characteristics; above all, they both were very stubborn people.

Coming back from the hospital, I was in total care of my aunt Mado, who, on top of giving me all the medicines I was prescribed, had me on a special diet for my recovery. Coming out of the hospital, I was very weak and lost a lot of blood. To help me regain the blood I had lost from my illness, she made some special beverage for me, which I had to drink one full glass twice a day. It was a mixture of tomato paste and egg yolks, which she had turned into a beverage. The beverage was the grossest thing I ever tasted in my life. We fought every day for me to drink it. Even though I had a hard time taking it down, it sure did help me recover at a speed of light. About a month after being released from the hospital, I was up and kicking, thanks to my aunt Mado with her care and witty diet.

A few days after we came home from the hospital, my father finally moved in with us. This time around, he was more caring and even more affectionate than I could ever remember. Throughout my whole recovery process, we got to develop a very close relationship reminiscent of the old days.

Being hospitalized along with the recovery process led to me miss the rest of the school year. I missed the remaining of my sixth grade.

By the time I fully recovered from my illness, everything was perfect at home. With Aunt Mado at the helm of the household, nothing could have possibly ever gone wrong. I even got to be more acquainted with other family members, as most of them who pretty much stayed away from my father's home were now regulars at Uncle Danny's house. I got to see more and more of three of my other aunts, Aunt Monique, who was born right after my father, Aunt Euphrasy, and Aunt Martha, my father' eldest sister.

Aunt Monique lived about an hour and a half away. She lived with her husband, Mussa, an army lieutenant. Together, they had a daughter named Laetecia, who was about five years old at the time.

Aunt Euphrasy, who was born right before Uncle Danny, was a registered nurse at the city' second-largest hospital. Aunt Euphrasy had the reputation of jumping from relationship to another. She had the habit of showcasing whomever she happened to be dating at the moment to the world, especially family members who, after seeing so many of her "this is the one," were now being less supportive of, if not annoyed by, her showcases, to be quite frank. For her defense, I always thought that she was just unlucky in picking the wrong men who happened to be in a relationship with her for reasons that weren't as similar as hers; either that or she just was attracted to scumbags. One thing for certain, Aunt Euphrasy was the most successful independent woman I had ever known in that time. She was financially stable. She had it all except a healthy and long-term relationship. Aunt Euphrasy was the only female sibling who didn't have kids yet. She pretty much made me the heir to all her fortune. Everything I wanted was always provided by her. She was my all-year-round personal Santa Claus.

Aunt Martha, the third in line of all my father's ten siblings, and the eldest sister of all, was the bridge or escalator of the family. She was the first of all her siblings to be married and to move from her native village to settle in the city. She lived with her husband, Robert, who was once a prominent state official. Together, they had eleven children, four boys and seven girls.

As the very first of all her siblings to settle in the city, Aunt Martha's home played the host to most of her siblings who migrated from the village to the city for various reasons. Whether you came to the city for school or to embark on a new adventure or maybe you were just someone trying to find yourself, Aunt Martha's house was the ultimate halfway house. She provided for most of her siblings' needs, if not all of them. You were more than welcome to stay there until you were ready to finally fly on your own wings and take on the next challenge.

Just to name a few people who stayed at Aunt Martha's house: My father stayed there while trying to earn his master's degree in philosophy. Aunt Euphrasy stayed there while going through medical school. Uncle Danny stayed there while going through carpentry school. Aunt Monique and Mado both briefly stayed for whatever reason they were there for. Even I stayed there in my years as a toddler. Aunt Martha was more like a mother to most of her siblings, and what was so amazing about that woman was that she hosted and raised all those multitude in just a two-bedroom house, and never a day did she or her husband ever complain about anybody or anything. From her house came doctors, teachers, college graduates, nurses, good housewives, you name it. Above all, Aunt Martha was the best cook to ever step in a kitchen. She only cooked on Sundays, and when she did, it was always something special. With her around, the multitude always found themselves fully fed.

Aunts Mado, Monique, and Euphrasy were very close. Together, they formed what was like a gang, sometimes as a force for good, other times not so much. On a few occasions, they were responsible for fighting their sibling's wives or girlfriends whom they thought weren't a good match or fit to their siblings. They were also involved in many of their sibling's breakups. Although they were vehemently opposed to my father's marriage to Maggie, the fact was my father made it very clear to them that they had one option and one option only—either accept his choice and live by it or have absolutely no part at all in his family. My father's firm warning about any interference in his private life might have kept them at bay, as I can count with only two fingers how many times I saw any of them at the house. The only good act they had ever done came by when they decided to forcibly remove the wife of one of their uncles out of her home for having an affair. They did that while their uncle was away on a business trip. At least that one was justified, I thought.

Living on the other side of the duplex was this lady who was a close friend of Aunt Mado. She lived with her son and little niece. Her son Serge and her niece Esther were both my age, so we all became friends. We did pretty much everything together.

One afternoon, while Serge and I were sitting in the living room watching TV, we heard someone knocking on the front door. As I went to open the door, I was surprised to see the person on the other side. It was Uncle Danny, whom I haven't seen in years. The last time I saw him, it was when Jenny was born. Now it seemed almost like a decade ever since. As it has been my tradition, whenever seeing him, I always greet him by doing some boxing moves he had taught me and then jumping on top of him afterward. I was so glad to see him, and from the look on his face, he was just as thrilled to see me. He came in a cab with a whole lot of luggage, which Serge and I helped him unload. He had brought with him all kinds of stuff from clothing to some electronic apparel. It was as if he had bought some store out.

About a few hours later, Aunt Mado came back from her errands. Seeing that her brother was back from his long trip, she decided to go back out and do some more grocery shopping, this time perhaps buying some of Uncle Danny's favorites. She came back to the sound of loud music, and there were already two or three guests from around who came to welcome him back home, and by the time the night came, there were about fifteen people in the house, drinking and eating to the sound of some of Uncle Danny's favorite tunes from one of his favorite artists, one of our country's great, Tabu Ley Rochereau, and his African fiesta band. Uncle Danny was a notorious ladies' man, the ultimate bachelor. He had them coming in all types, shapes, and colors. He was the Romeo to all the Juliets he could possibly land his hands on.

If I had to take a guess, I would say Uncle Danny brought back with him about $20,000 in cash, of which about $5,000 went to a used car he just purchased, and he ended up spending about the same amount again in trying fixing it, as a few weeks after the purchase, the car seemed to generate more and more problems. On a daily basis, that car always seemed to have something that needed to get fixed. Not only that, but also he had all kinds of different mechanics working on that car. About three months later, he finally had enough with that car and ended up selling it to a mechanic for a fraction of what he previously paid for.

Uncle Danny spent his money very lavishly. He treated every day as if it was his last day on earth. The man was having as much fun as a person on a mission to fulfill his bucket list. He had different sets of women for each time of the day partying with him. Only Mr. Hefner and his notorious Playboy mansion came close to rivaling him in that department. From all those women, there was a particular one that seemed to be getting the most out of his affection. Her name was Corine. Corine was tall, light skinned, with a body structure identical to those women they have been showing in one of those after-dark hip-hop music videos. I couldn't quite figure out why she was my uncle' favorite. Corine made the best out of Uncle Danny's weakness for her by taking advantage of him financially. What Uncle Danny didn't realize at the time was that Corine was playing him all along for his money. She had a boyfriend whom she loved and cared for, and it sure wasn't my uncle. When my uncle Danny finally ran out of money, she was nowhere to be found.

There is something about money that makes the person with it either blind or immune to any advice that does not conform to his personal interest. My father tried as much as he could to reason Uncle Danny into investing his money into something that would help him generate some more money. Either my uncle Danny didn't think that was a good idea or he just had so much faith that he would never have to worry about running out of that money. Before he knew it, all the money ran out. He had no car and less friends than Hitler ever had during his last hour. It was very sad watching Uncle Danny going from hero to zero. Reading the Bible and meditating through gospel music were now the norm.

A few months afterward, we all had to go our separate ways as an eviction order was issued for being behind on rent. Just like that, it was all over again for me as Aunt Mado left to go live with some distant cousin of hers. My father, who had already left way before, during Uncle Danny's golden days, would have taken me with him had he had a bigger couch at his cousin's studio apartment. My father hated even more the fact that I was living at Uncle Danny's house. The moment Uncle Danny came back from Angola, he turned his house into a Playboy mansion, not a place suitable to raise a child. During those times, my father would come by occasionally and take me out to spend the day with him and bring me back at night. We would enjoy long walks together just like the old days and make trips to my favorite bakery to get my favorite croissant. I always looked forward to spending the day with my father.

Shortly after the breakup with Maggie, my father met a lady named Francine, who was working on her master's in finance while working part time as an accountant in one of the city' private banks. She was very nice and charming. I liked her from the very moment I met her. Something about her from the way she spoke to her smile reminded me a lot of Marceline, my father's former girlfriend whom he almost married before meeting Maggie. But just like in Marceline's case, just when I was starting to warm up to the idea of perhaps seeing my father and Francine taking it to the next level, their relationship ended, and just like that, I was left wondering about what could have been. I never knew the reason that led to their breakup. Seeing how happy and perfect they seemed together, I couldn't even guess even if my life depended on it.

Shortly before the eviction, I was sent to live with my aunt Monique. Aunt Monique lived in a small one-bedroom apartment, which was a part of a fourplex. Living with her was her husband, Mussa, her daughter Laetecia, who was about six, and her stepdaughter Tabu, who was about eight years old. Mussa had two wives. Aunt Monique was the second wife, while Tabu's mom was the first one. As a Muslim, Mussa was allowed to marry up to seven wives if he wished to. I slept on the couch in the living room, Tabu slept on a mat she set up in the living room every night, while Laetecia slept with both of her parents in their bedroom.

I was enrolled in a neighborhood school to start the seventh grade shortly after I started living there. Aunt Monique sold used clothing at the neighborhood market, which was about half an hour from the house. Mussa, a lieutenant in the armed forces, was only home one weekend in a month. As far as I'm concerned, Mussa was very nice and generous toward me. He treated me just like one of his own.

There was one particular thing about my aunt Monique that made me really uncomfortable. The way she treated Tabu, her stepdaughter, was very alarming. For whatever reason, she despised her stepdaughter so much that one would think the poor nine-year-old girl probably had committed one of the worst crimes humanity ever witnessed. I don't care what anybody says; there is absolutely no reason under any circumstance that a child should have to endure such treatment. At nine years old, Tabu was given the task of a maid. She had to clean the house daily, wash all the dishes, and on top of that, wash everybody's clothes.

Like that wasn't enough, she was constantly abused physically and verbally by Aunt Monique. She called her all types of names but her given name. She even accused the poor little girl of being a witch. My aunt Monique was trying to get pregnant for so long, and when she couldn't get pregnant, she blamed it on Tabu the witch. Tabu never had much to say. The poor little girl was as quiet as a mute, but one thing—she carried with her one of the most beautiful smiles I had ever seen. You could easily see the sky light up whenever she did smile. During each meal, Aunt Monique always made sure Tabu had the least amount of food among everyone else in the house. At the house, only my aunt's daughter Laetecia was given the privilege to eat brunch every day. Tabu and I had to wait until about 6:30 p.m. every day for our first and only meal.

I left home for school every day at around 11:20 a.m. I had about an hour walk, and class didn't start until 12:30 p.m. and finished at 5:30 p.m. I went to school every day on an empty stomach, making it hard for me to focus. As time went by, I finally got used to it, mostly thanks to Patrick, one of my classmates whom I became best friends with. Patrick would always share his lunch with me during the fifteen-minute lunch break we had at school. Since Patrick lived about three blocks away from school, I would stop by his house on my way to school and wait about five to ten minutes for him to get ready. Then we would walk to school together.

Patrick was a cartoon fanatic until this day. I don't think I ever met a biggest cartoon lover than him. As a kid, I never really liked cartoons. I was very selective, although I did have two favorite cartoons. I enjoyed watching *Lucky Luke*, a western comic series created by a Belgian cartoonist. Lucky Luke, the main character, was a bounty hunter who gave himself the task of ridding the communities out of the bad guys. Lucky Luke was my favorite cartoon until Patrick introduced me to *Jules et Julie"* a Japanese cartoon based on the characters Jules and Julie, two twins gifted with special powers who were separated at birth by the Japanese government who saw their power as a challenge to their ruthless ruling of the island. They kept them separate and away from each other for the simple fact that the twin's superpowers only worked when both of their hands were touching. I fell in love with *Jules and Julie*, which coincidentally was aired on TV every weekday from 11:30 a.m. to 12:00 p.m. I started leaving the house about half an hour early just to watch an episode of *Jules and Julie* with Patrick before heading for school.

Since I technically was only given one meal a day, which was dinner, Tabu and I would only eat half of our portion and save the other half to eat as breakfast. Even though there sure wasn't enough food to be split into two meals, we couldn't afford to wait twenty-four hours just to get another meal. The longer I stayed at the house, the more I came to realize how ruthless Aunt Monique was in mistreating her stepdaughter, making an amateur out of Maggie in the way she was abusing me. Although there were similarities between the two stepmothers, just like Maggie, Aunt Monique was so obsessed with the fear of witchcraft. She even was convinced that her stepdaughter was a witch. She accused Tabu of being responsible for her not being able to bear another child. She has been trying to get pregnant for a long time now, but for whatever reason, she wasn't getting pregnant.

One time, during one of the school breaks, Aunt Monique decided to finally do something about the whole ordeal. She has been trying really hard to find the cause of her misfortune everywhere else but within herself. It never occurred to her that perhaps maybe her body had something to do with it. The genius in her was telling her that it has to be somebody, and she was sure was not going to let anyone take away her ability to conceive, especially not the devil that was her nine-year-old stepdaughter.

Aunt Monique got an appointment to see this tribal spiritual healer, a fancy term for witchcraft doctor if you ask me. This guy was supposedly the best in his profession. He supposedly had more feedback than Steve Jobs ever had after inventing the iPhone brand. The self-proclaimed spiritual leader claimed to perform miracles such as healing deadly viruses, AIDS, cancer, just to name a few. Among all other miracles, he was mostly known for making barren women give birth and exposing witches. If you were a witch, he was going to expose you and rid you of all your witchcraft.

He held about four big healing conventions every year, attracting a multitude of hundreds of people each time. People with all types of sickness and personal reasons would attend, hoping to get healed. The healing convention took place at one of his residences, a very big house that looked like an old abandoned castle located on top of a hill about twenty miles away from civilization. It was a pilgrimage on its own just trying to get there. It was about a good ten-mile walk up the hill to reach the place. The healing convention, which lasted for a weekend only, began on Friday and ended by Sunday afternoon. There was a cover charge for participation, which I believe was something between fifty dollars and one hundred dollars per family, depending on the gravity of your illness. With all that multitude paying him off so well, it wouldn't have shocked me a bit to hear the man's name mentioned in one of *Forbes* magazine's world's top earner.

We arrived at the place very late on Thursday. Aunt Monique, her daughter Laetecia, Tabu, and I were very exhausted from the long walk up the hill. I just couldn't wait to get some quality rest. There were about hundreds of people scattered all around the big sandy yard. Groups of families picked their own spot all over the yard. The wealthier families occupied some of the rooms inside the house, while others had tents set up outside. The rest of us who were less fortunate financially had to settle for just setting up sleeping bags right in the open. We were so lucky it didn't rain that weekend at all.

As part of the ritual, everyone involved was required to drink one liter of palm oil along with twenty ounces of hot water each day until Sunday. Aunt Monique's daughter Laetecia was the only one exempt from taking part in the whole ritual. The only reason she came along was she was too young to stay home by herself; either that or Aunt Monique couldn't find a babysitter. Drinking a liter of straight palm oil was torture on its own, but since there was absolutely no way of getting out of it unless some very high power descended from the sky and knocked every bottles containing the palm oil out of the sight, we were all doomed to drink up.

Everything about drinking straight palm oil made me sick to my stomach. It felt like I was on an episode of *Fear Factor*; only this time, instead of competing for a $50,000 cash prize, I was forcibly volunteering. Instead of taking it sip by sip, I managed to drink it all up in two tries. Boy, was I looking forward to Sunday so I could just get over with this nightmare. It was the longest and worst forty-eight hours of my life. I was in total rebellious mode against my aunt for making me endure such a cruel and unusual punishment just in the name of getting healed. This was one of the very few moments in my life where I wished death upon somebody, not just a dying-in-her-sleep kind of death, no—I mean, a very painful one like getting hit by a train or getting stuck under the *Titanic* kind of death.

Although it seemed like it took Sunday longer than expected to come, but it sure finally made its way. On Sunday, the last day of the healing procedure, the spiritual leader finally showed up as part of the closing ritual. They had set up a special tent for the spiritual leader whom everyone called Baba. Dressed like one of those biblical figures from the Old Testament, he reminded me of the Moses I once saw in one of the biblical movies. He was bald, with very long beard almost touching his knees, dressed up in a long white robe while carrying a long cane. Everyone, after having drank the last portion of palm oil, has to go see Baba for the last procedure of the healing process. His tent, which was fairly big in size, was set up about one hundred yards away from everyone else. It was very dark colored, and no one could see through it from the outside. There were two chaperones at the door to welcome whoever was next in line. There was a very long queue of people lined up by families in a single line ready to be seen by His Highness, the man himself, the master healer Baba.

When our turn came to enter the tent, I was the very first one to go in. As I got in with Aunt Monique on my side, I went in front of Baba, who was sitting in a royal-like chair. There were three ladies in the tent. One was standing on one side carrying a bucket of hot water, and the other, who stood on the other side, stood by with an empty bucket and a towel. The third lady stood right next to Baba with a bucketful of very small palm leaves. I got in front of Baba. Coming out from drinking my last portion of the one liter of palm oil, he told me open my mouth wide just like at the dentist. With my mouth wide open, he took one of the palm leaves from the bucket and inserted it deep down my throat. After he pulled out the palm leaf, I threw up on the ground. Aside from food and liquid, I threw up a little object that was shaped like a very little Hacky Sack.

As part of the ritual, Baba had people drinking all that palm oil, and inserting the palm leaves in one's throat, as he explained it, would cause a person to throw up. In your puke, you will find the thing or things that were responsible for your illness. If you came there to get rid of cancer, you will be puking out the cause of your cancer. In Aunt Monique's case, who was there to find solution to her getting pregnant, she would have puked the cause of her sterility. Whatever it was, Baba would give you a thorough explanation of his findings, and in some cases, he would prescribe some divine ritual as a follow-up.

For some reason, when it came to the residue found in my puke, His Highness Baba couldn't explain the meaning of that little object that came out of my stomach. He did say he never saw anything like that before and that I was a special case; whether that was a good thing or a bad thing, that was for Baba to figure out.

Tabu threw up a little chunk of meat-like object. He explained that someone had been using her body spiritually every night to hunt people to kill. The meat-like object is some of the people's flesh she ate after killing them.

Aunt Monique did throw up a piece of coal, which he explained was what kept her from getting pregnant. But now that the coal was out of her, she should be able to get pregnant at no time now. Although Baba never did label Tabu a witch for Aunt Monique, she still maintained that she had been proven right about her labeling her stepdaughter a witch. As for me, I never understood why, out of all those hundreds of people who threw up something, I was the only one that threw up something that the so-called spiritual leader, the guy that has the power to perform all types of miracle, was not able to identify or give any explanation as he had so successfully done in the past and most recently. But once again, Baba was just one of the savvy scammers around. Once he got his money, he could care less whether you were healed; and since the money given wasn't refundable, if for whatever reason you didn't get healed, the only explanation was you didn't get healed because you performed some of the rituals wrong. With his satisfaction rate being at 100 percent, he sure wasn't taking any responsibility for any failure or shortcoming.

When we got back home from the healing convention, everything was back as normal. We were still fed one meal a day, and Tabu was still being worked like a slave, just the usual. Whenever Mussa was home either for the holiday or the weekend, Aunt Monique treated Tabu just like a mother would treat her daughter, which was pretty, but sometimes, I wondered, only if those walls could speak up on what really goes on in that house in Mussa's absence, only God knows what would have happened.

Even under those rough circumstances, I did manage to finish the seventh grade. I finished fifth in my class. I was very proud of myself as it had been a while since I was able to finish a whole school year. Most importantly, I did it under one of the hardest circumstances. But one thing became certain. I was not going to start the eighth grade under those same circumstances, at least not in this lifetime.

A few months earlier, I got to spend the entire fall break with my father. His roommate happened to be out of town for work, allowing my father to have the space to host me for the weeklong break. Being away from Aunt Monique's house came as a relief for me. Spending time with my father never felt so great. Besides, I got to see Jenny, my stepsister who was about five years old this time around. The last time I saw her, she was still crawling around and couldn't fully pronounce my name. She was even more adorable now that she knew how to speak and walk.

I took the time to address my displeasure at living with Aunt Monique during a conversation with my father. He assured me that he was working on getting us a home. "Hang tight for few more months. Before you know it, we will all be in our home" were his words to me. Every day I felt like giving up. All I did was think back about my father's words. I was able to turn to those words to help me going.

Although my father never came through with his assertion on getting us our home, he did come up with an alternative to my grievance. Shortly before the start of the new school year, I was sent to live with Aunt Martha. Even though that wasn't what I had anticipated, I still found some relief in leaving Aunt Monique's home. Aunt Martha's home was uptown and very farther away from everything I have been accustomed to. On the day I arrived at the home, the very warm reception from the rest of the family made me feel right at home. I was later told that I had previously spent a few years as a toddler in this very house. I still never had any recollection of ever being a part of this scenery. The house had three bedrooms and a very large kitchen.

Aunt Martha and her husband, Robert, had a very big family. They had seven daughters and four boys, for a total of eleven. There were Robert's the firstborn, who was about twenty-five years old; Mbuyi, who had a twin sister that passed away during birth, who was about twenty-three; Ndaya, who was about twenty-one; Misenga, who was handicapped from having suffered polio at a very early age, who was about nineteen; Meta, who was about seventeen; Amba, who was about fourteen; Mama, who was about twelve; Clementine, who was about ten; Rolly, about eight; Rodrigue, about six; and the baby of the family, Odia, who was about three years old.

I was so happy to see Amba, who just happened to be around my age. I was looking forward to live in the same house with a friend who happened to be a relative. It felt like I just hit a hole in one. Jean Paul was about three to four inches taller than I was. He was very crafty with his hands. He was able to make all kinds of stuff from scratch. He was a very good swimmer. He knew how to fish, just to name a few things from his list of abilities.

Although little Robert did stay on campus while trying to earn a degree in architecture, he occasionally spent some weekends at the house. The same went for Mbuyi, who was also in medical school about to become a pediatrician. Aside from the master bedroom, the eldest girls occupied one room, while the younger girls shared a room with the two younger boys, Rolly and Rodrigue. Amba and I both slept in the living room. While he slept on a couch, I slept on top of a wooden dining table. The very first nights were really uncomfortable. Putting my bare back against that wooden table the entire night was pure hell until my body finally got used to the table.

Aunt Martha and her husband used to be financially well off about a few years back. Everything took a wrong spin when her husband, Robert, a former city employee, was laid off as a result of a big government spending cut following the country's economic meltdown, which brought about the Great Depression throughout the whole country, almost wiping out the country's entire middle class, bringing up a very big gap between the haves and the have-nots in the country.

Aunt Martha's husband, Robert, hasn't been able to find another job ever since the layoff, leaving his wife the responsibility of being the family's sole provider. Trying to make ends meet, Aunt Martha took up a new gig. She started selling bags of water at one of the city's ports. When asked how she came about with this idea, she said, one day, while on her way to meet up with a friend of hers who ran her own little restaurant at the port for a chance to eventually become her partner, she saw a lady who was about her age that had caught her eyes. The lady was selling cold water, which she had in little plastic bags. The lady who happened to be alone at the time attracted a lot of customers, making it obvious that selling water was a high commodity around there. She went out and introduced herself to the lady and asked her if it wouldn't cause any inconvenience if she was to potentially set up her own little kiosk next to hers. The lady didn't have any objection to the idea. Besides, she was even more supportive and offered to help Aunt Martha throughout the whole process. A few days later, she officially became a water lady.

I started school about two weeks after my arrival. Amba and I were in the same class. we walked to school together every day of the week. Lumiere, which was the name of our school, was an all-boys school sponsored by this Orthodox Church next door to the school. The school was known for its very strict and harsh disciplinary method, which many found unorthodox. Students were given up to twenty lashes for being late to class repeatedly. Any minor or major disciplinary infraction resulted in lashes followed by mandatory attendance to Sunday's mass. The mandatory church attendance as means for punishment made the least sense to me up until Amba and I had to attend three consecutive Sunday masses after being late for class.

Aside from the few rituals, everything from the building, the setup, to the priest's clothing was just similar to the ones found in Catholic churches. For a church building that was big enough to fit up to two hundred faithful, there were only about twenty people in attendance—that is, with the priest and his staff included. The rituals were so boring that it would take some spiritual help or perhaps a big paycheck for anyone to stay awake throughout the majority of the mass. After having survived three masses, I made a vow to myself to never be late to school ever no matter what the circumstances might be. That was my first year at the school and Amba's second. Although we both hated it equally, the walk to school was just as painful as we had about a fifteen-mile walk to and from school every day of the week except for the weekend.

Every Saturday, Meta, Amba, and I had to wake up as early as 5:30 a.m. to go help sell some water at the port with Aunt Martha. We would leave the house at around 6:30 a.m. and walk about ten miles to a bus stop, where Aunt Martha would try to bargain for the cheapest fare that would have the four of us ride to the port. Aunt Martha and I would get out about a mile away from the port to purchase two blocks of ices, which came in rectangular shape and weighed about forty pounds each. After picking up the ice, we stopped to the nearby flea market on our way to the port to purchase a pack of plastic bags the size of lunch bags.

A plastic bag contained about two hundred small baggies. We filled the small baggies with about twenty ounces of cold water to be sold.

By the time Aunt Martha and I got back to the kiosk, Meta and Amba already had everything set up. They had already filled up the barrel with water. All we had to do was dump the big ice inside the barrel. The two blocks of ice were broken into four pieces each, which usually would last a whole day on a regular day, half a day on a busy day. While Aunt Martha and her daughter Meta were filling up the small baggies with about twenty ounces of cold water each, Amba and I would load about thirty to forty bags of water into two separate plastic basins, which we each carried on our heads, going around opposite ways to each other near the cargo ships, shouting, "Mayi ya malili mayi," or "Water, cold water," catching the attention of any thirsty merchant in need of some cold water under the ferocious sun. One bag of water was sold for the equivalent of about fifty cents each.

Once we were sold out of the water inside the basin, we would make our way back to the kiosk to load more water to be sold. We began selling the first load at around 10:00 a.m. but didn't have a set time at which we stopped selling. It all depended on how busy or slow things were that day. On a busy day, we didn't leave the port until around 8:00 p.m.; 6:30 p.m. was about the norm.

Trying to sell the water bags to anyone from merchants to anyone that was thirsty under the very hot sun, at twelve years old carrying around a fifty-pound bucketful of water bags on my head all day was one of the hardest things I ever accomplished in my lifetime. Selling water was very challenging for me aside from the heavy weight, which I had to carry around. Working under the very hot temperature of about ninety to one hundred degrees didn't make it any easier, and the fact that there were about twenty other people selling the same product, sometimes even better product than ours, the very fierce competition did nothing but add more fuel to the hard challenge.

The lady who introduced Aunt Martha to the water selling business went by the name of Mama Mapasa, which means "Mother of twins." She had about four elder boys between the ages of fifteen and eighteen working for her. She had her kiosk right next to ours. Not only did she have the edge from being in the business a little longer than Aunt Martha, but she also had the upper hand on the number of loyal customers. Most customers preferred her product than ours, since hers looked a little cleaner than ours, and she seemed to put a little more water in the baggies than we were, and most importantly, she was very flexible with customers who didn't have enough money to pay. She was very easygoing and sweet; whereas, Aunt Martha was all about business. She didn't play when it came to her money.

The ports had the same vibe as the port in New York in the movie gang of New York with all types of people around from thieves, gangs, law enforcers, the good and the crooked ones, merchants, you name it. The water business went hand in hand with the port. Whenever the major commercial ships made their way into the port unloading all sorts of merchandise ranging from corns, beans, starch, coffee beans, oil, etc., from their trip, it attracted more workers, merchants, and buyers. The more people coming into the port for various reasons, the more customers we had. The more sunny it was, the more we sold water.

The downside of it was when most if not all the major commercial ships were gone, business was really slow; either that or rainy days. The difference was very remarkable financially during the good days when the major commercial ships were docked in. We grossed about the equivalent of one hundred dollars a day. That figure would drop dramatically to about twenty dollars on the days the major commercial ships were away. I hated those days when the major ships were away. Since there was not a lot of attraction at the port, it meant that we had to work twice as hard to come close to meeting about half our quota, which meant we were taking longer routes around neighboring ports carrying the heavy weight longer as there were less customers. I even found myself going too deep into the water inside docked ship trying to make sales. Sometimes, we even have to stay as long as past eight o'clock while still trying to sell the last round.

My greatest fear was falling into deep water while trying to make my way from ship to ship carrying that big basin full of water on my head to make a sale. Even though I was as acrobatic as a Russian gymnast, knowing that I couldn't swim was very risky on my part. During my time as a water boy at the port, I had witnessed three people who had drowned in the water and never made it alive. One of them being a fourteen-year-old boy who coincidently didn't know how to swim either. There was also the very bizarre belief going around the port, which was that the water around the port needed a human as a blood sacrifice once every three months for business to be booming. Even though I never really put too much into those beliefs, it was very hard to just brush it aside, since about every three months, there was at least one death by drowning or a person being reported missing in the water. Whatever was the leading cause of those deaths and disappearances was too coincidental to just be swept under the rug.

At around three thirty, Aunt Martha would order a bunch of food from her friend who was running one of the small bistros among many others that were set up all around the port. Amba and I were given about fifteen-minute break to eat, which was not until about close to four o'clock. The fifteen-minute lunch break, which pretty much seemed like two minutes, was very desirable, as that was about the only time during the day I was able to actually sit down. I found life as a water boy very hard to adjust to, but there was something about making money, or should I say making Aunt Martha's money, that kept me going. At first, I thought that Aunt Martha was withholding a share of the revenue allocated for me until it was the right time to hand it to me. It took me a while to realize that was nothing but pure illusion. There was no such thing as a personal fund set up for me.

About few weeks into the start of the second school trimester, I was sent home from school for being behind on tuition. The tuition for the school year was $150, or $50 per trimester. From school records, it was said that I still owed about $35 from the first trimester. Until I came up with at least $35, I wouldn't be allowed to attend school. When I broke the news back home, I was a little disappointed to find out that there wasn't $35 lying around the house for that purpose, and no one around had anything close to $35. Aunt Martha promised to track my father down, and hopefully, he could come up with some money to put me back in school, but in the meantime, before that happens, since I won't be attending school, I had to help out full time now as a water boy.

Those words were as sharp as knife, and they sure went straight to my heart; I almost fainted. My being a full-time water boy—I already had a very hard time managing being a water boy once a week to become a full-time water boy six days a week—had death written all over it. The decision was final, and there was no getting out of it. I had no choice but to comply to the fullest.

Life as a full-time water boy was hell on earth for me. I would wake up at the very first sound of the rooster, sometimes between 5:30 a.m. and 6:00 a.m., and take a cold shower, and by 7:00 a.m., Aunt Martha and I would head out the house. We had to walk about ten miles to catch the bus that would take us to the port. I know you are probably asking why such a long walk just to get to a bus stop. Here is why. From Aunt Martha's house to the nearest bus stop was about a three-mile walk. From the first bus stop, we had to get out to the next bus stop, which was about seven miles away. That stop was on the main road, and from there, we were able to catch the bus leading us to the port. Aunt Martha was the cheapest person I ever met. She would bargain her way to anything. She was the only person I knew who tried to bargain her children's tuition. Aunt Martha was so cheap. To cut the fare cost by half, she had us walk all the way to the main road just to catch only one bus to the port.

The ten-mile walk in the morning wasn't as bad as the one at night after a very long exhausting day carrying about forty pounds of water all day under the scorching sun with the average temperature being one hundred degrees. To make matters even worse, the long walk back home from the port was more exhausting because I always had to help carry some things back, whether a twenty-pound bag of flour or rice or whatever it was that Aunt Martha had purchased from the port.

Being a water boy was seen as the worst and shameful profession there ever was. It was so embarrassing to be known publicly as having anything to do with selling water. Even a public restroom janitor was one step above being a water boy. Although on the good days, the money coming out of it was good enough for Aunt Martha to be feeding a family of eleven and put nine of them through school. Her children graduated from high school, and some were almost college graduates;

all that from the water money. Even with the fierce competition, I still managed to put up good numbers as a full-time water boy. During those days, I was working so hard both physically and mentally from Monday to Saturday for about two months straight, leaving home as early as 7:00 a.m. and coming back home at around 10:00 p.m. I would go to bed in pain and wake up to even more pain.

I only had one dream and one dream only, which was to see my days as a water boy come to an end, whether by luck or by miracle. I couldn't wait to see such a day. Until then, I was settling to praying for Sunday to come by as fast as possible. Sometimes, I even wish the calendar mistakenly had two Sundays in the same week. Sunday was the only day when I could actually get some rest, but for whatever reason, it always felt as if Sunday was the only day in the week that had fewer hours in it than the rest of the days of the week.

Sundays at the house were very vivid as those were perhaps the only days of the week when everyone was at home at the same time. Sunday also had its own special vibe and flavor as it was the only day of the week when the kitchen was only reserved to Aunt Martha. With Aunt Martha at the helm of the kitchen, dinner was always guaranteed to be full of flavors and in abundance. Sunday's dinner was served in four portions. The first portion was reserved to Aunt Martha's husband, Robert, who ate alone. The second was allocated to Dorothy and Rodrigue, the two youngest of the family. The third was for Aunt Martha and the adults, along with any guests if there were any that day. Finally, the last portion was pretty much for anyone sixteen and under, who were Meta, Amba, Mama, Clementine, Rolly, and I. We all ate together. Unlike at Aunt's Monique's house, where I pretty much stayed hungry every day from not eating enough, that never was the case at Aunt Martha's. Over here, not only did we eat twice a day but also we ate to a full stomach.

There was something that caught my attention the very first weeks I moved into the house. It has something to do with Ndaya's, Aunt Martha's third child, demeanor toward everyone else in the house, or vice versa, which I found very peculiar. Although she shared the same room with four of her other relatives, there was no interaction between her and anyone else in the family except for occasional talk with the two little ones. Moving into the house, I was about the only person she sometimes spoke to. I never understood what exactly had happened in that house that led to her distancing herself from the entire family. She was almost a different entity within that house. She was to that house what the Vatican is to Italy. She also made her own food. Sometimes, she would even give me her leftovers in exchange for doing her dishes for her.

There were stuff around the house that were marked hers that no one was allowed to lay hands on, not even if their lives depended on it. The rest of the family respected her wish very piously to make sure that the peace that came from both parties' containment, which was very fragile, wouldn't be broken. Tension between both sides were very highly reminiscent of the cold war between the United States and the former Soviet Union. Even a fool could see that at any given moment, something as little could possibly trigger something as major as a nuclear war in that house. I gave up on my quest to trying to figure out the reason beyond such animosity within these relatives. No one seemed interested in briefing me on anything. Perhaps it was a family secret that no one was allowed to discuss.

Months later, still, no one had paid any of my tuition—meaning, I was still out of school. I became so desperate. I started reminiscing about those days at Aunt Monique's house as being one of my golden eras. At least at Aunt Monique's house, I went to school. I said to myself that was probably how the Israelites must have felt a few months into the desert. After the Exodus, they started looking back to their days under Pharaoh as being perhaps their best days compared to life in the desert.

Every time I asked Aunt Martha about when I was going back to school, she would reply by saying, "The minute I hear from your father. He has been MIA for as long as I could remember. Now, he is nowhere to be found. Not one seems to know where he is," she said. If words were bullets, those words were coming straight out of a 12 gauge caliber. I haven't seen my father ever since the day he dropped me off at Aunt Martha' house for a short stay, as he told me.

Looking at where my life stood at the moment, not only was I out of school, but also the fact that there seemed to be no actual plan or will from anyone around to have me back in school to be just like the other kids around, it was now becoming more and more obvious to me that Aunt Martha was more than comfortable with the idea of not having me back to school anytime soon as I was an asset to her as a full-time water boy, while Meta and Jean Paul had the luxury to only work on Saturdays.

I felt both trapped and betrayed at the same time—betrayed by my father once again for not coming through with his words and being nowhere to be found when I needed him the most. Here I was hopelessly being exploited by his own sister. I felt trapped by the circumstance I was facing. I hated everything about being a water boy, from the shame to the pain it brought to my body. Every morning I woke up, I couldn't wait for the chance to get back to sleep. Every night before falling asleep, I prayed that there will be an endless rain just like the one in Noah's time that would keep me from going to the port that day. Every day I woke up as disappointed as the last one.

School was out for the summer—meaning, I have missed yet again another year of education. During the long summer, I was joined by Meta and Amba as full-time workers, each respectively on their off duty. By the time they got back full time, I have already become master of my domain. As a full-time water boy, I perfected a few ways to make myself some cash, since working for Aunt Martha didn't provide me with either an allowance or a salary. I came to develop a few ways of making myself a little cash on a side. I had a couple of methods that I applied piously. The most common one usually involved Meta. By observing Meta, I came to realize how she wasn't too bright in math and used it to the best of my advantage. Since Meta was basically the second in command, her duty consisted of bagging water, loading up our basin with bags of water, and collecting money from our rounds. When loading up, she often miscounted. A lot of times, she would be off by two to three bags; instead of forty, she usually had it at forty-two or forty-three. Sometimes, I would purposely throw her off into putting extra bags.

There was another method that I only used when there was very tight security, which mostly occurred when Aunt Martha was on top of her game and was less distracted. Occasionally, when making rounds, a bag or two would burst inside the basin from all the commotion. When that happened, we were required to bring back the burst bag as a show of proof. In this case, I would just look for two bags on the floor and bring it back as evidence while pocketing the money as there never were any burst bags in the first place. Even though Aunt Martha didn't subject us to a pat down, I always was very clever in hiding my money. I would hide my money in my underwear near my genitals.

On average, I made about fifteen to twenty rounds daily, making myself some good pocket money. Once I got home, I had dug up a hole by the garden outside. That was my little private bank. Every night, I went to the hole and made deposits. Some nights I made bigger deposits; others, not so much, depending on how busy the day was at the port. My goal was to come up with my own tuition by the time school is back in session. No way was I going to miss out on school again. How I was going to justify the source of such big income in my possession, I had no idea, but I said to myself, when the time does come by, then I would have come up with an explanation to the IRS—in this case, Aunt Martha.

Aunt Martha was very strict about the water business, at least when it came to me. There was no getting out of selling water unless you were either puking blood or severely ill as if pretty much dying in the next few hours. Going to the port from Monday through Saturday was mandatory. I remember twice she had me come in a few hours later after I was running a fever. One time she even forced me to go even after I have been complaining of stomach pain throughout the entire night.

One sunny day at the port, as I was slowly coming back from my rounds, as I reached the kiosk, Aunt Martha welcomed me with a few slaps to the face while endlessly screaming at me for slowly making my way back to refill since it was a busy day at the port and there was a lot of money to be made out there. My taking my time instead of hustling back was making her miss money.

I wasn't feeling too well that day as I was running a temperature the night before, causing me to still feel a little woozy by the morning. After mentioning it to her in the morning, she put her hand against my forehead, gave me two aspirins, and told me to get dressed—I will be just fine. The aspirins didn't help as much. I was still feeling weak throughout the day, but I still put up a great fight in working through it all, but my efforts were still being taken for granted. I didn't know whether to cry or else, but since there were a lot of people around, crying would do nothing but bring more embarrassment my way. I just swallowed my grief and went on to finish the day as if nothing happened.

Going back home that night, I couldn't help but rethink about the whole day. As I lay down on top of the wooden dining table, which was my bed, waiting to fall asleep, I felt tears coming down my eyes. Whether those tears were tears of anger or sorrow, I never gave it too much thought, but one thing was certain—those weren't tears of happiness. What I hated most during my childhood was crying and seeing anyone crying. Just like in ancient times, when the bell sound was applied to mark the time of the day for me, tears always brought about awareness to what time it was. From my happiest moment to my saddest one, I always found time to shed a few tears just to reminisce. I shed a few tears the day I ran away from my father's house. I also did shed a few more the day I opened my eyes for the very first time after a week in a coma. The greatest moments in my life have always been marked by tears. This time, the message was very clear. I was not happy with no one to turn to. Once again, I was left with very little to no other option but to take matters in my own hands, as the time was becoming very critical and now my well-being was now at stake. I had to act as quickly as I could.

What kind of action I was going to take, that would lead me to a state of partial relief, if not a total one. I had yet to come up with a concrete plan that would bring about a much-needed solution to my dilemma, but ready I really was!

It was on a Wednesday afternoon, during the summer of 1996, about a few days after I was slapped for not hustling fast enough even though I was still battling a fever. After coming back from making a round, I gave the money to Meta and told her I had to go to the bathroom. There weren't any public restrooms around, so people settled for the bushes that were way far back to do whatever they had to do. If you were a male, you wouldn't go in too deep into the bushes unless you were in for a number two; but for females, they had to go very deep into the bushes just to get some privacy, regardless of whether they were in it for a number one or two. I had no intention to do either. I just told Meta that as an excuse to get away. I had decided shortly before that was the perfect moment to run away since Aunt Martha went away to go buy one more block of ice as water was in very high demand that day and we were almost out of ice.

By the time I left that day to go to the bathroom, I had already pocketed myself about the equivalent to ten dollars, which was pretty good considering that it wasn't even close to the end of the day yet. As I made my way out of the port, even though I didn't know where to head, the sense of total freedom, along with the extra cash I just had now shifted from my underwear to my pocket, gave me a great state of security and hope. I had enough ammo in me to face about anything that would dare come my way.

As I continued my walk, I stopped by this little market on the way and bought me some grilled peanuts. Also known in my city as the journeyman's best companion, grilled peanuts in my city was of a great asset to anyone traveling long distance by foot. As not everyone had the luxury to own a car or was able to afford bus fare just to get around, to most people, grilled peanuts, which was sold to almost every corner of the city, was your ideal travel buddy. One toss in the mouth was followed by a few good steps with the foot, and the more peanuts in the mouth, the more ground was being covered on foot. Therefore, grilled peanuts was just as good as your personal Uber. With it, one could go a long way at a very affordable price. It had the ability to make a ten-mile walk feel like a two-mile one. That was the miracle grilled peanuts was able to perform on journeymen.

As I continued my walk, inspired by the great power bestowed upon me by each nut that entered my mouth, an idea came through my mind. Having no concrete plan on what to do or where to go next, with plenty of freedom to go along with almost ten dollars in my pocket, which seemed like a fortune to me at the time, the only thing lacking was some inspiration on my next move, and what better place for a runaway to find some inspiration than under the mighty baobab tree. FEZADI! I made my way to FEZADI, hoping to catch up on the latest gossip while contemplating on what my next move will be.

Once I got there, I was once again reunited with the great Khumalo, whom I haven t seen in years. We both were very happy to see each other.

"Where have you been all my life? Look at you, all grown. Where do you work at now?" he joked.

"Your girlfriend's bedroom," I replied.

He playfully tried to chase me around the mighty tree. Boy, it felt great to see him again. Khumalo was still the greatest debater there. He hasn't lost a step. He was still well respected this time around. He was even nicknamed the mayor of FEZADI. I guess you can say that he was gifted in a way, as he pretty much had the ability to prove you that his dollar was worth about twice as much as your five dollars.

I was in for a good bargain that day. About an hour later, the city derby was about to kick off at the main stadium, which was about a half-an-hour walk from FEZADI. The city derby or the football match between the two city rivals, the Dolphin and the Immaculate, was the biggest football event of the year as it involved the two most popular and successful teams in the city. The kickoff was scheduled for 7:00 p.m., local time. Kids fifteen and under were allowed in the stadium free of charge, only when in the company of an adult with a ticket. So all I did was look around for an adult who was making his way to the gate alone and asked him to hold my hand so I could enter the stadium without having to pay. Once inside, the environment was crazy. No one was sitting down. Everyone was up. The ninety-thousand-seat stadium was completely sold out with half of the stadium in green and black, while the other half was in white and green. There were team flags everywhere. Supporters of each teams painted their faces in their respective team colors. From the first whistle marking the kickoff, the stadium was so noisy you couldn't even hear the person next to you.

About fifteen minutes into the game, a riot broke out in the stadium. The referee signaled for a goal before the ball has crossed the goal line. The ball was on its way in the goal when a defender from the Immaculate acrobatically cleared it on the goal line, but before the defender even got to the ball, the referee had already pointed to the center of the field, signaling that a goal had been scored. That call from the referee ignited the biggest riot I ever witnessed in my life. Immaculate supporters were rushing into the stadium trying to have a piece of the referee. Police shot tear gas and gunshots in the air, trying to dissuade the crowd from rushing into the field. There was a big stampede of people vying for the small exit door by the hundreds. People were stepping on other people just trying to get away from the sting coming from the tear gas. It was a catastrophe. The game was called off. The death toll stood at around twenty-three with hundreds of wounded with some in critical condition.

I got out of there untouched without a single scratch in my body, and how that happened will forever stay a mystery or a miracle, which ever suits the best. On the way out, I went on and followed a crowd heading toward some unknown direction. Games involving the two most popular teams in the city always brought about traffic in a city where public transportation was more a luxury than a commodity. So whenever there was a large influx of people on the streets from major events such as a football match or concert, taxi drivers and bus drivers were now charging double the price for a fare. As a result, the majority of football fans and music fans always opted for a walk home rather than paying double the fare. After every football match, there would be a large crowd of people making their way home from the stadium on foot.

After the game, with no specific place to go, I followed a group of about one hundred people who were heading toward the Victory Place, the city's biggest intersection. It was a very fun walk as everyone was shouting and chanting their team songs and reminiscing about the tragic incident at the stadium. The more we walked, the more the crowd started to get smaller. About an hour into the walk, the crowd was broken down to even smaller groups as different groups started heading opposite ways to whatever direction led to home. I found myself still following a group of about fifteen people who were still heading toward the Victory Place.

The Victory Place was in the center of the city. It was by far the busiest place in the city. It was like our city's Time Square, with a chain of bars and nightclubs along the way covering about a two-mile long radius, operating twenty-four hours nonstop. It always felt like daytime no matter what time of the night. That was the only part of the city where no one slept. The liveliness and loud music around the Victory Place was a major attraction to many types of people; from homeless kids, drunkards, thieves, and prostitutes, the Victory Place was home to them all.

By the time I got to the Victory Place, I was the only one left from the crowd, so I decided to just cruise around since I wasn't yet of legal age to have a sit at bar and order me a drink. I settled for a small walk gazing at those half-naked women that were lined up along the street selling their goodies. I still had about seven dollars left in my pocket. I went on and spent about two dollars on some junk food. Before I knew it, it was already past midnight. As I started walking again, this time feeling a little sleepy, I sat down on some concrete that was a bit off the main street. It was dark, and no one was on sight. I just sat down, tucked my harms under my shirt, balled my head down against my knees, and closed my eyes, hoping for the first sign of the crack of dawn to get here.

About close to half an hour, I felt a hard slap in my face catching me by my left eye. I quickly got up and looked around. There was no one around within my sight; nor was there any movement. For a person to come and slap me as hard as I was slapped in my face and disappear as quickly as a wind without leaving any trace, it would have been impossible for him or her to be characterized as being human. There is no one on earth with that kind of speed or might. I was left with no choice but to get away very far away from that place. Whatever it was that had slapped me that hard had a very clear message for me. It didn't want me there, and I sure wasn't going to challenge such mighty force. I wasn't ready for that. I slowly picked myself together with my left eye still blurry and painful. One thing for sure, I sure wasn't sleepy at all afterward.

After making about three rounds up and down Victory Place, it was about close to 3:00 a.m. I saw a group of about ten people standing in front of this house located just along the street. They were all arguing about the football game that just cost about twenty-three lives. I stopped there and started listening, hoping to kill some time until the first crack of dawn. As I got closer to them, no one seemed to care much that there was a twelve-year-old among them until after about thirty minutes into the heating debate, which was split between two groups, with one group blaming the referee for the incident, while the other group blaming the Immaculate supporters as being the ones who instigated the whole melee by trying to rush into the field, causing the police to react with tear gas and shot fire.

There was this guy who looked like he was in his midthirties who, after noticing me, asked who I was. After introducing myself, I told him that I had nowhere to go. I was just hoping to kill time until the morning got there, and I would be making my way to my next adventure. He was very supportive and welcoming. After everyone left, he welcomed me inside his house, a small studio apartment in which the bed took about 75 percent of the space available, and the rest was a small chair and a table with a small stove on top of it, while the rest were his clothes hanging around everywhere. He was making bouillon potato at 4:00 a.m. He made me a plate. While we both were still eating, he asked me where I lived and why I was out and about so late. I told him I was homeless and didn't have a place to stay as I just ran away from my aunt's house. He felt sorry for me and told me I was welcome to stay with him if I liked. I told him I would love to, and I thanked him for the much-needed hospitality. He told me to feel free to lie down in his bed if I was sleepy as he went out the door and told me he would be back.

About an hour later, he came back and hopped up the bed next to me. Next thing I know, I felt his hands slowly moving up and down my thigh, and I couldn't help but hear the sound of his belt as he was undressing himself while attempting to undress me also. I quickly got up. He got up slowly after me. My very first instinct led me to go for the doors. I quickly unlocked the door while keeping an eye on his movement. I could see him reaching for the knife. As he got closer to me with the knife, I quickly opened the door, and before he could get closer to me, I was already out the door with no one around. I just took off running as fast as I could, fearing he might be coming after me. Thank God, as I looked back around two blocks way, there was no sight of him or anyone chasing after me. As it became apparent to me that I was now safe, I was catching my breath while pacing myself.

By the time I made it back to Victory Place, it was already 5:00 a.m. You could see the sun slowly making its way into the sky, marking the beginning of a new day—in my case, the end of perhaps the most eventful day of my life. A day that started as me being a water boy and a runaway, surviving tear gas and gunshot, getting slapped by a mysterious creature, and to top it all up, escaping an attempted rape by a thirty-five-year-old man at knife point—all that in one day. You name me another twelve-year-old in this universe with a worse day; I will guess all the numbers right from today's lottery.

At around 6:00 a.m., I found myself heading toward FEZADI. When I got there, I was happy to see that I wasn't the only one there. I got there somewhere around seven o'clock, and there were already about ten people gathered around the big tree. Usually, the early birds mostly consisted of either homeless people or people who were on their way looking for one of those temporary jobs that paid daily. They would stop by the tree for a few minutes to gather themselves while catching up on the daily gossip on either politics, sports, or entertainment before continuing on their routes. Sometime around noon, I joined a group of about seven street kids who were playing soccer barefooted not too far from the tree. By the time we were done playing, it was already close to three o'clock.

I made my way back to the tree where. By this time, the crowd around the tree was around thirty people or so. I could hear the loud voice of Khumalo echoing from afar. *It was showtime at the Apollo,* I told myself. I spent about two dollars more and bought me a loaf of bread, some grilled peanuts, and a bag of cold water. I made the mistake of going straight around the tree, where I was welcomed by a crowd of hands, all wanting a little bit of what I had. As it was the tradition around the giant tree, I had no choice but to break bread with the multitude. As a result, I was left with about two inches out of the twelve inches of bread I just bought. I vowed never to repeat such careless mistake ever again.

When the night came around and everyone began parting away, I found myself following the wind. Once again heading toward Victory Place, I spent about three hours just walking around from street to street around the vicinity. By this time, I had spent my last dollar on my last meal of the night. As I was walking, I remembered passing by a street with a palm leaf planted on the street corner. Just like a yard sale sign on a street corner directing people to the location of a yard sale, a palm leaf planted at the corner of a street meant that somewhere on that street, there was a funeral being observed. Then I remember talking to two of the kids I was playing football with earlier who told me that they have been living on the streets for over two years now. When I asked them where they have been sleeping throughout this whole time, they told me they didn't have any specific place where they spent the night regularly, but often, they would randomly spend the night at funerals.

"How would you know where a funeral was anyway?" I asked.

"It is pretty simple."

They both looked at me with astonishment as if to make me realize that I just asked the dumbest question that even a newborn baby would literally know the answer to. It was almost synonymous to not knowing where babies came from as a teenager—very pathetic.

"All you have to do," one said, shaking his head, "is look for a street with a palm leaf planted on its corner, which meant there is a funeral in one of the houses on that particular street."

In the city, funeral homes were only reserved to the rich ones, so about 98 percent of the population could never afford funeral homes, so it became a tradition to have the obsequy held at the deceased's residence. Most obsequies lasted between three and six days at the most, giving a chance to family members, friends, and acquaintances a chance to pay respects and say their farewell to the deceased and his or her family. Usually during the days of the obsequy, there would be a very big gathering of family, friends, and acquaintances camped around the deceased body, which would be put on display for a period varying from three to six days before the burial. Most immediate family members and close friends will be sobbing to the tune of some gospel music that would be playing nonstop all throughout the obsequy. Hot coffee was served to people attending the obsequy to help them stay up throughout the night. The fourth day is usually the day of the burial. The burial usually marks the end of the gathering for everyone but the immediate family, who would still gather for one or two more days.

On the fortieth day after the burial, as a tradition, a feast was held at the residence of the deceased, marking the departure of the deceased's spirit to an everlasting resting place. According to the traditionalist, from the time of death, a person's spirit still roam around for about thirty-nine days for whatever unfinished business. Then on the fortieth day, the spirit was gone for good. It was a tradition practiced by almost everyone I had ever known. During the feast, free food, drinks, and a lot of alcohol were served to anyone in attendance.

All those words were like music to my ears. Now, all I had to do was find myself a place where a funeral was being held. In a city with a population of about eight million people, with about 80 percent living below poverty level, death was no stranger. There were funerals every day somewhere. Sometimes, one street even had the luxury of having more than one funeral, which was nothing but good news for me, since to me, a funeral meant the perfect place for me to stay the night.

After taking my way back, I decided to ahead toward that way. I finally found the funeral, which was about twenty houses down the street. Upon arrival, I just grabbed myself a seat and joined the crowed that was gathered around paying tribute to the deceased, who appeared to be an old man in his late fifties. With no one around to question me, I just made myself comfortable on a chair, tucked both hands inside my shirt, with my legs stretched out on another chair, and closed my eyes. Sleeping on a chair wasn't comfortable at all, but at least it did the trick as it beat not sleeping at.

The following morning, I made my way back to FEZADI, where I once again spent the whole day listening to all variety of arguments and daily gossips. When it got dark, I found myself roaming around Victory Place as I was very hungry, since the only thing to go down my stomach besides my own spits all day was some water I had drunk earlier. My stomach was now craving for some food. With no money in my pocket, getting myself something to eat would have required some Robin Hood–like moves or a miracle from the sky. I couldn't come up with anything. I just went around and headed back to last night's funeral, walking as slow as a mummy with my stomach growling every time I took a step. I spent the night at the funeral once again. That family's loss was, in a way, my gain as through the loss of their loved ones, the stranger I was, was able to find me a place to stay the night.

Even though the night seemed very long as I was having a hard time falling asleep from the hunger, I must have fallen asleep. Somewhere around 2:00 a.m., I was awakened by a lady who was serving hot coffee and bread to everyone around. The sight of coffee and bread that was being handed to me by the lady felt more like a mirage than reality. I must have been dreaming because this was very far from being real, I thought, after I have given up all hope on seeing anything resembling food going down my stomach. That coffee and bread felt like a Hail Mary in American football or a buzzer beater shot in basketball. It sure was a lifesaver. I devoured that bread and sipped on that hot coffee as if it was the last supper.

The next morning saw me take a different route than the one I have been accustomed to in the past. About a year into living on the streets wherein my days were mostly split between attending FEZADI and roaming the streets, I was fortunate enough to never sleep on an empty stomach. Whatever it was, I always ended up eating something by the end of the night. It might have not been a full meal, but at least I got to tease my stomach every day with something, whether it was piece of bread and water from the FEZADI's faithful, mangoes I got from climbing mango trees along the ways, or sugar canes I got to take out of stranger's garden. During the day, I was in a Tarzan-like mode trying to feed myself with whatever nature had to provide, and at nighttime, I was a funeral hunter so I could have a place to lay my head. During all that time, I got pretty dirty. My skin, which used to be somehow of a lighter complexion, turned into a darker one from lack of showers. Although I did manage to shower at nearby rivers from time to time, but the lack of soap didn't do me any justice.

One morning, instead of heading back to FEZADI, as it has been my routine, I decided to roam around Victory Place, hoping to bring about better luck. As I was walking around passing through shops and bus stops, there was this young lady who caught my eyes. She looked like she was somewhere around her early twenties. She was making omelet in what looked like a mini restaurant set up right in the open across the bus stop. She had set up a few chairs and tables all around her. She had about six or seven customers all waiting to be served. From what I could see, she was working alone, and I thought she could use some help. Without wasting any more time procrastinating, I walked toward the lady and hung around just a few feet away from her while waiting for a chance to get her attention whenever she got less busier.

About twenty minutes later, I just got the guts to walk up to her and told her that I will be willing to help out around if she could use my help. Most to her delight, she said, "Yes, sure. You sure can help clear the table after each customer."

Before she even was done with her sentence, I spotted a customer who was just getting up after having finished his meal. Like a hungry lion after a prey, I quickly jumped into my new task of a busboy. About half an hour through my new gig, I was already in love with life as a busboy as I was enjoying filling myself with leftovers from the dishes I was bringing back. Apart from clearing and cleaning the tables, I occasionally made some rounds to the water fountain, which was about ten minutes away, to carry some water that was used for either cooking or washing dishes.

The young lady's name was Laurie. She was very nice and sweet to me. At the end of the day, which was around 4:00 p.m., as she only had her little restaurant open for just breakfast and lunch, she thanked me for the help and told me that she and her best friend Anna, who wasn't there today, just started this business about a month ago. She told me that she would love to have me around only if I was comfortable with the fact that I may be working mostly as a volunteer as she wasn't making much to be having me on a salary, but on most days, she would provide me with some tips depending on how good of a day we had. I also will have free meal. As she was done speaking to me, she opened her purse and handed me what was the equivalent of a ten-dollar bill. I was as happy as I could be, as with that, I could now mark this day as being one of the most successful days of my life as a street kid. After thanking her for her generosity, I went straight to FEZADI to feed on some daily dose of gossips and hang out.

* By the time I got to FEZADI, it started pouring down heavy rain. People were running left to right, trying to find cover. The heavy rain came somehow as a blessing in disguise for me. Having not showered in days, I took advantage of the heavy rain by showering in it. After the rain had ceased, I went to the open marketplace, which was about twenty minutes away from Victory Place.

Being soaked by the heavy rain, I needed a change of clothing. With the little money I made myself earlier that day, I went on and bought me a pair of used pants and one used shirt and pair of underwear, which I put on immediately. When the night came, I went back to my routine of funeral hunting. While funeral hunting, I always made sure not to go so far away from the vicinity of Victory Place since I had to be at work as early as 6:00 a.m. Given the importance of the restaurant to my survival, I tried my very best to stay really close by. I did manage to find another funeral about forty-five minutes away from Victory Place. It was a funeral of a local man in his late thirties whose cause of death was unknown, but the rumor going around the block was that he might have died from AIDS, a very deadly virus. To me, I could care less whether the man died from cancer or from a mosquito bite. I just was there to stay the night. I couldn't care less about the rest.

At the very first crack of dawn, I was already on my way to the restaurant. I worked with Laurie and her friend Anna for about three weeks until one day when checking in on a typical day at restaurant with all the commotion and noise all around the place. It was about ten minutes past 6:00 a.m. I found Laurie already on-site setting up for the first order. She introduced me to a young lady named Brigit, whom I saw for the first time. She was sitting down cutting up onion. Brigit was Laurie's cousin. She came in filling in for Anna, who was out sick. After the greeting, I quickly went on my daily duty as a busboy.

It was a very busy day. I was worked like a horse that day. By the end of the day, I was very exhausted. We got to stay two more extra hours than the usual. As I was helping closing down and packing while everyone else had their backs turned away from me, I grabbed a box of eggs and hid it under my shirt. About fifteen minutes later, just when I thought I got away with it, Laurie, having noticed the missing box of eggs, began looking thoroughly for it. After she had no luck finding it, it became apparent that something might have happened to them, or better yet, someone might have taken them.

She asked both Brigit and me if, by any chance, we saw or misplaced the box of eggs, which was now missing. None of us admitted seeing it or knowing its whereabouts. Something about my composure gave Laurie the impression that I might have something to do with the missing eggs as I was becoming more and more uneasy, and my face, just like that of a dog that has been bad all day during its master's absence, could barely leave the ground even for three straight seconds. Laurie's instinct led her to try to pat me down. As she reached for my shirt and pants, she was delighted by her discovery—a box of eggs tucked in halfway in my pants with the other half next to my belly.

The moment of truth brought about five seconds of complete silence, which to me felt like an eternity. It felt as if the world had ceased to exist for as long as that was. There were no sounds or any movement from any living organism to be heard by the average ear. I was shamefully numb standing in a complete state of hypnosis. After having regained all my senses, I was left to face reality. I was caught red-handed. There was nothing I could say or no explanation I could have given to get me out of this. Even Johnnie Cochran, along with the whole dream team in their glory days, couldn't manage to get me out of this. I dug myself into one of the deepest holes ever with nowhere to get out.

In that instance, I could see it written all over Laurie's face, which was filled with both anger and disappointment. The verdict was clear and firm. I was fired on the spot. It was all over. Laurie said she didn't wish to ever see me around again. Just like that, I was out of a job. *What a careless and dumb mistake I made,* I thought to myself. *Life goes on. We just down one, that's all! This is not the end. It is perhaps the end of a life that wasn't meant for me to excel at,* I said to myself.

The next couple of days that followed my firing weighed pretty heavily on me since working at the restaurant was very vital for me having a place where I was guaranteed a decent meal every day with unlimited access to any leftovers by customers to top it all off. The occasional pocket money I got from Laurie from time to time made life a little sweeter for me. Now that it was all gone, I was back to square one trying to find a way to feed myself on a daily basis. At times, it was way easier for me to find a place to spend the night than to get any meal. At this point, whatever I ate, I always made sure to follow it up with a ton of water to create a fake sense of fulfillment. I was basically tricking my stomach in thinking that I was stuffed. I became the very first person to set his foot in FEZADI and was the very last one to leave each day.

One day, while walking, I ran into Mr. Masanka, a good friend of my father who was a Catholic priest. Mr. Masanka was as shocked to see me in such a very bad shape. The lack of decent meal, along with a combination of bad hygiene and filthy clothing, made me look as a total different kid compared to the very brilliant and blossoming child he once knew. As he approached me after catching up with the very latest, I briefed him on my situation. Within half an hour of conversation, I was able to inform him of my homelessness and everything that came along with it. He was really moved by my condition and asked me to follow him. Mr. Masanka was one of the heads of a group of priests who were in training in a seminary, which was located about five miles away from FEZADI.

After taking me with him at his residence, he took me to the cafeteria, which was the size of a school cafeteria. In there were a lot of variety of one of the best cooked meals I ever had. He instructed one of the caterers that I was his guest and to guide me to the shower and afterward serve me whatever food they had prepared for the day. It felt very liberating taking a shower. After all, I couldn't remember the last time I took a shower, let alone a great one. Eating home-made meal for the very first time in a year felt just as good as spending a whole weekend at the Playboy mansion as Mr. Heffner's special guest. I stuffed my stomach with food like this was my last meal on earth.

Aside from being a mineral-rich country, the Congo is also one of the world's richest countries in gastronomy. For a country made up of about 450 different ethnic groups all divided into four linguistic regions, the DR Congo is a paradise for those who are big fans of good food and amazing meal.

The northwestern part of the country was home to the Bangala ethnic groups, who are known for their traditional signature dish, *Liboke*, meaning packets of food cooked in banana leaves. Although there are many different types of Liboke, the three most popular ones are the *Liboke ya Mbisi* or the fish Liboke, *Liboke ya Ngulu* or the pork Liboke, and also *Liboke ya Pondu* or the vegetable Liboke. In either cases, steaming fish, pork, or vegetable, usually cassava leaves are baked into banana leaf packets holding the steam while it penetrates the fish, pork, or vegetable amazingly to create moisture into them with flavors from different spices mixed into it.

The western part of the country is home to the Bakongo ethnic groups. They are masters of *Kwanga*, cassava sticks with a form of bread stick, and *Fumbwa*, a type of wild spinach cooked with a creamy stew made from a combination of peanut butter and red palm oil. The southern and central parts of the country, home to the Baluba ethnic group, are some of the few places on earth where dinner is really celebrated. The Baluba takes dinner very seriously. Their main traditional dish are *Fufu*, which is dough made out of mixing boiling water and cornmeal flour, and *Pondu*, pounded cassava leaves stew mixed with garlic, chopped onions, eggplants, red palm oil, and other traditional spices.

Last but not least, the eastern part of the country, home to the Baswahili ethnic groups. They have beans and plantain as their main dish. This region holds the art of making the best meal out of beans and plantain, which they cook religiously in so many different ways to perfection.

As perfect as the day seemed, it still lacked one very important thing. After having consumed what seemed like the meal of the century at the seminary, I still had to get the stepping since I couldn't spend the night there. As big as the seminary was, it was against seminary policy to have guests stay overnight. All the rooms in the dormitory were equipped with one twin-size bed, an office desk, and a mini fridge. There was absolutely no room for me to sleep in. Leaving the seminary that night was just as painful as seeing a young sailor leaving his loved one behind to embark on a mission. Before leaving the seminary, I made my way to Mr. Masanka's room, which was all the way at the end of the hallway in the dormitory, just to show him my gratitude and thank him for being such a Good Samaritan.

When I got to his room, there was no one inside, and right in front of me was an open briefcase with its back turned toward me. Just out of curiosity, I made my way straight to the briefcase. I was left in awe. I couldn't' believe what my eyes were seeing. I was staring at a briefcase full of money. The look on my face told it all. This was the very first day I ever saw so much money in my entire life. This was the kind of money that could easily change a person's life, I thought. But for whatever reason, among the many thoughts going through my mind at that moment, putting my hands on that briefcase wasn't one of them. Why would a priest have so much money in his possession was the main question going through my head. At that point in my life, living on the streets taught me to become so many things at once for survival purposes, but becoming a thief or a burglar wasn't one them. I wasn't tempted at all by the briefcase.

I decided to wait in the room for Mr. Masanka. Based on my CSI instincts and considering the open briefcase full of cash right in front me, it was a safe bet to believe that he wasn't that far away and that it was just a matter of minutes, if not seconds, before he came in to the door. Surprisingly, it took about a full hour before I saw him entering the room, looking somehow surprised to see me sitting there next to the cash. His words to me were "Did you get enough to eat?"

"Yes. I had more than enough. As a matter of fact, I think I ate enough food to last me until Jesus comes back." We both had a big chuckle after that.

"You know you are like a son to me, and as much as I would like to help you out even more, I am afraid there isn't much I can do to help since I cannot provide you with any shelter, but I tell you what—I instructed the catering crew to provide you with a meal anytime you wish to show up. That's about all I can guarantee for you." He put his hand in his pocket, grabbed what was the equivalent of a twenty-dollar bill, and handed to me. "Come back and see me sometime" were his words to me. I thanked him for such a wonderful day, hugged him good-bye, and then left the seminary.

Despite all the uncertainties surrounding my next move, unlike any other night, I had one thing going for me. At least tonight, I will be roaming around funeral hunting on a very full stomach. There is nothing more reviving and uplifting to boost the morale of a vagabond than a full stomach. With a full stomach, I was doomed to find any solution to whatever problem I was to face, big or small. Having acquired so much energy from the meal, I ended up finding another funeral to spend the night in after my long-distance walk.

By this time around, it has been about fifteen months since I left Aunt Martha's house, and during that period, I held three jobs. One as a water boy, which I only held for about three days. Right after leaving Aunt Martha, I worked for this old woman who had a lot in common with Aunt Martha. She ripped me off on the profit. She only paid me about five dollars for every one hundred dollars I made her. She basically took great advantage of my youth and innocence to have me work like a slave while paying me little to nothing. That's why I didn't hesitate to quit. My second job was bussing tables for Laurie, which I only held for about three weeks before getting fired for trying to steal a dozen of raw eggs. My third job was pushing this amputee on his wheelchair around town while he begged for money from various places such as gas station, small businesses, grocery stores, bus stops, etc.

The latter was the most intriguing gig I ever had. I was pushing this guy who went by the name Rambo. Rambo was in his late forties. Aside from the daily long-distance push, which was at times very tiring especially on sunny days, it was indeed a full-time job with very high dividend. Rambo made a lot of money begging. He made, or should

I say we were making the equivalent of about two hundred dollars a day. I started pushing him around town at around 7:00 a.m. right after breakfast and stopped at 11:00 p.m. during the weekday and around 2:00 a.m. on weekends. We did take lunch and dinner breaks eating hot meals in some of the city's small bistros. At nighttime, we would ahead to the city's main railway station, which was the headquarters for all the city's amputees. Their whole community was based there. They all spent the night there in groups along with their pushers. I pushed Rambo around for about four months before quitting.

At first, working for Rambo was somehow challenging as he was very demanding. Rambo was the biggest hustler I ever met with no legs. What the hell, he was the biggest hustler I ever met. Aside from him not having any legs, he was built like a wrestler. The man even lifted weights from time to time. Above all, he was a nympho. He did hit on every woman he laid his eyes on. His lack of legs never slowed him down in trying to lure women his way. To be honest, most women did find him attractive with his lighter complexion and big muscles, and he had money from begging. Rambo was mostly feared by most of his fellow amputees. He gave out the vibe of a ruthless man who didn't play games. ___ the amputee for about four months before quitting as I tried to embrace new challenges. Working for Rambo didn't pay much dividend for me financially, but having three meals a day on a daily basis while wearing clean clothes was a good bargain for me.

During my tenure with Rambo, I got to meet his family. Rambo had eleven kids and a wife. Of the eleven kids, only six were his biologically. The other five were former street kids whom he adopted as his own after they had worked for him for a while as I was doing. Rambo owned a house on the outskirts of the city, which was a five-bedroom house. His kids were all between the ages of six and twenty-five. They all were in school. He would go away begging for a period of about three months and then go back home to his wife and children for a whole week with all the money he had amassed during that time. He had a good family.

While there, he introduced me to his family as his new acquisition. He even asked me to stay with his family and become the twelfth member of the family. As the twelfth member of the family, he will have me back in school so I could return to a normal life for a kid my age. Although I was getting a warm reception there, I just felt uncomfortable accepting this golden offer. My decision to decline Rambo's offer really caught him by surprise as he never anticipated it coming, since during our time together, we got to develop a very good relationship. We developed a father-and-son relationship. He loved me very much and had a lot of praises for me to his friends and family. He always reminded me that I was very smart, therefore his favorite son. I felt bad breaking the news to him that I was parting my way from him to pursue my own dream, better yet to embark on another adventure that perhaps would lead me to my dream. Rambo was a great man. I did learn a lot about life being by his side, but I was more intrigued about the idea of recuperating my own freedom more than anything else. We both had our "It's not you, it's me" kind of moment together before saying our good-byes.

After leaving Rambo, I went back to the usual roaming around the city during the day and finding funerals at night for a spot to spend the night. On nights where I failed to find a funeral, I had to settle for junkyards. I would look for a junkyard but instead found a wrecked car with the least damage, get in its backseat, and bundle up like a fetus in the womb until the very first sound of the rooster. That's when I would wake up and be on my way for another inspiring day.

About two weeks after quitting being Rambo's pusher, I heard that the government was recruiting volunteers to go fight against the rebels who were gaining a lot of ground in their quest to overthrow the regime. With the regime unpopularity at a record high, the army facing defection after defection in almost every battalion, and with the well-trained and better-equipped rebels' advancement to the capital city becoming more imminent, so to keep the rebels from marching into the capital city, which would mark an end to the regime, a lot of money was poured into the streets to recruit volunteers to go fight the rebels and keep them from further advancement. Two hundred dollars in cash was given to anyone who was willing to volunteer taking a two weeks' boot camp training. Then another $300 in cash was given the day of deployment to the battlefront. Out of desperation, military recruiters were now going to middle and high schools, forcibly removing children as young as twelve years old from school and taking them to military bases where they were given military training and sent to the battlefront to keep rebels from making further gain on the ground.

The sound of making $500 in less than thirty days at twelve years old, which was perhaps the equivalent of being the first twelve-year-old to crack the *Forbes* magazine world's top one hundred wealthiest men, was music in my hears. I wasn't going to miss out on such a golden opportunity. I made my way straight to the recruitment location, which was at one of the military bases about eighty kilometers on the outskirts of the city. At twelve years old, with everything I was going through, living on the streets all these years day by day made me become fearless. I was so emboldened by hope that fear had no place in me. Whether at night while sleeping inside a wrecked car in the middle of nowhere or sleeping in the company of strangers at funerals, fear had never been the factor then and sure wasn't going to be a factor now regardless of what was at stake. Carrying a gun with a license to kill or a chance to be killed never fazed me.

By the time I got to the base and enrolled as a new recruit to go fight the rebels who were now approaching the capital city, everything has already changed. The cutoff age for recruits, which was once eighteen, now was lowered to sixteen, and since there wasn't no form of identification available for minors, one's word was good enough. A ten-year-old could claim to be sixteen, or vice versa. Those recruiters didn't give an F about it as long as they were fulfilling their quotas. Embezzlement was also a big factor by the time I got there. Now the $500 incentive allocated for the recruits was now reduced to a mere $100 if that, while the recruiters and trainers pocketed the rest. Instead of receiving $200 for signing up, I was given $25 and promised $250 more the day of deployment to the battlefront. At this time, the base was filled with a lot of gangbangers, street kids with ages ranging from nine years old up to boys and girls in their twenties.

The teenage female recruits had it tougher than everyone as they were subjected to constant sexual abuse and rapes by those recruiters and military trainers. Trainers would make their way to the female tents in the middle of the night, each picking one or two recruits who were as young as fourteen years old and having their way with them. Those who tried to desist were threatened with severe punishment. The more fortunate ones were bribed with a few dollars. Most were told that the sexual abuse was a part of military drills associated with hazing within the military. It had nothing to do with pleasure. It was one of the most efficient military training drills aiming at toughening up the moral of a female soldier. A lot of those female recruits ended up carrying unwanted pregnancies as a result of those top-secret military drills, which, by the way, were only carried out late at night when everyone was supposed to be asleep, I'm guessing between midnight and 2:00 a.m. That's when the enemy is more vulnerable; it makes perfect sense.

For most of us who weren't lucky enough to benefit from those special after-dark drills, our trainings consisted of waking up every day at 5:00 a.m., doing about one hundred push-ups, sit-ups, jumping jacks, pull-ups, and running about five kilometers around the base while chanting songs full of obscenity.

In the afternoon, after the break, we were broken up to groups of eleven. The afternoon session consisted of about ninety minutes of shooting drills, an hour of cleaning and dismantling weapons, and finally, the last hour of training was dedicated to government propaganda, which was nothing but rhetoric about how the rebels are very bad and evil and they all deserve to be killed to save our nation. By 6:00 p.m., we were all free to do whatever until curfew, which was set at 9:59 p.m. We were fed twice a day. We had brunch right after the morning training and dinner at around 6:30 p.m. The food, which mostly consisted of rice and undercooked beans, was terrible, but there was plenty of it, which kept our stomachs full.

I hated everything about the boot camp. I thought about quitting almost every day. Thanks to Jo, my drills partner, who was about fourteen years old, who kept me from quitting; that and the fact that we were told that anyone who quits will be sent to prison. Jo and I became very close. We slept next to each other. Just like me, Jo was a runaway who had been leaving on the streets since he was eight years old. Jo had been at the base for about two days prior to my arrival. He was physically fit. He had no problem doing one hundred push-ups and did all those drills with ease; while I, on the other hand, was basically on life support after each drill. Luckily for me, by the time I got to the base, the training was now lasting five days instead of the usual two weeks.

Now that the military was getting thinner and thinner by the number with all the defection and the rebels just two hundred kilometers away from reaching the city main airport, on the sixth day of training, about seven military trucks made their way to the base at around 1:00 a.m. Everyone was told to report to the yard. We were told they will be calling names. If you hear your name, you were handed an M16 weapon with two-cartridge magazines, ammo pouch, and a pair of military gear. After receiving all the equipment, we were told to board the assigned military truck. We were about eighty people all smooshed up in that truck like sardines. There was barely any room to breathe, let alone any moving room. Everyone was handed a twenty-dollar bill upon boarding the truck—yes, you heard it right, twenty dollars only. The much promised $300 was nothing but a mirage. Everyone was mumbling their displeasure under their tongue, but no one had the balls to voice it out loud.

The twenty dollars was the least of my worries. I was more disappointed that Jo and I weren't boarded in the same truck. This only meant one thing—we were each going to a separate location. Shortly before boarding the truck, I could hear someone shouting my name, "Timu! Timu!" From afar, it was Jo who was boarding another truck. "I will see you later, pal. Go kick some rebels' ass," he said. That was the last I heard from him.

At around 3:00 a.m., our truck was among the first to leave the base en route to Kenge, a village about 250 kilometers from the city. The ride to Kenge was the worst nightmare I ever lived. The dirt roads leading to the village were basically a death trap. I couldn't quite choose what would have been worse—dying from a wreck, which was bound to happen at any moment given how overloaded the truck was and how bad the dirt road was, or dying at the hands of the rebels. There was no easy choice there. The worst was yet to come until we had to cross the Mai-Ndombe bridge, a man-made bridge made centuries ago by the indigenous. Legend has it that the spirits usually take about twenty lives on a daily basis from cars and trucks crossing the bridge for sacrifice. From the looks of it, the spirits were in for a bargain. It looks like the whole truck was having a hard time crossing the bridge with its weight. Some of us were asked to get out the truck and walk our way to the other side of the bridge, which to me looked like it should be among the top five world's deadliest bridges.

By the time we got to the other side of the bridge, it was already daylight, and we could hear heavy artillery coming from about fifteen kilometers far ahead. We were broken up into groups of eleven and sent toward the bushes to the heavy sound of what sounded like nonstop lightning. We were told to advance and start firing our weapons. I was given a walkie-talkie since I was the only one among my peers who knew how to speak French, and all the commands were supposedly given in French.

As we pushed a little farther into the bushes, I realized that we were abandoned to fight for our lives as everyone was retreating, and there were dead bodies lying around along the way, and the lightning sounds were getting even louder. Halfway into the bushes, I heard a loud noise, like the biggest firework had just exploded. I looked back. Two of my fellow volunteers just caught a bullet, one in his head, the other in his neck. I had never seen so much blood pouring out of somebody's body before. It was like someone had just opened up a champagne bottle.

I didn't know what to do. No one was answering my SOS call from the walkie-talkie. I just threw away my weapon and took off my military gear; I had a pair of football shorts underneath. I just started running as far as I could toward the bridge, which by this time was about fifty kilometers from the bushes. As I was pushing back to the dirt road, I managed to hitchhike on a military pickup truck, which had about fifteen people in it running away from combat. Those people inside the pickup truck spoke Portuguese. I came to realize they were part of an Angolan mercenary battalion sent by the government to help keep the rebels from reaching the capital city. They have been fighting for five straight days, and the rebels just happened to cut off their supply line, and they had no choice but to retreat.

"It's a lost cause," one of them stated. "Some of your fellow soldiers are in contact with the rebels. They are telling the rebels what position to hit and which route to take. It's just a matter of time until the rebels march onto the capital city."

I got to ride with them up to the international airport, where they were waiting to board a military cargo plane that was going to take them back to Angola. From the airport, I caught a bus back to the city, marking the end of a very wild week.

The year 1997 was by far one of the most important years in our country's history and a very busy one for me. In May 1997, as I was now approaching two years as a street kid, a coalition forces mostly made up of Rwandan and Ugandan militias was led by a former rebel to the Mobutu regime who has been living in exile since his multiple failed attempts to overthrow the Mobutu regime. Laurent Desire Kabila ousted the longtime dictator Mobutu after thirty-two years in power.

Laurent Desire Kabila is a self-proclaimed nationalist who fought alongside Che Guevara during the '60s in an attempt to overthrow Mobutu after the latter had ascended to power by means of a coup d'état with the help of the CIA. His early attempts to overthrow Mobutu were brutally crushed as Mobutu, a then western and U.S. ally during the cold war against the former Soviet Union, was able to subdue the rebellion, leading Laurent Desire Kabila to flee to a neighboring country into a self-imposed exile.

Paul Kagame, a former military leader of the Rwandan Patriotic Front (FPR), a Tutsi-led militia, according to many sources, was responsible for triggering the genocide in his country, Rwanda, by downing a plane carrying Juvenal Habyarimana, the former Rwandan president who was from the ethnic Hutu tribe, along with his counterpart, Cyprien Ntaryamira, the former president of Burundi. The Rwandan genocide was allegedly triggered by Paul Kagame in April 1994 with the death toll standing between five hundred thousand and two million dead, mostly women and children, making it the world's most devastating tragedy since World War II.

Right after the assassination of the Rwandan president, which led to the genocide and ethnic cleansing in Rwanda, Paul Kagame, a former alumni at the U.S. military training camp in Fort Leavenworth and former staff chief of the army deputy director of the Defense Intelligence of Uganda under Yoweri Museveni, took over power in Rwanda. After rising to power, Paul Kagame's vision was to establish a Tutsi-led empire around the region. He had a strong ally in his quest in Yoweri Museveni, a fellow Tutsi with Rwandan descent who was now president of Uganda. Paul Kagame and Yoweri Museveni had very strong ties dating back to 1979 when a then twenty-two-year-old Paul Kagame joined the National Resistance Army (NRA), a militia led by Yoweri Museveni and supported by the United States in its fight to overthrow the then ruthless Ugandan dictator, Idi Amin Dada, whose character was made into the movie *The Last King of Scotland*, played by the American actor Forest Whitaker.

After helping Yoweri Museveni to power in Uganda, in return, Yoweri Museveni reciprocated the favor by leading Paul Kagame to power in Rwanda. In October 1996, both men, Paul Kagame and his fellow mentor Yoweri Museveni, who was now the U.S. most docile regional ally, drew a plan to invade Zaire and take control of all its natural resources and perhaps annex some of its lands to theirs. Might for might, Rwanda and Uganda were no match to Zaire militarily, but with the U.S. national interests and many western multinationals involved and siding by those two aggressors hoping to secure big mining contracts when everything goes according to plans, it became a very different ball game.

Since invading Zaire militarily would have been in total violation of the United Nations chart prohibiting military intervention against another nation unless acting in self-defense, doing so would have caused an outcry from the international community, which would have been forced into actions ranging from economic sanctions to possible military strike against Rwanda and Uganda. With the help of a prominent military adviser to Paul Kagame, the name Laurent Desire Kabila was brought up. He was a Zairian national and former rebel to the Mobutu regime now turned exile in the neighboring country of Tanzania where he has been making a living as a gold trafficker and ransom collector.

Laurent Desire Kabila, a self-proclaimed Lumumbist or one who follows the doctrine of the late Patrice Lumumba, was a former rebel who once fought alongside the great Marxist revolutionary and guerrilla leader, Ernesto Che Guevara, in the '60s. According to certain sources, Kabila's collaboration with Che Guevara didn't last long as Che Guevara accused Kabila of lacking a concrete vision and not being disciplined enough to sustain the requirement of guerrilla warfare. Che Guevara found Kabila to be more passionate about women and alcohol than anything else, thus leading Che Guevara to cut ties with him.

Laurent Desire Kabila was chosen by both Kagame and Museveni to play the role of a puppet to their diabolical plan. Both Kagame and Museveni put Laurent Desire Kabila as the face of the new "rebellion" against Mobutu. To the world, Kabila stood as the chief in command of a rebellion aiming at toppling the dictatorial regime of Mobutu that had been oppressing its own people for thirty-two years now; while in reality, this was nothing but a Rwandan and Ugandan military invasion of its much bigger neighbor, Zaire.

The Alliance of Democratic Force for the Liberation of Congo (AFDL), the Rwandan and Ugandan-led military movement, with its head, Laurent Desire Kabila, launched their first offensive in the Kivu, a mountainous region in the eastern part of the country bordering Rwanda and Uganda. While Kagame and Museveni provided the troops, the CIA provided military trainings and intelligence, and major U.S. mining company such as Adastra Minerals, formerly known as American Mineral Fields, in concert with other major western multinational companies such as Glencore kept the cash flowing for the purchase of heavy military equipment and arsenal.

The United States, Australia, Canada, Great Britain, Germany, France, Israel, and South Africa all had their hands dirty in this war. With about 90 percent of the population ready to rid themselves of the Mobutu regime by any means necessary, the news of a rebellion against Mobutu was like great music in people's ears, with Kagame and Museveni doing such a great job in masking their true intention by portraying Kabila as the ultimate rebel who was in charge of the AFDL movement, a movement with the sole aim of putting the Zairian people out of thirty-two years of misery by getting rid of their enemy number one in Mobutu. Every town and city was greeting those foreign troops as liberators.

While battling prostate cancer for years now, Mobutu was definitely at his lowest physically and morally. With the United States no longer providing him with any support, Mobutu's time in power was nothing but numbered. There was no army to speak of. What was left was nothing but a small militia of revolutionary guards whose sole purpose was to ensure his personal security and that of his family. Aside from them, the army was nonexistent—meaning, everywhere AFDL militia launched an assault, they didn't have to encounter any strong military opposition. With the rest of the population already fed up by the Mobutu regime, in each town and in every city, those foreign troops were welcomed as liberators.

After a few failed negotiation attempts, seven months from the time of its first military offensive, the AFDL militia marched its way into the capital city, Kinshasa, leading Mobutu, his family, and his closest entourage to flee into exile. As soon as the capital city fell under rebels' hands, Laurent Desire Kabila, from his stronghold city of Lubumbashi, the country's second-largest city and the economic capital beyond everyone's expectations, went on and proclaimed himself the new head of the state. As the new president, he went on to rename the country from Zaire to the Democratic Republic of the Congo. Kabila proclaiming himself president caught Kagame and Museveni by surprise. Those two wolves didn't know what hit them.

May 1997 saw a regime change in the country that was unheard of for over thirty-two years. Laurent Desire Kabila as the new president of the Congo with his nationalist vision and great speech, all that did nothing but inflate a great state of hope into the Congolese. To be honest, at this moment, even if you were a wild beast or even the devil himself, as long as your name wasn't Mobutu, you were good to go. The vast majority of the country that saw their freedom taken away and a rise in poverty under the Mobutu regime were glad to see him gone and welcomed the new regime as their savior.

As history has often taught us, change never comes cheap. Changes usually bring hard times. That was also the case in my country. The new regime, which was welcomed as savior, saw its honeymoon period short lived. Just a few months in it found itself facing a large number of unhappy population who were very frustrated about how slow the recovery process was going about. People were very frustrated by the large numbers of foreigners occupying key posts in all the institutions in the public sector. It was even worse within the government and military. The country's secretary of state was a certain Deogratias Bugera, an Uganda citizen; our foreign minister, a certain Bizima Karaha, a Rwandese citizen; the army chief of staff was James Kabarebe, a Rwandese citizen who now happens to be the chief of staff of the Rwandese army, just to name a few. All this was widely seen as a sign of occupation by the locals.

There was presence of foreign militias roaming around the city along with some unruly child soldiers who have been forcibly recruited and brainwashed by the militia at the beginning of the war. Those unruly kids with their ages ranging between ten and eighteen years old were allowed to roam the city heavily armed, terrorizing civilians, something that the locals were never accustomed to. They didn't have any manners. They were very abusive to women and elders. They were very confrontational. Those underage soldiers were known by their nickname, *Kadogo*, meaning "little one" in Swahili. Since they carried guns, they saw themselves as outlaws. As the newly crowned liberators, they enjoyed immunity against any persecution under their own law since there was yet any law as the country was in transition from the old regime of Mobutu to the new one of Laurent Kabila.

All this was going on a daily basis until the locals realized they had enough of their barbarism and took it upon themselves, since the authority seemed to keep a blind eye on the situation. But despite the popular belief of liberation going around the city as people were seeing more and more foreign troops speaking languages not similar to the locals, a lot of eyebrows started to rise up. Months later, those foreign troops were becoming more and more lacking morale and discipline. They started carrying themselves more as conquerors than anything else, leading the general population to become more resentful toward those former liberators. Now the popular belief was that Kabila had brought with him Rwandese and Ugandan troops who were becoming a pain in a butt to the general population.

There were many barbaric cases involving those foreign troops. In one incident, while walking with his girlfriend, a man got himself severely beaten to death as he refused to lend his girlfriend to one of those foreign soldiers who wanted to borrow her for a few hours to engage in a sexual intercourse with her. The boyfriend's refusal ended up costing him a few ribs and teeth along with a broken neck. On a separate incident, those foreign troops prohibited the wearing of miniskirts by women. Anyone caught wearing a skirt below the knee was stripped naked in public. There was now a public outcry demanding the return of all those foreign troops to their respective countries such as Rwanda and Uganda. Little did they know Kabila didn't bring those foreign troops with him. On the contrary, those foreign troops are the ones who brought Kabila along with them. This wasn't a liberation; it was rather an occupation, and they were in for the long haul. They traded the evil they knew well in Mobutu to the evil they knew nothing about in the Rwandese and Ugandan occupiers.

As the conflict between the locals and those foreign soldiers was growing, President Laurent Kabila took it upon himself and decided to part ways with his allies, who were the catalysts of him overthrowing the former government. Laurent Kabila went a step further by annulling all the previous agreements he had made with the CIA-backed coalition of Paul Kagame and Yoweri Museveni, which called for the annexation and exploitation of all the mining resorts in all the eastern part of the country and some parts of the north.

In August 1998, Laurent Kabila ordered all foreign troops, which were largely made up of Rwandan and Ugandan troops, out of the Congolese soil, prompting a breakup in relations with his former allies. Laurent Kabila, whose power heavily rested upon the presence of Rwandan and Ugandan troops, had previously verbally agreed to a deal that called for the exploitation of the mineral-rich eastern part of the Congo by both Rwanda and Uganda. He did that a few weeks before proclaiming himself president. The deal called for Rwanda and Uganda to be given full access to mineral-rich regions of the Congo along the Rwandan and Uganda border. Major mining companies such as Glencore and other multinationals would be guaranteed mining contracts with a higher percentage of the revenue going back to those foreign investors, while about 10 to 15 percent would go to the Congolese treasury.

Much to their surprise, there was a call for a revision of the previously agreed upon agreement. Laurent Kabila, who saw himself as nationalistic as the country's national hero Patrice Lumumba, the country's first democratically elected prime minister in 1960, told his counterpart, Paul Kagame and Yoweri Museveni, in a meeting that those previous agreements should be void, since not only were they verbal, and besides, at the time of the agreement, he was a rebel only in charge of a militia, but also now that he was the president of an entire country, those agreements did not reflect the interest of an entire nation, therefore needed to be renegotiated with about 60 percent of the revenue going toward the Congolese treasury instead of the 10 to 15 percent as previously agreed upon. "It wasn't personal, just a question of national interest," Kabila said.

Both Kagame and Museveni, along with multinational representatives, weren't too happy about Kabila's new stance. "A deal is a deal no matter the circumstances!" Kagame shouted. Just like that, the former allies now became enemies. You had Kagame, Museveni, United States, and western interest along with all those multinationals who felt ripped off after having financed the overthrow of the Mobutu regime on one side, Kabila and the Congolese people on the other side. One thing for sure, in politics, you do not want to go against United States and western interest. If history had taught us a lesson, it is that anyone who ever dare go against United States and western interest always found himself either assassinated, removed from power, or rotting somewhere in some international court prison. When dealing with those big dogs who run the world, you give them what they want and say as you are being told or else. With them, there is always the hard way or the easy way. Whichever way you chose, you better know they will always come up on top.

With Kabila totally isolated from the "world"—by world, it meant to be the western world—once again, Paul Kagame and Yoweri Museveni, with the blessing of their big ally, the U.S. government, decided to invade to Congo for the second time around. The second invasion of Congo by Rwandan and Ugandan troops happened on August 2, 1998, a few days after the Congolese president Kabila ordered the repatriation of all foreign troops back to their respective countries, Rwanda and Uganda. Few days later, those same troops, along with thousands more reinforcements, made their way back on Congolese soil. This time around, Rwandese troops occupied the eastern part of the Congo, while their Ugandan ally took full control of the northeastern part of the country.

It was peculiar how quickly things can turn in politics. Kabila's allies yesterday were now his most fervent enemy ready to topple him. Taking up the northern part left Laurent Kabila isolated. Those who were once his allies yesterday had quickly turned into his enemies today. With the departure of the Rwandese and Ugandan army, Kabila was left with a very weak army personnel. Now that his grip of power was more vulnerable than ever from a well-determined foe in Rwanda and Uganda backed by U.S. interest, Kabila had to resort to ask help from other regional powers such as Angola, Zimbabwe, and Namibia to come to his rescue and avoid being overthrown by a Rwandan-led attack that came within miles of his residence in the capital city. With the help of some heroes from Angolan commandos on the ground and a large arsenal of aerial firepower by both Angolan and Zimbabwean fighter jets, they were able to rid the capital city of those Rwandese insurgents, thus enabling Kabila to keep a hold on to power.

As history has always taught us, humans tend to unite strongly in the wake of tragedy or atrocity. So was the case with the vast majority of the Congolese people. In the capital city of Kinshasa, everyone was united behind the Kabila government in its fight to squash the Rwandan-led invasion, even though prior to the second invasion, Laurent Kabila's approval rating was among the lowest of any previous head of state in the history of the country. At one moment, some people were starting to wish for the old regime to make its way back as things weren't looking as bright as they thought it would following the liberation.

Laurent Kabila played all his cards right. He did a good job in rallying the whole nation against a common enemy, Rwanda and Uganda. During the second invasion of 1998, many locals took it upon themselves in chasing down the remaining pocket of Rwandese soldiers who made it to the capital city as a result of their failed attempt to overthrow Kabila. Rwandese soldiers were caught by the general population, with most being burned alive with tires and gasoline, while their bodies were displayed in main roads as a repercussion. With their long face and pointy nose, those Rwandese insurgents had a very distinct bodily feature that was very noticeable to the locals, and most importantly, the locals had never forgotten how badly they suffered at the helm of those conquerors. Watching them burning alive was sort of therapeutic. During that time, even the people who just happened to share the same facial feature as Rwandese were dealt with severely.

Shortly after Laurent Kabila took over as the head of the country, I was still roaming around the streets. Nothing much had changed except one day, as I was walking around town, I stopped near a crowd of people who were gathered around a TV outside a house. I joined those people in watching what happened to be the investiture ceremony of the country's new president, Laurent Kabila. It was about a two-hour speech held at the main football stadium where he was sworn in as the new president of the Democratic Republic of the Congo. After the speech was over, there were still pockets of people gathered around discussing their points of view on the new leader's speech, which was mostly marred by tons of promises and a very bright future, socially and economically.

As I stood there listening to everyone's comments, I began making my own reflection of the speech. I started impersonating the president while reciting excerpts from the speech that I found to be interesting. I repeated the part about rebuilding the country by making reforms such as building a stronger and unified army and creating a new currency that will be stronger than the previous one. He spent about half of the speech defaming the previous regime, while the other half was marred by many more promises. Most of them were very unrealistic, but as a good politician, he knew exactly what the masses wanted to hear, so he delivered. Kabila was very eloquent. He had a great gasp of the French language, which to many was synonymous to being very bright. Despite being a self-proclaimed nationalist, his presidency was overshadowed by a lot of amateurism and nepotism, He had as government officials people with very little to no public office experience. He himself was known to be a womanizer and drunkard. Rumor had it that he used to drink until he peed in his pants. For a person who was tasting power for the very first time after spending so many years leaving clandestinely from jungle to jungle, who could have blamed him?

As I was repeating part of his fascinating speech people all around were very impressed in both my ability to have memorized a lot of lines from the speech and most importantly I was sounding just like him. The more I spoke the more the small crowd were mesmerized and kept me going on and on. From that very moment it was official there I was a 12 years old young boy who was able to impersonate the president's voice there I was a star in the making who just happen to find himself a new gig.

I started going around town. Wherever I would see a gathering of people whether at funerals, party, bars, or any social gathering, I would just start impersonating the president in a loud voice, catching people's attention. After doing so, I started receiving a lot of tips from people who would ask me numeral times for an encore. With tips flowing like never before, I officially embraced the impersonating as my new gig. As time went by, I started getting a few negative feedbacks. My clientele started getting a little bored from listening to the same speech over and over. That's why I became aware that I needed to upgrade my materials. I was now in great need of new speeches from the president. Luckily for me, the president was very active in the media, giving out at least one interview to the local media at least once every other week, which was aired religiously on national TV, giving me the opportunity to acquire new materials.

As I roamed the streets walking from town to town, I would stop by houses that had TVs set up outside to catch on some new speech from the president. In the poorer part of the city, people usually have their TVs set up outside. In the evening hours up until 11:00 p.m., people would watch their favorite shows, which were usually aired after the 8:00 p.m. nightly news. It was the norm in poorer neighborhood to set up TVs outside on the yard since it was much cooler and relaxing outside given how hot it was during the hot summer with temperature flirting around forty degrees Celsius even at nighttime, and since conditioner unit was only a luxury, only affordable to the rich ones, watching television outside was one of the few only alternatives available. It was also used as a means to keep traffic at a minimum in and outside the house.

This time around, after acquiring new materials from the latest president's interview with some French journalist, I felt confident enough to take my gig to a bigger audience. I made my way to the Institute of Advanced Technological Study (ISTA), the city's biggest technical college. On my very first day there, I just placed myself near a group of college students who were gathered nearby after classes. I started impersonating in a loud voice, making sure to be heard by my targeted audience, quickly gaining their undivided attention. When impersonating the president, I always opened with an excerpt from his May 29, 1997, inaugural speech, which was by far my best seller.

"Que je leve la main la main droite ou la main gauche? Moi Laurent Desire Kabila president de la republic democratic du congo je jure fidelite a la nation et obeissance aux dispositions legales de l'autorite de la transition et notamment au decret-loi constitutional relative a l'organisation et a l'exercice du pouvoir."

With those words, I always managed to make the crowd go wild, and this new college crowd was no exception. No way were they listening to a twelve-year-old; they were perhaps witnessing a segment of Congolese Got Talent, they thought!

My very first day at ISTA campus was very successful moving from crowd to crowd around the campus, earning me the nickname Petit Kabila or Little Kabila for the very first time. I made about twenty dollars in tips that day. Life was good. As I became a regular at the ISTA campus, I started getting more and more clientele. I quickly became the new star on campus. I was known throughout the whole campus as Petit Kabila. After spending about a month roaming around the campus, people became more reluctant to tip as there was nothing new under the sun. I started having more people have me mimic on credit, stating they will pay me the next day or so, which they never did eventually.

One day, I was very hungry; I haven't eaten a thing the entire day. A student came asking me to hear some impersonation of the president. I asked him to pay up front since I was really hungry and didn't really feel like opening my mouth right now. He told me to go ahead and do it anyway and not to worry about being hungry; he will show me a trick that will have my hunger go away in just a matter of seconds. I went on and gave him about twenty minutes of impersonating, and after I was finished, he told me to take spit on my finger and then rub the spit around my belly button and wait for about five minutes; I wouldn't be hungry anymore. I did just that. I even gave it way past five minutes. I was still hungry. The look on my face after realizing that I have been made a fool of was priceless. That incident was a sign that perhaps my time there was up.

The next day, I moved to another college campus, the National Pedagogy Institute (IPN). In IPN, which wasn't as big of a campus as ISTA, I didn't have that much success gathering as big as a crowd as I had done previously. The reason being was that unlike in ISTA where about 99 percent of the students were males, about 90 percent of IPN students were females, and not that many females are known to have interest in politics. After lasting a day at the IPN campus, I decided not to come back there.

The following day, I decided to hit yet another audience. This time, I went to try my luck up the hill at the University of Kinshasa (UNIKIN), the biggest university in the country, which was nicknamed "the Hill" because it was built on a hill. UNIKIN campus used to be the most prestigious in Central Africa during the country's prime. It was now left to being a shadow of its glorious days where international students from all over the continent fancied it for its great architectural building and very high standard academic prowess. Built in the mid-1950s, the University of Kinshasa was among the leading academic power houses in the continent for quite some time until the people running the country decided that education wasn't a priority to the country's development anymore.

As the central government stopped its funding, there were no more buildings being built to accommodate the influx of students attending. The facilities were neglected, dormitories poorly maintained, and faculty members highly under paid, leading them to recur to corruption and bribes as a means to makes ends meet. A classroom that had the maximum capacity of about fifty students now had about 120 students in attendance. In some cases, students would even sit on top of windows, while others would be standing outside just to listen to a lecture.

The standard of living on campus was one of the worst that ever existed. The dormitories, which resembled shanty towns, were way overpopulated. A room set up for four students was now housing ten people, with very terrible insulation system, and public restrooms were inexistent. There were twelve dormitories on campus—two female-only dorms, nine male-only dorms, and the other one was reserved for grad school students only. Of all those dorm halls, only the female and grad school students had a somewhat working lavatory and working sewage system. For the majority of the students, the bushes around campus were about the only place reliable to dispose of their personal waste. The bushes around campus were later nicknamed Home Quarante or Hall 40. If a student was to tell you that he or she was on their way to Home Quarante, it was just them telling you they were going to use the bathrooms in the bushes. With the country totally in ruins in all aspects, UNIKIN being the biggest state-run educational institution in the country was still by far the one choice of many high school graduates who wished to further their education.

At twelve years old, one can say I was definitely the youngest person on campus, although I was not enrolled at the university, nor did I have any relative living on campus, during the days. I would roam outside school faculties attracting a big crowd of students while doing my gig. It didn't take long for me to become a star at the campus. Petit

Kabila quickly made his way into becoming the most popular figure on campus. I was ever grateful to the ISTA campus and its student body for helping me launch my mimicking career there, but I owed it more to the UNIKIN campus and all its student body because it was at the Hill where I reached the zenith of my career and was now forever known by all as Petit Kabila. The Hill being the largest educational entity in the country with about a minimum of fifty thousand students enrolled was by far the most profitable place for me after my daily rounds, which involved me going from faculty to faculty.

My day didn't start till sometime around noon and ended pretty much around 5:30 p.m. I always started from the faculty of medicine building, which was the second-largest faculty in enrollment and then went to the faculty of finance and economy. From there, I went to the polytechnic faculty, the equivalent of speed school, which also was the most shaded area of the campus with its building located around big trees and bushes, and then finally made my way up to the law school building, which was, by far, my biggest moneymaker as law students were, by a big margin, my biggest and most loyal customers. They even were jokingly calling me one of their own. They embraced me like no other. Law school students were in a league of their own. They fancied themselves being the most important faculty on campus. They never missed the opportunity to remind all the other students from different faculties that law was the only faculty among all the others that had its name in masculine form. Any other faculty's name was feminine—medicine, polytechnic, finance, economy, pedagogy . . . you name it; they all were feminine except, of course, the mighty law school.

On a daily basis, I would make around the equivalent of thirty dollars a day, maybe more on a good day, which was more than enough to pay for my daily meals and have some money left over for personal leisure. After my daily rounds, I would make my way down to the dorms. The dorm halls were housed by faculties. Halls 2 and 4 were only reserved for undergraduate students, halls 6 and 8 were reserved for students from the finance and economy faculty, halls 12 and 14 were for speed school student, hall 20 was for medical school, hall 30 was home to law school students, halls 10 and 60 were for grad students only, while halls 80 and 150 were female-only halls.

Since the campus was about thirty miles away from the city, it would have been harder on me to keep making it there every day back and forth. With that in mind, I decided to stay on campus. With my new status as the new little star on campus, Petit Kabila was welcomed in every hall, even the female-only ones. Having not reached the age of puberty yet, I wasn't a threat to the ladies, who were giving me total access to their dormitories given that most of them found me to be adorable anyway. I made sure never to reveal my status as a homeless kid. I made sure never to tell anyone that I was living on the streets, and luckily, no one ever suspected it.

After my daily rounds of impersonating, I would make my way to certain dorms, chilling and hanging out with the big boys. Life on campus was very vivid. Those students lived by their own rules. Campus was another entity within the city. Even law enforcement was kept out of there. A person could murder someone and run from the law. As soon as he made his way inside the Hill, he was now declared untouchable as law enforcement wasn't allowed there. Perhaps the murder illusion is a bit excessive, but the point I am trying to make is that the Hill was like its own little Vatican City inside the city of Rome.

Outside every hall, they had ping-pong tables and foosball tables. All around, you could see people playing chess and checkers. My favorite games to play was ping-pong and checkers. Living on campus, I got to become very skillful at both. I was one of the few twelve-year-olds in the land that could match up with any adult in both ping-pong and checkers, making myself even more friends among the big boys. In ping-pong, I had the best defense ever. I could return the ball back to the table from about almost anywhere. Being left-handed, I had the upper hand on almost anyone since everyone there was right-handed.

Weekends on campus were even more fun. Local bands set the roof on fire every Saturday nights with their performance at the esplanade of the campus pool, which was the place most entertainment events were booked. Life on campus was so much fun. I was like that student who was enrolled, lived on campus, and just never made it to any of his classes. Being very likeable and great at lying was what helped me live on campus for four straight months without anyone noticing that I was homeless. At nights, I would make up stories to stay the night inside the dorms. For instance, I would go in hall 2 and tell someone there that my brother whom I stay with in hall 20 went back home unexpectedly either for the day or for the weekend and that none of his roommates were there neither and that the door was locked. If I could just spend the night here until the morning, by then, my imaginary brother should have already made his way back from wherever he went to. The next night or so, I would move on to a different hall with the same story and so on. I did this for four months straight. On the days that I couldn't really find a suitable venue, I just spent the night outside staring at the beautiful stars in the sky. All this time, no one ever questioned my story.

As my audience was growing in number, so came the need for more updated material. On many occasions, I would have students walking up to me, asking me if I already had the latest speech given by the president, prompting me to start keeping up with the president's speech and interviews so I could stay on top of my game and feed the public the very latest. I found myself watching a lot of news on national TV to catch up with the high demand for the newest material. I would usually sit down with a pen and paper, writing down part of speeches or interviews given by the president. I would later edit it myself, usually adding certain things to fill in the gap on whatever I might have missed during my writing. Being exposed to politics at a very young age, I had no trouble doing so since politics was now my passion.

But just like in every business, there were times when business was booming, and there were also times when things weren't going so great. Some days, I would be doing my impersonation of the president for hours without getting any tips from people. On those days, I would go to some student dorms and help wash dishes or clean up in exchange for some meal. Doing chores in exchange for food was the most embarrassing job on campus only reserved to runaways and poor kids.

There were a few runaways who were known to perform such duties on campus. They were called *Moineau*, which was French for "sparrow." Being known as a Moineau was very embarrassing. Every day, I prayed that I didn't have to resort to being a Moineau for a day. Luckily for me, I only had to do it two to three times during my stay at the Hill; that was still two to three times too many. Living at Hill, my daily meals consisted of a lot junk food. Mostly bread, grilled peanuts, smoked fish, soy milk, and soda on the good days; while bread, grilled peanuts, and lots of water were what I had on my worse days.

Going on my fourth month at the Hill, I got the biggest break of my life. It was a certain Saturday afternoon on the biggest day of campus festivity, Open Day as it was called. Once a year, Open Day was celebrated on campus. Open Day was the only day during the school year that the female-only halls were open to guests of all genders for twenty-four hours. Male students or guests were allowed inside the female rooms for as long as twenty-four hours without any restriction. It started from 10:00 a.m. to 10:00 a.m. the next. Open Day was usually celebrated with big barbecue, live concert by various bands, plays, and also a big soccer game at the campus soccer field between the two major campus soccer rival teams, law school versus medical school.

Open Day usually brings guest appearances such as a star artist or a political figure. This particular Open Day saw the country's secretary of sports, youth, and leisure as the guest of honor, who happened to be a certain Vincent Mutond Tshibal, the president's nephew. That Saturday was not like any other on campus. It was a very special Saturday. Loud music was everywhere from different corners of the hall. Even birds were chirping louder than usual. They too knew it wasn't an ordinary day after all. perhaps were even louder on that may be as after all. The smell of barbecue coming from grill to grill could be smelled from a distance. As usual, I was making my way from dorm to dorm enjoying the day just as much as the campus residents were.

Not to be outdone by their counterpart from other dorms, the female halls were busy as well. Females halls were flooded by a huge amount of guests, friends, and family from all over the city lined up to see their loved ones. Boyfriends, fiancés, and husbands couldn't miss out on the opportunity to spend quality time with their loved ones beyond the lobby, which is normally the only place assigned for visitation in female dorm rooms. Open Day to the female dorms is as the Louvre Museum is to tourists, a great place of attraction.

As lively as was the whole campus with everything going in all four corners, there was only one place to be at as soon as the clock hit three o'clock, the campus football field. Three o'clock was the kickoff of the football match between the two campus rivals, the Faculty of Law against the Faculty of Medicine, even though their rivalry was mostly kept civil and respectful. There were a few occasions when there had been some isolated incidents that led to some physical encounter between members of the two factions, the future judges and lawyers on one side versus the future doctors as surgeons on the other side as it was known. There were friendly insults being traded between both sides. For whatever reason, law school students usually carried a big chip on their shoulder, anointing themselves as the most important ones on campus, which never sat well with their counterpart from medical school, who thought they were just as much important to society, if not even more important than their fellow future lawyers and judges.

Although law school students might have been enjoying their dominance off the pitch, it was a different story on the field. Within the past few years, the medical school football team had been enjoying such dominance against their nemesis from law school with a run of seven straight wins in all competitions this year; but with the arrival of the best striker on campus who happened to be on the law school team, this year was projected as the year the law school team would end their drought. Being six feet two inches and weighing around 195 pounds, the guy was so great in the air. His foot skills were out of this world with a speed only rivaled by the great Hussein Bolt. Only a bullet could stop this guy, and as far as anyone was concerned, the medical school team didn't have any, so if I was a betting man, I would have put up my neighbor's house betting on the law school team to take down the medical school.

I made it to the football field about half an hour past kickoff time. As I started walking through the crowd of about ten thousand students around the sandy field on a one-hundred-degree sun, I was greeted by a loud cheer from the students, chanting, "Petit Kabila," as I kept walking, blushing as not only did the cheer solidify my status as a campus star, but also at twelve years old, hearing a crowd of thousands shouting my name, or my nickname to be exact, made me feel extraterrestrial. As I was getting closer toward the sandy field, I found myself rushed in the air by a group of students and spectators and dropped right in front of the guest of honor, His Excellency, the secretary of youth/sports and leisure, Mr. Vincent Mutond Tshibal. Once I hit the ground, the students commanded me to let the guest of honor hear some excerpts from my impersonation of the president. One student whispered into my ear, "Petit Kabila, do what you do, my guy!"

Being in front of the young energetic government official, who appeared to be in his early thirties, with a group of bodyguards dressed in very intimidating military uniform, along with his entourage, which included the university president looking up, without fear, I started with an excerpt from the president's inaugural to one of his latest ones I had memorized. As I could see that I had him and everyone around him moved by my performance, it gave me even more strength and took the fear out of me and I kept going and going.

As soon as I was done, I was cheered by a loud ovation from the crowd, prompting His Excellency and his entourage to give me a big round of applause. After I shook hands with everyone around him, His Excellency gave me a big hug and asked for my name. "Timu," I said convincingly. He put his hands in his suit's pocket, took out a hundred-dollar bill and handed it to me, and said he wanted to see me at his office on Monday. I looked at the money. That was the very first time I ever touched an American dollar note, let alone a hundred-dollar one. The moment was surreal. I took the money, thanked him with every bone in my body, shaking like never before, and took off running as fast as I could.

A group of students who saw the money being handed down to me were rushing toward me, as were the group of students who lifted me and dropped me straight in front of His Excellency. All were rushing after me, hoping to get their cut out of that one hundred dollars as they felt entitled to it somehow. I ran my heart out of the football field straight to the nearby bus stop, avoiding all those students. Even Carl

Lewis at his prime would have had a really hard time catching up with me. Once I got to the bus stop, I hopped on the first bus on sight that I saw getting ready to leave. I took off to an unknown destination. Free from all those campus moochers who were all after my newly acquired wealth, I didn't have the slightest idea where to go next; but with a hundred-dollar bill in my pocket, in no way, shape, or form was I going to be short of ideas.

That night, I ended up hooking up with my old friends Rex and Patrick. We had the best time of our lives, thanks to a pocketful of cash. After having exchanged the hundred-dollar bill into the local currency, I had so much money. I could swear I was now among Forbes top 100 wealthiest men on the planet. At least that's how it felt at the moment. Rex, Patrick, and I had so much fun just like the old days with all that cash flowing out my pocket. We treated ourselves to about everything we ever wished for in life. It seems like no matter how much I was spending on toys, food, clothing, the money wasn't running out at all.

The following Monday, just like I was told, I made my way to the office of the secretary of sports. His office was located inside of the city's biggest football stadium, the Martyrs Stadium, which was once upon a time one of our country's jewels. Built by the Chinese, the stadium had a capacity of ninety thousand seats and was among the prettiest and biggest in Africa. Upon arrival at the stadium, I was denied entrance by heavily armed guards in military uniform. I was told by the guards that only people with appointment cards were allowed in; there was no exception. And since I didn't have an appointment card with me, I was not allowed in the building. I tried to convince them that the secretary was expecting me as he told me on Saturday to come see him at his office on Monday. All my efforts were met with skepticism and mostly sarcasm from the guards who perhaps were convinced that I was trying to put a fast one past them. They were unfazed.

As determined as I was to meet with His Excellency, I went out through the other side of the stadium. Using the skills I have learned throughout my days of sneaking into football matches by climbing the stadium wall, I did just that to enter the premises. While inside, I made my way to the secretary's office. As I got there, I was greeted by the receptionist, who asked me whom I wanted to see.

"I'm here to see His Excellency," I replied.

"Can I see your appointment card?" she asked.

"He didn't give me one. He just told me to come and see him at his office on Monday after meeting him over the weekend at the university campus."

She said, "As nice as that may sound, without any appointment card, I won't be able to do anything for you, little one."

The scenery inside the office looked very hostile. There were about ten people in the waiting room all dressed up in suits, very important people all waiting in line to meet up with the secretary of sports. One man who was sitting in the waiting room even shouted at me.

"Aren't you supposed to be in school instead of roaming around here, little boy!"

I just gave him that look as if to say, "You should be minding your own business!"

As I tried to have a sit back from the receptionist desk, one of the secretary's bodyguards who happened to pass by saw me and suddenly exclaimed, "Aren't you the little kid from last weekend at the Hill!"

I said, "Yes. I came to see him just like he told me to on Saturday, but they won't let me see him since I don't have an appointment card."

He went on and told the receptionist, "It is true. I was there. His Excellency wanted to see him."

But the receptionist replied by saying, "There is absolutely nothing I can do without an appointment card, and besides, he has a very busy day today. I don't think there is any room for him to be seen today."

The bodyguard took me by the arm, and we went outside. He told me to stand by the secretary's car, which was parked nearby outside the door. He said, "You can stay here by the car. When he comes out to get to the car at the end of his day, you can talk to him."

I was very happy. *At least I will get to see him today,* I thought to myself. I waited and waited for over six hours. I didn't want to move out of the spot, fearing I might miss him. I didn't even leave for a bathroom trip. I stood in one spot the entire time just like one of those Pontifical

Swiss Guards stationed at the Vatican's gate. Just when I started running out of patience, the man I have been waiting for over six hours came, making his way out of the door. Dressed up in a dark blue suit, a tie, with some brown dress shoes, he looked very sharp. The distance from the door to his car, a black Renault sedan with tinted windows, was about thirty feet, and he covered that distance as quick as a running back desperate for some rushing yard.

He came out of his office at around 7:00 p.m. It was already dark outside. As I saw him quickly approaching his car while his chauffeur held the door for him, I took a few steps forward toward him. With a very timid voice, I said, "Good evening, His Excellency!"

He smiled back at me, reached over his suit pocket, took out a fifty-dollar 50 bill, handed it to me, and said, "Come and see me tomorrow."

Everything happened so quickly in a matter of seconds. I didn't even get to have a word out of my mouth. Before I knew it, the car door was shut, and the car took off.

A man came outside right afterward, came to me, and introduced himself as Alfred. He claimed to have seen me at the ceremony last weekend while in company of the secretary of sports. He asked me if I needed a ride back home. I said, "Sure." I had him drop me off somewhere closer to my friend's house. Throughout the ride, I got to learn that Alfred, who was also in his midthirties, was His Excellency's cousin. He worked as an adviser within the cabinet. He asked me to come by and see him the following day. Alfred was very nice. I really enjoyed his company throughout the ride.

The following day, as I made my way back to the office, I asked for Mr. Alfred first. He came out and led me to his office, which was adjacent to that of his cousin, the secretary of sports. I spent most of the day hanging out with Alfred at his office, along with Alice, a very charming young lady, perhaps in her late twenties. She and Mr. Alfred shared the same office, but each had a personal desk. Throughout the day, I also got to meet the secretary of sport's younger brother, who happened to be His Excellency's vice chief of staff. He introduced himself as John. They all found me to be very adorable. I felt so comfortable around them.

Later on that day, I got to go into His Excellency's office, which to me looked very presidential. With all the decor and ventilation, one would think I was inside a private jet. After meeting with His Excellency, he asked me how I felt about performing in front of a crowd in the stadium during the festivity commemorating the one-year anniversary of the new regime. As a surprise to his uncle, the president, His Excellency was going to have me impersonate the president in front of him at the ceremony marking the one-year anniversary of his presidency, which was going to be held at the stadium.

"There will be a lot of very important guests from countries' presidents, government officials, ambassadors, to celebrities. They all will be there in attendance including the president himself, so don't you let me down," he said.

I was very happy to be a participant in such an event. I couldn't wait for the opportunity to showcase my skill in front of the president himself, the man I have been impersonating for quite some time now.

I came to develop a very close relationship with His Excellency and the members of his cabinet, which were mostly made up of his family members. I would stop by from time to time at his office, directly going straight to his office without having to go through all the trouble from the receptionist. His Excellency was very fond of me. On a few occasions, I got to go to his house and got to meet his wife, a very charming young lady in her mid or late twenties. His residence was in one of the city's most coveted neighborhoods, a very beautiful villa that was once the property of a former businessman who made millions of dollars under the former regime. With the arrival of the new regime, all the properties left behind by former regime officials or sympathizers were seized and overtaken by the new regime's elites and their families. That was the new regime definition of justice. The house was so beautiful, by far the most beautiful I have ever stepped my foot in with its amazing landscape, which included two swimming pools, a basketball court, and a playroom that included a ping-pong table, foosball table, and a pool table. That house was like a small paradise on earth.

I became very close with His Excellency. I even started calling him Tonton Vincent—*Tonton,* meaning "uncle"—instead of the usual His Excellency, which personified the closeness and fondness of our relationship. I also got to develop an even closer relationship with Alfred and Alice. I also started calling them Tonton Alfred and Tantine Alice—*Tantine,* meaning "auntie." Alice and Alfred gave me the impression of being a couple as they seemed to do everything together. If they weren't a couple, they sure were on their way of becoming one soon or later. Since His Excellency was always busy for most of the time, Tonton Alfred was in charge of making sure everything was going well with me. To be more exact, both Tonton Alfred and Tantine Alice took up my guardianship.

One day, Alice asked about my life—why I wasn't in school, where I lived, where my family was . . . I told her that I was an orphan, both of my parents have been dead, I was about three years old when that happened, I had run away from a home where I had been mistreated by my foster parents, and I have been living on the streets for the past two years. She was very touched by my story and became even more affectionate toward me ever since.

Around that time, I moved in with a group of high school seniors from a school I previously attended. For some reason, no matter which school I attended, I always was well known and well liked. I moved in with those seniors, helping them with small chores in exchange for room and board. In my country, high school students are required to pass a national test during their senior year to receive the state diploma, which was required for college acceptance. Failure to pass the test meant no acceptance to any of the country's colleges, so if you wanted to further your education beyond high school or just simply finish high school, you were required to take the national test. It was like the equivalent to the SAT. The national exam was given on a special day throughout the entire country. Fifty percent or above was required to pass the test. Failure to acquire such a mark meant that one had to retake the test the following year since the test was only given once a year.

The result of the national test was published the following day on a state-run newspaper, so to find out if you, a loved one, or any kin to you had passed the test, one had to purchase the newspaper and look for the name of the person, which was under whatever school he or she was attending while taking the test. Only the name of those who passed the exam and their test score were written on the newspaper. So if your name didn't get featured on the newspaper, it was bad news—you didn't pass the exam, which meant you were not getting your high school diploma and you had to retake the test the following year. While 50 percent meant that you passed the exam, 80 percent or higher guaranteed a scholarship to any of the state colleges or universities.

To guarantee their success on the state exam, it was a custom to a vast majority of the high school seniors in the city to get together in groups and rent a place for a few months where they would be doing some intensive studying and tutoring one another with limited amount of distraction. Doing so was a great step toward good preparation. A typical senior class of a certain school would break down into groups of four or six, rent a common place where they would all reside, and conduct study sessions after school until the day of the exam. Parents were mostly responsible for all the fees for room and board for their children.

Those places where high school senior gathered to prepare for their state exam were nicknamed Maquis. Although the sole purpose of the Maquis was to eliminate, if not limit, the amount of distractions that one may have to encounter while preparing for the state exam at home, for most high school students, male and female alike, being away from their parents, which also meant being out of reach of Mom and Dad's discipline, gave them a sense of freedom that most weren't exposed to, leading to bad behaviors. To most, being in the Maquis gave a carte blanche to do whatever they wished to do, whether illegal or immoral. For a place meant to be solely for studying purposes, the Maquis mostly turned out to be a place of intense debauchery rather than a place of intense studying. Instead of opening up more books and textbooks, males were opening up more zippers, while females were even busier opening up more blouses and legs.

Having your name featured on that newspaper the day the results were out meant a great deal for students, parents, family, and friends. It was about the same feeling as a father gets after hearing that his son has graduated from college, or the feeling a mother gets on her daughter's wedding day. The passing of the national exam was a very big deal in my country—that was, until corruption took over.

The national exam system became so corrupt that it lost its flare. School officials recurred to the bribing of exam inspectors to guarantee a better score for their school collectively. Those inspectors were expecting their bribe every time, so sometimes, those who didn't recur to bribing were penalized by being given failing grades no matter what. Now what was happening was a senior class of a certain school would either individually or collectively submit their bribe money to the school principal's office. The principal would take out a percentage of the bribe money and send the rest to the inspectors in return for a passing grade at the national exam. Since the most important criterion that parents judged schools to send their children to was based on the school's ability to graduate its senior class, having a senior class that had a higher graduation percentage even though acquired through bribe was still a great publicity stunt for the school.

The con of such a corrupt system was that most smart kids who couldn't afford bribe money were forcibly given a failed grade for not having paid their dues; while on the other hand, the dumber ones who did bribe were given a passing grade without merit, and it went on to show later on in college where more bribes were even required, and then after that in real life. You had people who were graduates based on their possession of a piece of paper stating so, which they have acquired not by merit but instead through bribe, while they have absolutely no notion of the subject in which they hold a master or a doctorate. You had doctors who didn't know much about medicine, and lawyers and judges who didn't quite have a grasp of the law. All this played a very important role in the destruction and demise of what was once a highly respected country that once had good working institution at its helm.

For a system that was so corrupt, it still didn't stop all the excitement from pouring down when a friend or a loved one managed to pass the national exam. For most students, they abstain from looking up their own name on the day of the exam since most thought doing so would jinx your chances of having your name featured on the paper. So to most, the news of having passed the exam was broken by family members and friends. As a celebration to mark the passing of the national exam, it was a tradition to pour flour on the person's head. So during the announcement of the result, anyone you saw with flour on their head had just passed the national exam. Having passed the national exam was a very big deal. It was celebrated with high loud cheer, the banging of doors, and very loud music. It was a party.

For those that weren't lucky enough and failed the test, it was a very sad day just reminiscent of losing a loved one or maybe even worse. Failing the test was pretty shameful. Not only will there be no fanfare, flour, or celebration, but also it meant that you were going to be repeating your senior once again and had to wait another year just to have another crack at the national exam the following year. What a big letdown for your family, and as for your family, what a shame to have raised a dummy that can't even get a 50 percent score on their exam—very painful.

For about three months, I lived in a Maquis with those high school seniors. They rented a few rooms out of an unfinished house. There was a certain businessman who was building a two-story house, but unfortunately, he ran out of money halfway through, putting all the construction work on hold for a long while. The businessman had hired a certain Gerome as a sentinel to stay on-site until the project was finished. Even after everything was put on hold, Gerome, a heavyset guy in his early fifties, with a wife and two small children, still lived in the small annex assigned to him and his family by the owner.

Behind the owner's back, Mr. Gerome went on and rented out rooms out of the unfinished two-story house to students who were looking for a place to set up their Maquis, making himself a good sum of money on the side at the owner's expense. Maquis around the city never last more than three months. It usually ends either the day of the exam or shortly after that. After the exam, everyone usually makes it back to their homes, respectively. In the same house, there was a group of female high school seniors who also rented one of the rooms across.

Living with all those seniors was very fun for me. I became very close with Lucky, one of the seniors there. Lucky was very fond of me. He would introduce me to everyone as his younger brother. He was my guardian at the Maquis. Lucky's mother, a single mother, was a businesswoman who owned a few clothing stores all around the city. She did a lot of traveling. With Lucky being her only child, she spoiled him with almost everything from nice car to the latest gadgets. Lucky had everything. Lucky was always well dressed and seemed to always have the ladies' attention. There was nothing he loved more than his music. He was one of the honorary members of a local band called Wenge el Paris and perhaps their biggest fan. Lucky went to all their rehearsals and never missed a concert no matter where it was.

There was also a girl named Ursile who lived across the street from the Maquis whom I became acquainted to. She was very shy, tall, with a lighter complexion, and very beautiful. Ursile had a thing for Lucky. One day, Lucky sent me on a mission. He asked me to deliver a message to her on his behalf. I did just as I was told by Lucky. Ursile was sixteen years old, a sophomore in high school, while Lucky just turned nineteen.

Ursile wasn't your typical sixteen-year-old. With a body of someone in her twenties, she had a shape of a Playboy model. She was taller than your average teenager, perhaps five feet ten inches. Her complexion was that of a mixed girl. She had a very lighter complexion. In other words, she was very beautiful and perhaps the most beautiful girl in the neighborhood. What also made her very attractive to anyone around was the fact that unlike any other teenage girl around, she rarely came outside; but when she did, whether it was on her way back from school or for a little walk around the neighborhood, it seems like that moment was everyone's favorite moment. Her walk was as majestic as a princess, and her vibe was as blossoming as a waterfall.

Ursile's family was very wealthy. Her father was a businessman who bought and sold diamonds. She was the eldest of seven kids. Most of all, she was her father's sweetheart. Her family was very strict. They weren't allowed to have any interaction with anyone around. She wasn't even permitted to speak to anyone, let alone another boy.

The very first day she encountered Lucky, it was love at first sight. She and Lucky got to develop a crush on one another. It was only a matter of time until those two began to see each other. Ursile would sneak out to come see Lucky. She would bring him hot cooked meals from the house, which were enjoyed by all of us. The two had sex on numeral occasions. Lucky even told me that he took her virginity the first time they had sex. *Whatever that meant,* I thought.

As Lucky's messenger, I got to gain access to Ursile's house whenever I wanted to. Mostly it was to deliver a message from Lucky. I befriended everyone in her family. Everyone pretty much liked me. At thirteen, to them, I was just this little sweet, adorable kid who meant no harm.

Being Lucky's little brother, as she was told, Ursile took it upon herself to set me up with one of her younger sisters, Evelyn, who was about my age. She did about everything in setting us up. Even though Evelyn seemed to like me, I really wasn't that interested in her; something about Evelyn's height turned me off. She was very tall. I never was attracted to girls my age who were taller than me; it made me feel small literally. Although Evelyn did like me a lot, I never really gave her the time or acknowledgment. She would often shower me with gifts. She gave me watches and necklaces, and she even gave me some of her brother's clothes. Even after all the trouble she went through to get me to like her, I still found ways to avoid her.

Sometime shortly before the national exam, Ursile ended up getting pregnant by Lucky. Since having a kid at sixteen years old by someone who was unknown to her family meant death, if not something closer in that line, with the help of Lucky's mom, Ursile ended up paying for an abortion before anyone in her family found out.

May 17, 1998, was a very sunny day. Birds were chirping as usual. It wasn't an ordinary day. It was the new regime's one-year anniversary, and there was to be a very big ceremony at the country's biggest football stadium. Upon my arrival at the office of the secretary of sports at around 10:00 a.m., I couldn't help but notice the heavily guarded premises. There were military tanks all around the stadium along with some of the most private and well-trained heavily armed military personnel, Special Forces from the Republican guards who delivered feared just by their posture; you can easily see that they meant business.

As I made my way through the heavily guarded office of the secretary of sports, I was welcomed in by Tonton Alfred, who was impatiently waiting outside for my arrival. I was dressed in an all-gray safari suit, which was bought for me by Tantine Alice and was meant to look identical as the one the president himself has been wearing. The president never wore anything but safari suit. He was also known as the safari man, and since I was going to perform his speeches on that day in front of him, Tonton Vincent though it was a good idea to be dressed as the president himself.

There was a big pandemonium at the lobby of the office of the secretary of sports. Security agents from both the Marble Palace, which is the equivalent of the White House, and the cabinet of the secretary of sports, along with various guests, all crumbled in respectively in the lobby. As the day went by, we encountered a big setback along the way. There was a big mix-up in the organization of the ceremony. As we sat in the lobby getting ready to enter the VIP lounge, shortly before the president's speech, there were words being passed around stating that order had been given by the higher hierarchy, perhaps coming from the secret service or the Marble Palace.

There was a security breach in the stadium, and for security reasons, no one was to enter or exit the VIP lounge, not until the president has made his exit from the stadium. There were armed security agents from the Republican guards to ensure that everyone was following those orders. As the president was getting ready to take the stage and address the nation and everyone in attendance at the stadium, any movement from the secretary's office to the stadium's VIP lounge where the president, with all his guests, was located was prohibited, so everything was quarantined. No one from the office could access the VIP lounge, and no one from the VIP lounge could make his way back to the office for any reason, at least not until after the president has left the stadium.

Tonton Alfred, along with some personnel from the secretary's cabinet, and I were stuck on one side of the stadium, being denied entrance to the VIP lounge to join Tonton Vincent, who was on the other side with the president and all his important guests. At that very moment, the Marble Palace was in control of everything from security to the event timeline, overriding everything that the sports cabinet had previously planned. Being stuck on the other side of the VIP lounge where the president was and seeing that everything was now running through the Marble Palace scheduling just like that, I saw my chances of performing in front of the president fade away. When we were denied access to the VIP lounge, that's when I realized my dream fading away right in my face. We had to listen to the president's one-hour-and-a-half speech from the lobby, and right after the president was done, he and his entourage took off immediately.

Few government officials and other guests hung around the lobby for some cocktails. I briefly saw the president exiting from the back door while surrounded by a group of heavily armed bodyguards. I was so disappointed. I felt so let down. There was no one to blame. I couldn't help but think how I came so close just to have such opportunity slip away. I did everything I could. I prepared myself to perfection for that very day. For whatever reason, as much as I was trying my very best to put the blame on someone, anyone, no one was at fault, not Tonton Alfred, not His Excellency, not even myself. I was there at the right place, at the right time, only to be denied the chance of a lifetime by fate.

I was inconsolable, not even the most comfortable words of love and wisdom by Alice and Tonton Alfred could dry up my tears. At around 6:30 p.m., I was called into His Excellency's office. After seeing how let down I was, he held me in his harms and said how sorry he was for what had happened today. He promised me that he would do whatever it takes to make sure I meet the president sometime in the near future. He reached out his pocket and handed me a fifty-dollar bill and ordered his chauffeur to drive me home that night.

The ride home was majestic. That was the very first time I had ever been in such a luxurious car. From its ventilation system to its soundless motion, with leather seats that felt like a bed, the car felt like a private jet. I felt like I was on top of the world. Every government official was driving that same model car, same color, with tinted windows as usual.

Something about being inside that car made me immune to any sadness or sorrow. I forgot everything that had happened that day. I did a total 180. I went from being the saddest person on earth to feeling like the most invincible person on the universe. How I wish the ride back was more like twenty-four hours rather than a forty-five-minute one.

Instead of having the chauffeur drop me off in front of the Maquis door where I had been staying, I had him drop me off in front of the neighborhood flea market to have everyone and their families see me getting out the government official's car. I wanted my moment of fame to be seen by the world, and what better place to be seen by as many people one can if not the neighborhood flea market, which operated twenty-four hours a day. When I got out of the car after the chauffeur had opened the door, the two to three steps taken getting out the car were done in a very slow motion, putting one foot at a time from the car to the ground outside. It felt like I was making an entrance on the red carpet as a nominee for multiple Oscars. Even Jesus's triumphal entry into Jerusalem, which is now celebrated on Palm Sunday, was second to mine as I was greeted by cheers from vendors and everyone that was around.

After the car had left, I was the topic of the entire market. Just like that, rumors were spreading from left to right, with some stating I was personally driven back by the president himself, while others could have sworn having seen a motorcade. Everyone and their mamas had their own version of the story, but above all, I came out as the big benefactor of all those rumors. With that, I became the most popular kid in the neighborhood.

About a week later, the students took their national exam. Lucky was among those who passed the exam, and three days later, the Maquis was disbanded. Everyone went back home. I still managed to stay in the neighborhood. I would sometime sneak back in that house very late at night where the Maquis was, which was now vacant after all the tenants had left after taking the national exam. I would sleep on the floor on top of cardboards very late at night without being spotted by Mr. Gerome, the heavyset guy who rented the rooms of the unfinished house to the students. He lived in one of the annexes with his wife and two young children.

During my time living at the Maquis, I came into contact with Rebecca, a girl who lived next door; a concrete wall separated the two houses. The Maquis being a two-story house, I saw Rebecca for the first time while I was in one of the rooms looking down her house. From the room, I could see her sitting in her backyard with her little sister. From where I was, I gently introduced myself. After she had introduced herself to me, I was once again mesmerized by her beauty. I fell in love with her the moment I saw her. To me, she was the perfect girl, from her very long curly hair to her perfect skin complexion, which reminded me of those girls in those beautiful islands such as Martinique, Cuba, Reunion, just to name a few. She had a voice of an angel accompanied by a smile that was as precious as the most expensive diamond on earth. She was flawless, a very well-crafted creature. Ever since I met her, I couldn't wait for the very next moment I would get the chance to see her, let alone talk to her.

Rebecca was in sixth grade in one of the most accredited private schools in town. She was born of a white father and a black mother. She lived with her aunt and grandmother. Rumors around the neighborhood had it that her mother, a very beautiful lady who lived a very fast life, has been working as an escort, just a fancy word for prostitute, to the wealthier ones. During her line of work, she came in contact with a Portuguese guy whom she ended up getting pregnant by. She was later paid off by the guy to have an abortion, but instead, she decided against it. She never saw the guy ever since, and the poor little girl who turned out to be one of the most beautiful girls was Rebecca.

Two years later, she got pregnant once again, this time by one of her former clients, a former government official who was a married man once again and didn't want to jeopardize his marriage or career by being known to have a sexual relationship with an escort, let alone have a baby by her. Once again, she was paid, this time not to have an abortion but to keep quiet about the whole ordeal. Her second child was also a girl whom she named Ardiette. She left the guardianship of her two children to her mother, who took great care of the girls. She would come visit them once a month and give her mother money for the girls. She took great care of the girls financially; as to physically or emotionally, that was a different story as she fancied her way of life better than being the much-needed mother to those little princesses.

Although Rebecca played really hard to get, from time to time, she did show some sparks of interest in me. I could sense from her demeanor toward me that I was a very good candidate to gain her heart. For whatever reason, every conversation we had always turned into an argument. We never did agree on anything, and to make matters worse, her little sister Ardiette hated my guts, and I couldn't stand her either. But it was very hard getting to Rebecca without going through Ardiette, who was the high-spoken one, while Rebecca was the shy type, and 99 percent of the time, they were inseparable.

I got to learn that I wasn't the only one after Rebecca. There was a kid named Miguel who lived in the same street but only a couple of houses down. Just like Rebecca, Miguel was of a mixed race. To everyone around, he was very handsome. He was the dream of every girl from the neighborhood, even Rebecca. Rumors even had it that Rebecca was Miguel's girlfriend. If Rebecca was the ultimate prize in this competition between Miguel and me, as everyone had it around, I was no match for Miguel. Miguel had everything in his advantage. He was tall, handsome, and very wealthy, and also he was the sole leader of the neighborhood. As for me, I was just your average Joe, the new boy in the block whom nobody seemed to know much about except for the fact that I was now occasionally on TV as the kid who did mimic the president. Just to add to my very boring credentials, I was also known to be a very smart kid for my age. My only weapon and most effective weapon was that even though I was nothing but a vagabond who barely had anything to show for, I was a very charming little poet. I had it in me. Romance was in my blood. I always knew what to say to take a girl's breath away.

At first, with Rebecca, it seemed like I was hitting a brick wall; but as time went by, I started gaining more ground with my soft-spoken words in which I had glorified everything about her from her smile, her walk, to the way she spoke and dressed. Even her shyness was magnified as being supernatural. When it came to Rebecca, I always went all out. Having an opponent of Miguel's caliber, whose dice were cast on his favor, was very hard, but to overcome both Miguel and Ardiette, that alone made it mission impossible for me. But when it comes to facing and overcoming challenges, I was the David to their Goliath.

Ten-year-old Ardiette was, by far, the biggest obstacle I faced on daily basis. She was a mean, self-centered, very conniving little creature. Being the youngest one, Ardiette was very spoiled by her grandmother. She was the center of attention in that household. Unlike her elder sister Rebecca, who was a shy like person, Ardiette was very outspoken. The way she ran her big sister, one would have thought that it was she who was the bigger sister. She lived in a world where pretty much everything had to go her way or she would make sure to bring hell upon anything or anyone that dare challenge her totalitarian mind-set. Ardiette and I never got along from the start. She hated my guts as I wouldn't bow down to her majesty, yet prompting a bigger setback on my quest to gain Rebecca's heart. She was very influential to her really shy sister. Another thing was that Ardiette was openly with Team Miguel, and she never failed to remind me of it.

The quest for Rebecca's heart between Miguel and me turned out to become a thing for the whole neighborhood, splitting up the neighborhood in two separate camps. There was on one hand Team Miguel, the most influential and more active, and Team Rossy on the other hand. Team Miguel, which enjoyed all the publicity and was way more popular among the neighborhood girls, had about every neighborhood kids in it except the two that were on my team. Teddy and Bobo were the only two kids on my team. Teddy and I were best friends, while Bobo was a good friend of ours.

Teddy and I were the same age. We became very good friends the moment we first met. Teddy lived with his mother and his eighteen-year-old sister Mireille. Teddy and I did everything together. We shared everything together from food to anything you could think of. His mother was a widow. Teddy's father died from natural cause back when he was five years old. Teddy's mother raised her two children single-handedly since by selling charcoal from her house. His mother wasn't too fond of our friendship. She never thought much highly of me, and the fact that I wasn't in school made matters even worse through her eyes. In so many ways, you could say she was against me being friends with her son, but that didn't keep Teddy and me from becoming the best of friends.

His elder sister Mireille, on the other hand, who was eighteen at the time and senior in high school, was very fond of me. Mireille was very tall, around five feet nine inches. She had some pretty long legs and long hair. I had a secret crush on her. We always enjoyed roasting and teasing one another on a regular basis.

Teddy lived four houses down from the Maquis, while Bobo lived a few blocks down the street. Teddy and I did everything together and shared about everything. Teddy's house was right across from Miguel's house. For whatever reason, Teddy never got to befriend Miguel. In fact, he disliked him so much even way before I came in the picture. With all odds pretty much against me, from Miguel's splashing of gifts to Rebecca every moment he saw her to Ardiette's hatred toward me, I have to admit that aside from getting Rebecca to give me a picture of her, which I cherished like treasure, I never did get to win over Rebecca. Even after emptying my romance clips, I still couldn't reach her heart. I gave it everything I had and still failed short. All that thanks to Miguel, who seemed to have won her over.

Losing her to Miguel was a very hard pill I had to swallow, but with Teddy on my side, reminding me every second that she wasn't worth all the trouble, it put me a little at ease. On the other side, I felt responsible as the captain of ship Timu to have failed my crew, but even with all that, this was about the only time in my life that failure didn't leave a bitter taste in its path. After giving it your all, if at the end your goal still isn't achieved, if after the biggest awakening, your dream still failed to come true, I strongly believe that within you, a hero is unleashed because in every situation encountered, big or small, only heroes give it their all no matter what. I felt a sense of great pride for challenging against all the odds. I had to give it to Miguel. He had it all going for him. He was biracial, which in my country was pretty much the equivalent of being white, and being white was a symbol of superiority. Aside from that, Miguel was handsome and most of all very arrogant and full of himself; being from a wealthy family, that came to no one's surprise.

After missing out on performing in front of the president, I still kept my hopes up. I still frequently stopped by His Excellency's office to hang out with Tonton Alfred and Tantine Alice. A few months later, His Excellency had me work on yet another project. This time, he had me on national TV reading some script his office had put together to celebrate the country's Youth Day. There I was on national TV dressed like the president reading a script while impersonating the president. I made more appearances on few other TV stations on numerous occasions, boosting my popularity across the city. I started getting offers from some show producers to appear on their shows. At thirteen, I enjoyed a status of a celebrity. I got to meet a lot of important people within the government, but my ultimate goal was to meet the president himself, and yet there was nothing pointing toward that realization.

On August 2, 1998, a war broke out. The former allies of the new regime, Rwanda and Uganda, decided to overthrow the person they once put in power after the latter decided to renege on a previously made deal that saw him at the helm of the country. The deal was that the Congolese president, Laurent Desire Kabila, had to give up some of the land in the eastern part of the country that was rich in strategic mineral such as coltan, a very strategic mineral very important in the production of mobile phones and all other electronic devices such as Xbox, PS4, Nintendo, etc. As part of the deal, Kabila had to give up that part of the country to be exploited by both Rwanda and Uganda through western multinational companies that helped fund the war that saw Kabila and his allies overthrow the former Mobutu regime.

On August 2, Rwandese and Ugandan troops crossed the border and invaded the long-coveted eastern part of the Congo in violation of international law prohibiting the invasion of a sovereign country unilaterally. After consolidating their foothold in the east, hundreds of Rwandese troops who were mostly made up of Tutsi ethnic group under the personal command of Col. James Kabarebe, with heavy artillery, took off for Kitona, an airbase about two hundred miles away from the capital city, Kinshasa. The capture of the airbase provided the Rwandese insurgents with more logistic supplies and firepower.

About a few days later, they captured the Inga hydroelectric dams, which is the country's number-one power and water provider. Rwandese troops, following orders from Paul Kagame, their president, who personally ordered the dam to be shut down in its entirety, did just that, cutting power and water supplies to about 70 percent of the country including the capital city, Kinshasa. Speaking of crime against humanity, with no means to generate power and lack of water, hospitals and clinics were unable to function properly, leaving hundreds of dead all across the region, mostly women, children, and elderly people. Kinshasa, a city of around eight million people, was left in the dark and without potable water over a two-week period. About three weeks later, the fight made its way to the capital city, Kinshasa.

The fight that lasted four days began as the Rwandese insurgents surrounded the city and infiltrated key areas within the city. Thanks to the great help of his new allies, Angola, Zimbabwe, and Namibia, the Kabila regime was able to foil a very ambitious, better yet very well-calculated plan from the aggressor of the Congolese people who came within reach of overthrowing his regime. The battle between Rwandese insurgents and government forces in the capital city, Kinshasa, ended after a brutal offensive led by five battalions of Angolan troops supported by tanks and aircraft was able to crush the insurgency, which was a few kilometers away from capturing the city's international airport and a nearby army base of Kibomango.

The Tutsi-led uprising, very cruel from its nature, left a very bitter taste among the Congolese people. With that came a vigilante hunt for any Tutsi or their collaborators. Shortly after the Rwandese insurgency was crushed, in Kinshasa, anyone who was either of Tutsi descent, even worse looked like a Tutsi, was lynched or burned alive on the street. The hatred of the Congolese people toward Paul Kagame and his Tutsi-led militants took off a different turn. It was now starting to affect poor innocent Rwandese that weren't even affiliated to the warmonger regime of Kigali. If you were a Tutsi living in Kinshasa, whether you were affiliated with Paul Kagame's regime, your life was now in great danger.

The minority ethnic Tutsi of Rwanda emerged as the most powerful in Rwanda postgenocide after the ascendance of Paul Kagame and his Tutsi-led click to power. Giving the international community inability or, just to be frank, its unwillingness to act to prevent the genocide that occurred in 1994 between Rwandan two ethnic groups, the Hutu, who were the country's majority ethnicity with about 85 percent of the country's population. The conflict that led to the genocide in Rwanda was pretty much an escalation of the bitterness that already coexisted dating back to postcolonization.

Just like the Congo, Rwanda was colonized by the kingdom of Belgium and gained its independence from it in 1962. During the colonization, the colonial power opted to work closely with the minority ethnic Tutsi while discarding the majority Hutu, thus leaving the latter isolated and rejected. The Belgians found the Tutsi to be smarter and sharper than their fellow countrymen. The minority Tutsi, which only represented about 14 percent of the population, were favored and put in key administrative position. During colonial rule, the majority Hutu were omitted from taking any part in the governance of their own country.

The conflict between the Tutsis and Hutus resemble that of the Palestinians and the Jews. The minority Tutsi, whose ethnicity are Nilotic, derived from the areas right along the Nile River, were nomadic shepherds who found their way from the northeastern part of Africa, pretty much following the path of the Nile River, eventually settling down in the central part of East Africa, with Rwanda being the place of most of their concentration. As they settled down in Rwanda, they were welcomed and given shelter by the local inhabitants of the land the Hutus.

All this occurred around the late 1800s and early 1900s. The friction between the two tribes who cohabited peacefully among each other didn't occur until Rwanda fell under colonial rule. The colonial power's policy that sought to elevate one tribe while completely dismissing the other was the leading cause of the conflict between the Tutsi and the

Hutu. Under colonial rule, the Tutsi enjoyed affirmatively an upper hand socially, politically, and mostly economically, while the majority Hutus were subject to a more deplorable condition, pretty much living as slave in their own country.

It wasn't until the '60s, after Belgium, along with all the other European colonial power, was pretty much forced to abandon colonialism in Africa, that Rwanda gained its independence. After Belgium left, the Hutu quickly stripped the Tutsi of all their power and took control of the country. Fearing reprisal, a massive exodus of Tutsi took place, with most opting to settle to neighboring countries. While most chose the eastern part of the Congo as their ideal place of settlement, others such as the group of Paul Kagame and his militants ended up in Uganda, where they would form a rebellion, vowing to come back and take over Rwanda once again.

Call him what you want, but Paul Kagame was indeed a visionary. For a man who is labeled by many as being the Adolf Hitler of this generation, he sure drew his inspiration from Hitler. Just like Hitler, Paul Kagame brainwashed his fellow Tutsi followers, making them see their ethnicity as being a superior one compared to all the others, and his vision was to establish a Tutsi-led empire all over Central Africa. About two decades later, he would have his dream come true, although partially, after unleashing the genocide that killed about nine hundred thousand people, mostly women and children, in Rwanda. Kagame did a great job selling himself and his Tutsi-led click as victims of the genocide to the world, while, in fact, it was he and his warmonger click who triggered the genocide by downing the plane that was carrying the Hutu president. That assassination is what led to the genocide; nothing else as Mr. Kagame and his blood-thirsty acolytes would try to have you think otherwise.

The four-week war had a big toll on me. I was still living on the streets, but now things were much more different than ever. Sure, the country had been through wartime before. Unlike every previous time, war never made its way into the capital city, Kinshasa. Every previous war always finds a political solution before reaching Kinshasa, but this time was different. The Rwandese insurgency was able to inflict hardship in the city by cutting off all water and power supplies for two long weeks. It was the worst thing the city had ever witnessed. There was shortage in everything, and the price of goods were sky high. A loaf of bread would cost about a dollar in the morning and jump up to three dollars by noon and ended up costing five dollars by sundown; it was unbelievable.

The insurgency made life very unbearable for the common person. Most families that survived off two meals a day were forced to make do with only one meal a day, and those who survived on one meal a day were now forced to pick and choose who of the family members was more deserving of a meal than the others as there was very little to no food to put on the table. A good example was a family of six, two parents, two small children, and two teenagers, was forced to only feed the two small children and have the rest of the family starve. That's how worse things have gotten.

During that time, I was lucky enough to have met two great young men. They were the best of friends; one was named Roger, and the other Olivier, who went by the nickname of Commandant. I met them about a few weeks before the war broke out. I told them a little bit about myself. By this time around, instead of telling people I was a runaway, I opted for a less-threatening label—an orphan.

The city was pretty much flooded with street kids. Children as young as eight years old roamed the city's periphery, aiming for survival. The reason behind such a high percentage of abandoned children was a combination of the lack of government assistance and a higher poverty rate for the majority. There was a small minority among those abandoned children who were orphans who didn't have anywhere to call home. Others were victims of sexual or physical abuse, sometimes both, while others were just plain runaways enjoying total freedom away from home. Being labeled a runaway or an abandoned child had a very bad connotation. It was seen as a very negative thing no matter what, and there was a good reason for that since about 99.9 percent of runaways and abandoned kids were either robbers, burglars, thieves, or gangbangers, sometimes even all in one. And now that it was being associated with witchcraft, it was now definitely bad news to be labeled as such.

Even I knew that at twelve, instead of telling everyone who seemed to care or at least pretended to care that I was indeed a runaway, to preserve my integrity, I told people I was an orphan who had lost both my parents when a boat capsized, killing all on board including my beloved parents. I would tell people that I have almost no recollection of either of my parents. As falsified as that story was, no one ever questioned me on its authenticity as it sounded believable to everyone who was hearing it. As a self-labeled orphan, I never got to experience any skepticism from any of my audience; if anything, I got more affection or pretense of affection in return.

One other major reason why I opted against labeling myself as a runaway was the fact that most, if not all, runaways were associated with sorcery or witchcraft. Being labeled a wizard made you automatically a "persona non grata," something I couldn't afford to be. In my city, there was nothing worse than being labeled a wizard. One would welcome being labeled a rapist or a cannibal rather to be called a wizard. If you wanted to bring damage to your worst enemy, all you had to do was to accuse them of being wizard.

Roger and Commandant grew up together in the eastern part of the country. They were in their early twenties. Their family relocated in the capital city following the arrival of the new regime. Roger's and Commandant's fathers were important figures in the new government. During the insurgency, I got to meet Commandant's aunt, who was married to a wealthy man. She was so nice to me. She had a son who was my age. We became friends. After learning of my situation from her nephew, she felt very bad for me. She told me she wanted me to come every day and share a meal with them. She gave me some of her son's clothes to wear. I was in heaven. While the majority of people were going without food, I had plenty to eat every day, but I was still homeless.

A few weeks after the defeat of the Rwandese insurgency, the Congolese president made a big shuffle in all the country's institutions, from his own security personnel to government officials. A lot of figures were either moved around, let go, or in some cases made to disappear from the face of the earth. Tonton Vincent was now promoted to secretary general of the ruling party AFDL, a position formerly held by Deogratias Bugera, of Rwanda, who fled the country on the eve of the failed Rwandan insurgency. Secretary general of AFDL was the equivalent to being the U.S. secretary of state. Within the country's hierarchy, Tonton Vincent became the third most powerful man in the country right after a certain Abdoulayi Yerodia Ndombasi, the president's chief of staff who was known to be the brains of the new regime at that moment and, of course, the president himself.

Tonton Vincent became a very busy man with very important decisions to make on a daily basis. It became impossible for me to see him as I have been more accustomed to at his previous position of secretary of youth and sports. I was now limited to only seeing Tonton Alfred and Alice. Every time I made my way to his new office, which was now in a more secluded part and the most fortified area of the city, he was either in a meeting, leaving to go to a meeting, or out of town on a mission. I did manage to see him on one occasion, which to me felt like pretty much winning the jackpot. At this stage, he was now in a way better position to help me meet the president since he was now in contact with the president on a daily basis as the country's third in command. At the same time, having a close friend who was now the country's third in command felt like a very big victory for me.

With him there, I thought it was just a matter of time before my dream of meeting the president came true with perhaps a chance of a way better future. To my big disappointment, as time went by, it became even more difficult for me to make it through the office as everyone around seemed to become busier than ever. I was getting more and more frustrated with myself as my living condition was still not improving. I was still homeless. I slowly began to wonder if fate had anything good stored for me in its bag full of wonders.

Instead of waiting for my dream to come knocking on my door, I took it upon myself to go find it instead. One morning, I decided to go to the Nation's Palace, the building that was once home to the nation's Senate but now was serving as the president's office. I went through the heavily fortified building, which was guarded by a battalion of elite Republican guards. It was a hassle making it through all those checkpoints. There were so many I even lost count. With a little bit of luck and savviness, I did manage to get through and make it to the side building where the receptionist was located. I timidly approached the receptionist, a young lady in her late twenties or early thirties, and politely asked to fill out a visit request sheet to have an appointment with the president. She asked me to state the reason of my visit with the president.

"He is my idol," I said. "I have been memorizing all his speeches and interviews from the first one to the very latest one. I breathe Kabila. I share the same vision of a prosperous and sovereign Congolese nation, a Congo that would once become the center of a highly developed Africa. I wanted to be his student just like he was one of Lumumba's students," I told her.

She wasn't too impressed with my presentation and respectfully denied my request, stating that I didn't have a good-enough reason to have a visit with the president. "Go back to school and don't you ever come here to waste my time ever again," she said, sounding as if I just handed her some counterfeit money.

I stood there for a minute numb as if I just got hit with a dose of horse tranquilizer. It took me a while to process her every word. After having recovered from my disappointment, I gathered myself and left the place.

On my way out, I made a stop at one of the military barracks that was on the outskirts of the building overlooking the river. There were about eight soldiers sitting around next to a military tent. Two were playing checkers, while four others were watching, and the remaining were cooking what seemed to be the biggest meal I had ever seen put together. There were two barrels put on fire. One barrel had fish in it, which was being cooked in the most unorthodox way you could possibly imagine. The fish were taken almost raw, barely washed, and dumped into the barrel, which already had water, tomato sauce, onions, peppers, and any other spice you could think of.

The other barrel had the traditional Fufu being cooked in it. Fufu is a course made from mixing boiling water, steering it with cornmeal, turning into a solid-like substance softer than corn bread but much harder than a mashed potato. Fufu is tasteless. You can't eat Fufu by itself. It has to be eaten with a side dish such as fish, meat, vegetable, or stew. The texture of Fufu is a very solid; it's between corn bread and mashed potato.

I made my way straight to the checkerboard where the other guards were. I asked to play a game. At first, they all looked at me with a very dismal tone as if to remind me that I was nothing but a little kid who wouldn't survive a match in a grown men's game. After pointing out a costly mistake made by one of the players, they realized that only someone who actually knew a thing or two about the game could point out such a thing. I was finally allowed to play. To everyone's surprise, after playing about fifteen games and not losing a single one, at thirteen, I was an elite checkers player.

In the city, checkers was also known as the unemployed's favorite hobby. I guess there was no irony in the fact that I was good in checkers given that I had no job and wasn't in school. Being homeless, a wanderer, also helped in making me a good checkers player as checkers was the number-one board game in the city. You could find people playing checkers in almost every street corner around the city.

After beating everyone, not only did I earn the title of champs but I also made me a lot friends after beating the so-called master, another guard who was sleeping inside the tent at the time. They had to go wake him up, and just like the others, I made a fool out of him by teaching him a lesson or two. After dethroning the king, I was crowned Gordian III, the youngest roman emperor at thirteen. My victory earned me a dinner with the lads. They actually welcomed me as one of their own and told me I could come every day and share a meal with them and pretty much hang out with them. They were pretty cool. All in their teens, with the oldest of the group being at most nineteen years old, they were all part of the child soldiers crew who were once recruited by the former rebels.

What started out as a bad day from being denied a visit with the president ended up as a good day after having made so many new friends. Most importantly, my belly was full to the maximum. No one in the world could eat to the fullest as the men in uniform. There was plenty of food, and I sure did take advantage of that. I went back there on a few more occasions, every time I got hungry. I enjoyed their company. They were like the coolest bigger brothers ever. They were from way out of the country. They barely spoke the local language, Lingala. They spoke Swahili, which I understood very well but had trouble speaking back to them. I tried my very best to teach them Lingala, which wasn't so hard. They seemed more interested in learning nasty words and pickup lines for girls than anything else.

Even after encountering so many setbacks in my quest to meet up with the president, which to me was becoming more than an illusion, a fairy tale, than an actual dream, I still didn't give up. As a matter of fact, I even put my foot on the accelerator and went on as far as going to the president's residence, the Marble Palace, trying to see if I could get to see him there. I couldn't make it past the heavily fortified Marble Palace's gates as only people who are expected by the president were allowed to reach past the gate. Being anywhere near the gate without having any concrete motive could have gotten me in serious trouble.

I did manage to make it to the building next door, which housed the office of the head of the Republican guards, Col. Eddy Kapend. Although I never got to meet Eddy Kapend personally, I did manage to meet up with one of his staff members, a certain lieutenant who, after seeing me roaming around the building, had stopped me to ask me if he could help me with anything. I told him I wanted to see the president.

"What for?" he asked with a very serious tone of voice. I told him all about me, and he was like, "Yeah, you are the little kid who impersonates the president on TV. I have seen you on TV before. I am a very big fan," he said. "Can you let me hear some excerpts from your impersonation?" he asked.

As I started going at it, a small crowd quickly formed around me who were very amazed by what they were hearing. After I was finished, he took me into his office and told me he will let his boss, Col. Eddy

Kapend, know that I wanted to see the president, and maybe the colonel could set me up to meet with the president. He told me to come back and see him around the same time next week. I was so excited. This meant I was now closer to seeing my dream come true. I made my way back up there the following week to meet up with the lieutenant. Unfortunately, he wasn't there. It wasn't until I had made about three more trips there that I finally caught up with him, which was about a month later.

Something felt out of place as he seemed less anxious to see me. Just in a matter of moment, all my excitement and high hopes were melting as fast as ice cube in a river. When I got into his office, he seemed very uncomfortable and uneasy as if he was bothered by something. He quickly broke the news to me by telling me that his boss, Col. Eddy Kapend, wasn't too fond of me and that he didn't want me anywhere near the president but didn't elaborate the reason behind his cruel decision.

To me, it was yet another blow to add in my collection of disappointment. Unlike the other failed attempts, this one sort of weighed a little heavier on me as it pretty much kept the door shut for me. I was now wondering if there really was a God, and if there really was one, why was he not on my side? The lieutenant might have felt the effect of his words on me as my head was almost hanging as low as my knees and my eyes were as red as Santa Claus's suit. He told me I was more than welcome to come by and visit him anytime, and if I needed anything, he would be more than welcome to do whatever he can to help.

After having received so many blows in my quest, I was still determined to achieve my goal. All those setbacks might have knocked me down on the ground, but knowing that I was still breathing and alive after suffering from those powerful blows, I still found in me the zeal to still fight no matter what. I was engaged to my struggle and married to my dream. Until death brings us apart, I vowed not to lie down.

I had a few more disappointing moments. I was turned down twice afterward. Once was by one of the most prominent producers in the country by the name of Mr. Suzy Kaseya. Suzy was a very successful music producer and well known throughout the whole country. He was the author of so many successful projects. His most recent masterpiece included the song "Franc Congolais" or "Congolese Franc," a patriotic song dedicated to the newly introduced national currency, the Congolese franc. He had various artists, all from the best the country could offer, participating in the making of the song. The song, which was likened to prominent songs such as the "We Are the World," sang by Michael Jackson and friends from star power standpoint, was a major hit. I heard from a very reliable source that Suzy was working on another project of that caliber, this time funded by the president himself. The project was a new patriotic song to mobilize the nation behind the government during the time of war.

I did my research and found out about Suzy's residence. After going back and forth trying to meet up with Suzy at his home, I presented myself to Suzy, asking him if he could include me as the voice of the president on his upcoming project, maybe having me read a script impersonating the president somewhere in the song. Well, for whatever reason, Suzy didn't think it was a good idea. Not only did he turn me down but also he basically shut me down. Although, to be honest, I was so disappointed and very angry at Suzy for not wanting to give me a chance, I was still thankful to have had a half-an-hour meeting face-to-face with one of the biggest names in Congolese music industry. Besides, he did promise he would keep me in mind if he ever needed me for any of his other projects. I wasn't going to hold my breath, I thought.

On another occasion, I went to a local TV station to see if I could get some airtime. I was turned down by the station executive director, Mr. Kibambi Shintwa, then an RFI correspondent and one of the leading voices of the Congolese press. He was like the Congolese Anderson Cooper who told me that he wasn't that impressed by my performance. He didn't think I sounded quite like the president himself, and that contrast to the president's voice, which is much deeper, mine was much softer. I even tried to impress him by rehearsing a script from one of the interviews he had with the president. He still wasn't that impressed. He told me to come back when my voice gets a little deeper. Maybe then

I would sound much more like the president. Getting criticism from one of the leading voices in the press was a bit of a consolation for me as it proved that I wasn't afraid to climb any mountain. It showed me that even though I haven't arrived at my destination, I was on the right path. With a little bit more prowess and work dedication, it would be a matter of time until I finally catch a break.

One day, I was roaming around the neighborhood not far from the Maquis. I was stopped by one of the neighborhood guys who has been looking for me. He told me that his mother was anxious to see me. The guy went by the nickname of Grand Chat, Wildcat. He was in his early twenties. He was the eldest of two sons. His younger brother Gaylor was eighteen years old. Wildcat and his brother lived with their mother, a lady in her early forties who was a widow and a single mother. Her late husband was a former captain in the army during the Mobutu regime. He died a few years back from natural cause.

Wildcat's mother was the vice president of the state fair committee. She was in charge of coordinating the staging of the state fair, which ran from July to September every year, and she also was in charge of overseeing all the revenues. Mrs. Jeanette was a very intelligent lady, well deserving of her position. She was sharp and very attractive for her age. I was well known to her two sons, especially Wildcat, the neighborhood mascot. He had stories for the ages. He was the neighborhood entertainer. He would gather people from all ages all around him every day, telling them old stories of his time in France. His most famous ones were his encounters with the former president's son who went by the nickname Saddam Hussein for his ruthlessness and, most of all, his encounter with the biggest name in Congolese music. He was good friends with the singers from a very popular local band called Wenge Musica, which had the whole city going crazy with a new generation of artistic ingenuity. Although about 80 percent of his stories seemed very phony to me or to any other ears out there, a vast majority seemed to be very intrigued and entertained by it anyway. On the other hand, you had Gaylor, the youngster who was eighteen years old, very shy and pretty much kept a very low profile and never really associated with his brother Wildcat.

On one occasion, at Wildcat's request, I was brought in to his home. He introduced me to his mom, who just had gotten out from work. As she was getting herself situated to relax on her couch, Wildcat told her he had a surprise for her; she just needed to relax on the couch and listen to this. After Mrs. Jeanette, Wildcat's mother, was all relaxed on her couch with her glass of wine by her side, I started my impersonation of the president in front of her. I could see I made a very good impression on her. She was amazed by it. After I was done, she grabbed her purse and took out what was the equivalent of ten dollars in local money and handed it to me. On my way out, Wildcat quickly followed me and asked me for his commission as he was the one who set me up for the payday. I took out about 20 percent of my earning and gave it to him.

One evening, I went back to see Mrs. Jeanette, who has been anxiously looking for me according to Wildcat. As I got there, she was even more excited to see me. She even invited me to join her for dinner. At the table, she told me that she wanted me to do my impersonation of the president at the opening ceremony of the state fair. I was going to do it in front of two very important guests who would be in attendance, His Excellency, Mr. Abdoulaye Yerodia Ndombasi, the president chief of staff, also known as the second-most-powerful man in the country, and Her Excellency, the deputy minister of education.

"I want you to be at your very best, and do not let me down," she said. She reached out for her purse once again and took out some money. "Buy yourself some nice clothes. I want you to look very sharp for the occasion."

I came in the next day at the ceremony marking the opening of the state fair looking very sharp, and most importantly, I had my game face on, ready to take over. It was showtime! It was your typical summer day, very sunny with the temperature in the nineties with the wind blowing cool air from the trees, making it a perfect day. The ceremony was held in the lot in front of about one hundred guests. Among the guests were notable city officials, the mayor, the state fair executive, the deputy minister of education, and the president's chief of staff.

After the president's chief of staff was finished cutting the ribbon, I was introduced by Mrs. Jeanette as the special surprise for the guests.

As I took the stand in front of all those guests, one thing and one thing only ran throughout my brain. I said to myself this was my time to shine. I pretty much had a fifteen-second pep talk with myself wherein I boosted my confidence level to an all-time high.

As I took the microphone, I started by reciting excerpts from the president's investiture speech, which I almost memorized by heart and had been the most comfortable with among his other speeches for me. I closed out with one of the president's latest speeches in which he described the country being at war against a common enemy. He identified the enemy of the Congolese people among a specific ethnicity, the Tutsi, which made up the core of the Rwandese government and promised to export the war back to its source of origin, back to Rwanda. In this speech, the president pointed out the difficulty and setbacks that the nation would have to endure and overcome; but with the help of a unified nation behind a common enemy, the war would be very long but a popular one, which will require everyone to fight with their heart and soul, and we wouldn't stop until the enemy is subdued or exterminated. With that speech, the president boosted his popularity and earned himself support from a large majority of the people.

My performance was greeted with a loud ovation from the guests, and everyone around was moved by my performance. Everybody was left in awe, prompting His Excellency, Mr. Yerodia, to leave his seat. He came forward to me with his arms wide open and gave me a warm hug. His hug went straight through my bones. I pretty much felt the energy coming out this powerful and influential figure transferring into my body through this thirty-second hug, which to me felt like two hours. I felt, all of a sudden, empowered by this iconic hug.

As he looked straight through my eyes while keeping both his hands on my shoulder, he asked me, "Is there anything you would like me to do for you for taking my breath away?"

Without even wasting any second, as if I was already programmed, I replied, "Your Excellency, I would like for you to take charge of my education and provide me with a place I can call home. I want to go to school, but unfortunately, I'm lacking the financial means to do so."

I don't know how and why I came up with that answer, but that was the only thing that came out of me, which was pretty much the only thing in me at that moment given this unexpected request from this statesman. This was the very first time in my life someone had ever asked me for a request, someone as high as the country's number two in command, someone that was well equipped to perhaps make any of my dreams come true.

Looking back to that very moment when I elevated the need for a great education above all possible needs or wants that could have been at the center of my life at that moment or ahead of me, I could have asked for a house, a car, clothes, or money, but none of those things came up to me, not even my dream of meeting up with the president. I never questioned my decision to come up with that answer as to whether that was the very best I could ever possibly come up with. I just find it to be very peculiar to have come up with such a brilliant answer so anonymously, making it perhaps divine as there was no script, and I never anticipated such thing to be thrown my way.

Mr. Yerodia took me by the arm and walked me toward this lady who stood next to him throughout the whole ceremony. This lady happened to be the country's deputy minister of education. He instructed her to take great care of me. He pulled a hundred-dollar bill out of his pocket and handed it to me. The deputy minister of education told me to stop by her office the following Monday to fill out some paperwork.

At the end of the ceremony, everyone parted ways. I went out my way as the happiest man in the world after going through what seemed to me as the perfect day. The stars did shine on me very brightly on that day. I couldn't wait for Monday, and most importantly, I couldn't wait to see my friend Teddy to share some of the joy with him. With a hundred-dollar bill in our disposal, only the sky was the limit for us.

After a very long weekend, which Teddy and I made the best out of having one hundred U.S. dollars at our disposal, we made sure to fulfill about everything we possibly had on our bucket list. We made it to Martyrs Stadium and watched our team play, and this time, we purchased our own ticket and sat in an actual seat for once. We went to some local movie theater and watched a couple of movies. Local movie theaters were nothing but empty rooms with a regular TV and a VCR hooked to it, which they usually set on top of a table. There was a cover charge to see whatever movie was being played from the VCR, which were usually American action movies. At nighttime, after hours, adult movies were shown in those places, which sometimes turned into motels during showings of people engaging in every kind of sexual activities. With so much money to spend, we felt so empowered. There was no stopping us.

That night, after taking Teddy to the bus stop to make his way back home, I ended up going the opposite way toward Victory Place. While wandering around with no actual plan but still with a whole lot of cash still in my disposition, I ran into a bride and groom making their entrance into a nearby hall hosting their wedding ceremony. With no hesitation, I got in one of the lines following the newlyweds. Just like that, I made my way inside a wedding in which I knew no one and to which I was never invited. Being well dressed, no one ever suspected me of being an intruder.

As the night went on, I found myself settling in one of the tables. It was a table of eight with two empty chairs. Sitting in one of those chairs was one of the most beautiful girls I had ever seen. She happened to be one of the flower girls, and I have had my eyes on her the entire reception. I couldn't wait for a chance to get closer to her. I sat down in one of the empty seats and introduced myself.

"I'm Timu!" I said to everyone. "You guys look amazing, by far the best table in this hall," I said. "And you, young lady," I said to the flower girl. "Heaven is on lock down at this very moment. Its most beautiful angel had left for a wedding on earth, and she said she might not be coming back to heaven tonight, and here I am looking at her right now. The best day of my life. What's your name, pretty angel from heaven?"

"Rodre," she said, with the prettiest blush I had ever seen.

At that moment, I became the star of the table. One of the adults sitting at the table looked at me and said, "You look quite familiar. You are the kid that impersonates the president on TV. Small world." He said, "Can you do some impersonation for us? After all, this is the best table like you said."

After doing some impersonation, I could see how amazed Rodre was. From that moment on, we didn't leave each other's sight. Sometime that night, she did ask me who I was related to, the groom or the bride. Realizing that she was related to the bride, I responded by saying the groom. I just made up a random name and said that I was so-and-so's son!

"Oh, OK," she said.

Things got even more cozy that night between us. At around 3:00 a.m., Rodre and her family made their way back home, and at around 5:30 a.m., I was one of the last people to leave the hall, marking a very eventful night. I couldn't stop thinking about Rodre, who would end up being my one-hit wonder as that was the first and last time I saw her.

The following Monday morning, just like I was told by Mr. Yerodia, I showed up at the office of the deputy minister of education. I told the receptionist that Her Excellency, the deputy minister of education, was expecting me. I was fortunate enough that she already knew who I was, courtesy of a note left by the deputy minister's chief of staff who was present last weekend at the state fair.

"Oh, so you are the little kid everyone's been talking about," she said. "Over here!"

She led me to the office of the deputy minister's chief of staff, who greeted me with a very warm hug. She asked me to tell her a little bit about myself. I felt very comfortable confiding to her. She made me feel like I could tell her about anything. I told her about my childhood and life as a street kid. I told her how I lost both of my parents at the age of three and then later ran away from a family that used to physically abuse me. She was very touched by my story. She promised me that she and her cousin, the deputy minister, would do the very best in their power to ensure everything is OK with me from now on.

It took me about half an hour to complete the paperwork she had me fill out. After I was done with everything, I was asked to pick which school I wanted to attend. I was given the option to pick among any school in the city, private or public. My tuition was going to be fully taken care of as a ward of the state. This time around, I was already going on my third year living on the streets. So I picked the very best school I could think of, Moliere, one of the best accredited schools in the city. Moliere was among the top five best private schools in the city and consequently one of the most expensive. The average tuition for a private school in the city ranged between $50 and $200 a trimester, making it $150 to $600 a year. Tuition fees at Moliere were at around $150 a trimester. Although I had absolutely no intention whatsoever to enroll at the school, since I was told to pick any school I wanted to, I just thought, *Why not go big?*

According to the paperwork they had me signed, I was to be given room and board money on top of my tuition money every three months. A week before the very first day of school, I was given around $400 in local money for my trimestral tuition and all other expenses including uniform and school supplies. I believe I was to use some of the money left over to find me a place.

After receiving the money, I decided to cut corners. Instead of enrolling in Moliere, I went on to enroll myself in the very least expensive private school whose tuition was only around fifty dollars a trimester, leaving me with one hundred dollars to spare. I took a very big gamble by doing so. I really never envisaged the consequence I would be faced with had I been caught, but without hesitation, I did pull the trigger. While according to the paperwork I had signed I was to attend Moliere as a seventh grader, I was in fact enrolled in another school, the Institute of October 14th, a very laid-back school.

I spent some of the money on uniforms and school supplies. I took Teddy with me. I got him uniforms and school supplies also. Altogether, only about fifty dollars of the money was spent on school stuff between the two of us, leaving us with a fortune to spare. I took most of my supplies and hid it back at the Maquis where I have been sleeping occasionally by sneaking in almost every late night and waking up at the very first crack of dawn. The rest of my stuff I gave to Teddy to keep for me, which wasn't much, only a few clothes and shoes. During my time on the streets, I never had a suitcase to put clothes in, and since I was a rolling stone with no particular address, I wear the same clothes for two to three days, get to the flea market to buy another outfit, which was always secondhand clothing, wear it for another two to three days, and then throw it away again and get some more. That was my cycle.

It was very exciting to be back in school after taking such a long break away from it. Something about those blue pants and white shirt, which were the school's uniform colors in the city, gave me a sense of purpose in life, a great sense of hope that maybe one day, through education, I can achieve greatness. There is nothing more personifying of a sense of purpose and a brighter future than a school uniform. I was really proud of myself. Even though I still didn't have a home to leave from to go to school and come back to after school, my love for school, which transpired in my determination to make it every day to school, helped me overcome all odds and still make it to school.

On days that I couldn't sneak my way back in the Maquis, I slept inside abandoned cars in junkyards; while other days, I would find me a funeral to spend the night at. One day I remember even walking my way throughout the whole night with my uniform on and backpack on my back until the very first sound of the rooster at dawn. I had a spot where I hid some of my extra school clothes, somewhere in one of those cars inside a junkyard that was near the school. I would wear one uniform for three days and the other for the other two, and so on. Whatever it was, I always made sure to look very clean. I would sneak in inside a church or a school at the earliest hour, at around 5:00 a.m., just to find a water outlet to wash my body off before heading for school, leaving no indication whatsoever of my living condition. The way I secretly kept my living condition from any of my classmates and school officials, that alone should have me qualify for a job as a CIA or Mossad agent.

I was very popular in my school. I was the funniest in my class. I also did manage to catch the eyes of the ladies by being a Romeo to them. I was the complete package. I was cute, smart, and funny, a complete hole in one. The very first two trimesters went smoother than I first imagined. I was among the first five among twenty-four students in my class academically. I always made very good notes in class. Unlike many of my classmates, I had a very good handwriting. I excelled in calligraphy. I never really developed the habit to study; therefore, I made sure to pay great attention during class for some reason whenever

I took notes. It felt like I was doing twice the studying. I had a good recollective memory. I could memorize about anything. I really never bothered doing any homework as it only represented a mere fraction of the grade anyway. Homework only constituted about 5 percent of the grades, while quizzes stood about around 30 percent, and the exams were around 50 percent. There was about 15 percent floating out there, which was available for class participation, attendance, and extra credits.

Not having a home didn't help but hurt any chances of me focusing on any homework. I was more focused on where I was going to sleep at night rather than care about an assignment that only constituted 5 percent of my grade. For some reason, for a big majority of teachers at those laid-back schools, homework never was a big part of their curriculum. Their argument was that homework never truly reflects student's knowledge on the subject learned since they thought there wasn't any evidence pointing at kids being the ones actually doing the work. There was stronger belief that homework was done by adults. Since they had very little interest in giving freebies, they just didn't grade homework that highly.

In seventh-grade, math, history, geography, science, technology, music, and French were part of my daily curriculum. Math, history, and geography were by far my favorite ones. I was second to none in my classes when it came to those three subjects, especially history since it involved memorizing places, dates, and events, and when it came to memorizing stuff, I was like a minicomputer. Science was my least favorite subject. I never really paid too much attention to it. I was more than happy to get by with a passing grade. I wasn't too fond of technology or music either. Within the national grading system, 50 percent was all that was needed to pass a grade. Students who had between 45 percent and 49 percent were given another testing session postfinals, which usually was much easier than the actual final exams to boost up their average grade perhaps to 50 percent or higher. This process where students who barely passed were given a second chance was called Repechage, probably the equivalent of summer school in the United States.

I got to develop a good friendship with two of my other classmates, a boy named Sefu and another who went by the name of Mashikote. The three of us got to forge a very close union. Everywhere I had been, I was always among the most influential people around; school was no exception either. I had the gift of unity. Not only was I popular but I was also a unifier. I had the ability to bring people together like no one else. I was the class charismatic leader. I exercised and followed my own credo, which was leading from the backseat. I loved playing the role of the unsung hero. I have always been so clever and highly manipulative in designing every personal decision and turning it into a collective one. I spoke softly but yet fearlessly. I only fought when the odds were in my favor. In conflicts where victory wasn't guaranteed, I was so quick to compromise only, in my favor, of course. I was the leader who presented his people with choices, but most of all, I made sure they were choosing between doing either what I was going to do for them or what I wanted them to do for me, just so everyone can be presented with a sense of democracy and diversity of ideas without questioning the legislator turned executive. Either way, the dice were already loaded.

Just like in the real world, leadership never went unchallenged whether internally or externally. There is always a challenging threat; sometimes imminent, other times not so pragmatic. There are always critics out there that always pose as a challenge to any given status quo. In my case, my number-one critic and self-declared public enemy number one was none other than a classmate named Amuri. Amuri was very smart, handsome to say the least. He always was first in our class academically, and he prided himself on it every chance he got. And most importantly, his father was our French teacher. Having almost everything going for him, Amuri hated my guts. Although he never personally informed me of this, he did find the importance in telling everyone else but me.

Amuri and his hatred toward me, which I mostly found to be more artificial than anything, was the least of my worries; but instead, I found it to be a little bit odd for the simple reason that I never looked at him as my nemesis. If anything, I had so much consideration for him as I had for any other of my classmates. As time went by, it became clear to me that Amuri had it in his agenda to bring me down to my knees. With a few of our classmates at his disposal, he sought to create a block opposite to ours, thus splitting the class in two blocks. He got down even dirtier by spreading numerous rumors about me and trying to incite the class to turn against me. He even challenged me to a fight after school.

After doing my homework, I found out that Amuri was motivated by jealousy. He was very jealous of my ability to have conquered the heart of the class in a very short period. I did all that without being the number one in the class academically. Unlike Amuri, who was one of the few people in our class who been in that school for a long while now, I, on the other hand, was only entering my first year at the school. I was almost unknown to the scenery until now.

In dealing with Amuri, I did what I had always done in the wake of conflict. I studied my opponent's weakness and capitalized on it. I realized that a physical showdown between Amuri and me wouldn't be going in my favor as he was more physically fit than I was. I sure wasn't going to risk playing into his stronger hand. I did what suited me best. I bought him out. I did it psychologically, not financially. I showered him with tremendous flattery on a daily basis. Amuri was a big showoff. He had a great passion for the spotlight. Being the center of attention was very vital for him. He wanted it at all cost. He hated me for having taken away the spotlight from him. Unlike him, I was naturally accustomed to the spotlight my entire life. As a natural, it was a given for me to be the center of attention regardless of whatever position I occupied. Being funny, charming, and easygoing had it going for me. By being both funny and charming, I gained the interest of all the girls. Being easygoing helped me extend my sphere of influence to different types of personality, even the ones that were totally different from mine.

I started showering Amuri with praises such as calling him "the big boss," "the man," "the man with all the ladies." By making him feel and think bigger than he was fueling his own fire, which was pretty much made up of more smoke than actual fire, I did myself a great favor; while, on the other hand, I was exposing his cockiness to the whole class, making him look bad to most classmates, especially the girls. Most importantly, I eliminated the threat he posed against me by making him dependent on me. He needed me to feed his ego. I didn't need him. I just used him to make him look more stupid than he ever looked, and it worked. I was able to bring the class back together as one happy click.

By the end of the second trimester, I was the most loved kid in the block. I put my friend Sefu in charge of organizing an after-school picnic, which was to be held on a Saturday afternoon after school. Our school hours were from 7:30 a.m. to 12:30 p.m., Monday to Friday. I specifically told Sefu to include some eighth graders who were willing to participate in our event. It should help bring the cost down since every participant was asked to bring in either food, beverage, or a participation fee.

Bringing the cost down had absolutely nothing to do with why I decided to include another class to our class event. It was pretty simple. I was secretly seeing an eighth grader. When I told her about the event, she wanted to bring along five of her friends to our picnic. Since it was strictly a seventh-grader event, bringing in guests without the whole consensus would have raised some eyebrows, so I decided that the event was also open to eighth graders who were willing to join to cut down on our cost.

Sefu was the most honest person I ever met. I would have entrusted him with my life. Although the picnic idea was mine, I decided to let Sefu do the planning and appointed him as the event treasurer. As a participant, everyone was required to come up with the equivalent of five dollars in cash, which will be given to Sefu, or five dollars' worth of a specific canned food and beverage.

Everything was going just as planned logistically. The only problem we had was that we had yet to decide on the venue of the event. We finally agreed with Mashikote to host the event given that he had been bragging about how big his house was and how they had a swimming pool. But for whatever reason, every time we tried to schedule a day to stop by his house and use the pool, Mashikote would always bring up something to keep us from coming over; whether the pool was dirty one weekend or his parents didn't want anyone at the house the next week. It was always something with that infamous pool that no one had seen except its owner. Enough was enough, we said. We are bringing the picnic to the pool, and we won't take no for an answer. Feeling pressured, Mashikote reluctantly accepted our demand and agreed to host the picnic at his house.

Sefu and I were very determined to bring about a successful event, which brought about our concerns about the event's venue. We realized that none of us had ever set foot at Mashikote's house. Aside from those multiple stories coming out of his mouth about how big his house was and how much he enjoyed dipping into his pool, I couldn't tell if we were more motivated by the annoyance of his stories or it was slightly out of jealousy, perhaps a little bit of both.

Even though the three of us were the best of friends at school, it seems like our very close relationship never evolved outside the school's vicinity. We seemed to never meet one another at any of the other's home. In Sefu's defense, he lived about fifteen miles away from school. As for me, I claimed to be living about five miles away from the school away from Sefu's way home. Which now leaves us Mashikote, whose home happened to be about three blocks away from the school, allegedly. All we knew of each other's home location was that Sefu lived very far away from us all, Mashikote's mansion was the closest to the school, and I, on the other hand, lived about five miles away from school in my imaginary home. But unlike Mashikote, who never ceased to brag about his home, I kept life inside my home very private, as private as a scientologist's life.

About a few days before the picnic, Sefu and I embarked on our secret mission, which was to take a sneak peek at Mashikote's home. As we arrived on his street, we didn't know which house might be his, so we decided to ask a group of kids who were playing outside. We told them we came to visit our classmate Mashikote. We knew he lived on this street, but we had trouble locating his house. They directed us to a gated house near the end of the street. As we got into the gated house, there was one big house that was located at the entrance and three little annexes at the end.

Before we got the chance to ask for Mashikote, we saw him coming out one of the smallest annexes, which looked the size of a one-bedroom studio. He was wearing shorts with a green T-shirt almost twice his size. As our eyes met his, the look in his face was a combination of look from a cheating wife caught red-handed and that of a husband caught by his wife masturbating in his room. That look had shame and anger written all over it. Mashikote was caught. His home was far from being the mansion he endlessly told us about, and to make matters worse, just like the WMD George W. Bush swore that Saddam Hussein had, Mashikote's swimming pool was nowhere to be found. There wasn't even a small swamp around.

With that being said, our mission was accomplished. We succeeded in putting to shame one of our very own who desperately went to all that trouble. He went as far as placing an imaginary swimming pool inside his imaginary mansion just to impress us. Why he went through all that trouble, we will never know, Sefu and I thought. As for me, I would have killed to have any place that has a roof just so to call home. How lucky he was, I thought to myself. We ended up having our picnic at a spot not very far from FEZADI. The picnic was a success, thanks to Sefu's planning and a very big turn out from eighth graders.

Midway through the second semester, I met a guy named Fidele Kinata on my way back from school. He recognized me from my time on campus at the University of Kinshasa. He was on his way to a meeting. "Petit Kabila!" he shouted at me. It had been quite a while since anyone referred to me as such.

I looked very surprised as I had absolutely no recollection of the person shouting at me. After shaking my hand, he introduced himself as Fidel. He claimed to have seen me a few times on campus. He was now starting a youth movement under the sponsorship of a certain government official, the deputy minister of mining and energy. He wanted me to join his new organization, Youth for a Better Future. Youth for a Better Future was a mastermind project, as he put it, whose goal was to promote awareness of the role of the youth in the country's rebuilding process. He raised the need for the youth to be involved within the country's politics not only as an area of interest but also most importantly as a pledge to their patriotism. His movement slogan was "Enlightened youths of today the fuel to a better tomorrow." Being sponsored by the deputy minister meant that his movement was built to fly within the government's ideology. I welcomed his invitation with open arms.

After making it to a few of his meetings after school hour, I became very fond of Fidele Kinata, a gentleman who was in his early thirties. Not only did his eloquence weighed volume in me, but also his ambition and character were that of a great visionary. Fidele was a very intelligent man who spent a few years studying in France. Feeling the sparkle from his fire from afar, I quickly put myself as close as possible to the man I saw as a great mentor. In a matter of time, I became an Aristotle to his Plato, thus making me his protégé. From then on, we became pretty much inseparable.

About two weeks from the time of our encounter, Fidele brought me to his mother's home, where he lived, and introduced me to his family. After briefing his mother of my living situation, Fidele persuaded his mother to welcome me in the house to stay as one of their own. I received a very warm welcome from the entire family, the Mampas. After Fidele's father's death, Fidele's mother married a military official in the former regime's army, a certain colonel Mampa, a well-respected man in the community who was now in retirement. Mr. Mampa, whom everyone in the neighborhood referred to as colonel, was an alcoholic who just lived off his rented properties. He would drink himself up from the sound of the rooster to very late at night. Aside from his drinking habit, the colonel was a great family man whenever he was around. He took great care of his kids. The colonel had three children and two grandchildren at his home. There was Patricia, whom everyone called Pathy, his first daughter, with her two children, Josué and Christelle; his son Andy, who was only about two years older than I was; and finally, Flore, the colonel's youngest daughter and perhaps his favorite child, who was about two years younger than me. Patricia's husband and his nephew also lived there at the residence.

The colonel's house was very big. Andy, Guy, who was Patricia's husband's nephew, and I shared a room; while Flore, Christelle, who was about nine years old, and Josué, who was about six years old, shared the same room. Patricia and her husband shared another room. Fidele had a room of his own, which he barely used as he barely slept at the house. And finally, there was the master bedroom. Mrs. Mampa was a very busy woman. She had her own little business, which kept her busy. She sold fried fish across the street from the house, just something to keep herself busy as she really didn't need the money that bad.

I enjoyed living with the Mampas. They made me feel right at home. I was about 90 percent comfortable being a part of their family. The reason I said 90 percent is one can never feel totally comfortable under someone's roof no matter what. It might have absolutely nothing to do with anyone's character or their heart. It's that one thing that is found within every individual living in this planet, that very thing that always pretty much forces you to pick sides willingly or unwillingly between certain colors, animals, sports teams, religions, women, men; that very thing that keeps you from loving your stepson or daughter fully and totally as much as you would love your biological child; that little thing hidden deep inside you that you never truly cared much about.

One day, a noble man was touring around town, taking a break away from his palace. He realized he was thirsty and stopped at one store to get himself a drink. On his way out from the store, he saw a homeless man lying down, begging for spare change. He reached out of his pocket just to realize that he didn't have any change or bills with him. He only had a credit card. He felt really bad in his head. He realized he didn't have anything to offer to the poor man. He went back to his palace, grabbed a mattress from his six empty guest rooms, packed a few pillows and blankets, along with some food, and quickly got back to the homeless man who slept under the bridge. He got back as quickly as he could, found the homeless man lying at the same spot, and gave the homeless man everything. The homeless man was very happy; so was the noble man. But one question remained to be asked: what is it that kept him from offering one of his six empty guest rooms to the poor homeless man? The answer is pretty simple. It is indeed that one little thing.

Even though it was obvious I wasn't a relative of the Mampas, they did about everything they could to prevent it from affecting our relationship. My relationship with everyone was at the zenith. The colonel, for the few moments he and I encountered one another at the house, treated me just as his own. His wife was a great mother to me. Patricia was a great big sister to me, but there was something about her husband that made me a little uncomfortable at times as he gave me the vibe as if he didn't really want me there. As far as I was concerned, his opinions meant very little to me.

Andy and I had the very best relationship. It was a combination between a big brother–little brother relationship and a friendship. I also had a good relationship with Guy as both Andy and I sort of looked up to him as our friendly big brother. Guy was about nineteen years of age. He was at his senior year of high school. Most notably, Guy played soccer for a second-tier football club. Guy was a very good defender. He was about six feet tall, weighing around 190 pounds. Guy had great potential. He was very dedicated to the sport. His ambition was to help his team gain promotion to the top flight division and then perhaps move on to a bigger club on his way to play for a professional team overseas. He sought football as being his opportunity to make it out of the country. Andy and I would walk about ten miles just to go see him play and walk back home with him after his game. We had a lot of fun doing so as it kept us from being at home.

Patricia's children were very nice to me. They were very respectful and well disciplined. Christelle was just as great as a little sister would have been, while her little brother Josué was just as good as a little brother. Flore showed a little indifference at first toward me. As time went by, she finally warmed up to me. She even went a little further beyond warming up to me by actually getting very cozy with me. At twelve, Flore was way too mature for her age. She would sneak around late at night while everyone was sleeping. She would enter our room, jump into my bed, and start to kiss me. On a few occasions, we would go around the back of the house and kiss for about fifteen minutes. One day, she took it a step further by coming into the bathroom while I was in it. She grabbed my genitals and began to rub it against her thigh. She even asked me if I could have sex with her. Although I was very tempted by such a golden offer, I knew better than committing such an act while everyone was literally a feet away. Chances of us getting caught were very high. One other thing that kept me from acting impulsively was the fact that I was a virgin myself, and from the looks of it, I would have bet on Flore being anything but a virgin.

Living with the Mampas made it very easy for me to make it to school and back. Now I had a place to come back to after school instead of wandering around all night looking for a place to lay my head. Living with the Mampas revived me. Now I could dream smoothly than ever. I was so excited. Now Sefu and I could walk back to school together. I invited him in a few times afterward for a drink of water. It felt so good to be a part of a family.

I continued to be a part of Fidele's youth movement, which was gaining more recognition in the neighborhood. The movement grew in number. Fidele went as far as getting us recognition from the city, making us a legitimate institution, with Fidele as the founder and leader of the movement. Being the very closest one to him, I was almost guaranteed this unspoken title of second in command, even though I never was given any responsibility within the movement, nor was I nominated or elected to assume any strategic position within the movement, yet my status in the movement was far from being questioned or challenged by anyone.

One day, Fidele took me with him at the residence of our sponsor, His Excellency, the deputy minister of mining and energy. It was His Excellency's birthday. There was a big party at the residence with a long list of guests ranging from family members, friends, and colleagues. Fidele had a great relationship with the deputy minister. I could feel the mutual respect they had for one another. Fidele was his right-hand man, just like I was Fidele's. About midway to the party, Fidele whispered to the birthday man that he had a present for him and that he would like for the live band to stop playing the music just for a few moments so he could get everyone's attention. After his wish was granted, Fidele walked back to where I was sitting and tapped me on the shoulder and said to me, "Go take over." I was caught between shock and happiness as I never saw it coming. Fidele never once told me of his plan. He put me right on the spot, and I sure wasn't going to blow it.

I made my way in front of all those guests standing in front of the little stage set up by the live band. I grabbed one of the microphones lying around. I was in front of a very silent audience who seemed to have absolutely no clue about what was going to hit them. I started with my impersonation of the president from his inauguration speech to the latest one. Not only that but also I was the best impersonator of the president. I never really had competition. There were also two comedians who were also impersonating the president but only underground as they were fearful of the repercussion in case the president wasn't amused by such a gig. But being thirteen years old, I had absolutely no fear whether the president liked it. I didn't quite see the president giving an order to arrest a harmless thirteen-year-old for impersonating him. But again, not only that this is Africa but also it's the Congo we are talking about here, a country with more surprises than a romantic guru. So basically, I really wasn't untouchable either.

The one-man show, which lasted for about fifteen minutes, had everyone in awe—I meant everyone, from the birthday man himself to anyone that was around him. They were all mesmerized by my performance. His Excellency, the deputy minister, got out of his comfort zone and came straight to me with a big hug. I could see the joy in his face, which transferred to Fidele's face like a magnetic transfer of energy, thus bringing back a big smile on my face. Not only did I steal the show from what I was seeing and feeling, but also His Excellency's wife better check herself; I just might have stolen her husband's heart also. I was indeed the man of the hour.

By the time the party was over, my performance was the topic of everyone's conversation. I couldn't have been any more proud of myself. His Excellency was so happy. He reached in his pocket and pulled out a fifty-dollar bill and handed it to me. On our way out, Fidele and I split the money together. He got thirty dollars, and I kept twenty dollars. Fair enough, I thought.

A few weeks later, the president shuffled his government cabinet yet again, the second time in less than a year, with almost two-thirds of government officials being either dismissed or reassigned to different positions. Of all the departments, only the Department of Interior,

Justice, and Press were left untouched. The rest were either reassigned to lesser roles within the government; whereas, others were practically relieved of their function. Among those who were let go were the deputy minister of education, whose department was in charge of my tuition, and the deputy minister of mining and energy, our dear friend and sponsor.

The fate of the former was of a great concern to me, as perhaps without her in charge, I wouldn't be able to continue my studies as I couldn't afford paying for my tuition, at least I didn't think I should. As for the latter, it wasn't so much of a loss for me, as apart from Fidele, who was personally the only one benefiting from most, if not all, of the financial support that was provided by him in the name of the movement, Fidele was the only one drawing a check from our sponsor, while everyone else pretty much volunteered. Hey, who could blame him? He's the one who came up with that idea. It was pretty much his thing. As for me, I never joined the movement for what it was rather than its potentiality. So as soon as our primary sponsor lost his status within the government, our movement folded.

I did manage to convince the newly appointed deputy minister of education, with its new team, that I was pretty much a ward of the department by presidential ordinance; therefore, they should carry on the duty of their predecessor by continuing paying for my tuition. The new undersecretary had no opposition to my request. When asked how much my tuition was, I told them it was $300 a semester instead of $150 a trimester, plus $50 for school supplies, which was given to me in a payroll at the end of each month. I was to start living a very sweet and comfortable life under this new administration.

One day, about midway throughout the last trimester, with about six weeks of school left, I was invited by this very nice, very sweet young lady whom I met a while back during my time at the university's campus. She was now an anchor at the national radio station. She had her own little show on the radio to help boost my popularity. She promised to give me some airtime on her show, to my great delight. I went to the station and did my little gig. At the end of her show, she offered me some lunch, and while I was eating my lunch at her office,

I asked to listen to her cassette player, which was sitting right on her desk. She handed me the cassette player. I told her I was going outside to get fresh air and I will be back in a moment. While outside, I don't know what demon possessed me. All of a sudden, I just took off with her cassette player. I came back home with the stolen cassette player.

About a week later, I was confronted by Patricia's husband about the stolen cassette player. I don't know if this was staged or just a mere coincidence. The owner of the stolen cassette player was none other than Patricia's husband's niece, and how in the world the two got in contact so quick was another mystery in itself. All I could think of is why God decided to put me, of all people, in such a smaller world. Patricia's husband publicized that incident throughout the whole house. He went as far as demonizing me for having stolen from his relative. He lobbied so vehemently to have me outcast from the family.

With all evidence turned against me, I was kicked out by the Mampas, and once again, I was back on the streets after a good run living under a roof. In a blink of an eye, it was all over. This time, I had no one but myself to blame, I brought it all upon myself. Although it would have been nice to be given a second chance, but from what I was told, I was already running on a very thin line as far as Patricia's husband was concerned as a result of an old incident that involved a pornographic material.

One day, I brought home with me a *Playboy* magazine I had borrowed from a classmate at school to share it with both Andy and Guy. I was very excited that day. I couldn't wait to get home and show Andy my new acquisition. I couldn't stop imagining it in my head how bringing home such a valuable prize would enhance my relationship with Andy. After showing him the magazine, he fell in a state of total awe, and from that point on, we would become the best of friends forever even in the next generation. It was like bringing a cellphone with service in a deserted island. Just like I had anticipated, I was given a hero's welcome by Andy after handing him the *Playboy* magazine. He was very amazed and thankful.

"How did you get this?" he said. "You are a god, a genius. How did you even come up with this? I have been looking forever to get my hands on such a treasure."

Any more praise coming out from him would have made my head explode. I am pretty sure that is how Steve Jobs's friends and colleagues felt after he unveiled the first iPhone to them. But as the day went by, it was just a matter of time until I moved from hero to villain. After having taken advantage of the *Playboy* magazine by doing God knows what with it, Andy forgot to hide it and left it in the bathroom.

Unfortunately for the both of us, Patricia found the magazine and told her husband about it. Andy, Guy, and I were summoned by Patricia's husband in the living room with only one question to answer—who that magazine belonged to and how in the hell did it find its way into this house. Before anyone could recollect any thought, Andy was very quick to point toward my direction as being the sole owner of what seemed to be a weapon of mass destruction according to Patricia's husband, and if we learned anything from the second gulf war, it is that people who happened to possess weapons of mass destruction are to be dealt with very harshly, first, with sanctions, and then . . . you get the point.

The pinpoint from Andy came somehow as a shock to me as I wasn't expecting the inquiry to end that quick. I was perhaps hoping for an "I don't know" from each of us, thus making the inquiry as dead as a cold case. I believed, with no camera or fingerprint, no one would ever know who the owner of that magazine was. If anything, it could have come from the sky as far as I was concerned. Just like in those organized mob family crimes, I was hoping for our motto to be "Never write off family." I was wrong. It took Andy less than five seconds to distance himself from me and walk out free as a bird. All the blame was rested upon me. I was at the mercy of Patricia's husband's fury, just like a poor little black accused of stealing from a white man in front of an all-white jury ready to be sent to the guillotine. He let me have it the very best he knew how, and it sure wasn't pretty. It reminded me that no matter how much love there was going around, when it came to it, I wasn't one of them. I guess from that point on, every little movement I made was scrutinized. It was just a matter of time until I was to get kicked out of the house.

I started the last trimester of the school year back on the streets. The very first week was a little bit harsh on me as I had to transition from living in a house back to being homeless once again. School-wise, the last trimester is the hardest of all as it may well determine your school grade as a failure or it may guarantee you promotion to the next grade level.

Few days after the start of the school's last trimester, while watching the local news at my friend Papi's house, I saw a lady on national TV, a certain Agathe Mulimbi. From some sources, she was a relative of the president. Some were saying she was the president's aunt, while others had her as being one of the president's many concubines. I wouldn't doubt the latter since the president himself never officially endorsed anyone as his wife. He had never been seen in the company of a woman in the public eye. He was known to be an alcoholic and, above all, a womanizer. Some rumors had it that he was secretly seeing one of the country's famous pop singers, Tshala Mwana, the Congolese Madonna who was nicknamed "boneless belly" for her belly dancing and dance moves that were strongly sexually motivated. She did things back then that even Beyoncé and Shakira in their prime couldn't have been a challenge to her dance supremacy.

In one interview with the local press, the president, when asked by one of the journalists when he will introduce the country to the first lady, or if there even was a first lady, the president responded with a big chuckle by saying that the country wasn't in need of a first lady; instead, it was in great need of stronger statesmen and women. "And besides, why does mine have to be the first lady? Who is coming up with all those rankings? And yours, which position is she occupying, second, one hundredth?" Just like that, the president was able to put that question to rest.

Mrs. Agathe Mulimbi, a lady who appeared to be in her late forties or early fifties, was the face of family value and women development within the new regime. She was very active. She pretty much took up the role of a first lady. She was involved in taking care of military wives, taking care of army veterans, advocating family values, visiting orphanages, etc. Her latest project was the launching of the fight against homeless kids. She wanted to take all those homeless street kids out of the streets. She was shown on national television helping out needy kids who were homeless. After seeing her on TV, a thought just popped up of my head. I thought maybe if I were to see her and seek for her help, maybe she could help me by finding me a place to call home.

The following day, I made it my priority to find out about her residence and try to make an appointment to see her and ask her for her help. I made my way to her house, which was in one of the nicest neighborhoods of the city, the Gombe neighborhood, which was inhabited by only upper middle class and the upper class. All the houses there were very fancy, with fancy gates and architecture. When I came knocking at her gate, I was met by her guards who were dressed up in military clothing. They were soldiers carrying Russian-made AK-47 weapons. I was asked to state the reason why I was there. I told the guard that I wanted to see Maman Agathe, as she is known to everyone.

"I am here to seek for her help. I am a homeless kid who is in need of a home," I told the guards through the gate. I even told the guards a little bit about my life story and gave them a little sample of my impersonation of the president.

They went on and told the person who was in charge of her appointments, who came out and spoke to me regarding my request. She told me she will relay the message to Mrs. Agathe, and I should come back the next day to find out if and when I was going to meet up with her. I was very excited as her words seemed very promising.

I came back the very next day and sat outside the gate for about three hours. The lady came out to me saying that she wasn't seeing anyone for the rest of the day as she just got an emergency call from the president, who wanted to see her. She asked me to come back tomorrow. Then again, I came back the next day only to be told this time that she wasn't home and that I should come back the following day. I made about six more trips. All were very unsuccessful same disappointing result. She was either not there or very busy, or I just missed her by a second. I became very frustrated as it became clear to me that I was purposely being given the runaround for whatever reason that was unknown to me. It seemed to me that Mrs. Agathe Mulimbi had absolutely no intention of seeing me. But why she didn't just say so instead of wasting my time and energy and feeding me false hope, only God knows why, I thought. Enough was enough, I said to myself. This was the very last time I will ever set foot in this place wishing to see this lady. After giving it about ten tries, I had to eventually move on.

On my very last day leaving from Mrs. Agathe's residence, I was so exhausted, and even worse, emotionally drained. I couldn't stop but think about how anyone can be as selfish as to not be as honest as possible with a thirteen-year-old especially in such a critical situation. I couldn't stop but beat myself up even more for having made all those trips in vain. If anything, I should have given up earlier than that. What was so hurtful was the fact that her residence was way out of my way. It was about twenty miles away from my school, and each time, I had to make the trip there by foot and, most of the time, on an empty stomach. I was enduring the painful trip there with a heart of a warrior only thinking about the potential of the reward. Little did I know that all those sacrifices were simply being made in vain, or were they?

I took the back street, which led me to another street that was to take me all the way to the main road. There was something a little different about this street that caught my eyes. Every other residence in this street had military men guarding its gate. This only meant two things: one, it was the residence of a high-ranked military official; or, two, it was the residence of a government official. About midway to the street, I stopped in front of a small group of soldiers who were gathered outside a gate playing checkers. I stopped and stood by nonchalantly with all eyes directed to the checkerboard while evaluating the two players, seeing if they were any match to my skills. I was still wearing my school uniform, a white polo shirt, blue pants, white tennis shoes, and a backpack strapped in my back. I got in line waiting for my turn as only the winner stayed while the loser would go back at the back of the line for another turn.

Checkers was the city's most popular board game. To some, it was a very interesting hobby, especially to guys between the ages of thirty and sixty. To others, it was a getaway drug. Some husbands would go out and play checkers for hours just to get away from having to deal with the everyday nagging and yapping from their spouses, while others would simply take their everyday shortcoming to the board. To a few, it was a source of revenue as it was also used for gambling purposes. To the journeyman, seeing a checkerboard along the way was an invitation to take a little break from the long walk and rest up a little either by watching as a spectator or joining in as a participant before getting back up and continuing the journey. There were no strangers when it came to joining a checkers match. Challenges were welcome regardless of age, social status, or background. Skill was all that mattered. If you had the skill or the ability to put up a challenge, you were welcomed at any checkerboard around the city. And it was also agreed upon that there isn't any other game that would best checkers in its ability to kill time. Checkers was indeed your ultimate time killers; PlayStation and Xbox wouldn't stand a match.

After having played a few games, I held a pretty good record against a pretty stiff competition. Seven wins, one loss, and three draws was quite impressive. There was a total of eight players, including me, six guards, and one civilian. Four guards were from the residence of a certain colonel Papi, a twenty-eight-year-old who was an officer of DEMIAP, the country's intelligence agency. The other two guards were from the next-door residence of the president's secretary, a lady who took notes during all the president's meetings especially with other foreign officials. The civilian was a guy named Michel, who was also a security guard for this pharmaceutical depot owned by the Red Cross, which was located a few houses down on the same street. The two secretary guards were Willy and Oliver. Colonel Papi's guards were Djeshy, a.k.a. Cascadeur, the most animated of all, and Michel, a.k.a. pretty boy. Unlike all his other mates who were of a darker complexion, Michel was of a lighter complexion. He looked like a model. He had the neatest uniform and kept his permed hair very nice. Above all, he had the hottest girlfriend. There was another guard who went by the nickname of Bourro for being chubby. And last but not least, Momo, a.k.a. Silencer, who was known for being the quietest of all. He usually does not open his mouth very often, but when he does, the whole world ought to listen. The checkerboard belonged to Michel, the civilian guard from the pharmaceutical depot.

Playing checkers with those soldiers was very fun. The way they made fun of each other's game was hilarious. There was a good vibe among the group, pretty much something like a band of brothers, which they pretty much were. What made it even more fun was the fact that they weren't that much older than me. The oldest in the group was Bourro, who was twenty years old; while the youngest, Oliver, was seventeen. At thirteen, I wasn't that much younger than them. There were a part of a very large group of child soldiers that the new regime recruited as they mounted their rebellion to increase in numbers. As they made their military gain from town to town on the way to ousting the former regime of Mobutu, they recruited children as young as eight to reinforce their numbers. Those child soldiers were nicknamed Kadogo. They were all country kids who lived in a shanty town way out in the villages. For the very first time in their lives, they were now exposed to the city life, and they were loving every bit of it.

As time went by, I got to know a little bit about each one of them, and I got to tell them a little bit about myself. I even let them hear some of my impersonation of the president. They were all left speechless. When I told them that I was homeless and that I had been endlessly trying to be seen by Mrs. Agathe Mulimbi, who lived at the corner of the street, for the past week or so unsuccessfully, they all felt sorry for me. They even ate their dinner outside just so they could share it with me as they couldn't have me come inside since it was a security breach. We had a little difficulty communicating as they spoke only Swahili fluently, and their Lingala wasn't good at all. As for me, I spoke Lingala but couldn't speak Swahili as fluently as they could. I tried to expand my Swahili with them as they tried to work on their Lingala with me. It was a little easier for them as they were mostly interested in learning pickup lines to pick up girls more than anything else. They reminded me of the soldiers by the president's office. They were very funny and kind, some attributes I could never think a person carrying arms could possess. They were all concerned about where I was going to sleep that night, but as much as they all wanted to help me, none of them could provide me with a place to sleep as they would all get in deep trouble.

As I started saying my good-byes to them, Michel, the security guard who had left earlier, just came back to get his checkerboard back. As I was getting ready to head out, Michel asked me if I wanted to play again, only this time we had to play in front of his work as it was already time for his shift. Michel was pretty much a sentinel. He looked after the place at nighttime, from 6:00 p.m. to 6 a.m. the next day. He worked in a rotation with another sentinel, an old guy, perhaps in his late fifties, who went by his nickname, Papa Mapasa, meaning "father of twins." Anyone who fathered twins went by that nickname. For a woman, the nickname was Mama Mapasa, "mother of twins." Michel, who was in his midthirties, was very cool for his age. He had no problem mingling with the youngsters. Michel was a good match for me in checkers. He was the only one to beat me that day. I enjoyed playing against him as he was always bringing the very best out of me. As we played game after game while exchanging life stories, I got to find out a little more about Michel. More importantly, I found out Michel was a player. He had more stories about girls than I could ever imagine. I sure was enjoying every one of them.

Around midnight, Michel set up some cardboards in one of the office's rooms inside the depot for me to sleep in. He told me I could stay the night there every time he is on duty but only to make sure I'm out of the building by 6:30 a.m. before any of the employees started making their way in. If anyone ever sees me coming out of there or catches me sleeping there, he would lose his job. He also told me that he would talk to Papa Mapasa to see if I he could allow me to stay the night on his days on duty. From what he told me, he and Papa Mapasa had a really good relationship, as he put it. Papa Mapasa was one of the few people in this world that only comes once in a generation.

I got up the very next day at around 5:30 a.m. and took a shower on the lawn outside by filling up water in a bucket. Michel gave me soap. He didn't have any towel, so I just hand dried myself. At around 6:00 a.m., I was on my way to school. It took me about two hours to walk to school even after taking the shortest of all the shortcuts available to me. I did manage to make it to school about twenty minutes after the bell, which wasn't bad at all considering the distance.

I went back and spent the rest of the afternoon and some of the evening playing checkers with the soldiers while listening to the animated Djeshy entertaining us with his war stories. Sometime around 6:00 p.m. I walked over to Michel to pick up where we last left off. I got to hear more stories from Michel. When it came to stories, not even the Bible came close to being a match to Michel's.

At around 9:00 p.m., this lady came by with a plate containing food in her hand and handed it to Michel. The lady who looked like she was in her late thirties or early forties came from two houses across. She spoke with Michel in private for a good fifteen minutes and left. On her way back, she said good-bye to me. After she left, Michel told me that the lady was the wife of the ambassador of Angola. He told me that she always brings him food whenever he worked. The two were very good friends. Judging from the way they went by to speak to one another privately, they sure were more than friends; at least that is what I was hoping. Michel and I took a little break from the checkerboard to eat. The meal was very delicious, smoked fish with potato stew, with a jar of cold water to sum it all up. The next day, she came once again. This time, she brought even more food. This time, she brought some plantains with some grilled chicken.

Michel and I took care of business just as usual. Hanging out with Michel was the coolest thing ever. At nighttime, we would stand outside the door with our eyes all pointed toward the main street where I would watch and listen to Michel hit on almost every girl passing by. One of the differences of hitting on a girl back in my country is, unlike here, where telephone is something that is available to almost anyone in my country, a phone was a luxury. I could count with one hand the number of anyone I knew who had a mobile phone, let alone a house phone. With that said, instead of asking for a girl's number, one would ask for her address instead or a point of reference to meet up there. One thing about Michel—he never seemed to have any particular taste when it came to girls; neither did he care about their ages. He would hit on either a piece of stick or a statue as long as it was a female. Whatever it was he was telling them seemed to work sometimes as I would see him bring some girls inside. He would eventually sleep with some.

About the fourth day, it was time for Michel to rotate shifts with Papa Mapasa. Michel was taking the day shift, while Papa Mapasa took the night shift. As promised, Michel did speak with Papa Mapasa about letting me sleep there. Most to my delight, Papa Mapasa was perfectly OK with that idea. I spent about three nights with Papa Mapasa, who was nothing like Michel but a good man on his own. Papa Mapasa was a very respectful, honest family man. He was married and a father of seven kids, with the youngest being about four years older than me. Papa Mapasa was a very wise man. He knew a lot of tales. I enjoyed listening to his tales. What was so astonishing about him was the fact that the highest grade he ever accomplished was second grade. He never went beyond the second grade. I couldn't stop but think how anyone with almost no education can be so enlightened and full of wisdom.

Papa Mapasa's spirit was always in its zenith. Nothing ever seemed to bother him. He was, for all I know, the happiest man alive. He always seemed to have the answer to any question, problem, or life crisis. "You going to make it just fine." That always was his favorite words to me. Papa Mapasa was the coolest sixty-year-old I ever knew. He never used any profanity. I learned a lot more by being around him those few nights than I ever did being around anyone in my entire life. Papa Mapasa might not have been blessed financially in his life, but he sure was one of the richest persons I ever knew when it came to having the purest spirit, along with the greatest heart; all that wrapped around a King Solomon-like's brain. He was one of a kind, a living treasure.

Staying the night at the depot wasn't bad at all. Aside from sleeping on those cardboards and having to get up at around 5:30 a.m. every day, the hardest part was getting to school. The depot was located on the corner of the street across from the ISC, a technical college that specialized in accounting. There was the main road, the November 24th Avenue, separating the technical college and the depot, which was on the corner of Citronier Avenue. In front of the technical college was a bus stop. So every day at around 6:00 a.m., I would cross the street and wait at the bus stop, begging for a ride.

While in the western hemisphere, public transportation availability isn't a luxury, that wasn't the case in my country, where finding transportation was part of the daily struggle. The transportation available to the public was each privately owned. We didn't have buses. We had the Kombi, which was a microbus made by the German automaker Volkswagen. About 99 percent of the Kombi in the city were out of date and poorly maintained. Owners would rip out the original seats and replace them with wooden benches, creating three separate rows just so it could seat about four times its original capacity. They would have people all squeezed up like sardines just to make more money with no government regulation. Everything was fair game to those Kombi owners.

The Kombi was divided in four parts. The front part had the driver and two front seats, which were not replaceable since the two front seats had cushions. It cost more to sit in front. You had the middle in which they took all the original seats and replaced them with two wooden benches to accommodate more people. The last part was the back, which was connected to the trunk and made up another row of seats. And finally, there was the trunk area, which was now turned into a spot for people who couldn't effort to pay the full price of the fare. They were given a spot in the back of the truck, which was the warmest spot in the minibus since it was one of the few automobiles around that had its engine on the back instead of the front like most automobiles.

The Kombi was managed by two people, the driver, who did the driving, and the driver's aide, who was called *receveur* or receiver. The receveur's job was to load people inside the Kombi while the Kombi was at the bus stop. While at the bus stop, the receveur would be yelling the destination of the Kombi, hoping to attract passengers. After all the seats were filled, he would then signal the driver, letting him know that it was time to take off. While the Kombi was in motion, the receveur would proceed by giving out tokens in exchange for money for the fare. After the Kombi had taken off, he would then proceed by selling tickets for the fare while the Kombi was in motion. After letting out anyone in their stop, his job was now to attract more people on board.

His most critical job was to ensure that every passenger paid his or her fare, and for anyone who didn't, it was his job to personally inflict a penalty to that individual. The most common penalty inflicted by a receveur to an imposter was to confiscate whatever possession the imposter might have, whether his belt, shirt, shoes, etc. But whenever one didn't have money for the bus, it was always good to try and beg the receveur for a free pass. If he's full, the clever thing to do is to ask to ride in the trunk, which five out of ten times always works. The other advantage I had was being in school uniform; it always made it very difficult for them to turn down a little school kid.

The only thing was that it was way easier to get a free ride to school than to get one coming back from school. Those Kombi receveurs were more compassionate in the morning than they were any other time of the day. Luckily for me, it never bothered me much walking about twenty miles from school. My feet did the best they could to get quickly used to it. I tried to make the walk back to the depot less challenging by occasionally stopping along the way. I usually walked back with Sefu, who lived about two towns away from the depot. Walking long distance never felt more exhausting while with a companion than it really is while going at it alone. With Sefu, the walk back home was always fun as we entertained each other along the way with unlimited amount of conversation.

One day, on my way back from school, I stopped to play checkers with the Kadogos. As Oliver and I were the only ones playing—everyone else was busy doing their own thing—Oliver came up with this very brilliant idea. He told me that his boss, the president's secretary, was very sweet and that she and her husband, who was a few years younger than her, didn't have any kids. They lived in that big house alone until her two teenage nieces moved in with them. The two nieces, Ariel and Sorine, were around eighteen years of age. Oliver told me it wouldn't be such a bad idea to ask the secretary to help me out as much as she could. "You never know, she might even try to adopt you." Those were his words.

I really welcomed that idea with very high enthusiasm, but how in the word I would meet face-to-face with the secretary, that was a great challenge by itself, since technically, I wasn't allowed inside her property being the stranger I was. Although Oliver's suggestion seemed to be very exciting, I wasn't very upbeat about it after my latest experience with Mrs. Agathe Mulimbi, who gave me the runaround for a week without even considering at least hearing me out. The thought of another repeat and the fear of another disappointing result kept running through my head. Looking at what was at stake, one thought overruled any other thought I had in mind. I had more to gain from trying. If this time the sky would show a little more mercy toward me, the reward would be overwhelming. On the other hand, if nothing was to ever come out of it, I wouldn't be in any worse shape. Now the only thing standing in the way was the plan of attack. How in the world was I going to get to meet face-to-face with the president's secretary? The closer I had ever been to her was playing checkers outside her residence. To make matters worse, Oliver, who came up with this brilliant idea, couldn't figure out how I could personally meet with the secretary without having to jeopardize his job.

After shooting plenty of blank ideas, I finally landed a winner. I will write the secretary a letter and try my very best to hand it to her either on her way to work while the gates are open or on her way from work while awaiting the gates to open. I found it to be more convenient to hand her the letter on her way back from work, which would usually be between 4:30 p.m. and 5 30 pm almost every day. Oliver and I agreed that it would be best for me to stand by the gates around that time on the opposite side to rule out any thought of complicity. He didn't want her to know that he had any part in it as it could consequently get him into a lot of trouble.

That very same night, I went to work. I wrote a two-page letter, double spaced, very neatly handwritten, with the very best autograph I could possibly come up with. I had asked Oliver to give me some change to buy an envelope. I put the letter inside the envelope and wrote on the envelope "To Her Excellency, the Secretary." I started the letter by giving a little background on how I was orphaned from both parents since I was three years old and how I basically lived on the streets for a big majority of my childhood until now. I also shared a little bit on how

I first found my passion of impersonating the president, and I pretty much concluded my letter by sending an SOS toward her.

"At fourteen, all I wanted, my greatest dream of all, was to find me a place to call home. I have been very less fortunate throughout my childhood not to ever experience a place I could comfortably call my home, a place to store all my memories, a place to dream. The only place I could ever afford to have one, I would do whatever it takes to cherish such a place if given the opportunity. My only wish is to have the Almighty God use you be the one to make such a dream come true for me, and from the day that happens, I will work twice as hard as I ever did just to ensure that your kindness will ever get rewarded by being whatever you aspire me to be."

I let it all out the very best I possibly could. I put the envelope in my backpack, said a little prayer, got on my cardboard, and finally closed my eyes for a good-night's sleep, hoping for a much better day tomorrow.

The next day was just like another typical day. I woke up at around 5:30 a.m., took a shower in the back of the building, and got my uniform on. At around 6:00 a.m., just like every day, I was out of there on my way to the bus stop. Along the way, from the time I got to school to the time the bell rang for dismissal, I had one thing in mind and one thing only—tonight's showdown with the secretary. I would occasionally get the letter out of the envelope to reread it a few more times while playing scenarios of the outcome in my head over and over, and each time, my heart was beating just as fast as the last.

Not even once have I mentioned anything to anyone else, not even to Sefu, my best friend. When it came to my life, I kept it as personal and private as possible. I made sure I gave as little information as possible as I could. I gave out exactly what I wanted the world to know. No one knew anything about me that I didn't want anyone to know. They never knew my father, my mother, or any of my siblings. I kept my life as vague as possible but without giving out any reasonable doubt. The reason behind that was purely simple—I despised charity. I loved being charitable. I just hated being the one at the receiving end of it. I always thought of charity as being a sort of loan with a long-term payment option that could ultimately take a lifetime to repay. My philosophy was simple—give as much while receiving as little as possible.

I was going through one of the hardest phases in my life. I had no support, no family to count on, no place to call home. There were days when I didn't even know if I was going to eat anything. My everyday life was as much as a miracle as seeing a flying cow. With all that going on, I never thought any less of myself, nor did I ever set any limit to what I could ever accomplish. The sky was still the limit for me, and I wanted every soul that came in contact with mine to see it just as I did. To me, no matter how low the glass might have looked, I always gave away the feeling of a glass being half full—better yet, on its way to getting filled up, nothing less.

Never a day have I ever backed down from any challenge, big or small. My everyday life was a bigger challenge by itself. While the daily challenge of your average fourteen-year-old in Europe or America was which video game to pick or what color shoes to put on, my daily challenges were not knowing if I was ever going to eat that day or where I was going to sleep that night, and most importantly, how was I going to sleep that night with one eye open to make sure I don't oversleep my welcome, or was I going to sleep lying down on the floor or sitting down? Those were some of the challenges I faced regularly.

I got back from school at around 3:30 p.m. that day and quickly made my way to see Oliver, who seemed more excited than ever to see me. He even had a lunch plate he had saved for me. It was white rice and beans with some pig's feet. After I was done eating, we played a few more games of checkers. As we were playing, we were also talking about the letter. I showed him the letter. He looked at it and gave me a nod as to tell me how good of a job that was. When he asked me what I said in the letter, that was when I realized that Oliver didn't know how to read or write at all.

About half an hour later, it was time for me to assume the position and stand by the gate to wait for the secretary's car to stop by the gate on its way into the residence. The secretary was chauffeured in a dark green Honda CRV. It was just a matter of time. At around 5:00 p.m., the dark green Honda CRV made its way to the gates. Before Oliver could open the gate, I rushed to the car's passenger seat window, where a woman who looked in her late thirties appeared to be sitting. She looked very marvelous with that professional look on her face. I quickly said my greeting and gently handed the envelope to her. She motioned back to me, telling me to give her time to read it tonight, and she would definitely get back to me as soon as she gets a chance. I came out that moment a happier man as half the battle was already won; the other remaining half was out of my hands. I did everything in my power to ensure a positive result, if not a victorious one.

The next day, I got myself ready for business as usual. By three thirty in the hot afternoon, I was already outside the secretary's residence. It was a very busy and exhausting day for me. On that day, I didn't have any luck finding a free ride to school, which meant I had to walk to school. I didn't get to school until around eight thirty, missing the entire first period. By the time I got in front of the school, the gates were closed. It always was the school policy to shut the gate about half an hour after the bell that marked the beginning of the first period. If you were half an hour late, you were just as good as absent since there was pretty much no way you were getting through the closed gates unless, of course, you were as savvy as I was.

I decided to go next door to this construction company. While inside, I was able to climb the wall from the back of the school. While inside school property, I was able to keep an eye on my class from a hidden position to make sure I could see the first-period teacher leaving the class before trying to sneak into the classroom. I had to make sure I was inside the classroom before the second-period teacher had set his feet in the classroom; otherwise, I would be forced to get a write-up, which was ten lashes.

One of the differences between schools in the Congo and schools in the United States was that in the United States, teachers were assigned their own classroom—meaning, in each period, students have to travel from and to different classes depending on their class schedule; in my country, it was the opposite. Every grade level was assigned a permanent classroom in which teachers had to come in and out of. Depending on the number of students in a graduating class, some classes were bigger than others or they were simply broken up into several other classrooms. For example, there only was one ninth-grade class, while we had two eighth-grade classrooms and three seventh-grade classrooms.

I got in safely into the classroom after watching the French teacher leaving the classroom right about five minutes before the math teacher was set to take over. I was able to dodge a bullet, a very big one this time. As soon as the bell that marked the end of the school day rang, I was already on my way, wasting absolutely no time.

When I got in front of the secretary's residence, I noticed that Oliver wasn't guarding the gate. It was Willy, the other guard, who went by Willy Manono; Manono is the name of his native town. Willy Manono was the weirdest of all. First, he claimed he was only nineteen years old, but his face told a different story. Judging by his face, he was most likely to be in his early thirties. In his defense, coming straight out of the village where there is no birth records, he probably didn't know his real age. Unlike Oliver, who was the smiling and easygoing type, Willy Manono always looked angry and mean; you wouldn't pay him enough to get a smile out of him. He was all business unlike Oliver with whom I had a lot of interaction with. Willy Manono was the most antisocial of all. I never held a conversation with him. Willy Manono had the look of a person who would shoot someone for accidently calling him the wrong name.

I sat on the bench with the other guards until about 4:30 p.m. By then, I got up and stood by the secretary's gate while waiting for her to come home from work. My heart began to beat faster than ever when I saw her car making its way to the gate. By the time her car made a stop in front of the gate, I was standing still like a statue. Even though the rest of my body was as numb as a mummy, that didn't keep my eyes from wandering toward the backseat of the car where the secretary usually sits. All of a sudden, I saw the backseat window roll down. Before I could even open my mouth, she greeted me with a very warm "Hello there." She then asked me to follow her inside the house.

As I got inside, I was welcomed by the secretary's niece, who introduced herself as Sorine. She looked like she was about eighteen years old or so. I was quickly escorted around the back of the house. I couldn't help but take a good look at the house from the outside. The house was very big with an annex in the backyard. The veranda looked very fancy to me as it has all these ornaments and flowers all around it. To sum it all up, it was a very beautiful house. I was seated in this little dining place like, which was on the other side of the house.

About ten minutes later, Sorine came with a hot meal, which she set on the table for me. She led me inside the kitchen to wash my hands. She told me to take my time eating, and she would come back to let me know when the secretary was ready to speak to me. Everything was happening so fast. I was becoming more and more anxious and nervous at the same time. I had no clue what to expect, although from the way things were going thus far, I couldn't possibly imagine anything worse. As I was thinking, who would have the courtesy to take their time to feed someone's stomach before feeding their spirit some bad news? *No sane person*, I thought. But then again, anything is possible in this crazy world we live in.

After I was done eating, Sorine came back, took the dishes away, and came back, sat with me, and started chatting with me. Her very first question to me was if I spoke Swahili. Swahili was one of the four main national languages. The languages were Lingala, which was the most spoken language in the country with its base predominantly in the capital and the northwestern region; Kikongo, which was seen by many as being the original native language and was spoken in the western part of the region; Tshiluba, the language spoken in the central part of the country and also in some parts of the south; and finally, there was Swahili, a language that has some of its roots from Arabic and is a mixture of native African dialect with some Arabic.

Few centuries ago, Swahili, which has its very first roots in Kenya, started up as a trade language between Arabic merchants who came to Eastern Africa through the Nile River and the African natives along those trade routes. Swahili, the most spoken noncolonial language in Africa, is spoken in about eight different countries in Africa, Kenya, Tanzania, Uganda, Rwanda, Burundi, Sudan, Somalia, and the Democratic Republic of the Congo, my beloved country. Swahili is the main language in the northern, eastern, and southern regions of the country.

Even though Swahili was such a popular language in the country, it didn't make its mark into the city until the current regime took over power. The new president, along with the majority of his crew, was native of the Swahili-speaking region, so with him came a big influx in Swahili-speaking population in the city. And given the fact that he kept most of the power within his region of influence just like most African leaders, his arrival at the helm of the country made Swahili pretty much take over the more popular Lingala, which very much ticked off a lot of the locals who until now knew very little of the language, if anything at all. It became even more and more apparent with the number of influential government officials who were all Swahili speakers.

This time around, being a Swahili speaker was a very big advantage. It was almost as good as having a degree from any Ivy League school. Lucky for me, I spoke a little Swahili, although I wasn't fluent. Spending time playing checkers with those Kadogo, who pretty much spoke nothing else but Swahili, I did pick up a lot. I told Sorine that I spoke a little bit. Sorine was very interested in me. She gave me that impression that she saw me as a little brother figure to her, and I was ready to embrace her as a big sister. Being years younger than she was, I had no shot at being anything else but her little brother.

As we were chatting, we heard a voice from the inside shouting Sorine's name. I recognized that voice as that of the secretary's. Sorine quickly went in. She came back a few minutes later telling me that the secretary was now ready to see me. She escorted me to the front porch where the secretary and her husband were both sitting.

"Have a seat," she said to me. I sat down. Just like in a job interview, I was on the other side of the table, while the secretary and her husband were on the other. "How was your day?" she asked me.

"Good," I said, "but it could be better."

"What made it a good day, not a bad one?" she asked.

"I woke up, made it to school, ate the best meal I had in a long while, and here I am sitting next to you," I said.

She gave me a smile that only a mother could give out. "I read your letter. You have a pretty good handwriting and very good grammar," she added, "but I am more interested in hearing your story than reading about it. Tell me a little bit about yourself."

I started by stating my name and proceeded by telling her how I became an orphan and lived on the streets. I told her how I started impersonating the president and finally that all I was dreaming for was for a place to call home.

She looked at me in my eyes and said, "Is everything you're telling true? Because if I find out you lied to me, you will be in a big trouble," she said.

"I do not tell lies," I said to her.

"OK," she said. "My husband and I welcome you into our house for now. I will have someone look into your references. If we happen to find out that you lied to us, like I said, you will be in big trouble. Now you can get your stuff, and Sorine will show you to your room, but before that, my husband and I would like to hear a little bit of your excerpt from the president."

To most of my delight, I began. "Moi Laurent Desiré Kabila President de la Republic Democratic du Congo Je jure fidelité."

She was all smiles throughout. After I was done, she had Sorine escort me to the annex, which was occupied by the guards. I was so excited I couldn't wait to share the big news with Oliver, who wasn't on duty that day. I couldn't wait till he saw me coming out the house. I took a real shower that night before going to bed. This time, instead of sleeping on cardboards, I had a real bed. I knelt down by the foot of the bed, said my prayer, hopped on the bed, and closed my eyes, and a few minutes later, I would open them back up from time to time just to make sure this wasn't a dream. After a few times, I finally convinced myself it was as real as a dollar bill. I finally closed my eyes for the night.

There were two separate rooms in the annex along with a shower and bathroom. One room belonged to Willy Manono, while the other was Oliver's. Unlike Oliver, who rented a studio about ten miles away from town, Willy Manono lived in the annex, so even when he was off duty, he still stayed there. Given that Oliver was off duty that day, I was told by Willy Manono to put my stuff in Oliver's room and sleep there. He said it in a way that gave me the impression that he didn't want me sleeping in his room; better yet, if he had it his way, he wouldn't want me there, period. What he didn't realize was that I was glad to be sharing the room with Oliver rather than sharing it with the evil being he was anyway.

I did find it a little bit odd that I had to sleep with the guards in the annex instead of sleeping in the main house with the secretary, her husband, and her two nieces, Sorine and Stella! I didn't make anything of it for the simple reason of staying in the annex beats sleeping outside or on top of cardboards; in other words, it's never wise for beggars to be choosers. All the meals were served to us by Sorine or Stella, depending on who was doing the cooking that day. Oliver, Willy, and I mostly ate together. I was given an allowance from the secretary, which was handed to me every day by Sorine at around six thirty during breakfast. My allowance covered the bus fare to school and back home from school, including lunch money. Now, instead of waking up at 5:00 a.m. every day, I had now the luxury of waking up an hour later. Life was becoming a little sweeter to me.

About a week into my new life, I was settling in just fine. My relationship with Oliver was becoming more solid than ever now that we shared the same roof. I also got to develop a good relationship with John, the Kombi driver. The secretary had a Kombi. She had hired John, a driver in his thirties, to drive it on a daily basis running the business. Every morning at around five o'clock, John would pick up the Kombi, take it for business, and bring it back at around ten o'clock every night. Every night, John had to deposit a set amount of money to Sorine from his daily revenue. His daily deposit money was set at the equivalent of about one hundred dollars; therefore, while working, John had the responsibility to make at least one hundred dollars every day. Whatever he made beyond the one hundred dollars was his to keep. On average, after having to pay the hundred-dollar deposit, setting aside gas money, and having to pay his receveur, John took home around one hundred dollars every day. The Kombi business was among the city's most profitable businesses.

I became so close to John that he took me with him in some of his runs on some weekends. I always had so much fun while out and about with John. The experience was enjoyable. It was like riding in a car all day. He would have me sit in front next to him. The most exciting part of being on a Kombi run with John was lunch break. John's favorite place to eat was at Mama Mapasa's bistro near Victory Place. Mama Mapasa, a lady in her fifties, was a great cook. She ran a small kitchen, which she had set up right in the middle of the city's infamous flea market, Gambela. She was the best at her job. During lunchtime, there was a long queue of people waiting to get served. Her signature meal, curry duck and smoked fish with either fufu or plantain on the side, was out of this world, and according to the myth she helped spread around, it was her cooking that finally ended WWII, she often joked. She was very funny. She and john always enjoyed roasting one another. For a woman in her fifties, there was nothing shy about Mama Mapasa. She enjoyed making sexual advances to younger men. She often teased her male customers about how none of them could satisfy her sexually and that the kitchen wasn't the only room in the house where she excelled at.

John and I were very close. All our conversations were in Lingala; whereas, with anybody else in the house, it was either in French or Swahili. Most of the time during school days, I wouldn't go to bed until I have spoken with John, which usually was around 11:00 p.m. from his time back from his Kombi runs. John would always have something for me every night, a magazine, ball . . . That's one of the reasons why I stayed up late almost every night waiting for him, and when he didn't have anything, he would usually give me some pocket money. He was the coolest big brother.

John dropped out of school in fifth grade to support his family after his father's sudden death. His father was a mechanic, his mother a stay-at-home mom. John was the eldest of three children. He started out by selling cold water in plastic bags at one of the city's ports. He then learned how to drive from one of his oldest friends, and a few years later, he got a job as a cab driver and later became a Kombi driver. He was inspired by his father, who, according to him, was the hardest worker he ever knew. His father was a good provider to his family. After his death, his family went through a lot of struggles just to get food on the table. With absolutely no help coming from anyone, not even their closest family members who all turned away from them, he and his two little sisters were kicked out of the school as his mother couldn't afford to put food on the table for them, let alone pay tuition. He and his two little sisters only had their mother, who was struggling to make ends meet by selling flour dough on the street corner.

As the eldest, he sought to help out the best he could by picking up a gig selling water in the market, just like I once did. With the money he was making selling water, he was able to provide food for the whole house and buy some clothes for his sisters, while his mother took care of the rent and utility. When he became a cab driver, he was able to finance his mom's business and help send his two sisters through high school as he was now making decent money. Now at thirty-two, he had his own place and helped his mother and two sisters move into a bigger place. His two sisters both graduated from high school and were now in college. His only regret was that his father never lived long enough to see him take great care of the family.

Life at the secretary's house was great. I was well fed and well clothed. I slept great, but even with all that, there was still this vibe I was feeling. It felt like I was with them without actually being among them. It was plain and simple. I stayed in that house but never felt like I lived in that house. You may ask me, but what is the difference? The difference was that I was in search for a place to call home, but instead, I was put in a house. A house cannot always be a home. Good examples are prisons, hospital rooms, college dorms, army barracks. They all may be housings, but I guarantee you none of them give you the feeling of being home.

One night, while waiting on John, I was in for a bigger surprise. After finishing his transaction with the Sorine that night, John came to the annex holding a puppy.

"Here!" he said to me. "I got this for you. Make sure you take good care of him. What are you going to name him?" he asked.

My joy was out of this world. I couldn't hold still. I was going crazy. As a child growing up, I always loved dogs. "Rocky!" I said, while petting my new friend. I couldn't dream of the day when I would have my own dog, and there it was. One of my wishes was happily barking at me, wishing to be pet.

I took good care of the dog. In my country, there wasn't such thing as pet food. So pets were fed leftovers, meat bones, and chicken bones. They even ate fufu. In most cases, I had seen dogs eating vegetables. Just like everywhere else, I fed Rocky leftovers. Sometimes, I even gave him all my food since I never really enjoyed Sorine's cooking, who was so terrible at cooking; even the whole house knew it, but for whatever reason, that never stopped her from cooking. I felt for her future husband who would have to endure her cooking for the rest of his life. Then again, it says for better or worse; I guess that's what the worse was going to taste like.

One day, there were no leftovers, which meant there was no food for little Rocky. I took it upon myself. I went next door to the Angolan ambassador's wife, whom I have known during my time with Michel, the sentinel. I asked her if she had some bones or any leftovers I could feed to my dog. She told me she was busy at the moment but to give her about half an hour and she would get it together for me. I went back and waited for about forty-five minutes outside our gates, waiting for her to come out her house. She never did. I went back inside. During the time I was inside, she came out with a plastic bag filled with leftovers. Since I wasn't around, she gave it to Willy Manono and told him it to give it to me. There were some meat and rice mixed together inside the plastic bag.

After handing me the bag, Willy Manono went on and told the secretary that I went to ask the Angolan ambassador's wife for food and she brought it to me. The secretary was furious. She let me have an earful of her fury, which was out of this world. She was very concerned of what kind of implication this could have with her job. She lambasted me for having committed a very embarrassing diplomatic faux pas. She was worried that the front page of tomorrow's local newspaper might read, "The wife of the Angolan ambassador comes to the rescue of a starving Congolese kid who happens to be none other than the adoptive son of the president's secretary!" or something in that nature. I tried my best to explain that the food wasn't for me; it was for the puppy instead. To her hears, it made no difference. To her, not only did I humiliate her but also furthermore I embarrassed the whole nation with my actions. As a punishment, I wasn't allowed outside the house ever again. The only exception was going to school and coming back from school.

One day, I decided to play a dirty trick on Willy Manono for having told on me. As I saw it, the food issue, which was completely blown out of proportion, could have been avoided had Willy Manono not opted to tell it to the secretary. There wouldn't have been any harm had he not said anything at all. Willy Manono was so overzealous in harming me any way he could. There had been bad blood between us from the start. I never quite understood the reason behind his hostility toward me. I never recalled any wrongdoing from my part. I did what the only realistic thing to do dealing with his stance—I totally ignored his existence by avoiding any sort of contact with him. I wouldn't say hello to him or speak to him even if he was the last person on earth and my life solely depended on him. He was just mean, isolated, and unhappy at all times, which to me was a very bad combination for a person who carried a weapon all the time.

It has always been my motto in life to make myself as fewer enemies as possible. I hated confrontation. I did everything possible to be less confrontational with anyone, big or small. Ever since at a very young age, I lived a very steady genuine diplomatic life as it was. I enjoyed being in great relation with everyone regardless of their social, ethnic, or religious background. But with Willy Manono, it was something that was out of my reach. A lost cause. He made it clear through his actions that he despised me. Aside from the very short greetings and direct conversations with Sorine, John and Oliver were the only two people I was constantly interacting with. To me, Willy Manono was as good as a ghost. He hated me, and I hated his guts even more.

One morning, I have decided to get close to getting even with him. I took both his walkie-talkie and his 9 mm pistol to school with me, bringing all my classmates in a state of awe. Bringing those two items to school was like bringing the hottest female celebrity as a date at a local school dance. All eyes were on me during lunch break. Everyone wanted to hold the gun, and we spent a few times listening to military conversation on the radio, one of the coolest things to ever happen to some. Unlike in the western world where such action could have landed me in jail or at the very least led to my expulsion from school, in my school, after the rumor had spread all over the school, one of my teachers even asked me to show him the gun and proposed to buy it from me. I never was tempted by the offer, which made it very easy for me to decline.

Ever since it was known publicly that my tuition was paid for by the Department of Education and that I lived with the president's secretary, I did enjoy quite a special treatment from all the school officials. At one point, my history teacher even gave me his twenty-page-long résumé to give to the secretary, seeking employment, which I never even gave to the secretary. Every time he asked me about the secretary's reply to his résumé, I always told him she had been very busy and that she said she was going to get back with me as soon as she got some free time. In my defense, even at fourteen, I knew that wasn't the smart thing to do to give a fourteen-year-old kid your résumé in hopes of landing a more prestigious job than the kid's parent. I couldn't understand what was going through his mind while coming out with such a ludicrous decision. I wasn't the one to point it out to him, and I definitely wasn't going to hurt his feelings by declining his résumé; even worse, I was never going to hand his résumé to the secretary, not with all that was going on at the moment.

I came back home from school that day to a very furious Willy Manono, who, the very minute I stepped into the gate, welcomed me with a very angry shout, demanding if I was the one who took his pistol and walkie-talkie. I bluntly denied such allegation. I quickly went inside and laid his pistol and walkie-talkie right by his bed in his room. He was even more furious when he went to his room just to see the pistol and walkie-talkie lying right next to his bed. He came back shouting and menacing me and threatening to beat me up. He even took it a step further by telling the secretary about how he was fed up with me and he was going to kill me if they didn't act quickly.

I was called in by a very angry secretary, who was once again very furious at me, asking me what in the world was going through my head when I was taking something that didn't belong to me—better yet, it had to be Willy Manono's stuff, for God's sake. Once again, I swore up and down that I had absolutely nothing to do with Willy Manono's allegation.

"He is just trying his best to get me in a lot of trouble with you, that's all," I told the secretary. She seemed more annoyed than anything, and I could feel she was now showing me less sympathy now that I was bringing her more trouble than ever before.

As days went by, the atmosphere between Willy Manono and I was becoming more and more like that of the USA and the Soviet Union during the Cold War era. We both kept the distance while keeping a very closer eye on one another, preparing ourselves for an imminent showdown, which could prove to be very catastrophic. Given his nature, which was that of a lunatic, I knew I was in for a long and unpredictable tussle. I lived in constant fear, mostly fearing that the mentally deranged Willy Manono could opt to put a bullet in my head, perhaps during my sleep. I would brush off such a thought by paying less attention to the worst that has yet to happen and perhaps would never happen.

I came back from school one day just to hear Oliver telling me, "The secretary has sent her driver to come pick you up around noon to have you in front of the president. Unfortunately, you were at school, and no one here knew where your school was, let alone the name of your school."

I just felt like someone had just shot my brain off. I couldn't realize what I was being told. This couldn't possibly be an April fool's joke or perhaps a very sour joke from Oliver. But two things were certain: it definitely wasn't an April fool's joke as we were few weeks past April already, and to make it more surreal, Oliver never was the type to pull pranks on someone. Everything coming out of his mouth was true. I was left speechless. I didn't know whether to cry, curse the sky, or punch the wall for yet another missed opportunity. I was more devastated when later on that night, the secretary herself told me about it. She said she had sent for me as a surprise for the president. She later told me she would give it another shot sometime in the near future. I really needed that assurance to lift my spirits up anywhere near where it was prior to that bad news. It was the third missed opportunity I had to meet up with the president. *Oh, well, may be the fourth time will be the charm,* I calmly said to myself.

One day after school, my French teacher pulled me aside to talk to me about an upcoming event that was to take place in one of the city halls. It was a competition sponsored by the Belgian embassy marking the anniversary of the Francophonie, the international organization representing countries and regions where French is the customary language. There were a lot of prizes to be won, notably scholarships from schools in Belgium and France. My teacher thought that with my impersonations of the president, I had a shot at winning a prize. He gave me all the information I needed to successfully sign up for the event.

I went the next day right after school to sign up for the event. I took my friend Sefu with me. When I got there to sign up, I was sent to the office of the event coordinator, a white man who looked in his late thirties or early forties. When I got into his office, he told me that I just missed out on the deadline by a few days. Once again, I was so disappointed at myself for encountering yet another missed opportunity. Just when I was about to leave the office, the coordinator stopped me by asking what was I signing up to do, if I don't mind telling him.

"Impersonating the president," I said.

"Impersonating the president? Like how?" he asked me. I told him about how I have been impersonating the president for quite a while now. "Let me hear something he said." I went on and did some impersonations for about fifteen minutes. After I was done, he was so amazed that he couldn't barely refrain himself from his excitement. "I tell you what!" he said. "I have something in mind for you. Instead of signing up as an individual, I would like for you to join me in my little project I put together. I will have you play a role in a gig I set up that includes four other kids. I want to include you in it. I will make a script for you. It won't be long. You shouldn't have any trouble going through it." He told me to come in the next day. He would have everything ready for me.

I went back there the following day. This time, I was alone. Upon arrival, which was around 2:30 p.m., the coordinator took me in a hall located in the building behind the one we were on. I got to meet the other kids who were part of the coordinator's crew. After introducing each other, I have learned that the three kids who were about two grades above me were from one of the most prestigious high schools in the city, College Boboto, an all-boys Catholic school. Among them was also a girl who was from a nearby all-girls school. You can say aside from me, who was just from one of the city's average private schools, the other kids' credentials were very impressive. They were all among the top of their classes. I felt like I was being introduced to the big league. Those kids were from schools where you have to qualify academically to be enrolled. Honestly, I was very impressed but far from being intimidated. I might have come from an average school, but I sure didn't have an average brain, and if, above all, the coordinator, a white man, thought I belonged, more importantly, if I had it in me that I belonged, then damn whoever would think otherwise.

We were all given a script of a mini play written by the coordinator himself. It was a very short story about all the different branches of the United Nations, UNESCO, UNICEF, especially working together in union to promote peace in all the French-speaking countries in the world. My role in the script was to be the voice of the Congolese president giving a message to the Congolese nation to adhere to this new concept, or something like that.

For the next three days, we have been rehearsing for about two hours each day, with everyone getting accustomed with their lines. It was a well-written play. Everyone was getting the hang of it. On the third day, the rehearsal took a little longer than usual. We didn't finish until around 5:30 p.m., which meant, with only about half an hour left of daylight, there was no way I was going to make it home before dark. Just the thought of it already was getting me sick to my stomach. The fear of being reprimanded for getting home past dark was already wearing me down. As much as I was trying to keep my cool, I couldn't keep my face from looking worried. Fortunately, not only did the coordinator sense the uneasiness in me but also he was kind enough to ask me what was bothering me. I told him I was afraid of getting home late, which could mean I would be the subject to some sort of punishment.

"Don't worry," he said. "I will take you home. "You just have to show me where you live."

Those words brought up a big relief. Thank God I was going to dodge a bullet. I got in his car, a gray Peugeot, a pretty nice sedan. We got to chat along the way a little bit about politics. From our conversation, I could see that the coordinator was not too fond of the president. Well, so did everyone within the international community, which pretty much only meant the United States and its Western European allies. To them, the Congolese regime was nothing but a dictatorial regime aiming at bringing suffering to its own people, which pretty much could best be translated as a regime that wasn't serving their "best interest." I tried to defend the regime the best way I could, but every little argument I raised was met by a well-put-together and stronger one. The intellectual disparity between the coordinator and me did have a lot to do with that. Even though our political opinions were very different as he tried to portray the international community as a force of good, while I tried to stand my ground by labeling their interference in our country's domestic matters as detrimental, we both enjoyed the exchange of opinion with one another in a level branded by mutual respect for one another. The coordinator was a very good man, with a very pious and energetic persona. I was never bored with his presence.

When he dropped me in front of the gates, there at the gate was Willy Manono sitting in his chair with his AK-47 branded across his lap. I got out of the car and waved good-bye to the coordinator. As soon as the coordinator left, as I was opening the gate to get inside, I heard a voice from behind my back asking, "So who is your new friend?" It was Willy Manono asking me that question.

I just ignored him and went inside. I took my school clothes off and jumped into the shower. As I was getting out the shower, I was told by Willy Manono that the secretary wanted to have a word with me. I got myself together. As I was headed toward the big house, there was the secretary and her husband sitting on the patio. I went on the patio.

"Hello, Mom. Hello, Dad." I greeted both the secretary and her husband.

"Sit down," she said. "So who was the white man who dropped you off?" she said. I told her exactly who the coordinator was and how I came into contact with him and the reason why he offered me a ride home tonight and, to be more precise, my relationship with him.

After I was done talking, she said, "We did the very best we could with you. We were very patient with you, but I don't see this working out. I would like for you to get your things together, and by tomorrow, I want you out of here."

I was left speechless. All I could manage to say was thank you. I couldn't quite understand what I did wrong. As I was headed back to my room, I saw Oliver heading toward the gate. I stopped him to tell him what had just happened. That's when I found out from Oliver that Willy Manono went on to tell the secretary that I was dropped off by a white man who could eventually be one of those European spies trying to gain access to some classified information about the president. For all he knows, I could possibly be working with white people plotting to kill the president. Wow! I couldn't imagine what my ears were hearing. This was beyond choking. I went back to my room. As I sat there in bed, I started thinking back about all the moments that got me in trouble with the secretary, playing it back in my head like it was the movie *Titanic*.

By this time around, the country was under a sort of state of emergency. With the military occupation of Rwanda and Uganda of Congolese, with Rwanda occupying the eastern part, while its ally, Uganda, took care of the northern part, the country was war. The regional conflict involving six different countries drew a similarity to that of the war in Syria. You had on one side Angola, Zimbabwe, and Namibia fighting alongside the Congolese government, which controlled only about 60 percent of Congolese territory ranging from central, west, a big majority of south, and, of course, the capital city; and on the other hand, you had Rwanda, Uganda, and Burundi, sponsored and financed by western multinationals and some American special interest groups such as the Clinton Foundation occupying the mineral-rich part of the country the east, occupying the eastern regions of the country, which were rich in minerals. Among many other minerals found in that part of the country, gold and tin, just to name a few, there was the most important of all in the name of coltan, a mineral used in all electronic devices. More than three-fourths of the world's deposit strictly lies in that part of the country alone.

North and a small part of the South. Just like before, to mask the true face of the occupation from the average eye, once again, Paul Kagame, Yuweri Museveni, and their small Tutsi-led click went and picked up a few washed-up Congolese dissidents and put them as the face of a new rebellion against the Congolese government, while Paul Kagame and Yuweri Museveni and all those multinationals and American special interest groups plundered strategic minerals found in those occupied territories. While the Congolese government tried vainly to rally the international community against the Rwandan and Ugandan aggression, in return, the Rwandan and Ugandan governments, through their proxies, were denying any interference by labeling their occupation a rebellion. They would present those Congolese puppets as rebel chiefs, knowing that it was truly them, Rwanda and Uganda, who were the real masters and creators of the charade.

To make matters worse, those Congolese territories under Rwandan and Ugandan occupation saw a large influx of atrocity to the local population. Regional cities such as Beni, Ituri, just to name a few, were living in constant fear of foreign troops and militias under the special command of Paul Kagame and his click. There were massive rapes, beheadings, and ethnic cleansing being carried by troops and militias under the command of Paul Kagame, also known as the twenty-first-century Pol Pot. A genocide of the Congolese people with a death toll ranging from eight to twelve million people, mostly women and children, had been under way since the late 1990s and still going on today. On many occasions, Tutsi-led militia, under the command of Paul Kagame's generals, would come into a village, burn all the huts and homes, and commit mass rapes to women and young girls as young as four, while they beheaded and executed the men. Some boys as young as seven were later forcibly taken away and enlisted as child soldier with the simple mission of committing more atrocities in other towns and villages. The more fortunate ones who were able to flee in the jungle usually ended up either dying there or making it out to a neighboring country and settle as refugee. It is all part of Paul Kagame's master project of getting rid of a large majority of Congolese people out of their land and replace them with Rwandese population, who will later be claiming those land as their own.

This is going on today, and why haven't you seen it on CNN, Fox News, or read about it on the *New York Times*? Because a lot of American special interests and multinationals who have so much interest with the exploitation of this mineral-rich region are sponsoring those militias to carry on those atrocities to depopulate those areas known to have strategic minerals such as coltan, a mineral primarily used in every kind of electronic device. So next time you use your iPhone or Samsung Galaxy, or next time you or your child plays an Xbox or PS4, keep in mind that those companies are contributing in a genocide being carried on in Beni and other parts in Eastern Congo so they can have those minerals at a very low price. Just like the blood diamond tragedy that happened Sierra Leone in the 1990, now, blood coltan has been going on from late 1990s and still going on today. I don't know the statistics on blood diamond, but the death toll from the genocides from blood coltan has reached more than eight million lives. That's the equivalent of waking up one morning and everyone in New York is dead—I mean, dead, and they are never coming back.

One other reason why the world had been so silent to the Congolese genocide being carried away by Paul Kagame is that Paul Kagame has done a great job portraying himself and his small Tutsi-led regime sympathizers as being the victims of the Rwandese genocide that happened in 1994. Paul Kagame has used the label of genocide survivor bestowed upon him and his small Tutsi-led click to his advantage by carrying his evil plans, knowing that the world wouldn't dare hold him accountable for all those mass rapes, ethnic cleansing, and war crimes since he is a Holocaust survivor.

To those who don't know the difference, a rebellion is when a group of citizens take up arms against their own government for whatever reason. On the other hand, when armed citizens from another country, whether military or contractors, enter foreign soil, whether they disguised their true identity, and wage a war against the established institution of that country, that's not a rebellion; it is an aggression. And when those foreign troops or militias decide to stay in those conquered territories without invitation from the established government, that is called occupation.

Only two years into his presidency, Laurent Desire Kabila was already facing dilemmas. Only 60 percent of the country was under his control, while the other 40 percent was directly or indirectly under Paul Kagame's and Yuweri Museveni's control. The western world, which is made up of the EU members, Israel, Australia, and their ally, the United States, wanted him out of power since he wasn't serving their national interest as a result, leaving him isolated from the entire international community. When the soup Nazi says, "No soup for you," believe me, you would not be having any soup, at least not in this lifetime. The EU, Israel, Australia, and the USA—those are the world's soup Nazi. When they say dance, you dance, my friend. If you have any other thoughts that are not in conformity with theirs, you will end up dead like Saddam Hussein and Muammar Gaddafi, removed from power like Manuel Noriega and Laurent Gbagbo, or isolated like Fidel Castro and Hugo Chavez; but if you do just like you are told, you will be elevated just like Nelson Mandela. The choice is yours to make.

The war was taking a toll on Laurent Desire Kabila. The economy was reaching its lowest point in decades. Every two months saw government officials removed and replaced. Some army officials accused of treason were either jailed or just executed. Rumors surrounding perhaps a coup d'état within his own circle were swirling around. Every week, there was either a foiled assassination attempt or something in that nature. We were living in a constant state of paranoia. There was a feeling that it was just a matter of time before something was to happen. Any white man was seen as suspicious, perhaps as a CIA agent or a spy; while anyone who had a facial feature of Tutsi ethnicity was either put in secret jails mostly underground or executed. That sort of explained why Willy Manono, seeing me with that white man, might have thought that I was given a special mission.

That night, while I was packing, getting ready to be out of the house the next day, Oliver came and spoke to me. He had told me if I didn't have anywhere to go, I was more than welcome to come and stay at his place. Oliver rented a studio about ten miles away from the secretary, which he paid about ten dollars a month for rent. Having no other choice, I was forced to accept his genuine offer. Even though Oliver felt for me, I still could see a part of him acknowledging that I had it coming. It was just a matter of time as I had been walking on a very thin line for quite some time now. Luckily for me, the next day was a Saturday, and I didn't have to go to school.

The next morning, Oliver and I caught the minibus to his place. When we got there, we saw a girl lying down on his bed. It was Carine, Oliver's girlfriend and soon to be the mother of his first child, so he thought. After being introduced to Carine by Oliver, I pulled Oliver outside and asked him how in the world this was supposed to work out, how his girlfriend and I were going to sleep on the same bed while he wasn't around. He started laughing so hard. I didn't know whether to laugh with him or laugh at him.

"Calm down!" he said. "She doesn't usually stay here. She lives with her parents about five blocks away from here. She just stopped by from time to time when I am on duty to wash my clothes and keep the house clean. On my off days, she does stay the night."

Carine was pretty cool. We clicked right from the start. She was one of those fast city girls who lives in one of the most rural areas of the city. She was about seventeen years old and dropped out of school. She was one of those very independent girls who did everything they wanted. Being a teenage girl in a very poor family as hers meant that Carine had to pretty much take care of herself by providing for herself and perhaps some of her younger siblings since her parents couldn't do it for them. In a poor family such as hers, options were very limited. It was pretty much everyone for themselves, and if by any luck or savviness, a family member was able to gather a little more than enough to feed and clothe themselves, they were now given the responsibility of their younger sibling. Since most of them couldn't afford tuition, school was a luxury that one could have gone without.

For most teenage girls in those neighborhoods, prostitution was used as a mechanism to provide for oneself, sometimes for the family. Even children as young as twelve years old were forced to take up such desperate measure. With the influx of child soldiers and other teenage soldiers in the city with the arrival of the new regime, it became a very profitable business for those young girls coming out of those rural areas. They found it more profitable hooking up with those child soldiers who had a salary of one hundred dollars a month.

These teenage little girls were like mice in search for cheese, and those horny Kadogo were ready to give it out in exchange for some good times. Ninety-nine percent of the time, love had nothing to do with it when it came to their encounter. Those teenage girls from the city usually played their prey, the Kadogo, making them think that they were in love, while in fact, they were being cheated on by their city boyfriends. On some occasions, guys would even pimp their girlfriends out to those Kadogo just to gain access to their wallets.

That was also the case with Carine and Oliver. While Oliver thought Carine was the girl of his dreams and had all those good plans for them to be together as long as forever, to Carine, Oliver was nothing but a walking ATM machine, which she took great advantage of by sharing the proceeds with her real boyfriend, whose baby she really was carrying, the same baby Oliver thought was his. At the end of the day, that wasn't any of my business, and I sure wasn't going to be involved in it. I had a great relationship with Oliver and a good one with Carine, and I opted to keep it that way. That was diplomacy at its best.

I moved in with Oliver at a very tough time with the economy at its nadir ever since the new regime took over. The government was becoming more and more interested in concentrating about 80 percent of its budget to the war, constantly paying large bills to mercenaries from countries such as Zimbabwe, Namibia, and Angola. Having no reliable army of its own capable of securing its borders, the Congolese government sought help from those three countries to help fight against the Rwandan and Ugandan invasion.

Paying those foreign troops was proving to be very costly. With the war that was being fought on Congolese soil at a stalemate, while

Rwanda and Uganda troops maintained their heavy presence in the eastern part of the country keeping hold of those minerals, all the government's allies troops were good at was keeping Rwanda and Uganda from advancing any further toward the capital, which seemed like a semivictory only to those who didn't have a grasp of the game being played.

Rwanda and Uganda had what they always wanted from the Congo, which was to have full control of the eastern part of the Congo, which enabled them to have full access to its mineral for personal exploitation. With the eastern regions at their elm and mercy, they were less interested in making any further military gain, although they did from time to time launch some sporadic military offensive through their proxies to make it look as if it was a Congolese rebellion trying to march into the capital city to overthrow the regime. They brought up a few Congolese exiles and placed them at the head of their operation to mask the invasion and portray it as a Congolese rebellion. While that was Rwanda's and Uganda's strategy in the east, in the west, the government allies, Angola, Zimbabwe, and Namibia, sought to make more profit than intended on this war by making sure they were "fighting" an endless war. In which case, they would maintain their presence pretending to be fighting, while they drew big checks from the Congolese government. The Congolese government was paying about $400 a day to its allies troops, while their government was drawing even bigger checks from mining concessions in areas that were still under government control.

In all this, there were many winners and only one loser. The winners were Rwanda, Uganda, and Burundi on one side, and Angola, Zimbabwe, and Namibia on the other side. While the big loser was the Congolese people who was being impoverished gradually and systematically. The Congolese people were paying even a bigger price with their lives during this war of aggression. With about 80 percent of the country's budget going to the war, the government wasn't able to pay its workers anymore. While those mercenaries were being paid about $400 a day, the government wasn't even able to pay its own military's salary of $100 a month.

With all the government sectors forced to take major budget cut, not only did the Department of Education cut my monthly allowance of fifty dollars a month to twenty dollars—and that twenty dollars wasn't even guaranteed anymore—but also I was told that the department wouldn't pay for my tuition next year. I was now on my own. If I wanted to pursue my education, I had to come up with a way to pay for my own tuition. The way things were turning out, school was going to be among the least of my worries.

Staying at Oliver meant that I was now farther away from my school. Not to mention that I had to walk for about five miles just to get to the nearest bus stop. I had to come up with my own food somehow. Since there was no electricity in the house, my bedtime was now around 7:00 p.m. On Monday morning, I got up at around 4:30 a.m. and took a shower, and by 5:00 a.m., I was already on my way to school. I walked those five miles to the nearest bus stop and caught the Kombi to school on my way back. I had to walk all the way back, a walk that took me about six hours. To make it a little easier on me, I would stop occasionally whenever I saw a gathering somewhere along the way to play either street soccer or checkers. I often took the route that led me through FEZADI, where I often took a break as that was about the halfway point from school to Oliver's. Altogether, I probably walked about thirty miles every day.

There was nothing easy about walking through the hot sun each day. It felt like I didn't have any other life aside from walking to and back from school and sleeping. By the fourth day, I have already run out of all the little money I had. In the morning, I was able to hitchhike to school. On my way back from school, I was very exhausted as I didn't have anything at all to eat for the whole day. Out of energy, it was now taking me longer to get back as I was walking at a record low pace.

It was now around 8:00 p.m., and I was still on the road. I was so tired and hungry. I just burst out into tears. I was singing gospel songs with tears coming out of me like a fountain. After a while, I stopped singing. I began speaking to myself, mostly questioning God, asking him why he was allowing me to go through so much, why he wasn't showing any compassion to my misery, and why he was turning a deaf ear to my prayers. While I was also reminiscing my fall from grace, about a little less than ten minutes afterward, my eyes pointed me to a guy standing at the corner of the intersection. The guy, who seemed to be in his midthirties, was sharply dressed with a black overcoat and a briefcase just like those lawyers in the movies. He seemed a bit preoccupied as if he was getting impatient waiting on a certain someone. As I got closer to the guy, something told me to approach the guy. When the guy was right in front of me, I approached him.

"Excuse me, sir!" I said with a very timid voice. "I'm just getting back from school and haven't eaten anything all day. I'm very hungry. I was hoping you could help me out with some change so I can at least get me a loaf of bread."

Without asking any question, the man put his hand in one of his pockets and pulled out a bill that was the equivalent of a twenty-dollar bill. It felt like being handed fifty dollars after only asking for a dollar.

Wow! I thought to myself. *There sure is a God, and he sure has been listening to my prayers indeed.* I thanked the guy, who still stood there emotionless. All of a sudden, I felt a burst of energy all over me. All my tears quickly turned into tears of joy in a matter of minutes. As I started walking, I turned back to take one more good look at the Good Samaritan. To my amazement, the guy with the coat was nowhere to be found. How could he have managed to disappear in such a very short period? Unless he had wings, that was near impossible to pull such a stunt. What had just happened to me was a miracle, if not the closest thing to a miracle I had ever experienced. It seemed to me that perhaps the guy's only mission was to be there at that very spot just for him to hand me the money. If that wasn't a miracle, I don't know what is.

With that being said, I praised God by singing more gospel songs throughout the rest of the way until I got home, thanking him for the miracle he just performed on me. I bought myself a loaf of bread and some sugar and mixed the sugar with some water in a cup. I killed that meal as if it was the last supper. After I was finished, I said a little short prayer. At around 10:00 p.m., I was snoring my way through Disney World in my dreams.

I spent that money so wisely I could have easily been next in line to receive the budgeter of the year award. For the next ten days or so, I was able to buy a loaf of bread, one-eighth ounce of grilled peanuts, with one-eighth ounce of sugar dipped into a twenty-ounce water cup. That's what I ate once a day for about ten days. I also paid for the bus fare, only one way. I only paid for my way to school and walked the distance after school. Since I was on a one-meal-a-day plan, I chose to eat only at nighttime and drink up a lot of water in the morning. I guess you can say I had plain water for breakfast and bread and sugar water for dinner. When making me a cup of sugar water, I usually added a little salt to bring out the sweet flavor a little more, one of the most creative tricks I learned in my days being at the Hill.

When I spent my last dime on the usual bread and sugar, I named my meal for the night "the last supper of the orphan." Unless there was to be another miracle of that magnitude, I didn't see myself being the recipient of yet again another miracle that eventually will lead to a continuance of the daily meal. Still keeping my hopes up even though things weren't looking so good for me. That didn't keep me from enjoying that last loaf of bread from the money I got from the guy with the black coat. I just took a little time to praise God for the meal I was about to receive as I thought it to be a blessing rather than a curse. It might have not been the best meal, but at least I was lucky enough to have one. I knew there were thousands not so far from me and perhaps millions a little farther away who wished they could have what I was having, but to no fault of their own, they had nothing, so I have few more reasons to be thankful.

The very next morning, being out of money, I wasn't able to hitchhike to school either. I saw all my attempts to get me a mercy ride to school fail miserably for the very first time that morning. *There is a first time for everything,* I thought. With that, my consecutive days without being absent from school were snapped. Attempting to walk to school from Oliver's house was as good as trying to swim in the river without getting wet. *Mission impossible,* I thought. Instead, I went back and caught some more sleep.

At around 4:00 p.m., I was able to walk to Michel's. That was the very first time in a while I got to see Michel again. During my time living with the secretary, not even once I went back to see Michel since I was forbidden to go out of the house after 6:00 p.m., which was the time Michel usually got to work. Once I saw Michel again that night, I got an earful from him, basically lashing out at me for forgetting our past once I got my little moment of fame living with the secretary, which perhaps was short lived for being ungrateful. I tried the very best I could to launch a good defense on my behalf, letting him know how I was put on curfew the moment I set my foot within those gates. According to him, there still could have been ways around it; I just chose not to and made absolutely no effort. I gave it to him. He did perhaps had a point there, and all I could say was sorry. After finally letting it go, we were once again the best of pals. I got to tell him about everything that had happened to me ever since we last saw each other, and he got me caught up on some more of his never-ending stories. Everything was back to normal once again. I got to spend the night there on those cardboards. I couldn't really say that I missed them. What is there to miss about sleeping about half an inch above the concrete floor after all?

The next morning, I did once again miss out on a ride to school. After missing three straight days of school, I just decided to call it quits for the remainder of the year. Waking up every morning at around five o'clock just to have every Kombi driver deny me a free ride to school was getting to me, and I sure wasn't going to walk twenty miles to school and twenty miles back from school every day. I didn't have the passion to keep pushing myself anymore. Since getting to and from school every day was physically and mentally tougher on me, I decided to take the burden off me. As much as I loved and enjoyed being in school, I had to take a break from it.

With me officially out of school, I had to step up in coming up with other means to generate any type of income just enough to eat every day. What better way than doing about the only thing I knew how to do—impersonating the president. Just like I did during my time at the UNIKIN campus, I decided to take on the ISC campus, located right across the street from Michel's workplace. ISC stood for the Superior

Institute of Commerce, also known as the country's largest business management school. I started out by walking around the campus. Whenever I would see a group of students gathered, I would stop by and ask if they were interested in listening to the president's press conference or speech. Their attitude would be a little indifferent at first, but it always ended up with them giving me the stage. My very first day at the campus was a hit. I made about twenty dollars in tips money, and on top of that, I came into contact with Blaise and Martin, two of the most influential students on campus.

Blaise and Martin were the best of friends. They shared a dorm together. Blaise and Martin were third-year seniors who were also known as being ISC president's right-hand men. The head of ISC was known as the DG, short for director general. Blaise and Martin took great care of the DG by recruiting cute undergrad female students who were fresh out of high school so that he could have his way with them. In return, Blaise and Martin were allowed to run the campus. They had a free pass when it came to doing whatever they wanted and breaking any campus rules they wanted.

Blaise and Martin quickly took me up on their wings. From now on, they were to act as my manager, they told me. They will start up by introducing me to the DG, and from then on, they will promote me throughout every campus event that was to take place. I loved every sound of it. Blaise was skinny and taller, about six feet one inch, while Martin was about five feet nine inches with the average weight. Blaise was the more outspoken of the two. Blaise and Martin took me back to their room, where we all shared a meal. At around 7:00 p.m., we parted ways. I went back to Michel's.

The very next day, while coming back from meeting up with Blaise and Martin, at around 4:00 p.m., I saw two people playing checkers outside of a house located right across Michel's job. I quickly made my way to the checkers match. Just when I got closer, one of the two who were playing was getting up, leaving the game. Before the other one could also follow suit, I asked if he still wanted to play some more. To my delight, he said yes! We sat there playing for hours. As we were playing, we introduced ourselves to one another. He told me his name was Kevin, but he went by Daudoit. I told him my name was Timu. As we kept on playing and talking, Daudoit asked me if I stayed in the neighborhood.

"Not really," I replied. "To be honest, I don't have a home. I just stay here and there."

I told him a little bit about myself, how I was an orphan and how I got kicked out of the secretary's house not long ago. Now I was back sleeping next door in a cardboard whenever Michel worked. Daudoit knew Michel very well.

Being very touched by my story, Daudoit, who was about my age, maybe just a year or two older at the most, said, "We have an empty bedroom in my house that we never use. I will ask my mother and try to convince her to let you move in, but until I get the chance to talk to her, you are more than welcome to come share lunch and dinner with me whenever you want to."

Wow! I thought to myself. *This was exactly what I needed. God has once again sent me another angel from the sky.*

That night, Daudoit and I ate dinner together at his house. He briefly introduced me to his mother as his friend before bringing the meal outside. It was rice and beans in a big glass bowl with hot peppers on the side. After the meal, we hung out outside listening to some of Michel's endless stories. At around 10:00 p.m., Daudoit went back home, while Michel and I stayed outside for about an hour before I had to call it a night. While lying down on my cardboard, I couldn't stop but think about how lucky I was to have run into Daudoit. I couldn't wait to hang out with him again the next day.

The next day, after having spent the entire afternoon with Daudoit, I had to leave him for a little while to go meet up with Blaise and Martin at the campus. They were supposed to introduce me to the DG, whom they nicknamed the Godfather. At around six thirty that evening, Blaise, Martin, and I headed to the DG's office located in the school administration's building. I have been inside the offices of few important figures such as the secretary of sports, the deputy minister of education, and the deputy minister of mining and energy. I have to admit, none of these offices were as well equipped and prestigious as that of the DG's office. It was very presidential. We were introduced by the DG's personal secretary, a young lady who looked to be in her early twenties. Blaise and Martin took the lead by introducing me to the DG, a heavyset man who appeared to be in his fifties. He was very cozy and down to earth. He came out of his seat and shook my hands as if we have been former high school teammates.

Without wasting any time, Blaise looked up to the DG and said, "Here's the surprise I told you I had for you," and looked back at me and said, "Go for it."

I started my impersonation of the president with the president's investiture speech, which had always been my knockout punch, and ended up reciting few excerpts from the president's latest press conference where he accused Rwanda and Uganda of bringing war on Congolese soil and vowed to export it back to their front door.

I left the DG speechless. He enjoyed my performance so much that he even jumped out of his rolling chair and embraced me. He put his arm around my shoulder like a friend and looked up to Blaise and said, "Where in the world did you find him?"

"Don't you worry about where we found him. You need to worry about taking good care of him if you can," said Blaise to the fifty-year-old DG.

He went back to his desk and grabbed five notes of one hundred francs and handed it to me. The notes were brand new as if he just pulled them out of the printing machine himself.

"How did you learn how to impersonate the president so well?" asked the DG.

"Just by watching TV," I said. I stayed around for about twenty more minutes, while Blaise and Martin had a chitchat with him.

"Make sure you keep in touch" were his words to me as we all exited his office.

When we got outside the administration building, Blaise asked me to pull out the money and let him see the money. I handed the money to him. He took three hundred and left me with two hundred.

"As your manager, we are entitled to some of the money as well," he said. "Isn't that right, little brother?"

"Of course, yes!" I said.

"That's how business works," he added.

I went back quickly and got across the street looking for Daudoit. I found him standing outside his gate. I pulled him on the side and said to him, "Guess what?"

"What?" he said.

"I just made two hundred francs. Let's go enjoy it."

Daudoit was so excited. "I have an idea," he said. "We should buy a bottle of beer and split it."

"That sounds like fun," I said.

We both went out and got ourselves a bottle of cold beer. In my country, there's no ID requirement to purchase alcohol or tobacco. Children as little as five can be sent to purchase alcohol or tobacco. It's not against the law. As long as you have cash in your hand, you can even walk into a pharmacy without prescription and purchase any narcotics you want for the simple reason that very few people, I'm talking about a little less than 1 percent of the entire population, ever thought about narcotic or drug abuse. Your average drug abuser in the western part of the world would find himself/herself in heaven if he or she ever came to my country.

Daudoit and I split the beer half and half. After getting a pretty good buzz out of it, we went back to Daudoit's house. While inside the house, Daudoit told me that he spoke to his mother about me staying with them. She seemed to be OK with it, but the overall decision was still up to his dad, who was out of town and was supposed to come home on the weekend.

After meeting up with Daudoit's mother, who was very nice and welcoming, I told her a little bit about my life story, which she had already heard from Daudoit, only this time, it was from me. I told her how both of my parents died when I was at very young age, how I found myself sleeping on the streets a few years afterward, how I got kicked out of the secretary's house who lived about five houses down the same street, and finally, how Daudoit and I met. Daudoit's mother was very pious. She was a very devoted Christian. She was very moved by my story. She even shed few tears throughout. Her biggest concern was whether I believed in God and if I prayed from time to time.

"Yes, I do believe in God, and I do pray, but not as often as I ought to," I told her.

"It's OK," she said to me. "God had answered your prayer. God is the one who brought you to me through my son Daudoit. I will talk to my husband this weekend about getting the key to the other room so that Daudoit and you can share the room together. In the meantime, you can sleep on the couch in the living room. You are to me a part of this family as my other children are."

Daudoit had a little sister named Lena, who was about six years old. She was in her last year of kindergarten. Living with them also was their cousin Helene, who was about nineteen years old. They all gave me a very warm welcome and quickly embraced me as one of their own. Daudoit, Lena, Helene, and Mrs. Diane, Daudoit's mom, who went by her nickname Ma Dindo, and I all lived in this two-bedroom annex located at the far end of the house. In front was this big seven-bedroom house occupied by this other family whose father was an officer in the National Police Department.

Ma Dindo was a stay-at-home mom. Helene was on her senior year of high school, Lena in her last year of kindergarten, while Daudoit was supposedly in ninth grade, at least that was what he made everyone in house believe. Daudoit didn't like school at all. Knowing that there was absolutely no way he could have asked Ma Dindo to let him drop out of school, he came up with a way of staying out of school without alerting anyone at the house. His school offered what was called a second-shift school schedule. The second-shift schedule that was offered by some schools in the country was from 12:30 p.m. to 5:30 p.m., instead of the more common schedule, which was 7:15 a.m. to 12:15 p.m. Daudoit would get out of the house at around 11:30 a.m., pretending to be on his way to school, while in reality, he was just leaving the house to hang out with his friends at their favorite spot, a nearby barbershop located about five blocks away from the house, while collecting tuition money from Ma Dindo, which he spent with his friends mostly on marijuana and other things. Only twice during the entire school year had he ever set his feet inside a classroom.

Daudoit and Lena were half brother and sister. Ma Dindo gave birth to Daudoit during her teenage years. Daudoit's father, her boyfriend at the time, took off shortly after she broke the news of the pregnancy to him. He was never to be found ever after that. Few years later, it was told that he was found dead somewhere, with the cause of death still unknown till this day. About a few years later, after giving birth to Daudoit, she met a certain Joseph Kabala, a soldier in his midtwenties who was deployed at a military base in the eastern part of the country near the regional city of Goma. They both met in one of the flea markets near the city line. It was love at first sight the moment Joseph laid his eyes on the young beautiful Diane, who was very outspoken. After seeing each other on a regular basis for about a month, the couple was so in love with each other that they decided to privately tie the knot.

But a few weeks after their Vegas-like marriage, their love was given a big blow as Joseph's platoon was sent back to the capital city, leaving behind his newlywed wife. The two were very heartbroken to be dealt such a blow to their fresh love. But that didn't stop Romeo and Juliet from keeping their love intact. As he was being deployed back to the capital city, Joseph promised young Diane that he would do everything in his power to have them reunited, but in the meantime, he promised to keep in touch through occasional phone calls and mails.

About two years later, the couple was able to reunite when Diane's half sister Helene married a guy named Roger, a businessman who owned a couple of stores around the city. The wedding was held in Kinshasa, about one thousand miles away from her family. Being the bridesmaid, Diane had to make the trip to Kinshasa. After the wedding was over, at her sister's request, she was able to stay and live with her newlywed sister. Diane looked up to her elder sister Helene, whom she shared the same mother but had a different father. Helene, who was in her late twenties, with a master's degree in accounting, was very smart and, above all, a very devoted Christian. A younger Diane ended up staying at her sister's house to help out with daily house chores while both her sister and husband were out working. Now that she was in the city, she was able to reunite with her lover, who was now only a few miles away.

About three years later, the couple finally got a home together in one of the city's military housing, a one-bedroom apartment on a third floor. About a year later, the couple welcomed their first child together, a girl whom they named Lena, whom she named after her sister Helene. About four years later, following the fall of the old regime, they were able to move into a new home, which was left vacated by a family that had ties with the Mobutu regime and ended up fleeing the country for fear of repercussion for their allegiance to the deposed dictator.

Joseph, whom we nicknamed Papa José, was about six feet tall, weighing about a little over 220 pounds. He was a very quiet person but funny when you got to know him. He looked very intimidating at first given his robust military appearance, but up close, he was just your average head of the house. He enjoyed jokes and listening to music. He had a very special bond with his young daughter Lena, who was the light of his life. Papa José worked as a military instructor training new military recruits at one of the army bases located on the outskirts of the city. Being an instructor, Papa José was required to stay at the base for most of his time. He only came home every other weekend. I got to develop a good relationship with Papa José. He became the father I always wanted, and I was the son he always hoped for since Daudoit, his stepson, wasn't quite the obedient type.

I loved Papa Jose and Ma Dindo. They were the coolest parents a child could ever wish for. They were two of the most down-to-earth parents the world had ever seen, but at the same time, they still carried a big stick when discipline was required. Unlike Papa José, who was somewhat the quiet type, Ma Dindo was the very opposite. She was very funny and easygoing. There wasn't a soul in this world who didn't enjoy her company. She always brightened up whatever place she set her foot in. There was so much similarity between the two of us, as I was just as funny as she was, which made our relationship of mother and son even more pleasant. I loved her so much as she was able to give me something I never had growing up—a motherly love. She gave me so much affection, thus making Daudoit become a little jealous of me.

I was somehow the opposite of Daudoit, who always found himself in trouble, whether from stealing food from the house to give to his friends at the barbershop, getting caught smoking marijuana, to spending nights out without permission. To make matters worse, he had girls coming for him at the house, each at their own time, sometimes even at the same time.

Daudoit and I still have the best relationship. It was a mixture between best friend and brother. We first met as friends, but now that I was now part of the family, I was like a little brother to him. Cousin Helene was the big sister to us. She cooked and was responsible for doing most of the house chores; whereas, Lena was just this adorable little creature, a little angel. She was very sweet. She was the perfect little sister.

About two blocks away behind the ISC campus lived Aunt Solange. Ma Dindo's other sister, Aunt Solange, who went by Ma Manga, was Ma Dindo's elder sister. She was just a few years younger than Aunt Helene. Ma Manga, a single mother, worked at RVA, the Congolese equivalent to TSA. She lived in a four-bedroom house with her seventeen-year-old daughter Sandra, her younger sister Guylaine, who was about the same age as Sandra, and her cousin Charles whom we called Tonton Charles. Guylaine was both Ma Dindo's and Ma Manga's youngest sister, while Tonton Charles was their cousin.

Although Tonton Charles stayed at Ma Manga's house, he spent most of the day at our house. He would come by around the afternoon and would stay up until 9:00 p.m. Daudoit and I would usually walk him about halfway back. Tonton Charles, who used to work as an account at the Customs Enforcement agency in the port city of Matadi, about one hundred miles away west from the capital city, was forced to flee back to the capital city following the events that led to the Rwandese invasion of that part of town. Ma Dindo and her family were from Tutsi descent. Her mother, who passed away a few years back, was Rwandese, and her father a Congolese.

With the Rwandan government, which was predominantly Tutsi, waging war against the Congolese government while occupying around 40 percent of Congolese territories, mostly the eastern region, anyone who had a drop of Rwandese blood in them was under serious threat in areas under government control, especially in the capital city, Kinshasa, where there was a massive witch hunt on anyone of Rwandese descent. The witch hunt even expanded to anyone who just fit the description of a Rwandese national and anyone who was harboring a Rwandese citizen. So from August 1998, anyone from Rwandese descent was subject to the same treatment as the Jews in Germany during the Nazi era.

But even though Ma Dindo and her family were half Rwandese, they were spared the prosecution from the locals since Papa Jose, an official in the army, was able to assure their security, and besides, Ma Dindo and her family weren't known to have any ties with anyone within the Rwandese government; they also did not have such a strong Tutsi's physiology like the case with most Rwandese of Tutsi ethnicity.

Unlike Ma Dindo, Tantine Helene and Tonton Charles were both full-blown Rwandese, and looking at their morphology, there was no way of hiding it. Tantine Helene quit her job and went into hiding in her own house, while Tonton Charles was now living a clandestine life at Ma Manga's house. Their elder brother Carol wasn't so lucky as he was taken to custody straight to one of those underground jails where he was treated like a POW. He was tortured and denied food and medical care for a long period. The entire family was fearing the worst as rumors of his execution were going around. On the other hand, Tonton Besto, the youngest man in the family, was lucky enough to escape persecution since he mixed in so well with the locals and had a lots of friends, with some of them even swearing up and down that he wasn't of Rwandese descent at all. Ma Manga was also left untouched and was allowed to keep her job, thanks to her connection with a certain commandant Jean Louis, a colonel in the Republican guards who was a good friend of hers and the family.

Tonton Charles stayed hidden inside Ma Manga's house. From time to time, he would risk his life by walking about four blocks just to come spend the afternoon with us since he was very bored alone at the house with basically no one to talk to. Ma Manga usually didn't get off of work until 8:00 p.m. on weekdays and sometimes had to work on weekends. He enjoyed playing cards with Daudoit and me, and we also watched a lots of TV. And since he couldn't risk being seen in public given his morphology, sometimes he would send us to buy stuff for him. Tonton Charles was a character. He had a very good sense of humor, which made it very enjoyable to be around him. Above all, he was what I called a friendly snake. In your face, he was your biggest supporter, while at the same time, he was your most fervent critic behind your back.

On one occasion, he gave me some money to buy him a few undies at the market. Before I left, I told him to keep an eye on the beans that Ma Dindo had told me to keep an eye on and make sure to turn off the heat whenever the water had dried up. She specifically instructed me not to let it burn. Before I left for the market, I asked Tonton Charles to keep an eye on the beans. Back from the market after handing him the undies, he was so excited. He was so proud of me for having such a good taste. "Those undies are great and perfect" were his words to me.

While I was out shopping for his undies, Tonton Charles somehow got distracted and ended up burning the beans. I was somewhat shocked to see a very angry Ma Dindo, who couldn't believe I failed the easiest task given to me. All I had to do was turn off the heat as soon as all the water was gone from the bean pot, and I couldn't even manage that. Having Ma Dindo yelling at me for something I had no control of was harsh, but what was even more shocking was watching Tonton Charles comfortably keeping his mouth shut while I was getting the heat from Ma Dindo over something he did.

Not only did he not own up to his carelessness, which was now costing me an earful, but also he even went a step further, putting the nail in my coffin, by making some unnecessary comments, telling Ma Dindo, with his slow-paced yet articulated voice, "Why are you even surprised? Those kids of yours aren't too bright. They can't even follow the simplest instruction. One day, you might wake up to a burning house. I will tell you I told you so!"

I stood nearby motionless. I couldn't believe he was saying such things. Few days later, when asked by Ma Dindo how he liked his undies, with smirk on his face, he told her they were the worst pairs of undies he ever had.

"These are the only pairs I know that only cover one butt cheek while leaving the other cheek exposed. I am waking up more often now in the middle of the night just to find one butt cheek being colder than the other one." He claimed they were by far the most uncomfortable undies he ever had. He is not sure where in the world I got them from, for all he knows, I probably took them off out of a sick blind man somewhere.

Tonton Charles also had a way of asking for something that I found to be very sneaky. Whenever he was hungry and wanted one of us to fix him something to eat, he would say something like, "You guys look like you are hungry. Why don't one of you take this money and go buy some groceries so we can fix ourselves something to eat?" while in fact he was the one who was hungry. After I got to know him, I realized how funny he was. He had a great sense of humor to go along with his sarcastic nature. Being around him made the day go fast. Aside from his funny antics, he was a great card player. I even learned a few tricks playing against him. A day wouldn't go by without us playing cards.

Being a part of a family was the most sacred thing that could have possibly happened to me, especially being a part of this particular family. Never before have I ever felt a part of something as I felt being a part of the Kabala family. There was absolutely no difference in treatment from the way Ma Dindo treated Daudoit to the way she treated me. Even all the uncles and aunts treated me as if I was biologically related to them. They all embraced me as their very own. I had a great relationship with both Sandra and Guylaine, who were like big sisters to me. The same went for our cousin Helene.

I got to meet Ma Dindo's younger brother Besto, who was the family disciplinary enforcer. He basically kept Daudoit and me in check. Every time one of us was caught to be unruly, one had to face Tonton Besto's wrath as he was the only one who took charge of straightening us.

One afternoon, after being given grocery money by Tonton Charles to prepare a meal, I got Daudoit into gambling that money on a two-on-two soccer game against our neighbors. The plan was to win ourselves some pocket money by beating our neighbors. Unfortunately, everything didn't go accordingly. Daudoit and I lost the match and consequently the grocery money. Since I was the one to whom the money was given, also the one who came up with that stupid idea to gamble the money, it was my responsibility to find a way to replace that money alone. I went out for hours trying to find a way to come up with the lost money. I spent about three hours trying my best to replace the money. I went to the college campus across the street. After doing about an hour of impersonating, I was able to pocket some tips money, with which I went on to buy groceries.

By the time I finally made it back home with the groceries, there was no more daylight outside, and it has been about five hours since Tonton Charles sent me away to buy groceries. I had to evade punishment for being gone for so long when asked to explain the reason why I was got back home at 8:00 p.m. after being gone since around 2:00 p.m. There was no way I was going to tell the truth, not today, I thought. There are a lots of times when the truth does set people free. This time wasn't one of them. Telling the truth at this instance was as good as playing Russian roulette with bullets in all the chambers but one. I wasn't ready to die just yet.

So I went straight for a lie I have been working on along the way. I told Ma Dindo that I was kidnapped by some secret service agents who took me to a secret location to interrogate me about my impersonation of the president. They wanted to know the reasons behind my acts, whether I did it to make fun of the president or if I was working for any of the president's nemesis. Ma Dindo, who seemed to believe my story, was very concerned. She even showed her displeasure with the government, condemning such act. Tonton Charles, who at first was the one consoling me, quickly turned against me by raising doubt about my story. In my absence, he claimed that my story was the fakest story he had ever heard. He wasn't buying it a bit, he said. With Ma Dindo somewhat believing my story, I was able to escape punishment.

The other character of the family was Lena. She was sweet and funny always. At age five, she spoke the funniest French ever. Whatever she spoke were a few French words mixed with whatever words she had made up. It was so funny it had everyone dying from laughter.

One afternoon, while we were all at the house watching TV, three Jehovah's Witness missionaries came by the house. They had scheduled a bible study session with our cousin Helene on that day. Having already seen them from far away as they were opening the gate, without being seen by them, Helene went quickly and hid from them in the room. She told Lena to tell the Jehovah's Witness missionaries she wasn't home. Lena opened the door to the knocking sounds of the Jehovah's Witness missionaries who were at the door.

"We are here for Helene. Can you let her know we are outside?" said one of the missionaries to five-year-old Lena.

Lena nonchalantly answered by stating, "Cousin Helene told me to tell you guys that she is not home!"

From that statement, they realized that Cousin Helene had no intention of meeting with them since she had been avoiding them for weeks now. One of the missionaries told Lena to ask Cousin Helene to hand back the brochures she was given from them for bible studies since it became clear that she had no intention of pursuing bible studies with the missionaries.

Lena went back to the room and delivered the message. Helene pulled Lena to the side and told her, "Tell them I'm not here. I went out earlier this afternoon to visit Auntie Helene."

Lena went back out and told the Jehovah's Witness missionaries, "Cousin Helene said she went out early this afternoon to visit Auntie Helene." Lena would go back and forth, asking, Cousin Helene, "What should I tell them this time?" It was hilarious watching her going back and forth, thinking she was being helpful to Cousin Helene, while in fact, she was really destroying her unknowingly.

Living at the Kabalas was a very captivating experience. It was the most lovable atmosphere I had ever been in a very long while. My feelings, my wants, my thoughts were all put in consideration. The relationship with everyone in the family was great. I was loved by everyone. Ma Dindo, who didn't have much compared to the secretary, was able to give me so much love and affection I had been craving for since I was a child. She gave me that motherly love that I so grew up without, something very precious, something as precious to a child's growth as water is to organisms. She was the joy of my life. The way she managed to be both mother and friend at the same time was a thing of beauty. She would joke everyday with us while at the same time feeding us some wisdom. She was the best cook. She really knew her way around the kitchen very well. For a person that only achieved the third grade as her highest level of education, she was full of wisdom. She knew everything about us. Whatever she couldn't get out of us, she figured out on her own somehow. She never was that far off the pace with us. Never before have I ever had so much unconditional love from a person as I did with her. She was by far the greatest mother a child could have possibly wished for. She had the total package with her. I was back to being a kid once again.

One day, Blaise and Martin were able to sign me up at a special event that was being held at the city's capitol, also known as Palais du Peuple. It was sort of a talent show. I came in second place with my impersonation of the president, thus making me about $200 in cash prize. As soon as I was handed the money, I asked to be excused to the restroom. From there I took off and left Blaise and Martin waiting for me. I made it back all the way home.

A few hours later, Blaise and Martin came home to look for me, wanting to talk to me. I told Papa José about what happened last time when Blaise and Martin pretty much kept about 60 percent of the money that was given to me by the DG of ISC for being my agents. This time, there was no way they were going to take advantage of me once again, so I ran. After talking to them, Papa José pulled out about fifty dollars out of that money and handed it to them with a strong message that he doesn't want to see them anywhere near me ever from now on. They were to have absolutely no contact with me, and if they want to call his bluff, he would have them beat with two hundred lashes a piece at a military compound. Papa Jose was somewhat built like Jean-Claude Van Damme. He was tall and robust, so when he speaks, you listen and listen very carefully because he never repeated himself. Blaise and Martin took off without even looking back, and that was the last day I had ever seen them or heard anything from them.

Few weeks later, Cousin Helene was sent back packing to her real family. Ma Dindo had found that she was keeping a pregnancy from her while desperately trying her very best to get an abortion by applying some kind of herbal treatment, which eventually wasn't working. She also was caught taking a good portion out of the food provision to her boyfriend's apartment. It was then that I have learned that Helene was not related to Ma Dindo at all. Ma Dindo took her in from her struggling family who had trouble raising their children since they were very poor. Ma Dindo took her in shortly after she gave birth to Lena. Ever since, Helene had been helping around the house, while Ma Dindo paid for her school tuition. After Helene's departure, it was just me, Daudoit, and Lena, while Papa José was only home one weekend out of the month.

A few months later, under extreme pressure from the international community, the Congolese government was forced to create a new department, which they named the Department of Human Rights, with the country at war against the Tutsi-led government of Rwanda, who, after failing to topple the current government, ended up invading and occupying a big portion of the mineral-rich eastern part of the country, thus putting in danger the lives of anyone of Tutsi descent living in Congo. People who were of Tutsi descent were targeted. Their properties were seized. Some were put to death violently, while others were put to jail by the government supposedly for their own safety. Sometimes, even people who just looked like Tutsi were targeted as well and suffered tragic fate. The UN had to step in to protect any Tutsi still living in the Congo who were vulnerable to any attacks from either the Congolese government or the general population. The UN, through its branch, the UNHCR, ordered the Congolese government to set up a department that would strictly be dealing with such a case.

The Department of Human Rights had the task to enlist everyone from Tutsi descent. Even those who were imprisoned were to be released to be housed in a camp set up by the government under the supervision of some UN officials. The camp was set up as a transition site to house all ethnic Tutsi descendants or Rwandese citizens living in Kinshasa who were now classified as endangered after the Congolese government has unleashed a territorial witch hunt on them. The UN's goal, through its branch the UNHCR, which dealt with refugee emigration around the world, was to first create a no-strike zone for them and then safely remove everyone out of the country to another country of transit before finding countries that would be willing to host them as refugee.

About three weeks into August, Ma Dindo, along with his two sisters, Helene and Ma Manga, her brother Besto, and her cousin Charles all went on and enlisted at the Department of Human Rights. Few days after enlisting, we had to move into the site, which was set up as a camp to host all those families and individuals that had signed up. On September 2, 1999, we all moved into the INSS site. Our immediate family included Ma Dindo, Daudoit, Lena, and me. Papa Jose didn't enlist with us. Being an official in the military, he couldn't leave his position to join us. That would have been desertion, an act harshly punishable in the military.

Ma Manga had herself, her daughter Sandra, and Guylaine in her case. Tantine Helene's family included herself, her two daughters, Deborah and Syntich, along with her stepchildren, Sam, Francis, and Sarah, who were her husband's children from his first marriage, and Bienvenu, her husband's little nephew whose father died years ago. Tonton Besto and Tonton Charles each enlisted individually. So pretty much the whole family, as it was known, was now placed in a mini refugee-like camp. There was to be absolutely no movement out of the camp. Leaving the campsite without permission from the head of the guards in charge of security meant a termination of your case and an expulsion from the camp.

The site used to house all those endangered Rwandese citizens. Protecting them from government persecution was a huge mansion with such a beautiful landscape. In the front by the entrance, there was a little post set up for the guards. On the far right, there were about fifteen different rooms, each lined up next to one another like a motel. Those rooms were each used for women and children only. Around the back, there was this huge hall that was used to house all the men and young boys aged ten and up. We all slept on the concrete floor with everyone's belongings packed next to the assigned sleeping area. In the back of the men's hall was this huge swimming pool, the water of which was now being used for laundry and dishwashing. All around, the lawn tents were set up to house even more people. The INSS site was guarded by a military platoon rotating every week. There were about more than two hundred families placed inside the property. There were still more people arriving on daily basis. The very first groups of individuals and families who were placed there were people who did qualify to be there. Among those families were mostly couples whose wives were Rwandese or wives whose husbands were Rwandese. Those couples made up a vast majority of the site's population.

Since Papa José couldn't be with us being in the military, the plan was for him to desert the army once we have made it out of the country. As time went by, the enlisting process became more and more corrupt, bringing the criteria for qualifying for a spot in the camp to a very low point. With the country's economy facing its lowest point since the war, people were getting more desperate to get out of the country to find a better life elsewhere. The way things were turning for the worse in the country, one would have a better chance of survival anywhere but in the country.

With the UNHCR offering a gateway out of the country to all Rwandese families who were being prosecuted by the Congolese government and citizens through the Congolese Department of Human Rights, the department that was in charge of the enlisting became flooded with a huge number of locals pretending to be Rwandese just to have a way out of the country through the UNHCR-sponsored process. The system became even more corrupted when the department officials were now accepting bribes just to have anyone enlisted. Sometimes, even people who had all the criteria for qualification were being either denied or threatened to be denied unless they bribed the officials in charge of the enlisting. They were now charging between $200 and $1,000 just to get enlisted.

In other cases, those same officials would enlist their own relatives and send them to the INSS site, putting them in a position of being taken out of the country and later given a refugee status in one of those Western countries, perhaps the United States or Canada, at the expense of the UNHCR. In some other cases, the Congolese government, through its intelligence agency, would infiltrate the site with undercover agents posing as Rwandese in hopes of gaining some classified information from anyone there who could be related to anyone within the Tutsi-led Kagame regime. So it was all a big mix-up. With the Department of Human Rights officials making their money off people chasing a better life outside of the country, the UNHCR-sponsored site housing Rwandese families, which I was now a part of, was getting overcrowded. Each day, there were at least five families coming in through the gates, bringing the population way over the maximum capacity limit.

The Department of Human Rights, which was responsible for the housing, was now forced to come up with placement measures as all the buildings on the site were all full with people. Certain buildings had people sleeping right in the open piled up next to each other like sardines, leading other families to be sleeping outside. For most of those that were staying outside on the lawn with all their belongings, being outside in the open was the least of their worries. As long as they were on track to be flown outside the country, they could care less if they were to be rained on or anything. It is true that humans tend to become immune to any natural disaster or any dark moment when opportunity is in the horizon.

The property, which had the capacity to house about three hundred people, now had about close to one thousand people in it. The true vulnerable Rwandese families now found themselves outnumbered by Congolese dream chasers who had no business being there in the first place, thus creating a lot of friction between Rwandese and Congolese on the site. There were fights, constant bickering, taunting; all sorts of animosity going on. The fighting and bickering were mostly found among the older generations, while people between the ages of forty and sixty were constantly at war with each other, fighting over who really deserved to be there and who didn't.

That wasn't the case with the thirties and younger. They were all bound with love for one another. They respected one another. Together they ate, told jokes and stories, and listened to music with one another. Some were too busy hooking up with the girls. Overall, the younger generation did care less about who was well deserving of being flown out and who wasn't or who was doing what . . . all sorts of things. They somehow understood that what might be a given to some could still be an opportunity to others, and they were sure not about to stand in the way of someone's opportunity, whether their presence was legitimate.

As it was becoming more and more obvious to the authorities that things were getting out of control in there, the Department of Human Rights ended up opening up another site for future families that were enlisting. There were now two active sites in the city, which probably meant more money to be pocketed by those crooked agents. To prevent fraudulent people benefiting from being flown out of the country at the expense of the UNHCR, the UNHCR proceeded by conducting three series of interviews to each person and family enlisted on the site to flush out those who didn't qualified to be there and send them packing. The first round of interviews involved each person being interviewed individually, the second round had the entire family being interviewed together, and finally, the last one determined whether you were a fraud.

Fraudsters were sent packing right away. Sometimes, it only took one interview for a person or family to be found out, and at that very moment, they were sent packing. A lot of people who made it to the site through bribe were very frustrated. In some cases, you had people who sold their valuables and gave a lot of money to the agents just to see themselves being denied the opportunity to make it out of the country through the UNHCR process. We had a well-known and very successful photographer who sold his business and had himself enlisted through bribe just for a chance to sneak out of the country. You also had a lot of women who gave up their bodies to those agents in exchange for what they saw as an opportunity to get to Europe or America.

The sequence of interviews conducted by the UNHCR on-site exposed some of the corruptions within the Congolese human rights agency and also brought to light some creativity or lack thereof from Congolese opportunists posing as Rwandese just for a chance to be taken out of the country with the UNHCR procedure. During the interview, the UNHCR got a good look at the different types of families hoping to be taken out of the country. On one side, there were your typical Rwandese families composed of either both mothers and fathers who were Rwandese who had been living in the country for years prior to the war; while on the other side, you also had families who had one Rwandese parent. And last but not least, you had your fraudster, Congolese opportunists who couldn't even point out Rwanda on a map containing only three countries. They were there posing as Rwandese while hoping to get a free ticket outside of the country.

Another category that almost escaped my mind is what I named the artificial families. An artificial family was a family composed of a Rwandese individual man or woman who had taken bribe money from up to five different people forming a family and then enlisting all of them as being a part of his or her family. It was usually the case with men. A Rwandese man would take bribe from a woman to enlist her as his wife and take more money from two or three different people enlisting them as being his children or relatives. If it was a woman, she would be the mother or wife in the made-up family structure. A lot of those fake families were busted and sent packing after being found out.

What happened in some of those interviews was very comical. Some of those fake families, while being interviewed separately, couldn't keep the same story. The husband wouldn't know the exact birthday of any of his "children"; better yet, some even had trouble remembering their own names after acquiring fake names to sound more Rwandese. During the interview process, the agent would start calling a person's name repeatedly, and no one would even blink since they haven't gotten a grasp of their newly made-up names just yet. Some would just panic right in the middle and start out confessing on their own.

While others, when being asked why they were there and what the circumstances are leading to them enlisting, one guy's response was flat out "Well, I heard you guys were taking people to either France, England, or Canada. I am not really sure about the exact country, but I just thought maybe I can come over here and check it out for myself. I always dream of one day making it to some western country. So is it really true, or is it just one of those many scams going around?" he asked the interviewers. People like that were sent packing immediately.

As for me, I was enlisted as being one of Ma Dindo's biological kids. I was enlisted as Rossy, her second child. Daudoit was the eldest, followed by me, and then Lena, our little sister. So we were a family of four without our father, who was still serving in the military. There was a cutoff age for individual interviews. Children twelve and under were not required to be interviewed at all. Being fourteen at the time, it was going to be a problem for us since that made me eligible for a one-on-one interview. Not knowing anything about the whole Rwandese thing, I could have put our case in jeopardy by giving out the wrong information or giving out a wrong answer. So to limit any collateral damage that could have been done during the interview process, Ma Dindo found it easier to just lower Daudoit's and my age by two years. Instead of being sixteen years old, Daudoit was fourteen, and I was now twelve years old, thus making me ineligible to be interviewed alone.

Luckily enough, the plan worked to perfection without any reasonable doubt. Three interviews were conducted within a ninety-day span, and by the time of the last interview, about 60 percent of the general population were sent home packing. To some, it was a complete loss as many of them had to make a lot of sacrifices just to get there and they were sent home. Many of them had to sell their homes, valuables, cars . . . you name it, just so they could pay their way to a better life outside of the war-torn country. Those of us who were lucky enough not to have suffered such a fate were mindlessly thankful, as yet again, it was another miraculous sign of the grace of God shining upon me.

Life inside the facility wasn't bad at all either. My ninety-some days there weren't a complete waste. I spent it being the funniest kid I could possibly be. Even in there, I still had people who recognized me from my television appearances as the president's impersonator. They would, from time to time, ask me to perform some impersonation in front of them. I was as popular in there as I ever was anywhere else. My popularity took me as far as winning the battle to have the prettiest girl there all to myself. I was able to beat my brother Daudoit, our cousin Francis, and anyone else who had a thing for a girl named Salima.

If beauty, which is by definition a combination of qualities, such as shape, form, and color pleasing the aesthetic senses, most importantly human eyes, took up a human form and came in this world as a female, it would have been Salima. Never before have I ever lain my eyes on something so precious, so pure and beautiful as Salima. She was petite, with a light skin complexion. She was more like a clone of Demi Moore, Julia Roberts, and Jennifer Lopez all put together in a fifteen-year-old body. It never crossed my mind to give myself up completely for a girl, but if it would ever happen, she would probably be the only one I would do it for. She was indeed breathtaking. We exchanged love letters almost every day, professing our infatuation for one another.

Since the facility was very dense with people, we found it very hard to have any time of our own without any interference from sneak pickers, parents, or other adults. Everything had to be done in a camouflage mode. All we fed everyone was our constant praise and admiration for one another, while leaving the rest of the people to feed off rumors and gossips. As it has been so for generations, never in the history of mankind had a pretty girl travel alone. Salima was no exception to the rule of nature either. She had her best friend and companion in Mamiya, a very attractive girl, chocolate skinned, long legs, with a killer smile that spell the words "Stay away. I am too good to be yours, but you sure can keep the fantasy going." As beautiful as Mamiya was, to me, it didn't matter; she wasn't Salima. I left her for Daudoit and Francis to fight over. *May the best man win*, I thought.

Although Daudoit had the edge at first—it seemed from the beginning that Mamiya might have had something for the "thug like" Daudoit—but she ended up shifting her attention to Francis, the self-proclaimed Romeo to any Juliet that was still roaming around nearby. Francis was very preppy. I'm convinced that when looking up the word "preppy" in the dictionary, one should find a picture of him next to the word. Being the son of a successful businessman, Francis had it all. He was so arrogant and so full of himself. In his mind, he could get any girl in the planet to sleep with him just by snapping his fingers at her. He would walk around with his shirt half unbuttoned, whistling some American R & B song, which he barely knew the lyrics of, just to sound hip. He always walked around carrying one of those romance novels, which he used as a bait to attract attention to himself from the ladies.

As much as I hate to admit it, his strategies were always effective. I was just glad they weren't as effective with Salima.

Daudoit, Francis, and I were part of the most influential trio in the facility. All eyes were pretty much on us. We were three kids with no blood connection but were now bound by family ties. We were three different people with completely three different characteristics. Daudoit was the indisputable thug; Francis was the smooth talker and preppy boy—Mr. Princeton to be more concrete; and I was El Pibe de Oro, the golden kid and the joy of the people. We all somehow ensembled the most dynamic powerful triumvirate force.

Our loyalty was later put to the test when Francis decided to test me. As the youngest of the group and perhaps the most pacific of all, Francis, being full of himself as usual, took it upon himself to have a go at me by trying to lure Salima his way. During a conversation, Francis mentioned to me that the only reason Salima and I were a pair was he chose not to pursue her, but if he was to go for her, there was going to be absolutely no way that she was going to resist. With a snap of his fingers, she would be here sitting on his lap anytime he wishes her to. Those were fighting words. With those words, Francis went too far, I said to myself, dealing our relationship the biggest blow.

From then on, Francis and I were engaged in a cold war, which pretty much was dominated by completely no speaking to one another. He did try his very best in trying to take Salima away from me. Luckily enough, he failed miserably in his quest. With Daudoit's intervention, we ended up leaving our differences behind us. We were once again on good terms but every big wound always brings about a big scar after healing. I did forgive his action, which pretty much was the result of his cockiness and selfishness rather than an intent to be hurtful. Although I forgave him, I sure didn't forget. I still kept a very close eye on his every move from then on.

In December of that year, about three months from the time we were placed in the facility, about 80 percent of the entire population were bound for the airport. A UNHCR chartered plane was on the runaway waiting to take all of us out of the country to a nearby country. The previous night was the busiest night ever as there was a long line of people queuing in front of the facility's office window where the UNHCR officials had put up a list of all the names of individuals that were to board the plane the next day tomorrow. As people were so anxious to see their names on the list, it was total madness in the facility.

The list, which only contained about 80 percent of the entire population, brought a lot of joy to those whose names were featured on it, and a lot more sadness and disappointment for those whose names were omitted from it. Those whose names were on the list stayed up all night packing and praising God for such a grace, while those who were staying still stayed up trying to collect souvenirs or any items that those who were leaving were not packing with them. Friends stayed up as to have one last chance at perhaps ever seeing one another again.

The night was highlighted by a guy who went by the nickname Grand Pays, pronounced "gran pay e," meaning USA, which was the name the locals associate the United States with. Grand Pays was in his late thirties or early forties, married with two young children. He was among the few whose names didn't get featured, so he was bound to be sent home once the facility was emptied. He was the facility's biggest comic. He always lit up the place with his funny stories, which people would line up almost every night to hear. A great stand-up comedian at his best. A one-man show. He had as his best friend Tonton Charles, who wasn't a bad comic himself. That night, Grand Pays, who had never even set foot outside the Congo, proceeded by demonstrating how life will be like in the western world once we get there.

He said, "In the western world, everything is automated. They have machines for everything. They even have a machine for sexual intercourse. They have a machine that would literally grab your penis and insert it into a woman's vagina and do all the work for you while you only feel the pleasure, and during that time, you could be doing something else on the computer." He claimed, "Right upon you guys arrival at the airport, there would be an escort waiting for you. The escort, a white agent from the government, will ask you for your name and very quickly hand you your real health. You will be given your real age, weight, height . . . etc. You see, the person you see in the mirror here in front of you right now, that's not the real you. The real you is out there, drinking all sorts of juices, juices made out of the finest omelets, eating a whole chicken." He finished his sermon by saying, "Charles, my good friend, this is not you. Go out there and get the real you. Just don't forget about the people you are leaving behind, people like the one who is talking to you right in your face at this very moment," pointing at himself.

While in the INSS site, I did reunite with my good pal Jo from the boot camp. His mother, who happened to be a Rwandese national, checked into the site along with her entire family of ten, including my friend Jo, while fleeing persecution from the locals. I was glad to see Jo again after going months without knowing what had happened to him. We did catch up on our time in the boot camp, and he showed me a bullet wound on his thigh that was healing.

"I did kill some rebels," he said, "and while everyone around me left me, I was hit by a bullet in my left thigh, and the last thing I know, I was in a hut being taken care of by a group of villagers who happened to saved me from being captured and executed by the rebels."

"Well, it is all behind us now. I am glad you made it out of there alive."

"What happened to you? Where did you go? How many rebels did you kill?" After telling him my side of the story, he kept on teasing me for having not killed a single rebel.

Jo and I were the best of pals. We picked up where we both left off at the boot camp. We even slept next to one another in the male hall. After the dynamic three split up following Francis's and my dispute, I quickly formed a solid partnership with Jo. We were known as the Hunting Duo. We were always together. Wherever we went exploring and exploiting, we had no limits, which led us to trouble most of the time.

One time, I got in so much trouble Tantine Helene, who was by far the head of the family, decided to have me sent back home just to straighten me up. While I was out of the facility, some people within the family were even petitioning for my complete removal from Ma Dindo's case. Once removed from the case, I wasn't going to leave the country with the rest of the family. I was going to stay home, while everyone else was out of the country. After spending about three lonely weeks at home, I was pardoned and sent back to the facility, thanks to Daudoit, who has been pleading night and day for my return to both Ma Dindo and Tantine Helene. I came back a saint just for a little while until the real me kicked back again, only this time I was being a little more clever.

The following day, at around 10:00 a.m., we saw a convoy of around eight UNHCR chartered buses entering the gate of the facility with both the Department of Human Rights officials and UNHCR officials leading the way. One of the heads of the UNHCR mission stood in front of the first bus while calling the names of the people who were to board the buses. There were about four hundred people on board. As soon as the last person to be called boarded the bus, all the buses, which were all lined up in a single file in the convoy, closed their doors and were ready to take off.

The convoy was made up of two UNHCR official SUVs leading the way followed by a few cars carrying the Department of Human Rights officials, while behind the buses were two military convoys with heavy artillery protecting the convoy, which was bound for the airport. One thing was for sure—these weren't your typical refugees fleeing atrocity with their belongings on their head and children hooked behind their back as you usually see portrayed on TV. These were upper-middle-class Rwandese. They were doctors, lawyers, professors, businesswomen, former military officials, and their families who were being evacuated out of the country to a safer place.

The hour ride to the airport was marked by a reflection. As I looked outside sitting next to the bus window, I could see some locals shouting along the way toward the convoy, "Go to hell, Rwandese! Go to hell!" Here I was leaving my country as a Rwandese, not knowing if and when I will ever see this country of mine again. Everything still seemed like a mirage. It was almost too good to be true. As long as we were still in Congolese soil, I thought anything is bound to happen, leaving everything else to be nothing but a dream. Even while boarding the plane, I still had the slightest of doubt. It wasn't until the plane finally took off from the runaway that I realized that this was a done deal. I was embarking into a new chapter in my life away from everything I knew, away from everyone that was once dear to me, away from any of my blood relatives, away from the long-lived struggle.

This was far from being the end, I said to myself. It wasn't even the beginning. It was perhaps the end of the new beginning, the laying of a foundation for a greater future dominated by more hope than ever before. I couldn't help but look straight to the clouds from my seat by the window all throughout the flight. I kept on making the same wish. My wish was to one day come back to my country as ten times the man I left, to be as much influential to lead a movement that would help transform that country from the hell it had become into a paradise it ought to be. Yes, I said it—a paradise a place where each one of us would be more than proud to call home.

At around 9:00 p.m., we landed at the national airport of Garoua, the fourth-largest city in Cameroon, a country located in West Africa. We were very well welcomed by the local UNHCR officials. Upon arrival, we were all placed in the waiting room inside the airport where each one of us was given a snack with a bottle of water. After about close to an hour, we were later escorted out from the airport in buses to our new location. The newly renovated refugee camp of Langi was located in the heart of the village, about two hours away from the city's airport and about an hour and forty-five minutes away from the city itself. The UNHCR refugee camp in Langi was set up in a vast enclave with the size of about six football fields put together. The refugee camp in Langi was divided in three classes, the upper class, middle class, and lower class.

The upper class was housed in an area called Garoua, which had four different units. In each unit, there were about eight rooms with paved concrete all lined up in a motel-like shape. The units were numbered from G1 to the last one being G30. Showers and restrooms were all set up in the back. Each room was equipped with electricity powered by a generator courtesy of the UNHCR.

On the other side of the camp, there were about forty tents set up on each side of the dirt road, which started out from the camp entrance and ended up to the other side of the camp Garoua. The other side of the dirt road had about sixty tents. The side with about forty tents all lined up in straight line with ten tents in each street was called Langi 1. Langi 1 was home to the refugee camp's middle class. On the other side of the dirt road was the area that contained around sixty tents all scattered in a circle. This rural area of the camp was called Langi 2. Langi 2 was mostly home to the lower class, single men and women, teenagers who wanted some privacy from their parents, and also a few families that couldn't find a spot either in Garoua or Langi 1. A family of six or more was given two tents to accommodate. Unlike Garoua, there was no electricity in either Langi.

The newly renovated Langi refugee camp, which was once home to another group of refugees from the country Chad, was now turned into the Hilton of all refugee camps. It had electricity, a big screen TV in each area, and an updated well installed in the heart of Langi2. If it weren't for the sporadic snakes and scorpion bites, Langi wasn't far off from being a resort.

The moment we set our feet in the camp, my friend Jo and I quickly settled in one of the tents in Langi 2. Daudoit and Francis, along with two of their friends, took up the tent across from ours. Ma Manga, her fiancé Tonton Jessie, Sandra, and Guylaine all stayed in Garoua; while Ma Dindo, Tantine Helene, and Tantine Chantal, who was their cousin, chose to live a few tents away from ours in Langi 2. Ma Dindo, Lena, Tantine Chantal, and her five-year-old nephew Grady all lived in one tent. Next to them was Tantine Helene and her two daughters, Deborah and Syntich. Tantine Helene's stepchildren, Sarah and Sam, with her husband's nephew Bienvenu, slept in a tent next to Tantine Helene's. All three tents were about ten feet apart from each other. Tonton Charles and Tonton Besto shared a tent nearby, along with three of their other friends, Jimmy, Henri, and Oliver, who was nicknamed the Physician after having graduated from speed school.

The first three days in Langi were great. Lunch and dinner were catered to us. There were plenty to eat for everyone, potatoes, chicken, meat stew, fish, vegetable, and Kool-Aid, all were available. We were served in line by local contractors hired by the UNHCR. About two days after our arrival, we were joined by another load of refugees coming from the Congo. They were people from the second site that was opened after the first one, from which we came, was overcrowded. They all settled in Langi 2, bringing the total to 802. With the newest arrival, there was shortage in tents—meaning, the site was in great need of more tents to accommodate more people. The UNHCR hired a team of villagers to build more tents for the refugees. According to the UNHCR officials, about fifty more tents were greatly needed.

A group of refugees took it upon themselves to set up a contracting team of their own. Among the two major contracting teams from the refugees, there was one that stood up the most. They called themselves the Indigenous Trio. They all were friends who stayed together in a tent in Langi 2 right across from me. The Indigenous Trio included two brothers. The Munyakazi brothers, Toto and Bienvenu, with their good friend and roommate Marcelo Munganga. The Indigenous Trio was known for their passion and hard work. They were responsible for the realization achievement of about half of the projects inside the camp. Jo and I did get to help them out in a few of their projects, earning ourselves quite a good amount of cash since the contractors were very well paid by the UNHCR.

In about a week, a group of about thirty women, which included Tantine Helene and Ma Manga, all put up about US$10,000 and handed it to one local working as an UNHCR contractor to go exchange the money into the local currency for them so they could purchase things that weren't being provided to them by the UNHCR. Either $10,000 was too much for the guy who at the time seemed like a very trustworthy human being to give back or he somehow got lost on his way and couldn't find his way back to the camp to return the money to their rightful owner, putting the whole camp in a state of total disarray. The whole camp was left pretty beat down by the schemer who was never to be seen ever again after that. That was a big wake-up call to those families. It was a lesson learned for them, as next time, they would have to think twice to put their trust in anyone just because they were wearing a shirt with the UN logo engraved on it.

During the first days, each tent that was accounted for as a household was given a small portable gasoline stove, two aluminum pans, two plastic dishes, two bowls, two plastic cups, few silverware, a very tiny mattress, two jailhouse-like blankets for each person sleeping in the tent, a ten-gallon water container, and a five-gallon gasoline container, which was to be refilled once a week. Each person was given a weekly food portion, which included dry rice and beans, cooking oil, onions, tomato paste, and about a half pound of meat every Friday. Everything was given in a single file. If one was to get his weekly portion of gasoline, he/she would have to stand in the line. There were three lines: the gasoline line, every Tuesday; the main course line, which included rice, beans, onions, and tomato paste, on Wednesdays; and the meat line on Fridays.

Being very close to the desert as we were meant that we were exposed to a different type of weather that none of us were accustomed to. During the day, it was so hot as the temperature was nearing 45 degrees Celsius, about 110 degrees Fahrenheit, and at nighttime, the temperature would drop as low as 60 degrees Fahrenheit until about 8:00 a.m. the next day. Every day, it was a tale of two weathers. Water that was stored in the container at nighttime felt ice cold in the early morning until about 11:00 a.m. when the ferocious sun came up. That sun meant business when it came out and never once missed a beat. When I tell you it was hot, I meant it was hot.

The honeymoon didn't last very long as we were introduced to poisonous snakes, deadly spiders, and scorpions. Some people got to experience being bitten by a snake or scorpion for the very first time of their life, a very scary experience. Daudoit was among the casualties as he was bitten by a scorpion. Luckily for us, there was a care center inside the camp with two registered nurses on call twenty-four hours and a doctor who came in once a week from the nearest urban town. The care center was fairly equipped with antibiotics, pain relievers, and aspirin. Among all, there were two Pierre Noir, or "black stone." The Pierre Noir was a little charcoal-like stone that was used as a remedy to cure snakebites or scorpion bites. The Pierre Noir was employed to wherever area that contained the bite. Once put against the surface, the Pierre Noir would stick just like a magnet, sucking all the venom out of the wound. Whenever all the venom was out of the body, the Pierre

Noir would automatically drop, signaling that there was no more venom left in the body.

The villagers who lived in nearby villages by the camp were very nice and welcoming, thus making the interaction a little bit cozier. Jo and I were the very first people to lead an expedition way beyond camp fences exploring the villages. We would walk for miles deep inside those villages, looking in awe how carefree and shameless those female villagers were walking around with their bare chest with very tiny pieces of clothing covering their bottom. We were experiencing a live edition of National Geographic, and we enjoyed every bit of it. We did go in there for entertainment purposes and ended up coming out of there with an eye for business.

Once deep into the village, I realized that a lot of the things we were being given by the UNHCR in the camp such as gasoline, rice, beans, tomato paste, blankets, and mattresses were luxury to those villagers, thus making it high demand. Since Jo and I didn't even cook, I persuaded him to start out selling our food portion and gasoline. We made most money selling our gasoline to the villagers. As the demand for gasoline among the villagers were gradually increasing, we had to come up with more gasoline supply to keep the business going.

Every Tuesday, I made sure I was among the first in the gasoline line. I get my container filled up, sneak outside the camp where there was one of the villagers waiting for me, empty the gasoline into his container, grab the money, and hand the container back to Jo. He would get in the line, get some more, sneak it back out, and sell it, and so on. We would go back to the gasoline line about three times before the guy filling up the container would realize what was going on. By that time, we already made ourselves a little fortune.

Word started going around that I was making good money selling gasoline. I became well known throughout the whole camp, earning me the nickname of BP. At first, everyone was so afraid of getting caught selling supplies to the villagers since it was prohibited. So anyone who was interested in selling their gasoline supply would come to us to sell it for them, thus giving us the monopoly of gasoline sale in the camp. Since the vast majority of the refugees were very skeptical about getting in contact with the villagers, let alone going into the village, it allowed us to fix the price. For example, we would tell the refugee that a gallon of gasoline was selling for 200 francs, when in reality, we sold it for 350 francs to the villager. Out of the 200 francs, we took 50 francs for our service, making ourselves a killing in profit. We were making so much money smuggling gasoline to the villagers.

Jo and I would take trips on motorcycle to the nearest commercial town, Pitoa, where we would buy clothes and enjoy better food. We were living the villager's dream. In the refugee camp, I was also living it up. I did manage to take care of my family the best way I knew how. Aside from Ma Dindo, my two other aunts really didn't approve of the way I was making a living out of smuggling. To them, that was one of the most embarrassing things I could possibly bring to the family name. On the other hand, my two uncles, Tonton Charles and Tonton Besto, were neither opposed nor supportive. It probably had something to do with the per diem I was giving them from my business. Tonton Besto, the Godfather, was my number-one fan; Tonton Charles, not so much as I knew of his double-face nature. He was my biggest fan in my face and also my biggest critic behind my back, especially when in the company of Ma Dindo and all the other aunts. But that's Tonton Charles for you. I still loved him unconditionally.

More people got the hang of the gasoline smuggling business, resulting to a big crackdown by UNHCR officials on the amount of the gasoline that was being handed out. They implemented new rules on gasoline handouts. They now had a list of all the families and all the single people who didn't belong to any family—meaning, neither Jo nor I was able to get any gasoline as we were both listed as part of our family, respectively. The new rule really dealt our business a big blow, but just like in any given situation, we had to come up with ways to overcome our setback. Since we couldn't get any more gasoline of our own, we targeted everyone that was willing to sell their share of gasoline. In this way, we still kept the business going. The only difference was that now that everyone knew how to smuggle the gasoline out of the camp and with the price by the gallon not being a secret anymore, we weren't making as much as a profit as we were making before. We were now just making pocket money. As time went by, with more people jumping into the gasoline business, more supplies with less demand equaled lower price. Just like that, Jo and I decided to get out of the gasoline smuggling game. Although it wasn't a complete surrender, it was more like a retreat to put our focus on something else. We left smuggling gasoline to take on a new business.

We started smuggling mattresses out of the camp and selling them to the nearby village. Smuggling mattresses out of the camp to sell it in villages about ten miles away from the camp wasn't as easy as smuggling gasoline. Although it had about five times the profit, it also had about 40 percent higher risk. Unlike the gasoline, which we smuggled in bright daylight, we had to wait until dark to smuggle the mattress out of the camp to evade being detected by the camp guards and by some refugees. Our first sale was my mattress. I decided to sell my mattress and share Jo's mattress to sleep in.

Moving from smuggling gasoline to smuggling matrix out of the camp gave me more free time during daytime. Gasoline smuggling took up most of my time daily, leaving me very little to no time to spend with Salima, who had a real hard time seeing me at all. I had concentrated a lot of focus and energy on smuggling, leaving behind the love of my life. Salima didn't approve of my hobby. I had tried to shower her with money and gifts on multiple occasions, and every time, she turned me down. She hated my guts and didn't miss the chance to let me know of it whenever she found the opportunity. We were constantly fighting. Nothing I did seemed to have any positive effect on her.

Being as busy as I was never allowed me the time to try to fix things with her. As far as I was concerned, there really wasn't anything to be fixed. She made it clear she wanted me to quit smuggling, and I made it clear through my actions that I had no intention whatsoever to quit. In my defense, I did suggest to slow it down a little to have more time to spend with her. Even that was very unrealistic since spending more time with her only meant more fighting and more bickering. There was no doubt in my mind about our love for one another, but the more we were fighting, the more I started distancing myself from her, avoiding every little chance of an encounter with her.

One night, she called me up to our favorite place of encounter, which was at the playground located in the most isolated area of the camp. It was there that she broke the news to me that she was breaking up with me. At first, it didn't seem to bother me that we were no longer together until a few weeks later when I found out that she was now dating a guy named Steve. Steve was the lead singer in the church choir, which Salima was a member of. Rumor of the breakup spread throughout the camp just like a plague. It was being said that Steve took Salima away from me, which did nothing but add more salt to my wound. I did have a hard time coping with the breakup. I became more and more isolated. I even took up drinking. I would go to the village and get me some of that traditional wine called Bill Bill, which was made out of starch. It had a very sweet taste to it. One night, I even passed out on the ground on my way back to the camp just to be woken up by some Good Samaritan from the village.

To make matters worse, the news spread all over the camp. I was once again in the spotlight, prompting an emergency family meeting that took place in my absence. Tantine Helene, who acted as the head of the family, as the eldest, suggested that I should be sent back home to the Congo to save the family from further embarrassment. I found the family meeting to be very offensive, especially since during the same period I was going through my struggle, Daudoit was caught twice smoking marijuana with some guys from the village. He was also caught having sex in the back of the church, yet none of his actions called for an emergency family meeting, only mine. I responded to the outcome of the family meeting by isolating myself from the family. I cut off most of the ties with everyone except Daudoit, while I avoided both of my uncles every chance I got.

While almost everyone seemingly have given up on me, only Jo remained strong by my side. Even though he took a lot of heat from his own family about being best friends with me, it never kept Jo away from me. Our friendship was as strong as ever. There was never anything pessimistic about Jo. His approach to any given struggle or setback was always optimistic. He always had a bright side in every failure. Whenever he would get turned down by a girl, he always comforted himself by saying that the reason he got turned down was nothing but a sign from the sky that she never was going to be good for him anyway. From sleeping on the same bed every night to smuggling gasoline and mattresses together, Jo and I were inseparable.

One night, we borrowed a bike from one of the villagers we were friends with to go sell a mattress in a village about twenty miles away from the camp. About two miles into our destination, the bicycle's steering wheel broke on us. We were left in the middle of the dirt road very far away from the camp with our mattress, which we made look very thin after folding it up over and over. The way we folded the mattress to smuggle it out of the camp had one of the camp's biggest comic, Mawashi, telling jokes about us, saying that he once saw us fit a whole mattress in a beer bottle to smuggle it out of the camp. He had everyone laughing so hard.

From where Jo and I were standing, we could hear coyotes or some other type of wild animal from afar. Jo took a wooden stick from the dirt and connected the steering wheel back together. He did it in such a way that to me seemed as magical as a David Copperfield stunt. Although the bike still felt very shaky at time, it still took us to our destination and back. The ride back to the camp was still as miraculous as the one to the faraway village.

We got back to the camp at around 11:00 p.m., when most of the refugees were already in bed. We couldn't believe ourselves how we made it back safely. This experience was the highlight of Jo's and my friendship. Through thick and thin, we always managed to survive. As we got ready for bed that night, we joked that one day, we will share this experience with posterity, perhaps around a dinner table during a reunion, whether it will be in Europe, United States, or Canada. We will sit back enjoying every moment of it. A band of brothers, that is what we were.

About a few weeks later, Jo was forced to move out our tent. His family had enough of our reputation in the camp. To them, I was the one to blame as I was a very bad influence to their son. They told him he had to move out immediately or he would have to face dire consequences. Jo took his mattress with him—meaning, I had to sleep on the floor. It didn't take long for me to find another roommate. After making amends with my family by telling them how sorry I was and that they were now looking at a changed man, I persuaded Aunt Helene to let Sam and Bienvenu come stay in my tent. Now that both Sam and Bienvenu were rooming with me, I set up both of their mattresses together so that all three of us could sleep together. The poor kids didn't think anything of it. To them, it was cool enough they were out of their parents' sight and they were now rooming with the coolest person in the world. The pleasure was all theirs.

Jo and I still remained very close, except we didn't smuggle mattresses together anymore. Aside from that, we were always seen together. He eventually found himself a girlfriend, a girl from the nearest village. Her name was Damu. She was very pretty and neat for a villager. She was from a well-respected clan. Jo's relationship didn't affect our friendship at all as he only saw her once in a while when she was able to sneak out her parents' hut. I did take a little break from smuggling to appease my family.

Now that I wasn't smuggling anymore, I became more involved in life in the camp. Jo and I tried to join the camp's football team, Jo as a defender and me as a midfielder. At the time, there were three senior teams, two girls' teams, with one team made up of the residents from Garoua (the brick house) and the other team made up of girls from both Langi, and the men's team, which was mostly made up of Langi residents. There was a sandy football field inside the camp located between the brick houses and the tents. So one had to cross the sandy football field on the way to either side of the camp. The two women's teams played against each other, while the men's team played against teams from nearby villages. Since no one had football cleats, everyone played barefooted in the hot sand.

Jo and I found it very difficult to break into the men's team. Jo was a terrible defender, and I, on the other hand, was too fragile. I wasn't as bad of a soccer player; I just couldn't compete against the other players who were much older and who were more physical than I was. The oldest player on the team was Martin. He was in his midthirties. He was an ace of a soccer player. He was skinny, tall, and very quick with his feet. He was one of our best players. The other one was Prince, who was around eighteen years old, very fast and skillful. The two players, Martin and Prince, accounted for our strike force. They both were the start of the team.

Since football was the main recreational activity, people would usually gather around the field every time there was a game being played against an opposition team, which was either a team from the nearby village or a team from town. With Prince being the youngest star of the team, he had all the girls as his fans. Every woman, even the married ones, wanted a piece of Prince.

There was another player who received a lot of attention from the female spectators, Romeo. Romeo was a Congolese citizen with no Rwandese blood whatsoever but had a Rwandese morphology. He was tall, with pointed nose just like a Rwandese. He got to convince the UNHCR that his life was in danger. He claimed he was being harassed and receiving death threats for looking like a Tutsi. That's how he got to be flown out of the Congo as a refugee. Romeo got his attention from the female spectators not because of his football skill or looks but because of his football shorts. He wore a pair of tiny yellow spandex shorts during the game. He wore them with nothing underneath, causing his genitals to stand out, and according to the female spectators, there was nothing skinny about his junk, and they enjoy taking a peek at it every time he moved on the field. For that reason alone, Romeo became one of stars of the team.

There was competition in every position on the team except for the goalkeeper area. Not only was no one interested in playing in that position other than Bob, but also there was no one as good in goal as he was, and he knew it. Whenever we would lose a game because of one of Bob's mistake, the whole team would nag Bob about it for the rest of the day, prompting him to threaten to quit the team. Every time he threatened to quit the team, people were obligated to beg him not to do so. At times, they would even bribe him just to appease him. The situation worked perfectly for Bob as he knew that the team needed him more than he needed the team. He became very arrogant. He would get mad and very irritated by anyone who dared criticize him.

The whole team was somehow held hostage by Bob's arrogance but couldn't do anything about it since there wasn't anyone willing to step up and take up Bob's position. That was true until I decided to step up to the challenge.

One day, during a game, Bob decided to walk off the field in the middle of a game after being criticized for letting in a goal that could have been saved. As everyone was pointing to one another on who was to step in for Bob with no one seemingly willing to take over, I quickly jumped to the opportunity and finished up the game in goal. I did so well in goal that day that I received a lot of praises from all over for my gutty performance, thus earning me the job as the number-one goalkeeper.

I found my rise to the top to be very short lived as the following game saw us losing the game by three goals to none. The other team took advantage of my short height by chipping the ball over me every time they got the chance. My goalkeeping skills weren't bad at all, but my tenure as a goalkeeper was mostly overshadowed by my lack of height, which made me so much vulnerable in all the aerial balls. After that defeat, I was made fun of every time I walked by. Enough was enough. I decided to quit the team. They eventually convinced Bob to come back from his self-imposed exile and rejoin the team.

After leaving the senior team, I went on to create a junior team, which included every kid fifteen and under, with me being the goalkeeper. As the new team founders, Jo and I were both manager and coach. We held practice twice a week, which was mostly dominated by scrimmages. Every Thursday, we set up friendly games against teams from nearby villages. The junior team was quickly a success. I was doing so good as a goalkeeper in the junior team. After playing about seven games, we had yet to lose a game. I gained recognition for my work throughout the whole camp, earning me a friendship with Mr. Wara, the highest-ranked UNHCR official of the refugee camp. Mr. Wara was like the refugee camp's mayor. He and I became the best of friends. If I needed anything, all I had to do was walk into his office, and it was done. Mr. Wara was very fond of me. He even bought my whole team a pair of plastic cleats and gave us a few soccer balls. I felt on top of the world. The junior team became so successful they had us playing out of town against other teams that were more sophisticated than our usual opposition. Even then, we still came up on top.

As time went on, I finally got over Salima and focused my attention to a girl named Christelle. Christelle was about fourteen years old, very pretty with long curly hair. There was something about her looks that made me go crazy over her. She was stunning, a perfect replacement for Salima. If I had to choose between the two, I still would have chosen Salima, but it was going to be pretty close since they were both stunning. Unlike Salima, Christelle gave me the runaround with her princess-like attitude. She was very capricious. At times, it felt like I was forcing myself to her. I was so determined that I wouldn't take no for an answer. It took me about two months to finally get her to even acknowledge me, and even then, things still weren't as smooth as I was hoping it to be.

Christelle lived in Garoua with her father, her two elder sisters, and her younger brother Yuri. Her father was overprotective of her, being the youngest of all his girls, watching her every move, looking out against anyone preying on his jewel. Even then, I still found ways to break through the security system. Most of the time, I found our love to be very exhausting as I was the one doing most of the chasing, and I was getting very little affection in return. One day, I approached her with an ultimatum, telling her how tired I was with this hide-and-seek relationship. She looked somehow indifferent to my request of having to see each other more often, leading me to put our relationship on pause.

I later moved on to another girl named Lydia. There were rumors around saying that Lydia had a crush on me. I first heard it from Jo and then from other people. Lydia was good looking. Her skin complexion was a little lighter than mine. She was taller than me, which made me feel uncomfortable around her at times. I always found myself not committing to girls that were taller than me. I never went for any girl that was taller than me as it made me feel inferior to her. But there is always a first time for everything. Lydia and I did manage to somewhat make up a good couple. Although I was happy with Lydia, there was still a part of me that was wishing for Christelle to come along.

Life in the refugee camp was fun. There was no school and plenty time for entertainment. It was a kid's paradise. People started dating each other. There were couples being made from left to right and preachers spreading the gospel trying to convert everyone. Aside from football, there were two other sources of entertainment. One was a Larry King–like show hosted by a guy who went by the nickname of Colombo. Colombo, who was in his midthirties, was known for knowing so much about each person's private life. He somehow knew who was dating whom, who was secretly sleeping with whom, who was prostituting, and so on. He came up with an hour show, which he called *Plateau,* meaning "The Stage." He had guests appear on his hour-long show, which consisted of asking them a series of very personal questions, which mostly made everyone, including the audience, very uncomfortable. From multiple rumors to factual questions, he never held back all in front of a live audience. No one ever declined his invitation. On some occasions, he had people shedding tears on his show after seeing their private lives exposed. He was the Larry King of the camp, and with him, there was no secret uncovered, no mystery left unsolved.

The other source of entertainment was from Mawashi, a guy who was also his midthirties and also known as the most popular man in the camp. Mawashi was the biggest storyteller of all time. He had stories for all ages, and what made him even more intriguing is the fact that he never went back to the same story twice. He had a story for each hour of the day. People would gather around him every night just to hear his hour-long stories, which was always fascinating. Just like Colombo, Mawashi was very popular in the camp. I long time suspected that a lot of his stories were nothing but made-up tales, but he told it so good. He put his every soul in all his stories, taking the crowd in his wings. Football, Colombo's *Plateau,* and Mawashi's endless stories are what kept the camp together while waiting on everyone's final destination.

Aside from some sporadic friction between the small groups of people who sought themselves as more deserving of a refugee status than the ones whom they labeled as opportunists for not being Rwandese or having any Rwandese blood in them, one of the biggest challenges faced in the refugee camp was the rise of prostitution. Living without any sources of income led some young women and some teenage girls to turn toward prostitution as a means to support their everyday needs. Some were even taken advantage of by some UNHCR officials. Some willingly sold their bodies for cash around town outside the refugee camp, resulting in the rise of sexually transmitted disease cases for those who didn't use protection. For some, that was a very small price to pay as they had access to a free clinic located at the outskirts of the camp. Sometimes, even respectful women were also tempted by this practice as it was a very reliable source of income. Some got pregnant as a result, while others tried to get abortion. There were groups of women who were openly known by the public to be prostituting, while some managed to keep a very low profile about it. Fingers were being pointed at to who was doing what. Even girls as young as thirteen were also involved. But, hey, let who is without sin cast the first stone.

During the eight-month stay in the refugee camp, there were three interviews conducted by the UNHCR to help with the process of placing each family and person to the right host country. The total number of refugees, which stood at 702, was to be divided among different host countries, which were the United States, Canada, Sweden, Norway, and Holland. The United States took up about 50 percent of the entire camp, Canada took about 30 percent, while the other 20 percent went to those other Scandinavian nations.

One day, the UNHCR posted a list with people's names along with their destination for everyone to see. The list of about 150 people was posted on the wall outside of the camp's UNHCR office. The first load of people was bound to the United States, with the first flight set to leave within the next forty-eight hours. There were joys and cheers for those whose names were featured on that list. Before anyone whose name wasn't featured started to question the process, they were told to calm down. This was only the first of four lists, with the next list scheduled to come out a few days later. Among our entire family, we were the only names featured in the first list bound for the United States. The very first people to leave the camp was everyone going to the United States;

and then a week later, people that were bound for Canada; and then about a month later, everyone going to Europe followed.

Out of the 702 people from the refugee camp, there were two registered deaths from illness, and three were sent back to the Congo. The three that were sent back to the Congo were Francis, Sarah, and Sam, all of them Tantine Helene's stepchildren. During the placement interview, it was found out that they weren't her biological children, and since their lives weren't in jeopardy back home, they had no business being placed with her.

Tantine Helene, with her two daughters, Deborah and Syntich, and her husband's nephew Bienvenu, ended up in Sweden along with Tonton Besto. Tonton Charles found himself being sent to Norway. Jo and his family went to Amarillo, Texas. Colombo went to San Diego, California. Mawashi and his family went to Atlanta, Georgia, along with one of the boys from the Indigenous crew, Marcelo Munganga. His two friends, the brothers, went to Cedar Rapids, Iowa. Salima and her family went to Jacksonville, Florida; while Christelle and her entire family made it to Richmond, Virginia. Prince went to Austin, Texas; while Romeo, the lady's man, ended up in Holland. A few players on my team ended up going to Saint Louis, Missouri; while others were sent to Champagne, Illinois.

Looking back at my time in both camps, I realized one thing. Now that I was Timu Kabala, an adopted child of a Rwandese family, I got to experience living with Rwandese. I came to realize that not all Rwandese people were pro Paul Kagame. As a matter of fact, those at the refugee camp were one of his harshest critics. So instead of generalizing all Rwandese people as being the enemy of the Congolese people, which they are not, all fingers should only be pointed to one man, the one and only Paul Kagame and his click who has been holding the Rwandese people hostage during his two decades of tyrannical reign. I had people like my uncle Charles who shared the same ethnicity with Paul Kagame who couldn't stand Paul Kagame and his politics but, unfortunately, found himself forced out of a country he has been calling home for as long as he could remember.

I spent the night before our flight to the United States looking back at how far along I came to finally make it here. From being a physically abused kid in his own home to being a runaway living in the rough streets of Kinshasa, to rising up to become the president's impersonator, to getting kicked out from the president's secretary's house, to being adopted by a family that was later forced out the country, to being known as the refugee camp's biggest smuggler, to finally getting an opportunity to start a fresh life in the greatest country in the world, to being able to finally experience the real American dream.

My journey from the bottom up was an indication that there is a higher power who has set us on a mission, a mission to complete one another through love and harmony just like a puzzle. I believe in him or her watching over each one of us to make sure we accomplish whatever we were set to accomplish in due time. Some may call him or her God. But which God, you may ask?

I would like to believe my God is not the one with a big long white beard and a white robe, you know, the single father with a son with no wife, I think not. Not even the one that promises you a certain amount of virgins for killing so many innocent people. Definitely not the one being worshipped day and night in the Congo while turning a blind eye on the eight million plus Congolese people who have been killed in a genocide during the past two decades while the whole world still stays silent. Absolutely not the one who is letting children as young as five get massively raped while their parents are being executed right in front of them by militias loyal to Paul Kagame of Rwanda, while all that is being said of Rwanda is how much progress they are making economically from selling resources that aren't found anywhere in its territory but are tremendously found in the Congo . . . no, that's not my God.

I knelt down that night thanking my God for being the recipient of yet another undeserved grace. I did shed few tears in memory of the long journey that took me here, knowing that this wasn't the end; it was just the beginning of a new chapter in my life. What lay ahead of me was going to be much more powerful than what I just outlived. Starting with a new identity, with no regret for the past, I was enjoying every moment from the present. Never in my life has the future ever looked so promising. I made a promise to myself to one day become one of the most influential persons in the land. I will be the shepherd that will help unite my people, bringing them together as one people under love. Together, we will make Congo great again.

We left the refugee camp on July 19, 2000, at around 7:00 p.m. Our plane made a refueling stop in the Canary Islands, Spain. We landed in JFK airport. Never before have I ever seen so many planes at once, and that airport alone was the size of an entire city, I thought. From New York City, we took a plane to Cincinnati, Ohio. From there, we took another plane to our final destination, Louisville, Kentucky, sweet Kentucky home, home to the greatest boxer of all time! "Ali Boma Ye," I said. We landed in Louisville, Kentucky, on July 20, 2000. We got out of the plane a little bit after 8:00 p.m., and yet the sun was still on the horizon. It was very bright outside. I looked at myself and smiled. No wonder this is the greatest country in the world. It's 8:00 p.m. and the sun's still up. What a miracle. From the airport, we were escorted by officials from our sponsor, Catholic Charity Agency, to a home set up for us as a halfway house until they found us a more permanent place.

This was the greatest experience of my life. I went to bed that night opening my eyes every minute just to make sure I wasn't hallucinating. As I looked around, I realized this was as surreal as it gets. I wasn't dreaming. On the contrary, I was just partaking in the first phase of a greater dream. This is the very first step toward my ultimate dream, the dream of finding myself a place to call home.